Praise for David Bell and his Novels

"When six students are trapped inside Hyde House, so, too, is the reader—helpless to escape until the final page is turned. *The Finalists* is a smart and compelling look at the dark underbelly of academia."

—Charlie Donlea, *USA Today* bestselling author of *Twenty Years Later*

"*And Then There Were None* meets *Knives Out* in David Bell's latest astonishing thriller. With Bell's customary biting wit and razor-sharp social commentary, *The Finalists* will have you cackling one minute while racing through its short, propulsive chapters the next, desperate to find out whodunit. Utterly riveting with intricate plot twists. Bell has crafted the summer's most entertaining and masterful 'locked-room' mystery. I couldn't put it down!"

—May Cobb, author of *My Summer Darlings*

"*The Finalists* is proof positive that David Bell is one of the best thriller writers working today." —Alma Katsu, author of *Red Widow*

"[A] smart, highly entertaining mystery with red herrings galore and such perfect dialogue, you'll feel like a fly on the wall. . . . The characters will play tricks on your mind, the house will feel like it's closing in, and the story will keep you guessing until the very end. Not to be missed!"

—Hannah Mary McKinnon, international bestselling
author of *Never Coming Home*

"David Bell is a top-notch storyteller. . . . I flew through this twisting, riveting psychological thriller."

—Cristina Alger, *New York Times* bestselling author of *Girls Like Us*

"Terrifically tense . . . will keep you guessing until the very end."

—Riley Sager, *New York Times* bestselling author of *Survive the Night*

"[A] suspenseful, page-turning thriller."

D1104389

"A tale straight out of the psychological thriller territory blazed by the likes of Harlan Coben and Lisa Gardner."

—*The Providence Journal*

"A compulsive, twisty, race-against-the-clock thriller . . . [a] smart and unrelenting page-turner!"

—Lisa Unger, *New York Times* bestselling author of *Confessions on the 7:45*

"Grabs you by the throat and never lets go . . . will keep you reading late into the night, with a twist you'll never see coming."

—Liv Constantine, bestselling author of *The Last Mrs. Parrish*

"A dark, twisty journey . . . one of David Bell's most unique and engrossing novels."

—Samantha Downing, *USA Today* bestselling author of *My Lovely Wife*

"Only the diabolical mind of the talented storyteller David Bell could concoct this mind-bendingly twisty thriller! . . . Smart, audacious, and completely original."

—Hank Phillippi Ryan, *USA Today* bestselling author of *The First to Lie*

"A tautly told, heart-pounding read . . . every character's a suspect and no one can be trusted."

—Mary Kubica, *New York Times* bestselling author of *The Other Mrs.*

ALSO BY DAVID BELL

TRY

NOT

TO

BREATHE

DAVID BELL

BERKLEY
NEW YORK

BERKLEY
An imprint of Penguin Random House LLC
penguinrandomhouse.com

Copyright © 2023 by David J. Bell
Readers Guide copyright © 2023 by David J. Bell
Penguin Random House supports copyright. Copyright fuels creativity, encourages diverse voices,
promotes free speech, and creates a vibrant culture. Thank you for buying an authorized edition of
this book and for complying with copyright laws by not reproducing, scanning, or distributing
any part of it in any form without permission. You are supporting writers and allowing
Penguin Random House to continue to publish books for every reader.

BERKLEY and the BERKLEY & B colophon are registered trademarks of
Penguin Random House LLC.

Library of Congress Cataloging-in-Publication Data

Names: Bell, David, 1969 November 17- author.
Title: Try not to breathe / David Bell.
Description: New York : Berkley, [2023]
Identifiers: LCCN 2022056159 (print) | LCCN 2022056160 (ebook) |
  ISBN 9780593549957 (hardcover) | ISBN 9780593549964 (trade paperback) |
  ISBN 9780593549971 (ebook)
Classification: LCC PS3602.E64544 T79 2023 (print) |
  LCC PS3602.E64544 (ebook) | DDC 813/.6--dc23/eng/20221205
LC record available at https://lccn.loc.gov/2022056159
LC ebook record available at https://lccn.loc.gov/2022056160

First Edition: June 2023

Printed in the United States of America
1st Printing

Book design by George Towne

For Molly

TRY
NOT
TO
BREATHE

PART I

1

Anna stepped out of the Uber.

Correction—she *stumbled* out of the Uber.

She steadied herself in the parking lot, waiting for the world to stop tilting. The driver, relieved to have deposited his drunk passenger, drove off into the night, red taillights glowing.

"Thanks, man," Anna said.

The steps to her apartment rose ahead of her. One flight, but it might as well have been fifty. Why had she and Kayla signed a lease for a second-floor unit?

The night sky was clear, a million stars like glowing dots. No wind, but it was cold. Anna shivered, tugged her jean jacket tighter. Her body shook. *Just go inside, into your warm bed.*

The world stopped spinning. Anna mouthed a silent prayer of thanks. She told herself she'd never drink tequila again. She amended the statement right away—she would never drink *anything* again. She'd been partying too much, staying out too late. Failing out of school. Everything spiraling—

She shook her head, stopped the out-of-control thoughts. *Just get your ass inside.*

Anna started forward, stepping cautiously. *Don't rush, don't fall.* She dug in her purse, reaching for her keys. She knew Kayla would have locked the door. Dependable, reliable Kayla. Asleep at eleven, homework finished. Dishes washed and put away. The next day's clothes ready to go.

Anna lived with her opposite. She loved Kayla dearly, but how had they become and stayed such good friends?

Anna grabbed the keys. *Score.* She hated to have to ring the bell, get Kayla out of bed to let her in. That had happened a few times. Missing keys, lost phone. Forgotten credit card. But not tonight—Anna had made it home, and she gripped the keys as her foot hit the bottom step.

Something moved on her left. From the corner of her eye, she saw it. The breath caught in her throat.

A figure coming from the direction of the building next door. A dark blur. A neighbor? Another drunk student?

It couldn't be the Midnight Rambler, could it?

The Midnight Rambler. The town pervert. A guy who'd been creeping around outside girls' apartments, peeking in windows, watching girls sleep. But he hadn't been spotted in their complex, and Anna thought he'd get caught soon or go away, some loser who didn't know how to get laid on his own—

Then the guy said something, called out a word in the dark.

Did he really just say that? Her *name*?

"Anna?"

She froze, looked his way. His face remained obscured. He wore dark clothes, walked with his hands in his pants pockets. What was the name of the guy next door? The one who had helped her get her car started the day she left her lights on? Was that him?

Why was he slinking around outside the building at . . . It was after two. Anna had stayed out until last call, slamming back one more shot before summoning a ride.

And did the dude next door even know her name?

Maybe he'd said something else. Maybe he'd just said hello. Or maybe he'd said nothing, and Anna had just heard a branch scraping, or the tequila was causing auditory hallucinations. Her stomach turned when she thought of the number of shots she'd consumed. *Why do I do this to myself?* Inside. She needed to get inside. Bathroom, Tylenol, water, bed—

She started up the stairs, turning away from the shadowy figure. She dismissed him. He wasn't the Rambler. Just another drunken student, one of her brethren in late-night debauchery. He needed to get into his apartment, sleep off his drunk while vowing never to do it again—

"Anna?"

Anna stopped again, halfway up. She looked back into the gloom. The man stood five feet back from the lowest step, his face still obscured. How did he know her name?

And if he knew her name—if he was a friend—why did he linger in the dark? Why not come right out and speak to her in the light?

Anna started up the stairs again. She missed the next step. Her foot came down on nothing but air, and her knees pounded against the concrete. Her eyes watered with pain.

"Shit. Fuck."

She regained her footing, started up. Moving quickly, stepping carefully. She didn't look back.

She drew the keys out, eyed the lock. She prayed Kayla—who worried more about the Rambler than Anna ever had—hadn't put the chain up as well.

Anna's key hit the lock, and she tried to turn it. The lock stuck, as it sometimes did.

"Shit. No."

The guy behind her started up the steps, heavy shoes against the concrete. Sweat popped out on Anna's forehead. She jiggled the key, turned it again. Mercifully, it turned. Anna pushed, almost fell into the living room, then spun and slammed the door shut, shaking the walls. Her hands trembled as she turned the lock, grabbed the chain, and put it in place. Her heart jumped against her ribs like a bucking horse, and she collapsed against the door, holding herself up.

Tears sprang to her eyes, and she wiped them away.

She risked a look. She pressed her eye to the peephole. With a fish-eye view, she saw the dude on the landing, hands still stuffed in his pockets. He looked down, his face still obscured. He didn't reach for the knob, but Anna worried he might. Maybe he'd try to kick the door in.

"Anna?"

She jumped a foot, almost screamed.

Anna turned around, saw Kayla behind her in the living room. Her roommate wore sweats and a Titans T-shirt. Her eyes were puffy from sleep.

"What's going on?" she said. "I heard the door—"

"Look outside. Look. It's the Rambler—or it's . . . I don't know."

Kayla came over, rubbing her upper arms. "I was dead asleep. Are you okay?"

"Look."

Kayla pressed her face to the door, turned her head from one side to the other. "I don't see anything."

"Kayla, there was a dude. He was out there in the dark. He came toward me—and—and—I think he said my name."

"Do you know him?"

"No. I mean, I didn't get a good look at his face. Oh, God, Kayla. I think I'm going to be sick." She dropped her keys and purse on the floor, clutched her stomach. The tequila roiled like a stormy sea. "He scared the shit out of me." She had to wipe more tears away.

"Anna, I've never seen you like this." Kayla covered the distance between them, reached out, and took Anna in her arms. "My God, you're shaking. Let's call the police. Okay? Right now. That could be the Rambler. Or if he said your name—"

"I don't know. Maybe I imagined it. I don't know. . . ."

"Let's call the police, okay?"

"No, no. I feel . . . I had too much to drink. I need to go to bed."

"But, Anna, if you're so scared . . ."

"Just, just . . ." Anna moved back, out of Kayla's arms. "I can't involve the cops. My dad— It's just too complicated."

"Anna, are you sure? You look terrified."

"I'm just going to go to bed. I need to sleep this off, okay? I'm sorry I woke you."

"It's not about that, Anna. It's about you—"

"I'm fine. Really." Anna started for the bathroom, but she looked back once, studied the door.

She wanted to make sure—*really sure*—that the lock and chain were in place.

2

Morning light leaked through the blinds, assaulting Anna's eyes.

She pulled the pillow over her head, burrowed into the warm sheets. She willed the world away.

Until the bedroom door swooshed open. Kayla. Always on time, always prepared.

"Anna? Hey, Anna? Are your ready to talk about last night?"

Anna spoke into the pillow.

"Anna, I can't hear you." Kayla yanked the blinds open. More light poured in—bright, stinging light.

"Damn it, Kayla."

"This is serious, okay?" Kayla came to the side of the bed, tugged at the comforter. "Someone may be stalking you. We need to call the police now."

Anna pictured Kayla without seeing her. Hands on hips, frowning mouth. Frustrated by her roommate. Eager to help and protect her. Light pouring over her shoulder, illuminating her rosy complexion, her bright eyes. Kayla was sickeningly healthy. And competent.

"I've tried to get you to go back to class and stop this academic spiral, but we've moved past that now. This is much more serious. And dangerous."

Anna remained still. She couldn't outlast Kayla, who was too good a friend, too loyal. Too determined. Anna pushed the pillow down, squinted against the burning light. Her tongue stuck to the roof of her mouth, and a rhythmic pain beat time in her temple. "Oh, God . . . I think I'm dead."

"There she is," Kayla said. "Swing your legs onto the floor and then we'll call the police. We can worry about class later."

"You're overreacting, Kayla."

"I'm not." Kayla studied Anna for a moment, her eyes intense. "I heard from your parents too. We can deal with them after the police." She reached into her back pocket and brought out her phone. She held the screen toward Anna, pushed it closer to her face. "See this?"

"No, no." Anna shut her eyes. "I can't read that. It's too bright and hurts my head. Please, no."

Kayla pulled the phone back. "That was a dangerous situation last night in the parking lot. It could have ended up a lot worse."

"Let's just take a deep breath. We're not sure it's a stalker. And why are you bringing up my parents?"

Kayla's cheeks flushed. She shook her head, ponytail swinging like an ax. "I'll read you this text I received earlier." She cleared her throat. "'Dear Kayla. We've been trying to reach our Anna for several days now, and she won't answer. Her mother and I are both very worried. Also, we are both struggling with health-related issues and don't need the additional stress. The world is dangerous for young girls. And I know there have been a series of unsolved break-ins in your area. I know these things because of my—'"

Anna groaned. "'Because of my long career in law enforcement.'"

"Exactly. 'Please tell us if Anna is okay and ask her to call or text us soon. If there is no response, I will contact the authorities in your town, many of whom I know personally. Yours, Russell Rogers.' It's annoying that you've put me in the position of getting worried texts from your parents, but I'm kind of glad, because I've never received a message with a salutation and a closing before. It's like he sent this text from the 1950s."

"Ignore it. He'll go away."

"I can't just ignore it. And you know he's not going to go away.

Besides, I think it's sweet he cares this much about his baby girl. Did you know my dad forgot my birthday? And I'm an only child."

"Kayla, do you ever just look at your family and wonder where you came from? Like, how did these freaks produce me? We have nothing in common."

"Anna, everybody does. That's why I went away to college. So I didn't have to be around my parents all the time."

"Okay, okay." Anna sat up, the covers spilling around her waist. The movement caused more pain in her head. She winced. Her dad's words stabbed her heart, almost made her forget she didn't want to speak to him. "I'll call . . . or something. I'm on it."

"But that's not item number one. We have to call the police, so we can file a report about last night—"

"No, no. No police."

"Anna, you scared me last night. When you came in the door, you looked terrified. And you *never* look terrified. That guy could have meant to hurt you."

"He's just a creep. A Peeping Tom or whatever. The Midnight Rambler who's been all over town."

"You said he knew your name. *That's* a stalker. That's dangerous. And another woman could be targeted next. Or he could come back here. You were crying when you came inside."

"He just— He startled me."

Kayla looked at the time and put her phone away. "I don't want to give you a lecture, but I think we need to take care of this. I'm going to skip class, okay?"

"No—"

"We'll call the police, and then you can tell your parents you're okay. If you don't, your dad is going to flip out. And maybe he should after last night. I can't leave you alone here."

"I can't talk to my dad. About anything."

Kayla's hands returned to her slender hips. She moved with grace, like the high school basketball star she was, the one who had given up the sport to focus exclusively on school. "What's the deal, anyway?

You went home a few weeks ago, and you haven't been the same since. No more class. No contact with the parents. What happened?"

Anna sat back against her pillows. Her eyes trailed across the room to the manila folder on her desk. She made a vague gesture toward it, let her hand drop back to the bed. "We fought about school. I told them I wanted to take time off. Travel or just . . . do something different. My dad can't deal. He's pissed about the scholarship. Always the scholarship, never me. He thinks it's an affront to his service if I don't take advantage of it. Like I asked him to get his leg shattered by a psycho's bullet so I could go to college for less."

Anna's heart clenched. She pictured her dad hobbling around the house, dulling his pain with daily pills and more frequent pulls from his bottle of Jim Beam. How could anyone be so fearsome and so pathetic at the same time? Like a wounded lion in a nature documentary.

"I fight with my parents all the time," Kayla said. "It's par for the course. It will blow over. But they're going to worry if you don't call them—"

"*It* came up."

Kayla's right eyelid flickered. "*It?*"

"Tanya Burns."

"Why did you bring that up?" Kayla spoke to Anna like she was two years old.

"It was my dad who kept talking about it." Anna felt herself pouting. The gesture struck her as childish, but she couldn't help it. "He defended the shooting. Of course. I knew he'd do that. And he trashed the protestors. No surprise." Anna took a deep breath. She almost couldn't bring herself to say it, to form the words and push them out. "Shit, Kayla, do you know what he told me? He *trained* Officer Shaw. He trained him. He *trained* the cop who killed Tanya Burns."

Kayla's arms fell to her sides, limp. She looked like her energy had drained out of her, through her shoes and into the floor. "Oh, fuck. Really?"

"Really. And he said it like he was *proud* of it."

Kayla recovered herself, quickly resumed her role as the person who always tried to find the bright side in anything. "Okay, well, if he trained Shaw, then that was long ago. Your dad hasn't been a cop for, like, six years, right? So he didn't train Shaw recently. Who knows what turned the guy into a murderer?"

"That's not the point." Anna felt the tears stinging her eyes. "He trained him. He knew him. He defended him. He's partially responsible for what happened."

Kayla came forward, rested her hand on Anna's side. "I'm sorry, hon. I really am. That's just . . . I can't imagine. I don't want to leave you alone this way. You're upset, and that guy who was outside—"

"I'm *fine*. Just don't—don't mother me." Anna's voice came out more sharply than she'd intended, the words cutting through the space between them like a knife.

Kayla withdrew her hand, took a step back. She shrugged, her long arms stretching, hovering over Anna's bed.

"Kayla, look . . . I'm sorry, okay? I'll figure it out. I will."

"Okay, good. But . . . you should still get in touch with your parents. Think of your mom. Do it for her, if for no one else. She's going to worry, and her health isn't great."

"*She* married *him*. That's all I need to know."

"But this is your mom. She's so sweet."

"She's not always sweet."

"She cares about you so much."

"I don't want to hear it."

Kayla nodded, backed away like she was retreating from the presence of an explosive device. The two roommates had reached that point before—rarely, but it happened from time to time. Kayla always withdrew, gave Anna her space. Waited for her roommate to come back around.

Anna hated being the one to push such a good friend away, but her mouth had a mind of its own.

At the bedroom door, Kayla looked back. "I'm going to lock the front door when I go. You should get up and put the chain on once I'm gone. Seriously, it's not normal for that guy to know your name. And if you don't contact your mom before I'm out of class, I'm stepping in. And who knows what I'll tell them?"

"Kayla—"

"Your mom, Anna. That's who I'm talking about. Your mom. The woman who gave birth to you. Oh, wait. I think that sounded like a lecture." She raised her index finger, pressed it against her lips. "You know what? I don't care. Bye."

Anna listened, heard Kayla gather her things, then slam and lock the front door.

Everything grew quiet except the blood rushing in her ears.

"Shit," she said.

3

Anna tossed the covers aside, felt the chill in the apartment.

The October sun looked bright, but the nights and mornings were now cool. Kayla refused to turn the heat on until November in order to save money. Anna shivered and reached for a hoodie. She loved fall but dreaded the coming winter cold.

Anna's head thumped but with less force. She went to the front door, hooked the chain in place, as Kayla had told her to do. Just standing at the door, thinking about the night before, the creep in the parking lot . . .

It shook her. Her heart jumped like exploding popcorn kernels.

She stepped to the right, peeked through the living room blinds at the parking lot below. Her fellow tenants, backpacks slung over shoulders, shambled to their cars, sleepy eyed. Life went on. Like a little kid left out of everybody else's fun, Anna felt a pang of regret. She could easily go to her room, throw on clothes, grab her bag, and head to campus. Sneak into the back of class if she was late, take notes. Go to office hours and beg for Jenkins' mercy.

She shook her head, still staring at the lot.

No. She'd made her choice. She wasn't going to live somebody else's life anymore. Certainly not the life her dad pushed her toward. Not after what she knew.

The parking lot cleared. Despite the sunshine, the emptiness caused unease to ripple through her body. Anna scanned the area, taking in everything. Looking for the creep.

The creep. The guy—he just had to be the Rambler, right?

The Rambler was known for going through unlocked windows and sliding glass doors, only in apartments where female students lived. He rifled through drawers, taking clothing, brushes, makeup. No one had been hurt, but more than one woman woke up with the creep standing over her bed, breathing heavily in the dark night. The media had dubbed him the Midnight Rambler.

That had to be the guy on the steps. Right? The town pervert trying to get off.

But—

The guy outside had said her name. He had come after her.

The Midnight Rambler never did that. He never laid a hand on the women he creeped on.

She tried her best *never* to listen to her dad, *never* to do what he wanted anymore, but wasn't Kayla right? Didn't she need to call and file a report? Not for her dad or the cops. But to ensure that no other woman woke up with that creep looming over her.

Anna had put it off last night. She let Kayla calm her down, promised her roommate she'd call the cops in the morning. Kayla had even talked about going home, borrowing a gun from her uncle who had served in Afghanistan.

Anna let the slat of the blinds snap back into place. The creep never did anything during the day. And the chain and dead bolt served as solid protection.

Anna went back to the bedroom, grabbed her phone off the bedside table. "Shit."

Three more texts from her dad. One inviting her up for the weekend from her friend Rachel in Louisville. Again.

And one from her sister Alisha.

Kiddo, can you just let the old man know you're okay? He's threatening to drive down there himself, and you know he can't do that. Which means I'm going to have to get a babysitter and do it. Can you just tell him you're okay?

Alisha. Her sweet sister. The one who was always there for her. When Anna was about ten, her mother had told her that Alisha—who had turned eighteen—was named her legal guardian in her parents' will. Her mom had been emphatic that Anna knew she'd be taken care of, as if her mom and dad were both about to die at any moment.

Anna had asked why they hadn't chosen Avery, since she was the oldest. But her mom had said that Alisha was the better choice and left it at that.

"The key thing, Anna," she had said, "is that you know someone will be here for you. No matter what happens to us."

Anna hated thinking about her parents' mortality. And she hated thinking about Avery, who she never heard from. Who clearly didn't care.

Anna's stomach churned, and not from alcohol. Her guts roiled when she thought of Avery. Nine years older than Anna, Avery lived right there in the same town but never made contact. She always acted like they were distant relatives with nothing at all to say to each other. Anna bit down on her lower lip, felt a pleasant and painful pressure there. She hated herself for feeling that way, but she really wanted Avery to reach out to her now. If Avery showed the slightest interest in Anna's well-being, she might just go along. Return to school, deal with life.

She felt weak for so desperately wanting the approval of her oldest sister, who didn't give a shit about her.

Besides, Avery had been a cop. Just like their dad. What was the difference between them?

Anna ignored Alisha's messages. *Let the old man wonder.*

She wrote back to Rachel: Invite still open?

Rachel wrote back in a nanosecond: Hell to the yes, girl. Big march for Tanya Burns. Wanna go?

A march protesting the Tanya Burns shooting? That would piss the old man off. Big-time.

Packing my boots now.

I work late. Blergh. See you when I get off. Then: Til then you can hang with Eric. He keeps asking about you.

Ignoring that, Anna wrote back: I just want to get away.

Anna tossed the phone aside, checked the room to see what she needed to pack. The manila folder she had taken from her parents' house caught her eye. She went to it, flipped it open. She touched the yellowed clippings that covered every year of her father's career with the Kentucky State Police. They were soft beneath her fingertips, but the headlines assaulted her eyes like the sun. . . .

Police Kill Suspect in Chase . . . Fourteen Arrested in Drug Raid . . . Murders Remain Unsolved . . . KSP Captain in Critical Condition . . .

Anna shook her head. She hated that he kept these things, hated that he was proud of them. In the wake of the Tanya Burns shooting, she couldn't look at any of it the same. She never would be able to again. She closed the folder, stuffed the loose papers back inside, and started packing for Louisville.

4

The fight spilled out of the Lambda Upsilon house and into the middle of High Street.

Avery Rogers pulled up in her campus security vehicle, its spinning yellow bubble light likely almost invisible in the late-afternoon sun. The car, a late-model Hyundai, carried all the authority of a golf cart, and when Avery stepped out of it, no one noticed her. A beautiful fall day. Sunny, leaves just starting to change. And yet, two numbskulls had managed to start a fight?

A group of students encircled the combatants, who stood in the street throwing drunken punches that mostly missed their targets. One fighter, the smaller of the two, managed to pull his opponent's shirt up, obscuring the guy's vision. The smaller guy looked to be barely holding on, waiting for someone to break up the scuffle before he got killed.

Women made up half the crowd. One of them, a girl with long blond hair, was holding a can of White Claw and appeared to be crying. "Stephen. Stop it, Stephen. Oh, Stephen. Stephen, he didn't mean it."

The frat bros in the crowd egged the fighters on. "Dude. Get him. Get him. Try the left. The left."

Avery wore a white uniform shirt and dark pants. She flipped her sunglasses down, the better to see the melee, and approached, keys jangling on her belt, thick-soled shoes thumping the pavement. The gold badge on her left breast identified her as a member of the Gracewood College security force. Gracewood was too small to fund and staff an actual police force.

The crowd finally noticed her, started to part and make way.

"Okay, gentlemen, okay. Knock it off. Knock it off."

The small fighter craned his head, showed visible relief at Avery's arrival. He took a step back and let go of the bigger guy's shirt. The bigger guy continued to swing but, no longer supported by his enemy, he pitched forward, landing on his knees in the street.

"Oh, God. Oh, Stephen. Are you okay, baby?"

Avery bent down, leaned close to the guy who was battling his own T-shirt, trying to see. "Sir, are you okay? Do you require medical assistance?"

He pulled the T-shirt down, his head popping out like a giant turtle's. His bloodshot eyes widened, capillaries like a road map. His mouth contorted, saliva dripping from one corner. He reached up, wiped it off with the back of his hand.

"Where is he? Where is he?"

"Easy, sir. Let's not have any more fighting."

The guy stood up. At least six-three, he loomed over Avery by a good six inches. His enormous gut flopped over his belt. Likely had played football in high school and now devoted his time to daily inebriation and the perpetual torturing of pledges.

"Fuck. What the . . . Who are . . ." He squinted at Avery. Eyes glassy, his hair a mop covering his forehead. "Who the fuck . . . Rent-a-cop? Oh, Christ . . ."

The guy reached out, placed his giant paw on Avery's upper arm. He started to move her aside, trying to get past her and at his fellow combatant.

"Sir, don't put your hands on me, please."

He offered her a cocky grin. Perfectly straight white teeth, dental work that cost more money than she'd ever had in her life. The guy smelled like he'd bathed in Axe body spray and beer.

"Are you kidding me right now?" He applied more pressure, trying to move Avery aside.

"Stephen, stop it. Come inside."

"Dude."

Avery took a quick glance around. Ten students, one of her. Everybody likely wasted.

The sun gleamed off the neoclassical buildings. Gracewood looked like a college was supposed to look. The students had everything. So why did anyone need to get blotto in the middle of the day and throw punches?

Avery lifted her right hand, fingers splayed. She placed it in front of Stephen's chest, an inch away from the T-shirt displaying a logo from a ski equipment company. She remembered her training. *Never touch a student. Never yell at a student. Always use polite language: "sir" or "miss" if appropriate. Never curse. Seek nonconfrontational solutions.*

"Sir," Avery said, "can you please not touch me anymore? And can you please step back and stop trying to fight?"

A collective gasp rippled through the crowd. "Ooooooooh."

"Stephen. Stop it."

"That was the undercard. This is the main event."

"My money's on the chick. Stephen drank a twelve-pack."

"She can shoot him. Pull a Tanya Burns on his fat ass."

"Tanya Burns deserved it."

"She's just doing her job, Stephen. Come inside. Okay?"

Stephen blinked, acting like he was seeing Avery for the first time. Like he'd flipped the kitchen light on and come face-to-face with a roach. "Her job? Her job? I pay her fucking salary."

"Ooooooooh."

Avery leaned in, spoke low enough so only Stephen could hear. "Listen, you entitled tub of goo drinking up your parents' money, I dare you to try me."

Stephen's mouth opened wider. He'd probably have worn the same look if the caddy at his country club told him to carry his own bag. "Oh, you fucked up now."

Stephen's eyes cleared, and the pupils focused, fixing on Avery. He drew back his big left arm, prepared to sweep it forward and deliver a smack to the side of Avery's head.

Avery braced, ready for the blow. Anticipating it.

Car doors slammed behind her. The crowd moved farther away. Two of the frat guys fled the scene.

"Hey there," one of the cops said.

Stephen lowered his arm. His features softened, a sudden transformation. The anger left his eyes and his mouth unsnarled.

"What have we here?" the cop asked.

"Looks serious," said his partner. "You need a hand, *Officer* Rogers?"

Avery took a step back, turned her head. Two Breckville cops, thumbs hooked in gun belts, strutted toward them. One chewed gum. Avery didn't know him, but she recognized the other, Officer Washington.

All the energy drained from the crowd. The students wilted like day-old party balloons.

"What's the trouble?" the first cop asked around his gum.

"Nothing, sir," Stephen said. "We were— I mean, I was just . . . Hey, I respect cops, unlike a lot of people these days."

"Right, I'm sure you do." Officer Washington looked down his nose at Avery, his sunglasses reflecting her face. "We got a call saying an officer needed assistance. We thought it was one of ours, not campus security."

"I didn't need assistance."

"Sure, Avery. Things looked well in hand when we rolled up."

The first cop pointed at Stephen. "How old are you, big boy?"

"Nineteen, sir."

"You been drinking?"

"No, sir."

"Right. And I'm the attorney general. Everybody, get out your IDs. Real ones, not the fake shit. Why can't you all learn to keep this nonsense behind closed doors?"

Avery turned to Officer Washington, who drew out his pen and clicked it open with his thumb. "Do you want me to tell you what went down?"

He studied his pen, clicked it a few more times. "I think we've got it. Since you can only write students up and we can issue actual citations . . . you can go on back to patrolling. You know, the campus."

"Right. Yeah."

Avery backed away. *Slinked.* She wasn't sure she'd ever slinked in her life. Her cheeks burned.

"Officer?" The other kid, Stephen's opponent in the fight.

"Yeah?" Avery said.

"I just wanted to say . . . Well, Stephen isn't really a bad guy. He just— When he drinks . . . you know?"

"You're welcome," Avery said, moving back to her pathetic little security car, the yellow bubble light blinking at her in mockery.

5

Avery returned home to her cramped but clean apartment.

She lived among graduate students, young married couples, and the occasional downsized senior citizen. She stripped off her uniform as fast as she could and headed right to the shower, hoping to wash the shitty shift off her body. A couple of days off lay before her, time to concentrate on what she wanted to do.

When she came out of the shower, her hair dripping, her robe tightly belted around her middle, she felt calmer. The night was pleasantly cool. She opened the living room windows, let the light breeze lift the curtains.

Then her phone chimed twice in a row.

She picked it up, one water droplet falling onto the screen, slightly obscuring her sister Alisha's message.

You home?

Yes.

I'm in town. Coming over.

Avery dressed, pulling on a long-sleeved T-shirt advertising a 5K she had run in the spring, leggings, and slippers. She filled the kettle to make tea. She and Alisha always drank tea.

As to why her sister was in town and coming over, Avery guessed it was about their dad. She considered Alisha her best friend, the person she was closest to, even though their lives were so different. But lately, when they talked, they talked almost exclusively about the old man. His health, his mental state.

His drinking.

Alisha rapped on the door, three quick knocks, and Avery let her in.

"You look comfy," Alisha said as she slipped off her jean jacket.

"It was supposed to be a quiet evening at home. One devoted to me. I have a feeling things aren't going that way now."

"You'd be right about that."

While the tea was poured and the sugar added, Avery asked about the kids, her two nieces, who were now four and two.

"They're little lunatics. What do you expect? They know Halloween's coming, and they're out of their minds at the thought of all the candy."

Alisha had turned twenty-nine a month earlier, and Avery noted a few gray hairs, a few lines forming around her mouth. Not for the first time, Avery saw how much her younger sister looked like their mom—the same brown eyes, the same thin nose. The same height as Avery, just over five feet eight, but a curvier body. Avery always felt an irrational jealousy that her sister looked more like their mom than she did. As much as she hated it, Avery had always been most obviously her father's daughter. In every way, including looks.

"How about you?" Alisha asked as they settled around the small kitchen table. "How's work?"

"A laugh a minute."

"School?"

Avery nodded. "I have a paper due Monday, and this coming weekend is set aside to work on that."

Alisha's eyes slid away, and color rose in her cheeks. "I see."

"Al, I can't just blow it off."

"You seem defensive."

"And you seem like there's something you don't want to tell me.

And we tell each other everything, so . . . I'm guessing a giant shoe is about to drop. Something big enough that you left your kids at home with Rick or a babysitter and drove an hour to show up on my doorstep with three minutes' notice."

Alisha raised her eyebrows, put on a giant fake smile. "Maybe I just missed my favorite older sister. Or maybe I'm so sick of my kids, I'm taking any excuse to get away from them. Heck, maybe I turned them in at the fire station and ran away to start a new life here. Maybe I'm going to get a master's degree right alongside you."

"You hated school. When you graduated from UK, you swore you'd never set foot in a classroom again. And you never leave your kids unless you have to."

"You sound like a cop."

"I'm not a cop. I work as a security guard to pay my way through school."

Alisha blew on her tea.

"Is it him?" Avery asked. "Is something wrong with Dad? He pretty much dominates every conversation we have these days. Just like he's always dominated everything."

"In a way, it's Dad. You're in the right church, but the wrong pew."

"What is it, then, Al?"

Her sister took a moment. "Have you talked to Anna lately?"

Avery felt heat rising under her collar. "Anna?"

"Yes, Anna." Alisha leaned in, lifted one eyebrow. "You know, our sister?"

"Our stepsister."

Avery spit the words out. Not a programmed response but an attempt to dig, a blade she worked in even though her intended target—her dad—wasn't present to hear it.

Alisha rolled her eyes. "You know I fucking hate it when you say that."

Avery drained her tea, stood up. She went to the sink—to do what? To get away from Alisha's disappointed look. Avery ran water, rinsed her mug just to occupy herself.

"She's our *sister*," Alisha said. "Half sister, technically, if you want to get into that hairsplitting bullshit. Not our stepsister. Dad's daughter."

Avery drank the slightly brown water that swished in the bottom of her mug. "You know we don't talk. And we don't see each other. And if you're here in your role as family peacemaker trying to get me to reach out to Anna and make nice before Dad drinks himself to death once and for all or before whatever is wrong with Jane gets worse, well, I guess you wasted the trip. We could have had this chat on the phone or via text, but I'm always happy to see you."

"You've never really wanted to help Anna. With anything."

"Alisha—"

"No, really, Avery. When Dad and Jane asked you to be Anna's guardian, you said no. *No.* I never understood that."

"You're clearly the maternal one."

"Oh, bullshit."

"Why were they so worked up over having a guardian for Anna, anyway?"

"It's what parents do."

"No, they were insane about it. They acted like they were both about to get shipped off to the French Foreign Legion. It was such an emotional overreaction. By both of them. Jane practically begged me. It was obnoxious—and just came out of the blue."

Alisha was watching her, Avery could tell. Her sister's eyes seared the side of her face.

Alisha said, "I guess you don't really need or want me to tell you who you're acting like right now."

Avery put the mug down with a shaky hand. "How bad is he?"

"He's bad. He's in pain, and he's drinking a lot. I don't know how much time he has. I really don't."

Avery's knees felt like Jell-O. "What does this have to do with Anna?"

"She's not going to class. And she's not answering anyone's calls or texts."

"Doesn't she have a boyfriend? What was the guy's name? Tyler? Maybe it's boyfriend trouble."

"His name is Trevor. And they broke up. But that was months ago. Apparently, Anna and Dad had a fight the last time she went home. A pretty big fight. We're worried about her, and we—*I* was hoping you would track her down. Find her."

"Find her? You heard me. I can't—"

"Avery, will you just hear me out? This is family, okay? Don't blow me off."

6

Avery couldn't listen. She jumped up, retreated to the bathroom. She ran water in the sink, ignoring the weak pressure for a change.

She cupped cold water in her hands and splashed it on her face.

After the third splash, she stopped and stared into the liquid.

When Avery was five, her dad tried to teach her how to swim. Avery had always feared the water. If she stood near a swimming pool, her mind fixed on the sensation of dropping below the surface, sinking and sinking and never touching bottom. And never coming up for air again.

Her dad spent a few days taking her to a neighbor's pool, trying to show her how to float, how to move her arms and kick her feet. Avery refused to try anything. She just clung to her dad, her arms wrapped around his thick neck, the sun reflecting off the aqueous blue of the pool. The chlorine smell burned her nose.

On the fourth day, her dad took a new approach. Frustrated, he grabbed Avery by the back of her bathing suit and tossed her in the water. Over the years, her dad defended his actions by saying that she landed in only three feet of water, that he jumped in right after her in case she struggled, that sometimes the shock of an experience like that made a person stronger.

Avery remembered floundering on the surface, gasping and choking. She remembered slipping below the surface, feeling the water rush up her nose.

She still didn't know how to swim.

She splashed her face one more time, dried it off. When she came out, Alisha was sitting on the couch, knee crossed over knee, foot bouncing in the air.

"I'm sorry," she said. "I'm not trying to be a dick. I know it's complicated for you."

"Isn't everything with Dad complicated for you too?"

"Well, let's just say you and I have different . . . forgiveness thresholds."

"That's a polite way of saying I hold a grudge. At the academy, we learned those people are called 'injustice collectors.' It's a key trait of serial killers. Besides, Dad never threw you in the pool."

"Dad never thought I could handle being thrown in. And he was right. We all know you're the daughter he raised to be the son he never had. He did his best."

Avery forced her words out. "He was fiercely loyal. And fiercely protective. That's for sure."

"Right."

"I did want to be like him. Desperately. He casts a long shadow."

"Isn't that a good thing for a parent? To set such a high standard?"

"Don't defend him."

"I'm not defending anybody. We're a family, Ave. There aren't sides."

Avery stood in the center of the room, too wired to sit. "Why don't *you* go talk to Anna and find out what her deal is?"

"I went to her apartment already. Nobody home. Dad's been texting Kayla and not getting a response."

"Who?"

"Kayla. Anna's roommate. Have you seriously not even been to her place? She lives ten minutes from here. You go to the same school."

"I'm a graduate student."

"Still."

"Now you are judging me."

"I guess I am. And why don't you sit? You're making me nervous."

Avery gave in. She plopped onto the other end of the sofa and dropped her hands into her lap.

"You know Anna looks up to you," Alisha said. "She'd love to have a relationship."

Avery stared at the floor. Her body tensed.

"I'm sure she looks up to me too, in a way. But I don't inspire the same kind of worship. I'm not as mysterious and brooding. When you're nice, people tend to underestimate you. And I've been nice to Anna. You know, like a big sister should."

Avery forced a few words out. "You're more like Mom."

"It's not Anna's fault Dad cheated on Mom and left her. It's not Anna's fault Mom was so crushed she packed all our shit, yanked us out of school, and dragged us with her down to Florida."

"Ugh, Mom's Florida year. An extended spring break for a woman in her forties. How many different leathery-skinned boyfriends did she have?"

"Enough that by the time Mom had had her fill of the tropics and we moved back north, we had a baby sister. And it's not Anna's fault Dad spent more time with her and was more available to her than he was with us. That's just . . . fate. The wheel of fortune spun that way."

"Mm-hmm. Like Mom dying."

"Mom dying. And getting a stepmother."

"Don't mention her. It takes two people to cheat."

"I guess I can't say anything right. As usual." Alisha tapped her fingers against her mug. "You seem particularly on edge tonight. Have you taken my advice about trying to date again? Or at least get laid? It might help."

"I'm busy."

"Do you ever talk to Hank?"

"Al, please."

"Okay, I'm sorry. He was such a sweet guy. I thought you two—Well, okay. Never mind. What *is* bothering you? Besides our family history and the sound of my voice."

Avery shifted on the sofa, turned her body to face Alisha. Her sister, as always, showed patience. Openness. Receptivity to whatever Avery needed to say. Even as she started to speak, Avery recognized—

again—what a one-way street their relationship was. Alisha filled her life with people who loved and supported and listened to her. Mostly, Avery depended on Alisha.

"I had to bust some asshole today. An oversized frat boy who drank too much and started beating on his much smaller friend out in the street. The way that punk looked at me, looked *down* on me . . . it brought something back. Made me think of Dad. That look in the eye that's meant to intimidate. And does."

"I didn't know you were scared of anything. Besides water."

"I got myself into a bad situation. I goaded the guy into taking a swing at me. I *wanted* him to. I wanted an excuse to get out my frustrations."

"I'm sorry. What happened?"

Avery shook her head, embarrassed by the memory. "I had to get bailed out by the real cops."

"Oh, boy. I bet that felt good."

"I've had better moments."

"You could still be a real cop if you wanted to."

"You know that ship has sailed. I'm in school for something else so I don't have to arrest frat boys or drunk drivers or whatever else anymore. And with the Tanya Burns shooting, by a KSP officer, the job is never going to have the same luster for me. Maybe not for anyone."

"That's what the fight was about. Dad and Anna. They got into it over Tanya Burns. You can imagine Dad's take on the whole thing. Plus—"

"Plus, he trained Shaw. I'm sure he sang his praises to Anna. Dad's not going to back down. We know that."

"We do."

Avery turned away. She couldn't look at Alisha when she spoke again. "And I have a paper to write this weekend. Anna is a college student. She's probably off having fun. Maybe she's saying 'Fuck you' to Dad the way I always wanted to."

"I think he got that message from you, Avery."

"Did he? I'm not sure he ever heard anything I said."

Alisha planted both feet on the floor and placed her hands on her thighs. "So I guess you're giving me a hard no."

"The hardest."

Alisha slipped her phone out of her back jeans pocket. Her mouth scrunched. "And I have to head back. It's an hour drive." She stood up, reached for her coat. "I'll keep you in the loop. Let's hope we hear from Anna soon."

Something beat at the walls of Avery's chest. Words and gestures that wanted to get out but couldn't. A block of ice that wouldn't melt. A barrier existed between her and even Alisha, one she couldn't find a way around. One she didn't remember erecting but that had always been there.

"Do you remember what Mom used to say about Dad?" Alisha asked, her hand on the knob. "You know, after he left her."

Avery remained silent.

"She used to tell Dad he was going to die alone. Remember that?"

Once Alisha was gone, Avery said, "Drive safe, Al."

7

As Anna drove out of Breckville in the late afternoon—sun rays slanting, light catching the leaves just turning gold and red—she felt like a curtain had dropped behind her.

Something was finished. Completed.

Time to shut everything down and start all over again.

She breathed easier, opened the window on the driver's side of her thirdhand Corolla, and let the air stream in and blow against her face. Tiny Breckville receded in the rearview. On either side of her, fences gave way to fields, acre upon acre of rolling grass, bright green from the recent rain. Cows, moving like they were in slow motion, dotted the landscape. Giant round hay bales, as gold as the sun, covered the hillsides.

Relief.

Anna opted for taking back roads to Louisville. She wanted to avoid crowds and traffic, the endless, mind-numbing parade of fast-food restaurants and gas stations. She wanted to see something real, allow her mind to clear.

She'd done her due diligence before leaving town.

She had texted Kayla, honoring the request her roommate had made. She said she was headed to Louisville for the weekend to see her high school friend Rachel. All true. Anna had texted Rachel that morning, told her that she was planning to make the two-hour drive east and then north and that Rachel should put some beer on ice for her. Rachel had texted back raising-hands emojis, five of them in a row, and that was all Anna needed to start the drive.

Kayla wrote back one word: Cool.

A feeling of ease swept through Anna's body like a soothing balm. Was Kayla letting her off the hook? That was so unlike her. . . .

Then another text: Did you talk to your mom?

Anna's skin prickled as if she were lying on a bed of dull nails. She hated to lie. Kayla was the best friend she had at school. Kayla watched her back with a ferocity usually found inside families. The way a sibling should watch your back. Like Alisha. But Alisha's kids took precedence now. Anna couldn't blame her sister for that— obviously. The dynamic had shifted when her nieces were born. She still talked to Alisha on the phone, saw her whenever she could, but her sister always seemed distracted. Frazzled and tired, like someone who had just lost their to-do list and couldn't re-create it.

And Avery . . . Anna gritted her teeth. Fucking Avery, who lived in the same town. Who even went to the same school. Anna had texted Avery a few times when she moved to Breckville, asking if she wanted to get together for coffee or lunch or just to go for a walk, but her oldest sister always wrote back claiming to be too busy or tied up with something else, until Anna just stopped asking and accepted they wouldn't ever be close.

Fucking Avery.

No, no. No negative thoughts. Look ahead to the weekend. Enjoy the ride. . . .

But Anna had lied to Kayla. She texted back before leaving town: It's cool.

What does that mean?

I'm taking care of it. My mom.

Did you talk to her?

I'm going right by their house on the way to Lville. It's halfway. I'll stop.

A long break in the messages. Anna loved Kayla, loved her to death, but sometimes Kayla felt more like a parent or a teacher than a friend. Why did Anna always think she was letting Kayla down?

Are you really?

For sure. I'll let you know when I get there.

Was there any sign of the creep?

Nada.

And Anna consoled herself by thinking that she wasn't really lying about her parents. Not yet, anyway. She'd be lying only *if* she drove past her hometown—Upton—and just plain old didn't stop. Or, she could tell herself, she'd stop and see them on the way *back* to campus once she'd had a good weekend of fun in Louisville.

Right? That could also happen?

Tanya Burns. Officer Shaw.

The names made an uninvited appearance in Anna's mind. A bitter taste filled her mouth.

A grain silo, its roof collapsed or blown off by a storm, stood in the distance. It looked lonely, forgotten, with no farm nearby. No purpose to serve. Anna hated trying to lie to herself most of all—and who exactly was she kidding? She wasn't going by her parents' house. She knew she had no intention of doing it. Call it what it was—she had lied to Kayla. Just to make her escape, to slip away for the weekend without any consequences.

She kept her eyes on the silo as she passed. She pictured the old man collapsing in on *himself.* Nothing for him to do but nurse old wounds, curse the world that had passed him by. She felt pressure in her chest, heaviness. Her dad always sat there like a stone inside of her. Her grip grew loose and shaky on the wheel.

No, no. Don't fall for it. He milked his injury for all its worth.

What did Alisha call it? *Learned helplessness?* Her dad got everybody in his orbit to do exactly what he wanted. And right now he wanted Anna to finish her degree in criminology, go to law school, enter the family business of law enforcement. Her dad had started pushing her even harder toward a career in law the day Avery quit working for the Kentucky State Police. Before that, Anna couldn't recall the old man showing any interest in her career or major.

Something else to thank Avery for. Wasn't the oldest sibling supposed to absorb the heat? Clear the way for the ones who came after? Wasn't the youngest supposed to lie back and draft off the others, let the older kids get all the scrutiny?

Avery had made that impossible when she left her job. Alisha had always flown under the radar, and then she got married and started pushing out babies. So Anna's number came up. Dad elected her to carry the family torch. And Anna did it for a while. Was that why Avery hated her so much? Because Anna basically took over for her, stepped into the limelight that their dad seemed capable of shining on only one of them at a time?

No, it had started long before that. It started *before* Anna was born, when their dad fucked around on Avery and Alisha's mom, caused that marriage to fall apart before Anna's sisters were teens. Anna kind of hated the old man for doing that too, even though she—strangely— owed her life to his inability to keep his urges under control.

Whoop-whoop.

A blue flash in the rearview. "Shit."

The cruiser steamed up behind her, its lights and grille filling her vision.

Had her speed crept higher while her mind wandered?

Anna guided the car to the berm, her tires crunching gravel and who knew what else littered the side of the road. She shook her head, slapped the steering wheel, and added that inconvenience to the list of grievances she kept against her family.

"Fucking cops," she said.

8

Anna's heart thumped.

Two cars whooshed by in the opposite direction, sending a gust of air through her already open window. In the side-view mirror, she watched the cop step out, start to approach.

She recognized the gray shirt and gray pants, the ludicrous Smokey Bear hat the size of a flying saucer. KSP. Kentucky State Police.

"Score," Anna said. Her breathing eased. It could have been a county cop or a local yokel, but she had caught a break. KSP cruising out here in the hinterlands. She watched him come closer, smelled the tar and oil from the road.

The trooper leaned down. He wore reflective sunglasses, and beneath the silly hat, his hair was cropped close to his head. His jaw looked like it had been sculpted out of marble.

"Good day, ma'am," he said, voice laced with a gentle Kentucky twang.

"Hello there." She spotted his name tag. *Always spot the name tag. Officer Carmichael.*

"Do you know why I pulled you over today?" he asked.

It wasn't Anna's first rodeo. She'd been pulled over more than once. In high school, she'd liked to drive fast on the country roads near their house. But she'd slowed down since then, tried very hard not to overdo it. Of course, no cop had ever issued her a ticket. She needed only to mention her dad's name and occupation. . . .

"I do," she said. "I think I was going a little too fast back there, Officer Carmichael. See, it's been a while since I came this way, and I was looking at—"

"Can I see your license, registration, and proof of insurance, please?"

Rude. He had interrupted her. Carmichael looked to be just a few years older than she was. If he'd walked into one of her classes and sat down next to her, wearing a T-shirt and shower sandals, she'd have assumed he belonged there.

"Sure. But can I just say something first?"

"What's that?"

"Well, look, I know this is going to sound all entitled and everything, but my dad is Russell Rogers. *Captain* Russell Rogers. He's retired from KSP. Actually, he got shot in the line of duty and had to retire with a disability. The bullet just totally wrecked his knee. Maybe you've heard of him?"

The cop's lips pressed together. His head swiveled, turning to check out the back seat. Then the mirrored eyes landed on Anna again. He wore a short-sleeved shirt, and his arms were lean and sinewy. "Yes, ma'am, I'm familiar with Captain Rogers."

"Oh, good. He always told me to mention his name if I was ever pulled over by the KSP. I've never actually been pulled over before, so I didn't know—"

The lips spread into a cold smile. "If you don't mind just getting me those documents I asked for. Thanks."

Anna felt her mouth open. She knew she looked like a customer about to launch into a litany of complaints in a restaurant. She didn't want to be *that* person. But she'd dropped the old man's name more than once, and whenever she had, the officers had simply stepped back and wished her a good day. No need to see any documents. No need to talk or check anything else.

Why did Carmichael want to be difficult? Was he a rookie looking to earn some cheap points by catching a speeder?

"Okay, sure. Yeah."

Anna fumbled in her bag, found the things Carmichael wanted. She held them out in her left hand, thinking maybe he'd stand on the side of the road, look them over, and then hand them back. Let her go with a smile and a kind word, a gentle admonition to drive more safely. But he glanced at the license quickly and said, "Anna, are you a student at Gracewood?"

"That's right. Down in Breckville."

"But you're from Upton?"

"Yes. I grew up there."

"My dad went to school at Gracewood." He smiled again, and this time color rose in his cheeks. He took off his sunglasses, revealing eyes the same blue as the sky. "That was a while ago, of course."

"Okay, cool. Yeah."

"I went to UK myself. I studied criminal justice. But Gracewood is a really good school. I have friends who went there and said it was tough."

Was this guy flirting with her? This *cop*? Anna's friends took various approaches to getting out of tickets. One approach was crying. The other was to flirt—bat their eyes and smile and compliment the cop on how brave he was. She wasn't sure the cop was supposed to flatter *her*.

He was better looking than Trevor. Or Eric.

And if it got her out of the ticket . . .

"Yeah, it is. Totally. But UK's a really good school too. Both of my sisters went there."

"Really. Nice."

Anna waited for him to hand the stuff back and let her go. Instead, he tapped the documents against his palm. "Sit tight for a moment."

"Oh . . . okay."

He took one step, then turned back. "Do you mind if I ask where you're headed today?"

A car whooshed by in their lane, kicking up road grit, but the cop didn't seem to notice.

"I'm going to Louisville for the weekend. To see a friend. Can I ask how fast I was going? You haven't said."

"I clocked you at fifty-one in a thirty-five."

"Sheesh. Well, did you hear me say I don't drive out here that much? And you know, the speed limit changes from time to time, and I have a lot on my mind and everything. So you see how I slipped up. Right?"

"Yes, Anna." He smiled again, like she'd really amused him.

When he was gone, Anna said, "Fucking cops."

Like her dad. Like Avery. And now that guy was acting like he was going to write her a ticket. Sure, he claimed to have heard of the old man, but maybe he'd said that to be polite. It made sense her dad's name would start to fade, that younger cops wouldn't know who he was. A surprising sadness passed through her, and she again pictured him hobbling around the house, using a cane or even a walker to navigate the short distance from the living room to the bathroom. Her mom had asked Anna to take the trash out the last time she was home, and the number of empty bottles made the bag almost too heavy to carry.

She shut her eyes, dropped her chin to her chest. "Fuck. Am I a terrible daughter?"

"What's that?"

Anna's head popped up. "What?"

"I thought you said something."

"I thought *you* were back in the cruiser writing me up."

"Oh, no." The cop looked sheepish as he handed her things back to her. "I don't think there's any reason for that. You're right that the speed limit changes, and they don't always mark things clearly. Besides, your dad . . ."

"Right."

"You said something about being a daughter. I think."

"I was just talking to myself. Like I said, there's a lot on my mind." She put her documents away. "Thanks for understanding. Well, be safe out here. . . ."

"Do you really want to know why I started to go back to the car?" Carmichael looked down at the road and swallowed, his Adam's apple bobbing. "Once I heard about your dad, I wasn't going to give you a ticket or anything. Really, I was just stalling because . . . my shift's almost over, and I was going to get something to eat. And I thought, if you wanted to . . ."

Anna felt the tips of her ears burn. And a twisting in her stomach. He *was* flirting with her. "Oh, I see. Well, I am driving on to Louisville."

"Everybody needs to eat," he said. "And there's a diner right up the road in McCoy. It isn't fancy, but the food's good. My treat, of course. And I could get called back on duty any minute. You know, if there's a high-speed chase or a drug bust."

"Or a cat stuck in a tree."

He laughed, looked down at his shoes. "That's the fire department. I'm afraid of heights."

"You're right. Firemen are a lot braver."

"Seriously?" He looked back up, the smile wider to show he wasn't really offended. "Are you going to say that to me? After I let you out of a ticket?"

"I think my dad got me out of the ticket."

"And I bet your dad would want me to make sure you're okay, to make sure you had a good meal in a fine dining establishment. One of the finest in McCoy."

"Actually, my dad always told us not to date or marry cops. He said it was a bad choice."

"He sounds like a wise man."

"My sister dated a cop, though, a nice guy from what I know. But she never worried about what Dad thought." Her stomach started rumbling, kicked into gear by the very mention of food. And free food at that. Anna's funds were limited, since, when she had stopped going to class, she had also stopped going to her part-time job as the supervisor in a campus computer lab. "How far is this place?"

"Five miles. In McCoy, the next town." He pointed in the direction she'd been heading. North. "I'll be honest. There's nothing else in McCoy. You can't miss the diner. It's called Glenn's Place."

"Sounds very fancy."

"Glenn is a master chef. Actually, Glenn died in 1982."

"Did he give himself food poisoning?"

"Car accident. He was speeding on this road. Going fifty-one."

Anna laughed. "If that's not true, please don't tell me. Okay, meet you there. And I promise to stay below thirty-five the whole way."

9

Kayla's bedside lamp cast a soft glow on the book in her hands.

She'd been reading all evening, and as she read, she cursed herself for signing up for an elective literature class during her senior year. She'd done so in a moment of weakness, when she remembered reading during summer days as a kid and thought doing it again would be relaxing.

But the books chosen for this class were nothing like the Harry Potter or Divergent series. The one she was reading now, *White Noise* by Don DeLillo, was about a toxic leak that made a family flee their home. But a lot of the story focused on details. Many, many details. What exactly was the point?

But she plowed through. Her GPA hovered near a 3.8, and she refused to let it slide at the finish line. She had wanted to graduate with a 4.0, but with that option wiped out by some required science classes, Kayla saw 3.8 as the absolute minimum. Even if it meant reading late into the night a book that seemed bizarrely focused on the fictional family's trash compactor.

Did anyone even have a trash compactor in their house? Kayla had never seen one.

With Anna gone, everything seemed muted and hushed. Kayla tried not to feel guilty over Anna's struggles, tried not to dwell too much on what she should be doing as a friend to help. She'd known Anna since freshman year and really come to know her when they were roommates as juniors. It quickly became clear to Kayla that there was only so much she could do for her friend. A stubborn streak a mile wide ran through Anna, and when she decided she didn't want help or advice, nothing could move her. Kayla hoped Anna would come back to school, hoped it wasn't too late for her to salvage her grades and graduate with all of their friends in May. The way they'd always planned.

Kayla looked up from her book. She tilted her head.

Was that . . . ?

It happened again, and that time Kayla was certain. Someone was knocking on the apartment door.

"What the . . . ?"

The clock read ten forty-five. A half-full mug of tea sat nearby. Kayla's friends drank but usually not so much that they'd show up knocking late at night. At least not without texting first.

Anna would. She was prone to losing her keys or misplacing her phone, especially when drinking. But Anna had headed off to Louisville. . . .

The knocking again.

Kayla grabbed her phone, swung her legs off the bed. She put the book aside, wishing she could speed-read it and be finished. Why would someone be knocking at that hour?

She went out to the front of the apartment. A lamp burned in the living room. The kitchen still smelled like the remnants of the burrito she'd brought home for dinner. Kayla checked the door, confirmed the chain was attached. She breathed a little easier. Everything was locked. The fort was secured against anyone, including the Midnight Rambler.

Or the dude who had shown up last night. The creep who had spooked Anna so bad.

Kayla decided to ignore the knocking. She stood in the center of the living room, phone in hand. She wore no shoes and shivered in her shorts and T-shirt.

She expected—hoped—that they'd get bored and go away. A

drunken bro at the wrong door. A pizza guy with the incorrect address.

They knocked again. Then a voice muffled by the door. "Hello? Anna?"

A dude's voice. Asking for Anna.

Kayla took a couple of steps forward, her feet scuffling over the smooth carpet.

"Hello?"

"Who is it?" Kayla asked.

"Can you open the door, so we can talk?"

Kayla moved closer, spoke with force. "No way."

"Are you Anna?"

"Who are you?"

"Anna, I'm a friend of your father's. I'm a police officer. If you look through the peephole, you can see my badge."

Kayla *knew* it. Anna hadn't called home. She hadn't done what she said she was going to do. And now a cop stood at their front door waving his badge around. Anna had disappeared, leaving Kayla to straighten out the mess. *Typical* . . .

She went over, pressed her face to the peephole. Sure enough, the dark shape of a man. About thirty, wearing a sport coat and a button-down shirt, his face turned to the side. At the end of his extended arm, a silver badge.

Anna and Kayla had once spent an entire weekend watching a Discovery Channel marathon of shows about missing and murdered people. Who knew so many people were the victims of violent crimes, or how often they met their doom because the killer posed as a cop flashing a fake badge?

But the show never explained how to tell a real badge from a fake one.

Pressure grew in Kayla's gut. Even if that guy was a real cop, should she tell him anything about Anna?

"I think Anna's fine," Kayla said. "She's dealing with her family."

"Are you Anna?"

"I'm her roommate."

"Oh. Kayla, right?"

He knows my name? "Yes."

"Her father isn't well. You know that, right?"

"I know."

"He's a real hero, injured in the line of duty. If there's anything you can tell me about where Anna is or how to contact her, it would really help. Can you just open the door a crack? You can leave the chain on, but we can see each other then."

Kayla exhaled, but it didn't ease the pressure in her gut. Cops. Was it normal to freak out when you talked to cops, even if you were totally innocent of everything? "Okay, hold on."

Kayla undid the dead bolt but left the chain on. She opened the door a crack, felt the cold air rush in, stinging her feet.

The man's face clarified. Brown eyes, a hint of stubble on the cheeks. A little rough, not as clean-cut as other cops she'd seen. But this guy wore plain clothes, maybe was a detective trying to blend in on the mean streets of Breckville.

The guy craned his head around, looking past Kayla.

"She's not here. I promise."

"Where did she go?"

"Look, dude, I don't really feel comfortable talking about Anna's business, even if you're a cop and a friend of her dad's. Why don't I call her and let her know you're trying to find her?"

"Can you give me her number?"

Kayla started to answer, then caught herself. "Wait. Didn't her dad give it to you?"

Something flashed across the man's eyes, and then he smiled. "He did. But I want to make sure I have the right one. Kids change numbers all the time."

"Do they?"

His smile held, but it looked like the effort hurt him. "If I could just come in and talk to you more about this, it would really help.

There are people who care about her, and they want to know how she's doing. Do you see?"

The pressure in her gut rose, moving into her chest and throat. "I don't think so. I'm going to close this."

She pushed the door.

The man's hand rose, blocking it.

10

An unfamiliar noise woke Anna.

She bolted up. *Where the fuck am I?*

Dark blue walls, a thick blue comforter. She wore a blue UK T-shirt two sizes too big for her body. The closed blinds blocked out any light. The bedside clock read seven eleven.

Something beeped in the room beyond the closed door. *Coffee. Please, Lord, coffee.*

The previous night came back in a rush.

A meal with Officer Carmichael at the diner. First name—Justin. At his recommendation Anna ordered the dinner special—Salisbury steak (whatever that was), mashed potatoes, and green beans that looked like they were left over from World War Two. But she ate it all, every bite, along with three Cokes, since the waitress kept bringing refills. The whole place smelled like frying oil.

And against her better judgment, she enjoyed talking to him. Justin had majored in criminal justice at UK but minored in creative writing. He told her he wanted to take his experiences as a police officer and turn them into stories someday. When she asked how many he'd written, he admitted the total was pretty close to zero. But he figured he was still young and relatively new to being a cop. All he needed was more experience, more crazy stories to tell.

More important to Anna, he listened when she talked about her experience at Gracewood. She liked her criminology classes, found it fascinating to learn about the underlying causes behind crime. But the more she learned, the more she felt pushed in other directions.

"Doesn't the world need more people who are out there helping?" she asked between bites of Glenn's special. "I mean, can't I make a difference another way?"

"You don't think cops and lawyers make a difference?" Justin asked.

Anna knew what she would have answered any other time. Times when she wasn't sitting across a table from a uniformed officer who she actually liked. She would have offered a flip response about all the problems with the police—overzealousness, racism, violence.

Tanya Burns.

But could she so easily slap any of those labels on a cop who seemed to be fundamentally decent?

"And what about your dad?" Justin asked. "Did he make a difference?"

Anna waved her fork in the air. "Don't get me started on him. I know the kinds of things he did. The number of people he sent to prison. The cops he trained. Cops who shoot innocent people of color."

Justin chewed thoughtfully. Anna noticed he tended to be slow to speak, to consider his words before he said them. Maybe he wanted to impress her? Or maybe he feared hurting her feelings?

"I know your dad's reputation," he said. "He was a good cop. Very tough, I understand."

"Did you work with him?"

"No. He was already retired before I started, but I've heard his name. Old-timers talk about him." Justin looked like he wanted to say more but opted to swallow potatoes instead.

"What is it, Justin? I've read his collection of press clippings. I know the stuff he's done."

Justin nodded. "Sure. I guess I can't tell you anything you don't already know. He was . . . is . . . just a tough hombre. From the old school. Very much his own man."

"That's a polite way to say it."

"And you spending time with me right now, it's kind of . . . what? Are you acting out some Freudian revenge psychodrama?"

"Sheesh. Can't I just think you're cute?"

She did think that. And went back to his house after the meal. She'd been woken up by a polite knocking at the door.

It felt strange, since that was his house, and they'd slept together the night before, but Anna said, "Come in."

He did, carrying a steaming mug of coffee and a small plate with what Anna hoped was a piece of toast. She also hoped for it to be slathered with butter.

"Hey," he said. He wore his uniform already, every crease sharp enough to cut paper. "I let you sleep while I got ready."

"You *are* a good cop." Anna pushed herself farther up, then leaned back against the pillows, enjoying the humming, early-morning afterglow of good sex. "And you brought me coffee, so I'm all about the Freudian psychodrama. Or whatever you called it."

Justin sat on the edge of the bed, handed her the mug, and held the small plate out.

Yes. Toast. Lots of butter. He read my mind.

She sipped the coffee. *Bitter.* But it still smelled so good and tasted so warm.

"I've got to head out in a few minutes," he said. "But you can stay as long as you want. The door will lock behind you. And most of the neighborhood miscreants know a cop lives here, so they're a little less likely to break in."

Anna took a bite of toast, which caused a waterfall of crumbs to rush down the UK T-shirt and onto the comforter. "Oh, sorry."

"No worries." He wore that look again, the one that said he wanted to say something else.

"What gives?"

"I was thinking this morning that your family has had some bad luck. There's what happened to your dad, when he got shot, and I know about your sister as well."

"Oh, her." Anna swallowed coffee, anticipated the caffeine surging to the nerve centers in her brain.

"When I told you I knew her last night, you really clammed up. You seemed less interested in talking about her than about your dad."

"If it's possible, she and I have a worse relationship. Like it's almost nonexistent. My dad . . . at least he's my dad. He was always this superprotective papa grizzly, keeping an eye on me. The only thing Avery and I have in common is a dad and sharing a name that begins with an A."

"You said you all three did. Why?"

"My grandma. My dad's mom. Her name was Ava. The old man honored her by giving us all A names. Cute, right?"

"It's a nice tradition."

"I guess so. My sisters are older, and they're closer to each other. They have a tight bond. Oh, and they both got the height in the family. I'm the runt of the litter. Only five-four."

"It looks good on you. Is Avery doing okay? Does she have any lingering effects from that incident?"

"Like I said, I wouldn't know. But she seems pretty capable of taking care of herself. As long as you keep her away from water."

"Right."

"I know I sound like a bitch, but my family is a pain."

"Families usually are." He dug in his pocket and pulled out his phone. "It seems pretty likely we won't ever see each other again."

"You never know. I could speed through here another time."

"And even though you don't approve of your dad's career, you drop his name if it gets you out of ticket."

His words stung. Anna wanted to storm out but wearing a T-shirt and no pants made that impossible. "Where's all this coming from, Justin? Were you reading your psych textbook while I slept?"

"You might want to stop home when you pass through Upton. I know it's on the way to Louisville." He shifted his weight on the edge of the bed. "See, there's a private messaging app we use in the KSP. It's a way for officers to communicate with one another without using official public channels."

Anna felt cold despite the hot coffee.

"Say, for example, a cop has a child who is in some kind of trouble, and they don't want the whole world to know about it, but they want their colleagues to be able to help . . . maybe if a child is missing or hasn't been in touch for a while. . . ."

Anna set her mug on the bedside table. She took the phone from Justin's hand.

BOLO. Twenty-one-year-old Anna Rogers, daughter of Captain Russell Rogers (KSP retired). Last seen at her apartment—likely driving a—

"Did you report me?" she asked.

"No. I really don't have to. You see what this means, right?"

Anna sighed. "Yeah. Fuck. Every cop in the state is going to be looking for me."

11

Through her dirty windshield, Avery watched students streaming out of their apartment buildings like the undead.

They tugged light jackets around their bodies, yawned as they opened car doors, and threw books and bags into their back seats. They all looked wiped out, and Avery envied them the simplicity of their existences, the way worrying over a missed assignment or crushing on a fellow student consumed their thoughts. Simple, uncomplicated worries.

At thirty, she felt old. She understood how distant those days were becoming for her. Being a graduate student and working a full-time job just didn't feel like careless fun. Nothing felt like fun anymore.

She checked her phone. Nothing.

She regretted the message she'd sent earlier that morning, considered it a sign of profound weakness on her part. She'd managed to go weeks, almost a month, without initiating any contact with Hank. She exerted an iron will, kept her texting and dialing fingers under control. And then, last night, in a moment of weakness that she intended to blame on Alisha's visit and the news about her family, she wrote to him again.

Hey, how's it going?

In the history of texting, those four words rose to the top as the lamest ever strung together. And when Hank failed to respond, failed to so much as even write back and tell her to please leave him alone, her shame and embarrassment just grew. If there were only some way to reach out and pull a text back, reel it in like a hooked fish.

She imagined Hank leading an exciting new life. Without her. He'd been a serial monogamist before he met her, and she couldn't imagine he'd have changed. She could imagine him doing all the things for a new girlfriend that he used to do for her—flowers on random occasions. A surprise weekend getaway to Asheville. Volunteering together at the animal shelter.

She put the phone away, shifted her attention back to the lot. A maintenance guy in a red windbreaker rode a giant mower over the grass, a toothpick dangling from his lips. If Anna came out and headed to her car like she was going to class, then Avery wouldn't say anything. She'd chalk this up as a successful reconnaissance mission, report the results to Alisha, and get back to writing the paper she had failed to make any progress on the night before.

But if Anna didn't appear, as seemed increasingly likely, then . . .

"Crap."

Minutes ticked by, and classes started soon. It was possible Anna hadn't scheduled anything at that time, but did Avery want to sit in the parking lot all day looking like the Midnight Rambler? Or like a washed-up cop on a stakeout? She'd nailed the washed-up cop part a few years earlier. . . .

And she couldn't write her paper sitting in her aging Camry.

She pushed the door open, stepped out into the clean morning air. As she walked across the lot, dodging between the dinged and beat-up cars that could belong only to students, cars decorated with Gracewood College stickers and Greek letters from the various fraternities and sororities, Avery practiced what she was going to say.

Look, Anna, I know I've pretty much been ignoring you and the rest of the family for years, but I'm here at your door because I really do care.

Anna was too smart to fall for any bullshit. The two of them shared that trait. Although Avery had started to suspect she'd been bullshitting herself. How long could she pretend most of her family didn't exist?

Was she destined to die alone? At least Dad was married . . . and had a kid—Alisha—who would stick by him no matter what. . . .

At the top of the stairs, she knocked on the apartment door. Not the full-on cop knock she had perfected in the KSP, but a firm rapping meant to get the occupants' attention. She reminded herself of the roommate's name. *Kayla. Kayla. Kayla.*

She knocked again. Louder.

They were probably asleep, blinds closed and pillows over their heads. A memory from years earlier intruded on Avery's mind, one that she couldn't stop. Anna at age three or four, a tiny little girl rushing down the hall in footed pajamas, carrying a stuffed Winnie-the-Pooh in one hand. If something scared her, she came to Avery first, perhaps knowing her sister was an easy mark then and wouldn't send her back to her own room the way Dad and Jane would. Anna would jump in next to her, Pooh Bear clutched to her chest like a life preserver. She'd sleep through the night, curled next to Avery.

"Okay," Avery said, pushing the memory away. "Enough bullshit." She raised her fist and pounded on the apartment door. "Let's end this, so I can get back to my paper."

The apartment next door opened. A guy with a mop of dark curly hair stepped out. He wore basketball shorts and tall white socks, and he squinted at the sun like it was a newly discovered planet in the sky. An empty White Claw can sat near his feet.

"Sup."

"Nothing."

"You looking for them?"

"Anna, yes. And Kayla. Are they home?"

The guy scratched his balls and shrugged at the same time. "Don't know. But it sounded like somebody was having a good time last night."

"A party?"

He laughed, lifted his hand to cover his mouth.

Maybe wash that hand first?

"Maybe a two-person party, if you know what I mean," he said, winking.

"I think I do, boss. Kayla or Anna?"

"Kayla and I share a wall. Your girl, Anna, I don't know what she's up to. You a friend of hers?"

"Not quite. I'm kind of her sister."

"Oh, I see. Anna's cool, you know. I mean, she's a little . . ."

"What?"

"Moody, I guess."

"It runs in the family."

"I get it, man."

"But Anna had a boyfriend, right? Have you seen him?"

"I think that's over, isn't it?"

"Probably. But you never know. Some feelings die hard."

"No doubt."

Avery saluted him, hoped he'd take the hint. "Well, thanks a lot."

"Yeah, sure."

But he stayed on the landing. Watching.

Avery pointed. "I'm just going to see if this is open by chance."

"Everybody's locking their shit. Tight. That Midnight Rambler dude is all over the place. See, I think he's a cop, right? Who else could break in everywhere but a cop? Cops do all kinds of freaky shit. Like that stuff in Louisville. Tanya Burns and all."

"Well, your instincts are right about that. Always stay away from cops. They're the worst."

Avery turned the knob, expecting resistance. It gave way. She gently pushed the door open farther. No chain.

Nothing.

"It's open?" the neighbor asked.

Avery felt a prickling at the base of her neck. "Stay out here. I'm going to look inside."

12

The apartment sat in half darkness.

The blinds and curtains were drawn. Nothing appeared to be disturbed.

Avery closed the door behind her, groped on the wall for a switch to flip. A lamp near the sofa came on, casting a yellow glow over the thin carpet. Everything was quiet.

"Anna?"

Avery's right hand dropped to her hip. She'd grown used to having something there—Mace, even a gun. They acted as security blankets more than anything else. She moved forward to the short hallway that led to the bedrooms. Since she'd been playing the role of coldly disinterested older sister for the past few years, Avery had no idea which one was Anna's and which one was her roommate's.

Her sneakers slipped over the carpet. She smelled food—onions? Peppers? Nothing hung on the white walls. Everything in the apartment looked functional and temporary. Her own apartment utilized the same aesthetic. But Anna and her roommate were college students, young and unattached. What was Avery's excuse for having no anchorage at the age of thirty?

Ahead of Avery, one bedroom door stood open, the other closed. She went to the open one first, stuck her head inside. Messy but not ransacked. Avery looked for a hint to tell her if that was Anna's room or not. How would she know?

She stepped inside. Discarded clothes and shoes littered the floor around the unmade bed. A couple of criminology textbooks sat on the edge of the desk, stacked unevenly like a child's blocks, next to a plastic cup from a pizza restaurant.

And a framed photo. Anna smiling broadly, surrounded by Alisha and Rick and their two girls. They stood outside an ice cream parlor, one Avery recognized from downtown Breckville. When had the photo been taken? Last summer?

A needle lanced Avery's heart. Alisha and her family had visited there. They had all hung out together, posed for the photo. Where had Avery been? Why had she been excluded?

Hold it, now.

Avery put the brakes on her runaway thoughts. She remembered the time Alisha and her family had come to Breckville, knew for a fact that Alisha had called, informing Avery they were going to visit and wanted to see *both* Avery and Anna. Avery made weak excuses—work, school. Life. And Alisha let it go, just made the visit anyway and apparently enjoyed her time with Anna.

Besides, Avery thought, *you can build all the walls you want to keep people out. On the other side of them, life goes on.*

She put the photo back in its place. Anna clearly wasn't home.

A yellowed newspaper clipping sat on the floor. Avery picked it up and read about a KSP drug bust that had happened fifteen years earlier, while her dad was still on active duty. His name featured prominently in the story, which ended with a quote from the old man. "We just want to let the citizens of Kentucky know that this kind of illegal activity will not be allowed to flourish."

Allowed to flourish. Who talked that way? And why did Anna have the clipping? Maybe she studied the old man so she could continue on her path toward fulfilling all of their dad's dreams, the ones involving his daughter working in law enforcement. *Better her than me. Good luck with that, kid.* She put the clipping on the desk.

Avery stopped in the hallway outside Anna's door. On her right, the closed door to the other bedroom. She leaned close, listened. Silence.

What was she even there for? Was it worth waking a sleeping student on a Friday morning?

Maybe Kayla knew where Anna was. Maybe Kayla could get Anna to call home and then Alisha would leave Avery alone.

Avery rapped lightly on the closed door. "Kayla?"

She rapped again, pushed the door open. Thicker curtains blocked more light, creating a deeper gloom. Avery blinked, waited a moment for her eyes to adjust. This room looked much neater, much more orderly. A lone mug with the string from a tea bag dangling down its side rested on a coaster. *If Dad saw the two rooms side by side, he'd pick Kayla for the future in law enforcement.* Her dad made judgments that way, based on superficial stuff that didn't really matter.

One thing felt off—the bed wasn't quite made. A giant ridge bisected the comforter. As Avery's eyes adjusted, she saw it wasn't a ridge—it was a bump. Large. Person-sized.

"Kayla?"

As Avery moved forward, a chilling emptiness took over her body. Her legs slogged, like they were in quicksand, like the room— the bed—was zooming away from her.

But she reached the bed, reached Kayla. The girl lay on her back, head tilted to the side. Skin pale like ivory, bruises on her neck. No movement. No pulse.

"Shit. Holy fucking shit."

13

Avery sat sideways in the back of a Breckville police cruiser. Door open to the cool morning air. Her feet planted on the blacktop.

More than the crime scene itself, Avery served as the focal point of the increasing gathering of cops, crime scene technicians, and the morbidly curious, some of them with their phones out, snapping pictures or live streaming. When the van from the coroner's office rolled up, someone in the crowd gasped loudly enough for everyone to hear.

The Breckville detective, Vic Morris, came her way. He wore a barn coat and khaki pants. He leaned his right arm on the top of the open cruiser door, like the two of them were casually chatting at an office get-together.

"Ms. Rogers, I know you already gave an initial statement to the other officers, but I'd like to follow up on some things. And we may even cover the same ground."

"I get it."

"Right. So you were KSP. For how long?"

"Three years."

"And your dad was, of course."

"Do you know him?"

"By reputation. He was a captain, right?"

"He had a whole career until he got shot. He's a tough old bird."

Morris shook his head over the old man's injury. "And our victim, Kayla Garvey, is your sister's roommate, right? Your sister . . . Anna Rogers. Age twenty-one, if I'm not mistaken."

"You have a good handle on these basic facts."

"Thanks. I try."

Avery held up her phone. "Can I call Anna now?"

"You said you didn't know where she is, right?"

"I don't. But I can call her."

"No one in your family knows where she is?"

"No."

One side of Morris' mouth went up. A light breeze came through, skittering leaves across the parking lot. The maintenance guy stood by his silent mower, nibbling with more force on this toothpick as he watched the proceedings. "I'd rather you didn't call her yet. Do you know Ms. Garvey?"

"I never laid eyes on her before today."

"You've lived here a few years and so has your sister. But you never met her roommate?"

"We're not close." Avery felt defensive, felt the need to try to explain their complicated family dynamics to the police. But why? What did it have to do with anything? Sometimes her sister Alisha came to town to see her. Sometimes Alisha came to town and had a rip-roaring time eating ice cream with Anna. Avery had missed that boat, hadn't even tried. Families, right?

Officer Washington, one of the first cops on the scene, came over. Last time Avery had seen him, he was bailing her out of trouble with the frat boys. "Are you okay with the coroner taking control of the scene?"

"If the techs are finished," Morris said.

"They are."

"Then it's the coroner's show."

Washington nodded, but he didn't leave. "Are you okay, Officer Rogers? Can I get you anything? Water?"

"I'm good. Thanks."

Washington leaned closer to Morris and said, "Can I speak to you for a minute?"

"Sure."

The two men walked away, turning their backs to Avery. She looked at her phone, resisting the urge to just go ahead and call Anna. Or Alisha. She wanted to jump out of her skin. The old man would be hearing about this soon enough, and then he'd be roaring like a bear with a thorn in its paw.

Avery wanted to spare him hearing it from a stranger.

Washington showed Morris something on his phone screen. Morris took out a pair of half-moon glasses and still squinted. He nodded, dismissing Washington, and came back. He leaned on the door again, his right hand swinging free.

"Is there news, Detective?"

"This morning, your dad sent out a private alert about your sister. Did you know that?"

"No. I don't talk to him much either."

"Is there a reason no one in your family talks to one another? Your dad sends out an alert because he can't get ahold of your sister. You don't talk to your sister. Or your dad. But you were both cops. Your sister appears to be studying criminology, so maybe she wants to go into law enforcement in some capacity."

"We should call in Dr. Spock for a consult."

"I talked to my dad every day."

"I don't know what that's like."

"My dad's an accountant, so I didn't follow a hero into law enforcement the way you did. That would be a horse of a different color. And very difficult, I imagine."

"Can I call now?"

Morris raised his index finger in the air, like he was testing the wind. "I guess you don't know if your sister or her roommate was having any trouble with anyone."

"This is the Midnight Rambler, right?" Avery pointed at the crime scene behind Morris. "He went in there, and something went wrong. Very wrong. Or his urges have grown. Whatever it is, he killed a young woman. Maybe two of them."

"Maybe. I know you said you and your sister aren't close. And maybe no one is really very close to anyone else in your family. But . . . how did your sister get along with Ms. Garvey? Ever hear of any conflicts there? Problems?"

"Are you implying something?"

"Your dad had a reputation as a guy who handled things in a rough-and-tumble way. Maybe that runs in the family."

"Bullshit, Morris."

"Did either girl have a partner? Boyfriend or girlfriend?"

"Anna had a boyfriend, but they broke up."

"So you did know *that*?"

"I get periodic updates."

"The guy's name?"

Avery nodded. "I believe it's Trevor. My sister Alisha would know his last name."

"Are you sure you're okay, Officer Rogers?"

"All things considered, yes. Why do you ask?"

"Well"—he looked over his shoulder and then back—"I know a little about how your career ended. And I've been studying the effects of PTSD for my master's degree."

Avery shook her head. "I'm calling my sister now."

14

Anna drove with her phone off.

Completely off.

She had grown up with kids whose parents tracked their every move and message. Her parents had done it for a while as well. But when she left for college, she told them no more. The old man resisted, but her mom stepped in on her behalf. They bought her a new phone when she graduated from high school, and the creepy helicopter-parent app was gone.

But a phone could be tracked even without it. Anna knew it took a lot for the police to track someone's phone. It took warrants and the cooperation of the cell carrier.

Did she really want to put anything past her dad? Better to be safe than sorry. She believed Justin—word would spread among cops in the state. They'd have one eye peeled for her. What a way to curry a little favor with a hero cop—find his daughter who had run off and thrown a scare into her innocent, loving parents.

Anna doubted *Justin* would sell her out. Sex acted as a powerful motivator for keeping people in line. She had made sure to drop the little hint about driving through the area on her return home. Men gave up state secrets for the chance at getting laid. Wouldn't one KSP trooper turn a blind eye to a parent looking for his adult daughter if he might hook up with her again?

Anna navigated the back roads by memory and instinct, guiding the car around the gentle curves with one hand. She'd inherited a good sense of direction from the old man—and she silently thanked him for that, enjoying the one ability he had passed on that would likely allow her to evade him. She shared that sense of direction with Avery, who could always find anything. But poor Alisha . . . oh, Alisha. She once took a two-block detour on the way home from school and ended up fifteen minutes away. As the old man was fond of saying about his middle daughter, she could screw up a one-car funeral.

Anna drove east from McCoy, mostly taking State Road 58. It cut across two counties, winding through farmland and more farmland. Cows and horses and sheep watched her drive by, their dark eyes like pools of ink. Farmers disced their fields, sending up clouds of dust in the wake of their harvests. They left behind stubbled stalks, cut down like whiskers, as they prepared for winter. Anna stopped once, ordered a hamburger and fries at a drive-through. When she pulled around, a Cantwell County trooper sat in his vehicle sucking down a hamburger of his own. The guy was so intent on eating, he didn't lift his eyes to her, and why would he? But Anna's heart thumped so bad, her stomach flipped so much, she didn't feel like eating. The restaurant might as well have handed her a bag of sawdust.

Anna turned north when she reached Highway 177. It ran all the way into Upton and then to Louisville. Anna knew the way to bypass Upton, to swing around on an alternate route, but she replayed Kayla's words in her head. Anna wanted to freeze the old man out, punish him—if he even noticed such things—by giving him the cold shoulder. But what about her mom?

A complicated case, one that Anna could never quite wrap her mind around.

Her mom and dad had started carrying on while the old man was still married to his first wife, Avery and Alisha's mother, Margaret. Their dad had left their mother and moved in with Anna's mom—and then they got married when she found out she was pregnant with Anna, and she gave up her career as a paralegal. They moved away from Louisville, where Avery and Alisha had grown up, and settled in the much smaller town of Upton. That was where Anna had been raised, and where Avery and Alisha occasionally visited as moody teenagers.

Anna's mom liked to stay quiet and let the old man bluster. He took the lead in all things, and her mom stayed by his side, playing the role of a dutiful wife. But the tracking software on the phone wasn't the only time Anna had seen her mother stand up to the old man.

When Margaret died—brain cancer, only fifty—Anna's dad had acted like nothing happened, even though Avery had updated them all about Margaret's failing health anytime the chance arose. He said there was no reason to go to the funeral, even after Alisha asked him to.

Anna's mom sent a massive flower arrangement, having signed all of their names to the card. And then arranged for a catered meal for the reception after the funeral.

But that was her mom. She acted on her own if she had to. She tried her damnedest to smooth the old man's rough edges. And when Anna fought with her dad over Tanya Burns, her mom kept her mouth shut except for muttering once as her dad left the room, "Something like this should never happen. Never."

Kayla was right, as she so often was: *Don't hurt your mom in the process of hurting your dad.* Anna really thought about her mom. She always seemed to get her way when she really wanted to. Anna still couldn't figure out who was in charge between her parents. Sure, it looked like her dad. But was it really her mom?

Anna drove 177 by feel and memory. She'd done it enough times to anticipate every slight curve, every dip in the road. Anticipation built the closer she came to Upton, some primordial tug toward home, the place where she had grown up and from which she worried she'd never fully escape. Like gravity, some unseen force dragged her there whether she wanted to go or not.

And her mom's health wasn't great either. It was easy to fixate on the old man—his hobbling, his pills, the accumulated bourbon bottles. Her mom's memory seemed to be slipping faster than it should.

She was old—fifty-nine on her last birthday—and over the past year, she had forgotten things, including Anna's major a couple of times, at an accelerated rate. And she had totally spaced on the birthdays of Alisha's two children. Last summer, Alisha had wondered out loud—as she and Alisha's family all slurped ice-cream cones—if her stepmother had suffered a small stroke. Or was experiencing the first symptoms of dementia.

Anna shook her head, even with no one there to see her do it.

Her mom couldn't get sick. Or die.

She couldn't go away and leave Anna alone to care for the old man. Sure, Alisha would help, but with two small kids . . .

No matter what the old man said or did or stood for, Anna would find it hard to ship him off to a home. Or leave him in the care of strangers. It seemed to her he was trying to kill himself slowly. Could anybody really help him?

Decision time approached.

She was halfway to Louisville, one hour into her drive. The familiar turnoff to the bypass around Upton loomed ahead. Take it and steer clear of home and family. Stay on 177 and drive within half a mile of her parents' house.

"Fuck," Anna said, smacking the steering wheel with her palm. "Fucking parents. Fucking emotions."

How could she come so close and not at least . . . look at the house?

As she drove closer to her home, she surprised herself by feeling relieved.

15

The First Baptist Church, Reformed, of Upton sat on Highway 177, nestled in between an apartment complex called Bayside Estates and a strip mall featuring a vacuum cleaner repair shop, a pizza parlor, and a comic book store.

Anna pulled into the church lot and drove to the back, where the rear of the church's property met the subdivision behind. Close to the building sat a few cars, which likely belonged to a couple of secretaries and a minister carrying out the hushed business of the church on a weekday morning. On Sunday, the place filled up like a football stadium. Cars jammed the lot before services started, and then everyone hung around afterward, chowing down on fried chicken and fatty potatoes and cakes and pies baked by elderly women.

How did Anna know that? Her family had attended the church when she was a kid. Her mom woke Anna and even her sisters—during their occasional visits—early on Sundays, and rode herd on them while they brushed their hair and dressed in the nicest clothes they could find, and then the five of them walked—okay, her dad marched, her mom walked, the girls trudged—across the street and up the little concrete path to the parking lot and the church.

But the church had served a larger and more important purpose in Anna's life. Since their street ran behind the parking lot, it had made for a handy pickup and drop-off location when Anna and her friends started to drive. When Anna had wanted to go out with someone—and hadn't wanted her parents to know about it—she would meet the person in the First Baptist Church, Reformed, parking lot. Quite a few times, the lot had served as a convenient place to fool around with a guy while Anna tried not to think about a church on one side of the car and her parents' house on the other.

Anna took an empty spot in back. Leaves fell off the thin screen of trees, and she was able to see the familiar two-story house, white with black shutters. She yawned. The hamburger still sat beside her on the passenger seat, and her stomach rumbled, signaling the return of her appetite. She unwrapped the burger and took a bite, not even minding the lukewarm temperature, the congealed grease.

Two cars sat in the driveway. Anna recognized both. The white Impala belonged to her parents. Her dad drove the car with less and less frequency as his leg grew more and more painful. Her mom still drove, but even that seemed precarious. She'd started to get lost, and once parked the car in the middle of the yard and gone inside like what she'd done was the most natural thing in the world. Anna's dad told her she'd missed the driveway by twenty feet, and her mom looked out the front window, patted her hair, and said, "Oh, I guess I did."

Next to the Impala sat Alisha's blue SUV. She'd probably brought the kids over, as she frequently did, trying to lift her parents' spirits. Otherwise, their mom and dad spent their days in the house, the TV running continuously, the blinds drawn no matter the weather. A depressive weight pressed against Anna, making her sink into the seat. As she finished eating, she grew tired, her eyelids yielding to depression as well.

She tried to pump herself up, tried to reassure herself. *They're fine. Just fine. See? It's a normal day. Alisha's visiting. They're happy. Right?*

They weren't—she knew that. But if she closed her eyes, opted not to stare at the familiar house, then maybe she wouldn't think about it—

Clack clack clack.

Anna's eyes opened. She wiped a string of drool off her chin, turned to the left.

A kind face looked at her. The woman made a motion to roll down the window.

Anna checked the dashboard clock. She'd slept for only nineteen minutes, but in that time someone had snuck up on her. She rolled the window down. She knew this woman from somewhere.

"Hello," Anna said, wiping her chin again.

"Are you okay? We saw you parked back here."

"Sorry about that."

"No need to apologize." The woman's voice was soft, just above a whisper. A white poof of hair sat on top of her head, and she wore glasses in thin gold frames. "We thought you might need help."

"Oh, no. No help. In fact . . . I'm just passing through, on a trip. And I needed to take a nap, and this looked like a safe place. A church, you know? But I feel better now."

"Would you like to come inside? We have coffee made. That will perk you up."

"Oh, I don't know. I'm on my way to see a friend."

The woman tilted her head to one side, and sunlight reflected off her glasses. "It's Anna, right? Anna Rogers?"

Would lying accomplish anything? Lying to a literal church lady?

"Yes, ma'am. Anna. Aren't you Mrs. Delson?"

"That's right. Well, it's been a long time." Mrs. Delson turned her head in the direction of the house and then turned back. "You're awfully close to home."

"That's how I knew it was safe to sleep back here."

"But you're not stopping to see your mom and dad?"

"Well, see, I have to go to see my friend. And then I'm stopping to see my parents on the way back to school. At Gracewood."

Okay, you did it. You lied through your teeth to a church lady. Oh, Anna.

"I'm sure they'll appreciate that." Mrs. Delson leaned closer. "How is your mother?"

"She's good. Real good. Thanks."

"She's a strong woman."

"She is. Yes."

As if on cue, fifty yards away, the old man came out the front door of the house. He was using the walker and looked two hundred years old. He hobbled out onto the front walk wearing sweatpants and a yellowed T-shirt. His hair stood up like the bristles of a broom. The black grip of the ever-present nine-millimeter stuck out of his pants pocket. He carried it wherever he went, even if it was just to the mailbox.

Alisha came out behind him. She gestured back toward the house, trying to get him to go inside. But the old man looked determined to keep going. He pushed the walker toward the driveway. He stopped again, pointing down the street.

Anna turned her head that way. She wasn't certain but there might have been a car parked down there. Why her dad was agitated by the car, she couldn't say.

"Is he okay?" Mrs. Delson asked.

"He is. He's very protective. You know, that cop instinct doesn't go away easily."

"Protective of what?"

"The house. The family." Anna hadn't intended to say the words, but they came out. They perfectly summed up the best part of the old man. "He always made us feel safe when we were around him."

"But I don't understand what's bothering him."

Alisha reached their dad and placed her hand on his arm. He pulled free of her and pointed again. He was barefoot, and the wind moved the strands of his hair from one side of his head to the other. Alisha nodded toward the house, pleading. Anna could imagine she wanted him back inside quickly. Didn't want to leave her kids with no one but their grandmother watching them.

"Maybe you can go help them," Mrs. Delson said.

"Yes, I think you're right."

"I know your father hasn't been in good health since his injury."

"No, he hasn't. Thank you, Mrs. Delson."

"It's a shame, isn't it?"

"Dad's injury? Yes, it is."

"Yes, that. But I also mean the way police officers are treated these days."

"How's that?" As soon as she asked, she wished she hadn't. She suspected the conversation wasn't going to go in a good direction.

She was right.

"Like this Officer Shaw in Louisville. They're crucifying him for what he did up there. Dragging him and his family through the mud."

"He killed an unarmed woman."

Mrs. Delson's index finger came out. "That's what the media wants you to believe. You have to be careful about what people say on television. They're lying about her being unarmed."

Anna squeezed the wheel so tightly she thought her knuckles would explode. "I can't believe you're saying this shit."

Mrs. Delson looked like she'd been punched in the nose. "Please don't curse, young lady."

"Fuck off, Mrs. Delson." Anna started the car and dropped it into reverse. She backed out.

"I have your mother's phone number inside. I'm going to give her a call, tell her the way you've spoken to me—"

"Ask for my dad. The two of you have a lot in common."

"You should value and respect your father more—"

Mrs. Delson stepped back as Anna whipped the car around. The tires squealed as she left the lot, turning left instead of right, away from her parents' street and on up 177 toward Louisville.

16

Yates spotted the man in the park. He sat on a bench, knee crossed over knee, and held a newspaper that shook in the light breeze. The day turned slightly overcast as a cloud passed over the sun.

Yates hesitated, then went forward.

The man kept his eyes on the paper as Yates sat. He continued to read like Yates wasn't there.

Okay, Yates thought. *I get it. Make me wait, get me worked up. Okay.* That was the game they were playing. He could go along, play the game if he had to. He knew how to survive. He'd been doing it for years.

After all, Yates was the one who had fucked up. Even though he could explain it—

The man closed the paper with a snapping noise, folded it into a quarter. He tapped it with an index finger. "Young girl killed in her home. You've heard about that, right? You've *more* than heard about it. . . ."

Yates remained quiet. People went by on the sidewalk, heading to work. Women with small kids. Regular life. Better to stay quiet, let the man make his play, do his thing. Not to overreact or tip his hand . . .

The man dug around in his coat pocket and brought out a pack of cigarettes. He shook a few loose, held the pack toward Yates.

"No, thanks."

The man stuck one in his mouth and lit it, exhaled a long plume into the park. "So what happened?"

Yates had been thinking about it since the night before. He'd played it all out again before he fell asleep. And he slept pretty well. He looked down at his hands, which dangled and looked useless.

"She fought me, Hogan." He never called him Colby. Just Hogan. Calling him Colby would have been like calling your kindergarten teacher by her first name. But they were equals, weren't they? Coworkers? Hogan would try to intimidate, push him around. Yates needed to stand his ground. He brought skills to the table. "She— It was supposed to be simple, you know? Like you told me. But this girl, she didn't want to cooperate."

"You do know what the problem is, right?" Hogan tapped the paper again.

"I know. I knew that last night when she told me her name."

"But you killed her anyway?"

"I told you—she didn't cooperate."

Hogan shook his head. "Not only did you try to get information out of the wrong girl, but you killed her. You weren't supposed to hurt anyone. You were just supposed to *take* the girl, *get* her, and bring her to the farm, even if she didn't want to come voluntarily. The family thought you could handle this task, the way you've handled others for them. Admittedly, this one required a little more finesse, a little more precision. But you look younger than you are, so you could blend in on campus and maybe get close to Anna."

"It was the roommate who opened the door, okay?" Yates kept to himself that the girl had said she was Kayla. In that moment, Yates had thought she was lying, pretending to be the roommate. How did he know?

"That's a pretty low bar for killing someone. I'd hate to go trick-or-treating with you."

"I thought I could talk to the roommate, maybe get some information from her. I mean, she knew Anna as well as anyone, right?

Roommates, they talk all the time. I got a little eager. I forced it a little. Well, you know. . . ."

Hogan took a drag, held the cigarette out like he'd never seen it before and didn't know how it had ended up in his hand. He tossed it away into the grass, where it lay with a coil of smoke rising from its tip. "It's a problem."

"You saw the news. They're going to blame it on this Midnight Rambler guy."

"Anybody see you?"

"No, sir. It was dark. No one else was there."

"You hope."

"I'm sure. I was careful. I'm always careful."

"College kids everywhere."

"I waited until they were all gone."

A child started crying on the other side of the park. Yates watched the mother take the child by the arm and, shaking her finger, pull him toward a car.

"You hope so," Hogan said.

"I used the fake-badge thing. If not the Midnight Rambler, they'll blame a cop."

"Please. Cops don't blame other cops for anything."

Yates had no idea how old Hogan was. He looked to be middle-aged, maybe in his mid-fifties, but he was a tough guy to get a read on. Yates wanted to ask his age just to know, just to satisfy his curiosity about the man. But he couldn't bring himself to do it.

"I *do* have information," Yates said. "You wanted information, and so did the family. Well, I have some."

"Okay. But the family isn't happy about this. And neither am I. It makes *me* look bad, and they may be reluctant to give *me* work again in the future. And you . . ."

"I know where the girl's going, the cop's daughter. Anna. We can still do this. I can."

Hogan turned his head slightly toward Yates, like Yates might have grabbed his interest. He shook another cigarette out of the pack. "Okay. Talk."

"Louisville," Yates said. "She's going to Louisville."

The cigarette dangled from the corner of Hogan's mouth, but he didn't light it. "That's a fucking big city. Should somebody just stand on a street corner, maybe just walk up and down Bardstown Road until they pass the girl? How is this helpful?"

"I looked at the girl's phone. The roommate. She had texts from the cop's daughter. She said she's going to Louisville to see her friend Rachel."

"Okay. So we can stand on Bardstown Road and shout, 'Rachel.' What if she changed her plans? What if she stopped home in Upton?"

"No, no. There's more."

"Did you take the phone?"

"I did."

"They can track that."

"I tossed it. Maybe the cops won't know the girl's in Louisville, but we will."

"Okay. You said there's more."

Yates felt a flush of pride color his face. "I looked on the girl's social media pages. That was easy. And she has this friend in Louisville. A chick named Rachel Berger. From the same hometown, Upton. And her address is 1919 Humboldt Road. See? I've practically handed it to you."

Hogan lit the cigarette, and Yates felt relieved. He was getting sick of watching the cigarette dangle from the other man's mouth unlit. And he figured that lighting the cigarette meant Hogan was happy.

"You figured all that out, huh?"

"Yeah. I was hoping to make up for my . . . you know, overzealousness."

"I don't know if you can do that."

"Look, I'll go up to Louisville. I'll find the girl at this Rachel's house. I'll take care of what you asked me to take care of. I'll get her to the family."

"Or Rachel will be dead just for opening her door."

"Come on. Give me a chance. I look young enough to blend in with young people. You said that."

Hogan studied him, squinted. The clouds were shifting, more sunlight returning. "Maybe."

"You know I can."

Hogan puffed away. Some of the hard lines disappeared from his face, making him seem a little younger. He flicked the ash into the grass. "You sit tight for now. Don't do anything until you hear from me."

"How will you contact me?"

"The usual way." Hogan pulled up his sleeve and looked at his watch. "But I may not need you anymore. In the meantime, lay low. And I mean very, very low. The cops are lit up about this murder. They're dying to arrest someone."

"What about the cop? The dad."

"What about him?"

"Can anybody get to him?"

"Why are you asking that?"

"I just figure if you're tracking his daughter, it must trace back to the cop."

"Forget the cop. Ex-cop. Just forget about him."

"If you say so . . . I was just thinking—"

"Please, don't do that. It's dangerous."

"I know about the business the family is in. I understand that. It would make sense if they wanted to hurt this cop somehow. Or any cop who must have busted them."

Hogan held his index finger in the air. "You need to be careful about supposing things when it comes to the family. And their motives. It's not ever going to be what you think. Okay? Just push them out of your mind. This is way more complicated than you understand."

Yates tried to push harder. He didn't know if it would help to lift him out of the hole he was in. Or dig the hole deeper. It was time to try. "I've been to the farm. I know what goes on there—"

"*Once*. You were there once."

"—and they trusted me to do this job, so I feel like I'm involved. I have something on the line. And if the police were to track me down, I could easily tell them—"

"Like I said"—Hogan raised the finger again—"put thoughts of the family and their farm out of your head. It's best for everyone that way."

"I *want* this to work out the best for everyone." Yates felt a little better, like he had seized back some of the power in the dynamic with Hogan. It was always good to remind him of what Yates knew. "Don't you?"

Hogan studied him for a moment, his brow wrinkling. That made him look older again, definitely on the high side of fifty. The age seemed to settle on him, and it made Yates feel better, like he was getting a clearer fix on the guy. He hated when Hogan's age slipped around, when he couldn't tell exactly what or who he was dealing with.

Hogan looked like he'd reached a decision, accepted something about Yates. Maybe he'd just decided that Yates was going to be around for a little while, was going to be part of this now that the waters were muddied as they were.

"I do." Hogan smacked the paper against his own thigh, flicked the burning cigarette away. "And you need to wish for the same thing. Okay?"

Hogan didn't look back as he walked off.

17

As Avery pulled into the driveway, Alisha came out the door, her younger child in her right arm. The same old house—her *dad's* house with his *new* family—looked smaller every time she came, the white paint dingier, the roof more worn. Weeds grew in the unmulched flower beds on either side of the front door.

"Are you trying to stop me from going in?" Avery asked.

"Of course not. I'm glad you're here. Even a little surprised."

"I'm trying to help. It shouldn't be so shocking."

"No, no."

Avery wasn't sure who Alisha spoke to. Her kid, Eliza, had taken hold of a fistful of Alisha's hair and was twisting it in her tiny hand.

"No," Alisha said again.

That time Avery felt that her sister was speaking to her niece. Eliza unclutched the hair and stuck her fingers in her mouth.

"Can you say hi to Aunt Avery?"

Eliza looked away, buried her face in Alisha's hoodie.

Same, kid. Same. Avery never knew what to say to children, lacked the gift of speaking in a funny voice or making an appropriate face. Anyone under the age of sixteen might as well be an alien beamed down to earth, because Avery lacked the ability to communicate with them.

"What's going on here in Funville?" Avery asked.

"Dad just talked to the detective down in Breckville. What's his name? Morris?"

"That's him."

"Anyway, I guess this is good news. They made a thorough examination of the apartment, and it looks like Anna might have packed to go away. Did you know she's kind of a slob?"

"Of course I did."

"Okay. Easy. So, if she just went away, that's good."

"Or something happened to her, like what happened to Kayla."

Alisha smoothed a loose hair on Eliza's head, stepped toward Avery, and placed her hand on her sister's biceps. She lowered her voice. "Was it awful? I'm so sorry."

"Thanks. I'm okay." The image of Kayla tucked into the bed, head turned to the wall, skin pale and cool as marble, would linger for a long time. No shortcut existed to scrubbing certain pictures from the mind. "How are things inside?"

"Oh, yeah. That." Alisha looked back at the house, ran her hand through her hair. "Well, he's been drinking. And taking his pain pills."

"So, situation normal all fucked up."

"Something like that. Look, Avery, he's so around the bend about Anna. Earlier today, he came hobbling outside, using the walker, with his gun sticking out of his pocket. He was convinced a car parked up the street was someone coming to assassinate him. He thinks Anna's been murdered or kidnapped, and they're going to call and use her as bait to get him."

"I could have predicted all of that. But you seem to have an agenda. Spit it out."

Eliza tugged Alisha's hair again. "Ow, baby. Stop." She pried the little fist loose. "I know it's difficult for you to come here. It's been . . . a while. He's agitated enough."

"Christ, Alisha. I drove an hour to be with the family. After finding a murdered girl this morning. Can you give me a little bit of a break? And some fucking credit?"

"What does 'fucking' mean?" Eliza asked.

Alisha's eyes widened. "It's a grown-up word, sweetie." She looked at Avery and mouthed, *Thanks.*

Avery shrugged. She didn't feel like apologizing. To anyone.

Alisha said, "It's been years since we've all been on the same page in this family. Years. Since before . . ."

"Since before Dad met and married the Dragon Lady."

"Avery. We all want the same thing. Okay? We all want Anna to be safe."

"Where is Aunt Anna?" Eliza asked.

Alisha kissed her daughter on the top of the head. "She's not here right now."

"I love Aunt Anna."

"We all do, hon. We all do." She turned her attention to Avery. "Last night, you blew me off when I asked you to check on Anna. The hardest no, you said. But you went to her apartment this morning."

"So?"

"So, I know you care," Alisha said. "You big softie."

"Can we go inside before I puke?"

"Aunt Avery's going to puke, Mommy."

"She might if we're too nice to her."

Avery followed them to the door. Before they went inside, Alisha turned back.

"Just be aware . . . things have changed since the last time you saw them."

18

The house smelled musty, like it had been closed for too long.

As always, every blind and curtain was shut, making the house feel like a mausoleum.

Alisha's warning about things changing served Avery well. She noticed right away the scattered newspapers, the stained carpet. Every flat surface was covered with magazines or junk mail or soda cans. Potato chips littered one section of the carpet near the disordered sofa.

A TV played at a jet-engine decibel level. A news channel Avery hated. A red-faced anchor brayed about rising crime and lost liberty.

Alisha found the remote on the coffee table with her free hand and mercifully muted the TV. "Chelsea is sleeping, and I need to get this one down too. Jane?" She moved toward the door to the kitchen. "Jane? Dad?"

Avery looked around. The arrangement of the furniture remained the same. The artificial light cast a sickly yellow glow on the walls.

Something tightened around Avery's neck, like a choke collar. She started to find it hard to breathe. Like her air was slowly being closed off.

Like she was underwater. Flailing.

Jane emerged from the kitchen. "Oh. Oh, I see. It's Avery." She wore a pink robe, loosely belted at her waist, and dingy white socks. Her graying hair was pulled back, and her eyes looked slightly sunken. "Oh, thank goodness you're here."

"Hi, Jane."

"I wish you girls had told me you were coming. I was going to pick up."

Alisha placed her hand on Jane's upper arm. "You don't have to clean. It's okay. I can help you with that later."

"You're the only person who ever picks up here. Your dad can't do it anymore."

"It's fine, Jane. Where's Dad?"

"He was . . . I mean, he was right here. . . . I'm not sure. We heard you girls coming in. . . ."

The pressure on Avery's throat eased a little. A delay in coming face-to-face with him again. She was putting off the inevitable.

"Why don't you sit, Avery? Do you want something?"

"I'm okay."

Jane clutched her robe, gathered the two halves tighter across her chest. She was still nearly as tall as Alisha. "Avery, honey, was it awful? In that apartment? Honey, are you sure Anna wasn't in there?"

Avery tried to reconcile the scared, shaken woman before her with the home-wrecking monster she had considered her to be when she was younger. The two pictures didn't fit together. "I'm sure. And the police looked as well. They're very thorough."

"Avery, I was just telling Alisha that Anna's friend called us. Eric. You know, that kid who's been in love with Anna since they were in high school? He lives in Louisville now."

"Where was he last night?" Avery asked.

"Well . . ." Jane searched for the answer. "I guess I don't know."

"It's okay," Avery said. "Why did he call?"

"He can't get ahold of Anna either. And he's worried." Jane looked at Alisha and then behind her, like she wanted to make sure no one else heard. "I talked to him, instead of your father. Thank God."

"What did he say?" Alisha asked. "I thought he was just checking on her."

"Yes, that. He said Anna might be going up to Louisville, but he wasn't sure. He also said . . . he said he's heard that Anna was drinking a lot. And partying. And . . . other things."

"Other things?" Avery asked. "Like what?"

Alisha's brow furrowed. "We're all adults, Avery."

"You can imagine," Jane said.

"I hope it's true," Avery said. "She's a young woman. I hope someone is having some fun."

"Avery. Please?" Alisha said.

"I'm just thinking of Kayla's parents, what they're going through," Jane said. "Someone told them, right?"

"Someone told them, Jane," Alisha said. "Do *you* want to sit down?"

"To lose a child. To have your child taken away . . . so violently . . . And that lunatic is running around, maybe hurting other girls. Or spying on them. I was going to pick up the house a little."

"You don't need to do that. Would you like to go with me while I check on Chelsea and put Eliza down?"

"Yes, I would. Do you mind?"

"No, I'd like it."

Alisha took Jane by the arm and gently guided her down the hall, leaving Avery alone in the living room. She stood with her hands folded in front of her. She watched the muted TV anchor rage on the screen.

Family photos, framed and faded, still hung on the wall. Avery hadn't seen them in years, and she couldn't resist looking.

She and Alisha posing together as kids, wearing matching clothes. Anna in a few school shots, gap-toothed and braided. Dad, Jane, and Anna in a portrait.

Avery knew Jane valued those photos more than anything. Within the first year of their living in that house—while Alisha and Avery were still in Florida with their mom—there was a small fire, which destroyed most of Anna's baby pictures. Jane treated the photos that remained, and the ones taken since, like holy relics. She tried very hard to make everything seem normal. She never could, but she tried.

Avery's eyes landed on the photo she remembered best—her dad in uniform.

Since the day that photo had gone up in their home, when Avery was five or six, she'd been studying that image. Her dad, with a full head of hair, standing before an American flag. Badge shining, every button bright. He looked trim and strong, a force to be reckoned with. Avery hadn't read comic books or watched movies about superheroes. She had lived with one.

Avery had decided that far back that she wanted to be like him. Once she had even brought the photo to school for show-and-tell or career day or something—she couldn't remember which. But she remembered telling the class she was going to be a police officer like her dad. And the whole class applauded.

Whenever she'd told her dad, he always responded, "That's right."

For so long, it was. Right. An easy star to guide one's life by.

Until the day everything went wrong.

19

It happened on a Tuesday afternoon in February.

The call came over the radio: 10-46. *Accident with injury.*

Avery operated out of KSP Post Three in Bowling Green. The dispatcher added additional information: vehicle off road at mile marker thirty-three. Northbound.

Avery was close, just five miles away. She responded 10-96. *En route.*

Traffic was light. The interstate there cut through cattle farms, gently rolling hills with trees in the distance. Avery reached the scene, saw tire tracks leading off the interstate, a gaping hole in the barrier fence.

A burgundy vehicle bobbing in the dark water of a small pond.

"Shit. Fuck."

Avery flicked on her lights, pulled to the berm, skidded to a stop. She checked in quickly from the scene, requesting backup. *Vehicle in water. Passengers inside.*

Avery climbed out, ran to the pond. Two civilians stood on the edge of the water. It was cold but not freezing. About forty degrees. Avery's equipment jangled and creaked as she ran. She stumbled over a rock, partially turning her ankle.

"Damn it."

By the time she reached the water, the vehicle was almost submerged. *How deep is this fucking thing?*

"They went flying past me and off the road." The one guy wore a feed cap and heavy work boots. The man next to him, who wore a long wool coat and dress shoes, took two steps away from the water. "I think there's a kid in back. Maybe two."

"Shit."

The man looked at Avery. Waiting. Expectant. "Well?"

Avery dropped her belt, gun, baton, handcuffs, all on the muddy ground. She kept the flashlight to smash the windows. No time to remove her heavy shoes.

She stepped in. The freezing water stung her legs, even through her pants.

She felt like she'd swallowed water. Choking—an iron fist of fear around her neck. Cutting off her air. She swore she had smelled chlorine stronger than the rich odor of mud and brackish water.

All in. Just go all in.

Just like Dad said—dive in. All at once. That's the only way.

Avery stepped in up to her knees. The water around the edges of the vehicle bubbled and hissed. Her feet felt like frozen blocks.

A child. Maybe two.

Sirens approached. Still far away. It was on her. If you wore the uniform, sometimes it all landed on you to do something.

Avery swallowed. *I'm going to die. Just accept it—I'm going to die. This is how my life will end.*

She took two quick steps forward and dove, hands out, body flat. She splashed, disappeared under the surface of the water.

The light was extinguished. Avery paddled in the direction of the car—she thought.

She flailed but moved forward. The water rushed in her ears. But besides that—was she hearing things? Knocking against glass? Screams? Muffled screams and shouts?

A miracle occurred. Avery's hand touched something smooth and solid. Metal or glass.

She ran her hand over it, felt metal meet glass at a small seam.

She took water in, nearly choked. Then something popped into her mind. *The bottom. Let your feet touch the bottom.* And she did. Her feet found the bottom of the pond. She was anchored.

She held the flashlight. Competence overrode fear. She could do it. Smash the window, let them out. Adrenaline ripped through her body like electricity. She was doing it.

She gripped the light, pulled her hand back, and brought it forward.

But the water provided too much resistance. She couldn't swing hard enough to break the glass. No way. Why hadn't she thought of that?

She let go of the flashlight. It floated to the bottom.

Avery reached out, fumbled in the dark for a door handle.

She became aware of her hammering heartbeat, the pressure in her ears. Even in the pitch black, with her eyes closed, her vision clouded.

Get the handle. Get the handle.

But she couldn't find it. Her lungs burned. Everything burned.

She swallowed a gulp of sickeningly foul water. It choked her. Fingertips brushed the handle, tried to get a grip.

She felt like she had to vomit. She swallowed more water. . . .

Her hand, freezing and useless, couldn't grab the handle. Couldn't grab anything.

She started to float. She was losing it, slipping away.

The water above turned from oily black to bright blue. The surface rippled, drew farther away, the sun obscured in the distance. No one was going to help her. She was alone and sinking—

Avery started to flail. She slapped her arms around, and the more she swung, the more water she took in. Gulps and gulps filling her lungs and throat, leaving no room for air, no room to breathe. The bottom was gone. There was no bottom. Just a hole in the world below the water—

Something pulled her back. Up and toward the surface of the water.

Pulling and pulling while water went down her throat and up her nose.

Then she was out. And slopped onto the shore of the pond, a

soggy mess. Water ran off her body, Mud and rocks poked her through her clothes.

The sky was cloudy, pencil-lead gray.

Was she dead?

The guy in the feed cap bent over her. He slapped her cheeks a few times.

"Hey. Hey."

Avery coughed, spewed water into the air. She turned onto her side and vomited, a great flood of black water.

"That's okay. Get it out."

She was cold. Freezing. The guy took his jacket off and draped it over her.

"It's okay," he said. "You're okay."

"Did they . . . ?"

"Yes, ma'am. They're getting them out now. I think everybody's all right. Just scared and cold."

"Did you . . . ? Thank you. . . ."

"No, ma'am, it wasn't me. I didn't go in there. It was one of your fellow officers. He went in and pulled you out. To be honest, you were under so long, I kind of thought you were a goner. But then there you were. He pulled you out of there like he was noodling a catfish. You were about as wet and muddy as one too."

People trudged back and forth past her. Sirens wailed.

"Who did it?"

"That trooper there, the young guy. He took you out first, and then he dove right back in and came out with one of those babies."

Avery looked. It was Hank. Somehow she had known it would be. He was a hero.

Her heart galloped. It felt like it would never stop.

She'd almost died. She'd almost let go, almost slipped away. Holy shit—she'd almost fucking died.

20

"Do you know when that picture was taken?"

Avery knew. She felt her dad's presence in the doorway from the hallway to the living room. But she didn't want to turn. Did she want to see him now? See the wear and tear of the years on him? Couldn't she stare at the photo of him in his uniform and imagine he would always be that way?

She turned, saying, "I know."

"That's when I was promoted to captain."

The walker supported his sixty-two-year old body. The muscles in his forearms below the sleeves of his white T-shirt tensed, indicating the strain. He wore gray sweatpants and Velcroed white shoes. His cheeks were flushed—either from booze or effort or both—and the scarlet tint ran all the way up his forehead and showed through his much thinner hair. His blue eyes, glossy and small, took her in with wary intensity. He'd shrunk. In his prime, he had stood six-two, but he had to be under six feet now.

"Hi, Dad."

"Do you remember that?" he asked as though she hadn't just told him.

"I do. I was at the swearing-in ceremony. We all were. We were all proud. Very proud."

He nodded, then shuffled forward. His right pants pocket bulged. The nine-millimeter, always at the ready.

"Do you need any help?"

"No. I'm not an invalid. Not quite, anyway."

Avery begged to differ but kept her mouth shut. He reached the couch, awkwardly turned at an angle, moving the walker first and then his body. He started to lower his butt, but as if the effort grew too great—or gravity worked too hard against him—he just plopped onto the cushions, letting out a sighing exhalation as he landed. The sofa springs squeaked.

"Shit," he said.

Avery remained standing. Every surface that might have been suitable for sitting on, including the other end of the sofa, was covered with something.

He raised his index finger. "You're going to take me down to Breckville. Your sister won't do it. You're going to drive me down there, and I'm going to find Anna."

"Dad—"

"I can drive myself, but your mother worries. She hid the keys. Or she just forgot where they are—"

"She's not my mother."

The icy blue eyes expanded. "Okay, bullshit. Your stepmother. Who cares about the fucking semantics? Just take me there. I can pay for the gas."

"Hold on, Dad." From across the room, she caught a whiff of a sour smell. A combination of urine, sweat, and liquor. "I know how worried you are, and I know how much you care about Anna. The police are looking all over Breckville. Actually, *you* have the police looking all over the state. We don't know if looking in Breckville is the best thing. Anna talked to Alisha a lot. She talked about how much she disliked Breckville. Maybe she went somewhere else. Her friend Eric said she might be going to Louisville. Alisha says she goes there a lot on weekends."

Before she finished speaking, her dad started shaking his head. "That's not it. I told you girls this would happen. I warned you and I warned you. And you didn't listen to me or take me seriously. And now it's happened."

While they were growing up, her dad had kept a thick binder on a table near the front door. Pages and pages of photos—mug shots—of men he'd arrested. Men who might be getting out of jail or prison someday. If a person they didn't recognize showed up on their doorstep, they were to consult the binder and make sure someone hadn't come by to settle a score. Even after Avery's mom and dad had split up, the binder remained. The only time it didn't sit by their front door was the year they lived in Florida, in that dingy apartment with the tree frogs on the window and lizards in the bathtub. Florida was a freak show of its own, but they stopped worrying about an ex-con looking for the old man and ringing the doorbell. Yet Avery had missed her dad—his fierce protectiveness, his eternal vigilance. The sense his arm was always around her, holding her close. She wasn't sure she had ever felt that way again, even when they moved back.

"There was a car up the street earlier," he said. "They drove off when I went out there, but I saw them. Alisha was there. She saw it." Dad flipped up the couch cushion next to him, peered under it.

"Are you looking for something?"

"Forget it."

"Didn't Anna stop taking your calls because you had a fight?" Avery asked.

There were rules in the family—including not asking their dad about anything he didn't want to talk about. Long ago, Avery had decided the rules were stupid—and how much of a member of the family was she, really? Avery needed to talk to him if there were to be results.

"Oh, that's cute." He lifted the cushion again.

"Are you looking for a bottle?"

"Forget it." He adjusted the gun in his pocket. "Your sister—"

"Stepsister," Avery said, but so low he didn't hear her.

"—wants to throw everything away. She got a scholarship because of this." He pointed at his leg. He always referred to it as "this" or "that thing that happened," never "my injury" or "my knee" or "where I got shot." He acted like the shattered leg belonged to someone else. "And all because of this stuff in Louisville. That shooting, which was a good shooting by a good cop. I trained him."

"I wouldn't brag about that."

He laughed, smiling a bitter grin with yellowed teeth. "I see. Yeah. I have daughters who like to throw good things away." He jerked his thumb toward the bedroom. "At least that one in there is raising a family. She knew what she wanted and got it. The rest of you . . ."

"Are we going to do this now? Can we concentrate on the problem at hand?"

"You would have had a fine career." He pointed. "Your picture would be on that wall. You'd be a captain. Sooner than I was."

"It didn't work out for me."

"Damn, you were good, Avery. You were so good. You've always been smarter than me. More analytical too."

Avery's face flushed at the praise. Encouraging words from her dad still moved her. "Dad, can we not—"

"When this is over, and you find your sister, we're going to talk about your getting back on the force. I can still pull some strings, talk to the right people. My name still carries weight."

"If this is all we're going to talk about, Dad, I'm going to go."

Before she reached the door, he said, "You gave it all up, and why? Because you're afraid? Let me tell you, I was afraid every day of my career. Every fucking day." He tapped his chest. "Every cop is, whether they admit it or not. That's why you train. That's why you have this." He patted his pocket. "But you threw it all away because your boyfriend had to pull you out of a pond. And he's a good cop. That's for sure. Tougher than shit. Just to look at him, I didn't know he had it in him. Now you don't have the boyfriend. Or the job either. You're a rent-a-cop."

Anger caught in her throat, choked off the air. "At least I'm not sitting in my own filth, drinking myself to death."

"Oh, oh." He started reaching out for the walker. He placed both hands on it and tried to hoist himself up. But the sofa sat too low, and he lacked the strength to make the move. He floundered like a turtle on its back. "I need up. I need to say . . . Jane? Janie?"

"I don't know why I came here. Anna's going to be fine."

"She's not going to be fine. It's . . . Jane? . . . She's not fine. She's young, and she wouldn't understand everything that has happened."

"You're babbling. You've created a fantasy of your own importance."

Alisha and Jane appeared at the end of the hallway. "Dad, what are you doing? Why are you getting up? Avery, can you help him?"

"He's fine."

"Jesus, Avery."

"Janie? Go out and get me that bottle. I think Alisha moved it."

"Okay, honey, I will. Just sit, okay?"

"Dad— Avery. Crap, I asked you not to fight with him."

"Me? Why is it my fault?"

Jane left the room and quickly came back with a pint of Jim Beam in her hand. Russell took it, lifted it quickly to his lips, and guzzled, his Adam's apple bobbing. When he'd thrown back as much as he could, he wiped his mouth with the palm of his hand.

He stared at Avery, blinking. "Come here."

Avery didn't want to go. "What?"

"Come here."

Avery looked at Jane and Alisha. When she looked back at her dad, something moved on his face. Had his chin quivered ever so slightly? Had his eyes grown more watery and glazed?

She crossed the room, leaned down. Her heart thumped like a sustained roll of thunder. How did that weak man still scare her? How did he manage to make her do his bidding?

"Russ," Jane said, "be nice."

Avery's dad reached up, gathered the material of her shirt in his hand. He swallowed, air and not booze. "I need you to find her. Find Anna. And bring her back here. To me. You need to do that, Avery. The family needs protection. Okay? You need to do it. You're the *only* one who can do it. Okay? You're the one."

And then something happened that Avery had never seen before— her dad started sobbing.

21

Jane moved over and sat on the couch next to her husband. She placed her hand on his knee and spoke to him in a low, soothing voice. "Now, Russ, you've upset yourself. You need to take it easy. We'll find out where Anna is."

"No, no," he said. "This is bad. Very bad. You know. You know that, Janie."

"Russ . . . don't . . . We don't . . ."

"It's bad. For all of us."

"Maybe it's not what you think," Jane said.

"What does he think?" Avery asked.

"Maybe it's just not as bad as you're saying."

Avery felt like she'd just witnessed a plane crash. She looked at her emotionally wrecked father wiping his eyes with a grungy handkerchief and she couldn't turn away. As much as she wanted to.

Alisha's brow wrinkled with surprise and concern. "Dad, we'll figure this out."

"No, no. I should have protected you girls better."

"You always protected us, Dad," Alisha said.

"I tried to give Anna a gun, but she wouldn't take it. If she'd taken it back to Breckville with her . . ."

"Dad, you can't expect Anna to keep a gun in her apartment," Avery said.

"Why not? You do."

"I'm different from Anna. And I don't even keep it loaded."

"You don't? Did you bring it with you?"

"No, I don't tote that thing around everywhere."

"You all should have one with you. And loaded. Janie goes to the range with me. Always has. She knows how to protect herself."

"You know I don't like to talk about guns, Russ," Jane said.

"Do you still keep the binder by the door?" he asked. "I bet you all stopped doing that."

"Russ, can you just take a deep breath?"

He tipped the bottle again, took a long swallow. The phone in the kitchen rang. Avery and Alisha looked at each other.

"Maybe that's Anna," Jane said.

"I'll get it." Avery went out to the kitchen, found the ancient cordless phone sitting on a table cluttered with dirty dishes, prescription bottles, and a small bird feeder. "Hello?"

A cheerful voice responded. "Hi. Is this Anna?"

"No. Who's this?"

"Oh, is it Alisha, then?"

One more guess—the least likely one. "This is Avery."

"Oh." Surprise? Shock? "Oh. Avery. I see."

"Who is this?"

"Oh. You don't recognize the voice. It's been so long since you've been around. This is Libby. Your mom's—*Jane's*—cousin."

A picture popped into Avery's mind. A woman ten years younger than Jane and her dad, heavyset. Chipper. Always moving. Always talking. Always dressed like a Stevie Nicks impersonator. "Sure, it's been a while."

"I heard you're back in school."

"Graduate school. I'm getting a master's in history."

"Good for you. I've always advocated for as much education as a person can get. Are you thinking of teaching?"

"I don't want to teach. Did you need something?"

"Oh, yes. I was wondering . . . about Anna. I texted her a few times, and she didn't answer. And then I called. I thought maybe she got a new phone number or something. Maybe your— Maybe Janie has it? Or maybe you do?"

Jane continued to speak to her husband in soothing tones in the other room. And he continued to respond in the same way. "No, no. Everybody needs to be alert. If you let your guard down for one second—*one second*—it can all go away. That's what happened to my leg. It just takes a moment, and some bastard takes you down."

"Okay, Dad," Alisha said. "We hear you."

"I don't think she has a new phone number," Avery said. "To be honest, this isn't the best time for Jane to talk to you—"

"She's so dear, our Jane. And much stronger than she seems. Is she okay?"

"She's okay. Dad's in a lot of pain."

"I know. His injuries have been a cross to bear. He's such a brave man."

"Yes, he is." Avery wasn't sure, but he might have been crying again. "When's the last time *you* heard from Anna?"

"Let me see. . . . It's been a few weeks. I'm just worried something has upset her."

Avery heard something beneath the words Libby spoke. A slightly discordant note. "Do you *know* what upset her?"

"I get the feeling there are some tensions with Russ."

"That's true. Parents and kids, you know."

"But, really, maybe I should just talk to Jane."

Avery held the phone against her chest, muffling it, and went to the entryway to the living room. Jane remained next to Russ, her hand rubbing his back. He muttered to her, words Avery couldn't hear.

Alisha pointed at the phone and whispered. "Who is it?"

"Jane's cousin Libby."

Alisha's nose wrinkled. "Gold Dust Woman."

Avery went back into the kitchen. "You know, Libby, this isn't the best time. She's helping my dad right now. She's going to have to call you back."

"Okay." Disappointment. "Can she do that soon?"

"Do you want to talk to her about Anna? Is that it?"

"I just want to talk to her."

"Libby, if you think there's something going on with Anna, you can tell me. It might be important."

A long pause drew out. "Avery, to be honest, I need to talk to Jane. I mean, I might share this with Alisha, but I just don't . . . I mean, you just aren't, well, you know . . . I don't know how much you care about your family."

Avery held the phone out like it was a ticking bomb. She stabbed the end-call button with her index finger as hard as she could.

22

Avery went back into the living room.

"Who was on the phone?" her dad asked.

"Libby."

"Who?"

"Libby. Jane's cousin."

Avery might have imagined it, but some of the red drained from Dad's face. "What is *she* calling for?" He stared at Jane. "Do you know?"

Jane didn't answer.

"She wants you to call her back, Jane," Avery said. "And maybe you should."

"Why do you say that?" Alisha asked.

"She was asking about Anna. Kind of like she knew something, but she refused to tell me. She acted like I was a piece of dog shit."

"Oh, honey, Libby wouldn't think that about you. She's very understanding."

"Well, I kind of hung up on her."

"Oh, my . . ." Jane clutched her robe again.

Dad laughed. "Good. She's a busybody. She can't be calling about anything good. Just pretend she didn't call. That's what I try to do when she sticks her nose in things."

"Did you say she might know something about Anna?" Alisha asked.

"She was asking about her."

Jane's voice rose louder than it had all day. "Libby always cared a great deal about Anna. They were always close. When I had— Well, before Anna was born, she came and stayed with us. She was very helpful. You know, Libby is like a sister to me. She and Anna bonded when Anna was very little. Do you remember how sickly Anna was? People thought that because she was a bigger baby she was healthy, but that's not always true. I told you girls that back then."

"Well," Alisha said, "we heard about it. We were in Florida for some of that. Remember?"

"With Margaret," Dad said, "sowing her wild oats."

Avery felt trapped. The walls of the living room—dingy and faded—seemed to be closing in on her. Every time she went to the house, it felt smaller. Every time, her dad and Jane appeared to have shrunk. If she went back enough times, they'd eventually just disappear, along with the furniture.

She worried she might disappear along with them if she stayed.

Would it ever be possible to be completely disentangled from them?

No, it wouldn't. Family meant blood, DNA, shared history. A gnarled and tangled vine.

One with sharp thorns on it.

"Do you have this Eric kid's number?" Avery asked.

"I think I do," Jane said. "If I can find my book."

"What about her other friends in Louisville?" Avery asked.

"There's Rachel," Alisha said. "You remember her, right?"

"Oh, yeah. Sure. She's the one who never stops talking."

"I just remember Anna's graduation party," Alisha said. "Rachel has the wild red hair. I think she spiked the punch."

"I never trusted her," her dad said. "She wore all that red lipstick too. That's never a good sign."

"Do you have Rachel's number?" Avery asked. "Or address?"

"I can get it," Alisha said.

"How do you know Anna's in Louisville?" Jane asked.

"I don't. But she's not in Breckville, as far as we can tell. And she's not here. She has friends in Louisville." She looked at her dad. "And, you know, there's a march tomorrow. Protesting the Tanya Burns shooting. That might be the kind of thing she'd like to attend."

He winced but didn't say anything.

"A protest," Jane said. "That could get violent."

"Unlikely. Unless the cops show up in full force."

Her dad's face turned a darker red. Almost purple. Like an eggplant. "You were one of us once."

"I quit, though, remember?"

"Most certainly," he said. "We'll talk about that again."

"Will you just bring her back, Avery? That's all we care about," Jane said.

"Yes," Russ said. "You wouldn't agree to be her guardian when we really needed you to."

"Russ, not that—"

"Do this for us. And for her. Okay?"

"I'll try to find her, which is unlikely enough in a city that big. I can't promise I'll bring her back. She's an adult. If she wants to stay in Louisville, she can stay."

"She'll come if you ask her," Alisha said.

"It's needle-in-a-haystack time."

Her dad spoke through gritted teeth. "Louisville, that whole area, it's a cesspool. Crime. I hate it there."

"I'll tell them you said hello."

"Do me one favor," he said.

"You're *not* going with me." Avery looked around the room. "None of you are."

He shook his head, which was still purple. "Not that." He raised his index finger. "On the way to Louisville, do me a favor. Stop and see Charlie Ballard."

Avery nodded. "That's the first sensible thing you've said all day."

23

Two miles up 177, Anna reached a giant gas station. It looked newly built, the lights and all the surfaces bright. It occupied almost a full block, with about twenty pumps and as many parking spots around the building as at a sports arena. Anna parked on the side, near one of the air hoses that she could never figure out how to use, and decided to check her phone. She planned to look at her messages, reach out to Rachel, and then shut the phone off again before she moved on.

As she'd expected, an avalanche of notifications poured out of the phone.

"Fuck."

Texts, calls, voice mails. She almost shut the phone off.

But she needed to deal with the predictable messages from her mom and Alisha.

Call us. Call us. Call us.

"Shhh." As though the messages could hear her.

Then one from Eric: Babe, where are you?

"Babe"? The fuck.

And again: I hear your coming to Lville this weekend.

You did? Rachel . . .

She checked her voice mail. The usual suspects. She skipped the ones from her mom and Alisha. She might not be able to resist the sound of her mom's voice. The tentative pleading, the subtle guilt trip. *Your father is really wondering where you are. . . .*

Kayla was right—it was tough to resist her mom. Her parents knew Kayla's number—they'd already written to her once. Kayla—likely—wouldn't sell her out, but if Anna's mom and dad kept bugging Kayla, she could tell them Anna was okay.

And a message from her cousin Libby. Technically her mom's cousin, which made Libby her cousin too somehow. Second cousin once removed? Or first? Or what?

Libby was younger than Jane, and a lot more fun. Everyone needed that relative or friend, someone older but kind of outside the immediate family who could talk about things parents couldn't talk about. Libby filled that role for Anna.

Libby had married a guy named Dale when she was young. Dale had gone off to the army, and when he came back from overseas, he left her, telling her he just wasn't the marrying kind. Libby had remained single since then. She taught art at a high school in La Grange, traveled in the summer as much as she could. New York, Europe, even a trip to Japan. She promised to take Anna along some summer, but Anna could never scrape together the money, and Libby couldn't afford to pay Anna's way. Anna's dad disliked Libby, liked to call her a busybody and a know-it-all. He just didn't really like it that much when people he disagreed with expressed strong opinions. People he disagreed with and people who refused to back down from him.

Libby never backed down from Dad.

But Anna had started ducking Libby's calls and messages a few weeks earlier. It wasn't that Libby wouldn't have understood what Anna might be going through, but Anna felt like she would be letting Libby down if she left school without a degree. Libby loved school, always talked about going back and earning more degrees when she retired from teaching. Anna wasn't sure what she'd say to Libby to explain it all, and so, like a lot of things lately, Anna let it slide.

Libby's message said: "Hey, kiddo, I'm just checking in. I heard you had a falling-out with your dad. I know he's a tough nut to crack, so if you want to talk about it, I'm here." A long pause. "I mean if there's something else going on. Anything else . . . you know . . ."

Libby sounded like she had something in mind. Trevor? What?

And someone with a Breckville number, one she didn't recognize, had left a message. A telemarketer?

She ignored it, scrolled through everything else.

Nothing from Kayla?

Her dutiful, mothering friend had managed to go hours without checking up on her? And there Anna was, arriving in Louisville a day late, because of her encounter with Officer Justin Carmichael.

She wrote to Kayla: Hon, do you want to know what I did last night? Betcha can't guess.

What was the point of hooking up with a guy—a cop who had pulled you over, no less—if you couldn't tell one of your best friends about it the next day? Sure, Anna could—and would—tell Rachel, but Rachel didn't shock as easily as Kayla.

No response. Nothing.

Kayla wasn't in class, wasn't supposed to be at work. Had she run off to see her girlfriend, Emily? Made a spontaneous run to Nashville for some action of her own?

"Okay," Anna said, "you'll have to wait for the juicy news. Maybe until Monday."

She wrote to Rachel instead: Almost there. I have a story for you!

Rachel wrote back: Trying to get out of work early. I wish I had a bottle here. . . .

Anna laughed out loud. She started to turn the phone off, but curiosity won the day. She played the message from the Breckville number.

"Anna, this is Detective Morris with the Breckville Police Department. We've been trying to contact you—"

"Nope."

Anna deleted the message. Her dad had pulled out all the stops, but it was still a big state. And Louisville was a big city. He could call up Sherlock Holmes if he wanted. Anna clearly intended to avoid detection for the weekend.

She turned the phone off, backed out of the spot, and continued north.

24

Detective Morris pushed through the glass door of the Lunch Box Diner. The irritating iron bell attached to the arm over his head rang, alerting the scattered late-afternoon crowd to his presence.

He scanned the room. Lieutenant Paulson lifted his hand, index finger extended like he was signaling a waiter, and Morris went to join him. He'd missed lunch, and as he slid into the booth, his mind conjured up images of a hamburger dripping grease and a Coke jammed with ice.

He and Paulson shook hands across the table. Paulson wore a fleece pullover on top of a checked shirt. His hair was cropped close to his head, and a mug of weak-looking tea steamed in front of him.

"Thanks for meeting me," Morris said.

"Thank you. I know the day's been crazy."

"That's an understatement." He'd never met Paulson before, never even heard of the guy. But when the news had broken about the murder in Breckville—the murder of Anna Rogers' roommate—someone at KSP took note. And Paulson, who worked out of Post Three, reached out to Morris, asking if he had time to talk. "We get about two murders a year in Breckville. Usually it's domestic. Or knuckleheads having a fight over something worthless. This one doesn't quite fit."

The waitress came, and Morris ordered his dreamed-of hamburger, fries, and Coke. He pointed to Paulson. "You don't want anything?"

Paulson waved his hand over the table. "I'm good. Thanks."

"My treat."

"Thanks, no." When the waitress was gone, Paulson sipped his tea. He said, "So, nothing like drugs with this Kayla Garvey."

"Nothing of the sort. Unless she's really good at hiding it. She seems like the all-American kid. Good grades. Working to pay for part of school."

"No partner involved?"

"She has a girlfriend in Nashville. Kind of a serious thing, but the woman has an alibi."

"And you've got this Midnight Rambler creep. . . ."

"He's never killed. Never so much as laid a hand on a woman. It seems to be his goal not to lay hands on a woman. He just likes to stare at them while they sleep."

"But he could—"

"Sure, he could graduate. Something could have gone wrong. Kayla was a high school athlete. She was pretty fit and strong. There wasn't any sign of much of a struggle, but maybe she wakes up, sees the creep standing over her, things get out of hand."

"But you don't seem convinced."

"I'm not. It doesn't fit."

Morris' food came. His mouth watered, and he started to eat. He remembered his manners and thought about asking Paulson if he wanted anything. Again. But Paulson seemed like the kind of guy who knew his own mind and didn't need to be asked twice. He'd come into the Lunch Box and ordered Earl Grey. He didn't need to be nagged.

Paulson said, "And then there's the roommate. Anna Rogers."

Morris nodded as he chewed. Was the food always this good here? "Anna Rogers. Daughter of Captain Russell Rogers. KSP. Retired. I'm guessing you didn't get in touch because you wanted to monitor my cholesterol intake. You have some information to share."

"I guess I was hoping for a free exchange of information between different agencies."

Morris sucked Coke through the straw. "We've always had a good relationship with the KSP."

"True, true." Paulson squeezed lemon into his tea. Some of the juice sprayed onto the scarred tabletop. "It's also curious that Captain Rogers' *other* daughter found the body."

"Former KSP herself. You know her?"

"Some. Tough way her career ended as well. Probably some PTSD issues for both of them."

"A lot of bad luck in one family."

Paulson withheld comment. "How did that come about?" he asked. "The sister finding the body. I know Avery is working and going to school in Breckville."

Morris wiped his chin. "Basically, Anna ghosted her family. Had some kind of falling-out with the old man over the Tanya Burns shooting."

Paulson winced.

"Yeah, sorry to bring up bad news. For the past two weeks or so, Anna hasn't been answering calls or texts from the family. Also not going to class. She's pretty much dropped out of life. So the other sister—"

"Avery—"

"Alisha. The middle child. She convinced Avery to go check on their kid sister. Avery goes and finds Kayla's body."

"And my understanding is Avery doesn't really get on well with the old man."

"I get that sense too." Morris waited, and when Paulson remained quiet, he went ahead and said, "Sounds like the old man is a piece of work."

"I think you're right. I don't really know him, but he was a good cop. Highly decorated. As you know, he took a bullet that ended his career. He's still in a lot of pain, from what I understand." Paulson shook his head. "It could happen to any one of us, and you spend the rest of your life using a walker or a cane. Or worse."

"And that shooting? Of the old man?"

"Unsolved." Paulson stirred his tea, the spoon clinking against the mug. "Captain Rogers came across a vehicle abandoned on the side of the road. In the dark. He stopped to check on it, and somebody ambushed him. A shot came out of the trees, hit him in the leg. He was lucky. I'm sure they weren't aiming for his leg. By the time help arrived, the abandoned car was gone. No real evidence in the trees."

"What was a captain doing, checking on an abandoned car?"

"He just happened to be driving by."

"But someone could have been following him or setting him up. Could have been revenge for something."

"Possible. You bust enough people . . ."

The waitress came and brought Morris another Coke and Paulson more hot water.

"And there's no sign of Anna?" Paulson asked.

"Not yet. We don't know if she left town. If she's hiding somewhere. The kid's kind of a slob, so it's tough to tell if she packed to go. Her toothbrush looks like it's gone. She might have taken off for the weekend. . . ."

"And left her roommate's body behind?"

"Her phone's off. We're waiting for her to surface. Or for a cop to come across her somewhere. It's a big world."

"And no problems between Anna and the roommate?"

"None we can see. Anna has a clean record. We gather from people who know her that she was having a good time in college. Shit, I wish I were still in college having a good time. I don't have the stamina for it anymore. But she and the roommate were good friends."

"Hmm."

Morris finished his hamburger and made a large dent in the fries. He pointed to the plate, offering the fries to Paulson. The struggle showed on Paulson's face. It was real. Who could resist hot diner French fries? Gandhi, maybe. Paulson reached out and took a few, stuffed them in this mouth like they were manna.

"Good, aren't they?"

"Mmm-hmm."

"You know, Lieutenant"—Morris stifled a burp—"I get the feeling there's something else you want to bring up with me, but you don't know how to do it."

Paulson finished chewing and swallowed. He eyed his tea, which probably didn't mix well with the fries. "You're a good cop, Morris. There is something else. But I'm going way out on a limb if I mention it. You understand that?"

"I do. And I'm afraid of heights."

Paulson smiled. He signaled the waitress and asked for a Coke of his own. When he had it, he said, "It's about another case we've never been able to solve. And I want you to know about it."

PART II

25

Charlie Ballard lived in Pine Grove, a small community south of Louisville. Pine Grove had peaked before the Civil War. Distilleries started popping up in that part of the state, and the residents of Pine Grove made the choice to remain dry. The Bourbon Trail—and everything else—bypassed them, and Pine Grove's population remained steady over the years. About nine hundred people lived there at any given time.

Charlie lived in a redbrick farmhouse, one built around the time Pine Grove cast its lot with temperance. He owned ten acres and used the land to raise a few goats, a bunch of chickens, and one cow that he planned to butcher later in the fall. When Avery turned in to the gravel driveway that led to the side of the house, Charlie came through the door, as if he'd been watching for her.

Two large dogs accompanied him. One looked like a pit bull mix. The other a German shepherd. They danced around Charlie's legs, happy to be outside, and when Avery stepped out, they both made a beeline for her, ears peeled back, snouts forward like the tips of missiles.

Avery took a step back, uncertain of the intention of the charge. But while they both barked—and barked—they also quickly switched to sniffing, wet noses and tongues touching her skin and every inch of her shoes and pants. She waited out the investigation, and then started rubbing their ears. Charlie came right behind them.

"Get," he said. "Go on. Go run."

They did, their claws throwing up clumps of earth like they were stallions racing on a track.

Then Charlie was before her, hands on hips. He wore a bright red WKU hoodie and dirty jeans. Salt-and-pepper stubble covered the lower half of his face.

"Well, well," he said, "look at this."

"Hey, Charlie."

"Come here, girl."

He leaned forward, opening his arms. Avery leaned in, let herself be folded up. His embrace felt comfortable and familiar. Like home, even though she'd never lived there.

Charlie smelled like woodsmoke and earth.

When they let go, his smile grew wider. "It's been a minute, hasn't it?"

"It has."

"Three years or so, I would guess."

"About that," Avery said.

Clouds were building off to the west, the sky turning a darker blue. A flock of black birds went past in the shape of a V.

"You okay, then?"

Avery looked around, heard the dogs barking at something in the distance. "Okay? What does that mean exactly, 'okay'?"

Charlie exuded Buddha-like calm. She could have told him anything and his face would have remained the same. Ease and acceptance carved in rock. "You'd better come in, then. The old man called me and filled me in a little. But he's . . . Well, I don't have to tell you what he's like."

The rickety screen door slapped shut behind them once they were in. Avery followed Charlie to the kitchen, where a woodstove gave off heat in the corner. The smell of fried onions hovered over everything.

Charlie opened a cabinet and pulled out two glasses. He put them on the kitchen table and nodded to Avery, telling her to sit. So she did. He turned and came back with a bottle of Jim Beam. He poured for both of them, the liquid gurgling.

"I thought you liked fancier stuff than Dad."

"I'm retired too. Fixed income. Besides, some things are classics. Like a plain white T-shirt, a pair of jeans, a pickup truck."

"Has living in the country turned you into a redneck?"

"That's right, girl. You're looking at the world's first Black redneck retired cop. Cheers."

He extended his glass, and Avery clinked hers against it. They both drank.

While she enjoyed the pleasant burn of the bourbon, she looked around at the orderly kitchen. Charlie had never married, never had kids. When Avery and her sisters were young, Charlie spent the occasional Thanksgiving or Christmas with them. He always showed up with gifts for her and Alisha, and later for Anna. He never said no when they asked him to play a game or go down the street to the jungle gym at the park.

Avery used to go to sleep at night conjuring a fantasy scenario that lasted into her teenage years. She imagined Charlie was really her father, instead of Captain Russell Rogers. Charlie had easily mastered all the things her dad couldn't—natural warmth, openness, support, patience.

She wished she'd stayed in better touch with him over the past few years. She wished her shame at quitting KSP didn't control her.

"You didn't really answer my question about how you're doing," he said. "Of course, if you don't want to answer, that's your right."

"Can I have a lawyer present?"

He drank again, then smiled. "I don't think you need one."

"I like school."

He nodded, encouraging her. "History, right? Always one of your favorite subjects."

"It is. I don't know what I'm going to do when I finish. I'm going part-time, so no rush." She swirled the bourbon in her glass. "I could get a PhD, but then what? I don't think I have the patience to teach college students."

"You're seeing what they're like up close at your job."

"Tell me about it. Am I just getting old, or are young people more entitled than ever?"

"You're getting old," he said. "Don't fight it. Have you eaten yet? I have beef stew I made." He jerked his thumb toward the refrigerator. "It's my neighbor's beef, not mine. A little tough but good."

"I could eat."

He stood, but before he went to the refrigerator, he refilled their glasses.

"Don't I have to be sharp to look for Anna?" she asked.

"The food will lighten your load."

As Charlie went about warming the stew on the stove, a spoon scraping against the pot, Avery told him what she knew. As always, he mostly listened, asking few questions. He only interjected to offer his sympathy over finding Kayla's body.

"Brutal," he said. "Just brutal."

By the time Avery finished, bowls of stew sat before them. Charlie also brought out a loaf of homemade bread, and he cut thick slices off, then pointed to the butter on the table. "That's also from a neighbor."

Avery didn't realize how hungry she was until she dished the stew into her mouth. Perfectly seasoned and comforting. She followed it up with buttered bread, quite possibly the best bread she'd ever tasted.

"Do you eat like this every day?" she asked.

"I'm not your average bumbling bachelor. I know my way around the kitchen."

"And the farm."

"That too. I guess, when I retired, I decided I wanted to do something a little gentler with my time and energies. Something more . . ."

"Nurturing."

"Fair enough. No kids or grandkids coming my way. So . . ."

"Dogs. You can nurture them."

"Those big babies are probably whining at the door right now." He stood up, tossed his napkin onto the table.

Avery heard the door open, nails skitter against the floor.

"Easy, now," Charlie said. "Easy, you two."

A few minutes later, Charlie came back and sat at the table. "Do you want more?"

"I'm full. That's the best meal I've had in a long time. I'm not a cook. And I live alone."

"You're busy."

"Yeah. Something like that."

"What do *you* think is going on with Anna?" he asked.

"Remember how I said young people are getting more and more entitled?"

Charlie laughed. "You think that applies to Anna?"

"It's tough to imagine anyone growing up with Russell Rogers as a father and somehow turning out entitled."

"True enough." Charlie finished the bourbon that remained in his glass.

"But I do think she's just run away. She fought with Dad, got her feathers ruffled. Maybe she's having some sort of crisis in terms of what she wants to do with her life. That can happen during the last year of college."

"You never doubted what you wanted to do."

Avery groaned. "Yeah . . ."

"I'm sorry. I wasn't trying to bring up bad memories."

"It's okay. I just haven't accepted how many people I disappointed."

Charlie leaned forward. "You didn't disappoint me."

Avery looked out the window, at the view that showed the goat pen and the rolling hills beyond. The sun had started to set, the sky going over to a burning orange along the horizon. "You're not my dad."

"True enough. That man is one of a kind. You know, I worked alongside your dad for years. I think he'd consider me his best friend—"

"He would."

"I know a lot of things about him. But not everything. I'm not sure how much *he* knows about what goes on inside him."

Avery shook her head. "That's sad."

"Maybe it is. I don't know. But he loves you girls. I do know that."

"It's tough to love someone who withholds so much."

"He always sang your praises. To high heaven."

"He did?"

"Talked about how smart you are. How tough. Even after you left the job, he said those things about you. I understand it wasn't easy having him for a father. It's not easy having him for a friend."

"I don't know how you put up with him."

"We had work in common. Common goals. That's a lot to share with someone."

Avery watched the sky darken. The dogs came into the kitchen, and they each lapped water out of a giant bowl, then settled onto two large dog beds.

"You and Anna have never really been close," he said. "I know the family stuff is complicated with the second marriage and all. But if you're so distant from Anna that you don't even see her in Breckville, why are you going to Louisville? Do you want to find her? Or impress your dad?"

Avery tapped her fingers against the table. She watched the sky, couldn't look at Charlie.

She finally worked up an answer.

"They're the same thing, aren't they, Charlie? Aren't they the same damn thing?"

Charlie nodded sagely. "I guess I'm a retired cop. Not a licensed therapist. But I get it." He stood up, started clearing the dishes. "I'd offer dessert, but I don't have any. My friend was going to bring me blueberries for a pie, but they never arrived."

"Thanks a lot, but I need to get going anyway. Can you just tell me where to go or the names of any contacts you still have? Anything would help."

Charlie placed the dishes in the sink with a clanking of silverware. He turned the water on, let it get warm, and spoke over his shoulder. "I'm going with you."

"Oh, no, I can't ask you to do that—"

"You're not asking me. And your father certainly didn't ask me. Not in words. But things are going to get messy up in Louisville, with that march and everything else going on. I'm not sending you up there alone."

Avery felt relief, a lightening of the pressure on her shoulders—but she'd also imposed. And she hated to impose. "The dogs . . . Who's going to . . ."

Charlie turned the water off and came across the room. He placed his hand on her upper arm. "My friend is coming to take care of the dogs. And the dishes will still be in the sink when I get back."

"Dad said your blood pressure . . . You were supposed to—"

Charlie placed his index finger over his lips. "Shhh. We're family. This is what family does for one another. I'm going to grab a few things, and then we can hit the road."

26

Charlie drove.

He owned a gray F-150, and he told Avery it made more sense for them to travel to Louisville—and then to drive around the city—in that than in her little sedan.

"Are you expecting us to ram a barricade or something?" Avery asked.

In profile, Charlie smiled. They drove north, the sun almost gone on their left. "Maybe it will be some *Les Misérables* shit. Maybe we'll hear the people sing."

"So, you're a retired Black cop redneck farmer who likes musical theater?"

"Actually, at the risk of sounding really damn pretentious, I read the book. I didn't see the movie or the play. And I'm talking the un-abridged book."

"Impressed."

"In the last six months, a new lady entered my life. She's more sophisticated than I am, and she has me reading a little more."

"Are you serious? That whole time when we were kids, I don't think you ever brought a date around."

"Well, I—"

"Wait. There was that one woman. When I was really little. She had a funny laugh. . . ."

"Sydney."

Avery snapped her fingers. "Yes, Sydney. That was it. I think she came to one of my birthday parties with you."

"I can't remember all those details. Your dad didn't like her, not that he likes anybody. I don't think your mom liked her either."

"And now you have a girlfriend."

"It gets lonely on the farm. And believe it or not, I'm a catch now. I have a college degree. A pension. All of my teeth."

"You can cook."

"Exactly."

The cone of the headlights showed the edges of the road. The drainage ditches on each side, the barbed wire fences. Solitary farmhouses in the distance with single lights burning over the doors of detached garages.

"What about you?" Charlie asked.

She knew what he meant. "Oh, Charlie, such a sad question."

"Okay, okay, I'll change the subject."

"Do you know what I did this morning?"

The tires hummed against the pavement. The question surprised her by popping out of her mouth that way. But once it was there, hovering in the dark cab between them, Avery wanted to press on. Alisha was the only person she confided in. But there'd been too much going on at the house for them to talk. So Charlie found himself, unwittingly, in the crosshairs. What a statement on her life that she needed to confide details of her romantic life—or lack thereof— to her father's best friend, her surrogate uncle.

"Is it going to embarrass me?" he asked.

"No. Me." She looked out the window again, a ghost image of her face reflected back. "Right before I went into Anna's apartment and found that girl's body, I sat in the parking lot and I texted Hank. It's been months since we talked. At all. Over a year since we've even seen each other. I felt so alone for some reason that I reached out."

They rolled on in silence for a few miles, the headlights and the pickup eating the darkness.

Finally, Charlie asked a simple question. "And?"

"No response. Nothing."

"It seems from the outside like things cooled between the two of you after the accident at the pond. Right?"

Avery kept watching the world whiz by. "Yeah, pretty much. I'm not sure . . . I didn't feel he fully understood what I was going through after that. I had nightmares. And anxiety. I couldn't shake it."

"PTSD."

"I never labeled it, but yeah. I pulled away. We didn't communicate well. Not at all."

"I'm sorry to hear it."

"It's fine. I know he's working. Probably has someone else in his life. Why wouldn't he?"

A long shot, but she hoped this would induce Charlie to offer information if he had it.

He picked up his cue. "I hear he's doing well at work, but that's all. He's a good cop with a good career. He got the Lifesaving Medal from KSP because of what happened with you."

"I know that, Charlie."

"Sorry. But I don't know anything about his personal life. Obviously. I'm not connected to every KSP officer living out here in the hinterlands. Especially not young ones like you. And Hank."

Avery battled against the images in her head. The gray sky over her head. Lying on the bank of the pond while emergency workers swarmed.

Hank having to drag her out of the pond . . .

Before he helped the family . . .

"Did Alisha send you that contact info for Anna's friend?" Charlie asked.

"Got it, boss. I didn't call or text her. I didn't want to scare off our little squirrel before we arrived."

"Good. And Anna doesn't know about her roommate?"

"Not that I'm aware of."

"Hmmm. Notifications . . ."

"Nothing worse."

"Nope."

"Do you think what Dad thinks? That whoever killed Kayla was looking to hurt Anna, and it's somehow related to something he did when he was a cop?"

Charlie's index finger tapped the wheel. His lips pressed into a wire-thin line. "Why do you think I live with those two big dogs who bark as soon as someone comes near the property? Why do you think I have those acres? They make a nice barrier between the edge of my property and the house."

"A clear field of fire?"

"I have a couple of rifles, but I don't hunt."

"Why target Anna, then? Dad's a sitting duck in that house. He can barely move. And you . . . despite your dogs, someone could get at you if they were determined enough. Why Anna?"

Charlie remained quiet longer than she would have expected.

He finally reached over and patted her knee. "You never know—we might find something out in Louisville."

27

It took Anna nearly half an hour to find a parking spot within three blocks of Rachel's building.

She drove around—and around—and found one after just a few minutes, but a hipster guy with a beard down his chest and driving a Mini Cooper zipped into it ahead of her. She rolled down her window and said, "What the fuck, dude?" But he barely glanced back and kept on walking, acting as though Anna simply didn't exist.

She finally found a spot and lugged her duffel bag the three blocks to Rachel's. The sun was setting and the streetlights came on, starting with a blue glow that slowly turned white. Anna felt a pleasant tickling in her stomach, the anticipation of night coming on. Going out. Losing herself in a crowd. Being in another city where no one really knew her.

She huffed up the stairs to Rachel's apartment, her shoes thumping against the thin carpet. Three flights that made her feel like an old lady. The weekend in Louisville was just a reprieve, a break from reality, not reality itself. At some point, she'd come face-to-face with everything she'd been ignoring—school, the future.

Her family.

But couldn't she just get a break from it? A chance to breathe freely for a little while?

Rachel's roommate, Grace, opened the door to Anna's knock. Anna barely knew Grace, found her tough to read and to talk to. They'd spent time together on previous visits, but Grace always kept a wall up. And she frequently disappeared without saying good-bye, to spend the night at her boyfriend's apartment. Anna had never met the boyfriend.

"Oh, hi," Grace said, standing with one arm on the door, her body filling the rest of the space. She wore an oversized sweater and had her hair pulled back off her forehead. The apartment smelled like curry.

"Hey, Grace."

She made no move to step back and let Anna inside.

"Did Rachel tell you I was coming?"

"Oh, yeah. For sure." Grace's eyes were wide and brown. She looked ready to turn tail and run. "Did you know Rachel's at work still?"

"She told me she got held up."

"She said . . . well, she said she'd talk to you when she came home."

"Talk to me?"

"She said you could come in and wait. And then when she came home, she could talk to you."

"Grace, I just walked three blocks and then came up three flights of stairs."

"Oh, yeah." She looked at the duffel bag for the first time, noticed Anna's bright red cheeks. "Right. You want to come in."

"It would lift my spirits."

"Right." Grace stepped back—finally—letting Anna in.

Anna dropped the duffel onto the couch, felt the muscles in her shoulder scream with relief. The bag wasn't that heavy, but it hadn't been designed for long-distance hauling. "I'm just going to chill until she gets here. Check my phone. Is that okay?"

"Yeah. For sure."

Grace still looked at Anna like she might bite.

"Are you okay, Grace?"

"I am. I'm sorry. I just thought of something. I'm spending the night at Tanner's tonight. I mean . . . if you want to sleep in my bed, you can. The sheets are clean and everything. It's better than the couch. I know that's where you normally crash."

"Thanks. I don't mind the couch—"

"And maybe you won't even stay."

"I'm planning to stay. But I don't want to take your bed if you don't want me to."

"No, I do. Please." Grace still looked nervous, squirrelly. "I'm going over to Tanner's house now. So you and Rachel can have the place to yourselves."

Before Anna could say anything else, Grace left the room. And within a minute she came back out, hopping as she pulled one shoe on and then the other. She grabbed her coat and purse and rushed past Anna, who was sitting on the couch with her phone.

But Grace turned around at the door and came back. She bent down over Anna on the couch and hugged her. "Bye, Anna."

She left the apartment like it was on fire.

"Freak," Anna said.

She turned on her phone. The flood. Again.

"Ugh. I'll never turn my phone off."

She almost couldn't look at all the notifications. She couldn't bear the begging and the pleading of her family. Didn't they know she just needed a little space?

But she caught sight of a message Alisha had sent: Can you call me? Please? It's an emergency.

An emergency?

Anna's mind raced to the last time she had seen the old man. Hobbling and struggling. A wounded bear. In biology class she had learned about an old lion that got driven out of its pride by younger lions. Then the rest of the pride left him behind to die.

Alone.

Her dad wasn't alone. Her mom was there. But, shit, if the old man croaked while she was on bad terms with him, she'd never forgive herself.

She called Alisha, who answered almost immediately. Like she'd been waiting for the call.

"Oh, Anna, thank God."

"Is he okay, Alisha? Are they both okay?"

"Dad and Jane? Yes, they're fine. I'm right here with them."

"Then what's the emergency?"

"Oh, Anna. Are you at Rachel's?"

"What's the emergency?"

"Is Rachel with you?"

"She's at work. Why?"

"Oh, Anna. You're alone?"

"I am. What the fuck is going on, Al?"

"It's Kayla. I have to tell you something about Kayla."

28

Anna lay on the floor.

Her phone sat nearby. A voice came out of it.

"Anna? Anna?"

Was it Alisha? Why was Alisha on the floor?

A key rattled in the lock, and the door swung open. Someone came across the room, calling Anna's name.

It was Kayla.

Kayla had come home after class. She came into the apartment like she always did, using her key. And she locked and chained the door like she always did.

And the whole thing was a mistake. Alisha was wrong. Just like everyone in her fucking family was wrong about everything. They had screwed this up too.

Kayla was fine. She was there in the apartment—their apartment— and she bent down over Anna and started speaking to her in a soothing voice, taking care of her the way she always did.

Kayla was that kind of friend.

"Anna? Anna?"

She sat on the floor next to her and placed her hand on Anna's arm. She brushed Anna's hair out of her face, then wiped a tear off her cheek.

"I'm so sorry I wasn't here. I got caught up at work, and the traffic was so bad. I thought Alisha was going to wait to call. . . ."

"Kayla . . ."

"I know. I'm so sorry. It just doesn't make any sense, Anna. It doesn't make any fucking sense why some creep would want to hurt Kayla. I'm so scared, and I'm so sorry."

"No, Kayla . . ."

Rachel crawled over to the phone and started talking to Alisha.

"She's taking it pretty hard. . . . I'm sorry, Alisha. I didn't get home as fast as I could. . . . Maybe you shouldn't yell at me right now. I'm kind of anxious. . . . Okay, I'm sorry too. . . . No, I won't let her out of my sight. . . ."

Anna sat up, and her eyes started to focus. It wasn't Kayla. The girl had thick red hair. And she wasn't home. . . . She remembered coming to Louisville, coming to Rachel's apartment and Grace letting her in. . . .

And Grace acting like such a freak. Grace knew. So before Kayla's name came up, she had run out of the apartment like Anna carried an infectious disease.

Anna's stomach clutched. Her mouth felt dry and sticky. Her throat contracted.

"Oh."

She sprang up off the floor and ran to the bathroom. She made it just in time, then lifted up the lid and puked everything inside her into the toilet with a wretched gurgling. A violent eruption and rejection of whatever was in her body.

Rachel came in behind her, pulled her hair off her face. "It's okay, Anna. Let it out. Let it all out."

Then Rachel handed her a box of tissues, and Anna wiped the spit and vomit off her face. She felt empty, like everything was gone from her gut.

But not from her mind. Images of Kayla raced through like an out-of-control slideshow. Faster and faster the images went. Parties freshman year. Spring break in Panama City. Spending Easter with Kayla's family, her mom setting out a basket for Anna . . .

Her parents. *Fuck.* Kayla was an only child.

To lose a child, your *only child*, and in such a violent way.

"Here." Water ran in the sink, and Rachel handed over a cup. "Drink this. Or at least rinse your mouth out. Get all that shit out of there."

Anna did. She swirled water around in her mouth and spit it into the toilet. Then she swallowed some, enjoyed the coolness going down her throat.

"I'm so sorry, Anna. Alisha called me at work, and she told me what was going on. She wanted me here when she told you, so you wouldn't be alone."

"Grace . . ."

"I told Grace to keep an eye on you until I got here. But you know her—she can't stand any conflict. Remember, her dad died in an accident when she was little. She's kind of messed up by that still."

"I don't care." Anna put the cup on the floor. Her own hand shook as she reached out. "Oh, Rachel, I can't fucking believe this. I just can't . . ."

She leaned over, collapsing against her friend. Rachel pulled her close and held her. Anna squeezed her eyes shut, let the tears come. Kayla. Not Kayla. Anna shook, gasping spasms rocking her body. Rachel held on tight, wouldn't let go.

The crying ran down. Anne felt emptied of tears as well as the contents of her stomach. She was a hollow gourd, one with only a few seeds rattling around inside.

"She was such a good person," Anna said. "Way better than me. Way better than almost everybody I know. She never hurt anyone. I should have been there. If I'd been there, then the creep would have killed me. Or we could have fought him off together. Both of us. But I left her alone—"

"You can't think that way."

"We should have called the police. She wanted to call the police, and I said no."

"Call the police?"

"About the creep, the guy outside. The Rambler."

"I think you—"

"It's my fault. All my fault. She wanted me to start going to class again, to get my shit together. If I'd done that, then I would have been there and not driving up here. Fucking a cop."

"Doing what?"

"I fucked a cop on the way here."

"Oh. Okay."

"I should have been there for Kayla."

"This isn't your fault. A crazy person got inside and hurt her. You saw the guy, remember? He's been breaking into places all over Breckville. He's probably some pervert who's into college girls."

"I really didn't see his face. . . ."

"They're going to be after him now. Hard. The guy won't stand a chance."

"I should have done something more that night. My dad always wanted me to have a gun. I should have taken it from him, kept it in the apartment—"

"No, no. Please, Anna. Just take a deep breath. Don't blame yourself."

She heeded Rachel's advice. She took a deep breath, one that started down in her core and swooshed out of her mouth. She did that three times.

"Better?" Rachel asked.

"No."

"I wouldn't expect you to be. Not yet. You've had a shock."

"Did Alisha say anything else?"

"She's worried about you. Check in with her, okay? She's worried. And I know she's the sister you like. Even though she accused me of spiking the punch at your graduation party. And I totally didn't, by the way."

"Okay . . ."

"Although I always thought Avery was pretty badass when we were kids. She scared me, but I liked that about her."

"I don't want to hear about her."

Rachel sighed and appeared to be struggling for the right words.

"Well, you'd better get used to talking about her. She's coming to get you."

"What?" Anna jerked away from Rachel. "Tell me you're kidding."

"I'm not. Anna, they thought you were hurt. Or missing, or worse. They were worried sick about you. Alisha called me, and I told her you were here. She was so relieved. I guess they convinced Avery to come and find you. She's on her way—or maybe she's here. I don't know."

Anger jumped into Anna's throat. It burned more than the puke, and the flush spread throughout her body. "What is she going to do when she gets here?"

"I don't know. I guess she's going to take you home to your parents, and then maybe back to Breckville. I offered to drive you back, but they said Avery was on it."

"Why does anybody need to take me anywhere? I'm not a child." Anna realized her voice had grown louder and louder. It rang off the tile in the cramped little space.

"Then she can follow you all the way. This has been a shock, Anna. You're probably really wrecked inside, and it hasn't all sunk in yet."

Anna placed one hand on the tile wall and with the other gripped the towel bar. She pulled herself to her feet. A little wobbly, like a newborn colt. But she was up, standing over Rachel. "I don't want Avery anywhere near me."

"Why don't you just talk to her when she gets here?"

"Does she have the address?"

"She does."

"No, I'm going." Anna stomped out of the bathroom, started looking for her coat.

Rachel came along behind, her bootheels clacking on the hardwood floor. "Anna, I think you owe it to your sister to at least talk to her. She's probably worried."

She spun. "Do you know she calls me her stepsister, Rachel? That's what she tells people. She's done it since we were kids. Or she would say she had only one sister, or that I was adopted."

"So? Siblings can be shitty. While I was asleep once, my sister Nina drew a Hitler mustache on my face with a permanent marker. And it was the night before school pictures."

"She never accepted me. She never cared about me."

"She must care. She came all the way to Louisville."

"It's not for me. It's for him."

"Who?"

"My dad. She wants to impress him. Or she's trying to salvage any chance of having a career as a cop." Anna punctuated her words with jabs of her index finger. "She wants to rescue me and drag me back and then probably be a cop again. Since she flamed out before."

"Wow, Anna. That's harsh. Avery almost died in that accident."

"She fucked up. That's all."

Anna sounded terrible. Angry and bitter like her dad. But she couldn't stop the words that poured out—and the feelings that lay beneath them. They were there—a fault line waiting to rupture and crack.

Rachel's face showed concern, like she'd found herself in an enclosed space with a rabid animal. Her tone shifted, became more placating. "Okay, Anna. I hear you. We don't have to do anything you don't want to do."

"Good."

"So what do you want to do?"

"Did you say Avery's coming here?"

"She is. She could be right outside. Or walking up the stairs."

"Then I want to get the fuck out of here. Just take me somewhere. Anywhere. And if you don't want to go, I'll go alone."

"No," Rachel said. "I want to go with you. We're supposed to be hanging out, remember?"

Anna grabbed her coat, jammed her arms into the sleeves. "Right. Out. Anywhere, so long as it's out."

29

Yates studied the address on his phone one more time.

He was in the right place.

Young people moved around all the time, changed apartments as often as they changed clothes or got haircuts. But the address was the best lead he had, so he was going to check it out. He didn't have anything better to do. And staying in Breckville sounded unappealing. The cops were looking for him there, for the murder of the girl in the apartment.

Why sit around doing nothing, waiting for the police to kick in the door?

The streetlights were already on. People came home from work or school, and then they went right back out, walking their dogs, picking up the poop in little bags. Yates never understood that. Having a pet, sure. But having to walk around with a bag of poop in your hand? He liked to walk in the cemetery by his house. People walked their dogs there too, and sometimes he'd find himself talking to somebody with a dog on a leash and a bag of poop in their hand. They talked to him like it was no big deal, and gestured with the hand that held the little bag. Yates couldn't concentrate on anything they said. His eyes followed the bag like it was part of a magician's trick. Like it might hypnotize him.

Lights came on in the apartments, and blinds went down. He had to stay out of sight. The girl—Anna—had seen him outside her place. A couple of things worked in Yates' favor. For one, Anna hadn't gotten a good look at him. It had been late, and dark, and maybe she'd thrown back a few.

And the cops—and everybody else in town—pushed the idea that the girl had been killed by that Midnight Rambler pervert. Yates had done a lot of things in his life, but he'd never snuck into a girl's apartment just to stare at her while she slept. What was the point of that? Where was the thrill?

If Yates could pinpoint this as Anna's location and tell Hogan, maybe he could find his way back into the other man's good graces. He liked the work the family occasionally provided, and he didn't like—hated, in fact—anybody holding anything over his head. If Hogan wanted to, he could throw Yates right under the bus. Then back it up a few times and crush him just to make sure.

Yates could do the same thing to Hogan and his people, though. Tell the cops who it was who had sent him to the apartment in the first place. Yates knew what the family did. Hell, the cops did too. The cops were probably in on it, taking a cut of all the product the family moved. Yates could tie the family to the death of the girl in Breckville, and whatever they were trying to do to the daughter of the shot-up cop. He could try to bring everybody down. What did they call that in history class? Mutual assured destruction?

But why get into all that? Besides, when the shit started to fly, it always landed on the guy farther down the ladder. And right now he was that guy, standing at the bottom and looking up. Could he do something to get out from under it?

Yates positioned himself across the street from the correct address. He leaned against a metal post anchoring a street sign and took out his phone. The night turned cool, and he blew on his hands. To anyone walking by, he was just another dude talking to somebody, not paying attention to what was going on right in front of him. Distracted always by electronic devices.

A young woman had come home and gone into the building. He'd seen pictures of Anna's friend online, and that might have been her, but he couldn't tell in the disappearing light. And how many people looked in person the way they presented themselves online?

So he waited longer. The air grew even chillier. Leaves gathered in bunches in the gutters and against the buildings. He loved that time of year. It made him think of being a kid, of going trick-or-treating with his sister. Running through the neighborhood, begging for as much candy as they could, the only time it ever really felt like they had a bunch of stuff. A bag full to bursting. More candy than anybody could eat, even though they tried to devour it all . . .

Yates lost himself in the memory, so much so he was startled when the door of the building swung open and two women came pouring out. He recognized Anna right away. She came out first, her coattails flying up behind her. She walked quickly, a couple of steps ahead of her friend. She looked determined, leaning forward as she went, not looking back to see if the other woman was keeping up.

And the second woman—the redhead—was the one who had entered the building about thirty minutes earlier, the one he had thought might have been the friend. Rachel Berger. Now he knew.

"Jackpot."

They went down the street, heading toward the row of bars and restaurants on the main drag to the east. It was only a few blocks away—no need to drive. They could stumble home at all hours if they wanted to and not have to worry about drinking and driving.

Yates slid his phone into his back pocket and pushed himself away from the street sign.

He followed along, on the opposite side of the street, keeping his eye on the two young women.

30

Every light in the house burned. And every window was obscured by a curtain or a blind. Or both.

Morris walked up the front walk, rang the bell. Next to the door, a lone bulb glowed, illuminating the house number and the dingy siding. In the shrubs next to the porch, a yellowing newspaper rested, its rubber band snapped by the elements long ago.

Morris had made sure to call, to tell the Rogers family he wanted to stop by and at what time. Paulson had let him know what kind of man he was dealing with in Captain Rogers. Most cops hated surprise visitors. Morris figured Rogers—a man with a shattered knee— hated them more than most.

Morris waited, giving the hobbling cop or his wife time to reach the door. He knew where Anna Rogers was now, and that she was— *probably*—safe. He hoped that when he talked to her parents, he'd find out she'd called home, made peace with them. He still had a murder to solve, one with no obvious answers, but if Anna and her parents had talked, they might be in a better mood, more forthcoming with information.

When the door finally opened, Captain Rogers stood there facing Morris, his body leaning to one side where a cane offered support. Paulson had mentioned a walker, but Morris guessed Rogers discarded the walker when he wanted to project strength. Morris remembered his own father battling cancer in his spine. Seeing him using a walker yet *still* struggling had pierced Morris' heart. His dad had looked so—it was the only word that fit—*ashamed* to be using it.

"You alone?" Rogers asked. Light spilled past him onto the porch.

"I am. And I'm sorry to bother you in the evening, Captain Rogers."

The man wore a zippered fleece with a Western Kentucky University logo on the chest, sweatpants, and slippers. The textured grip of a nine-millimeter stuck out of his pocket, close to his free hand.

"I promise not to take too much time."

Rogers offered no response and extended no invitation. He stepped back from the door, leaving it open behind him, so Morris followed the man into the cramped and cluttered living room. The house smelled like a long-closed closet.

Wheel of Fortune blared on the TV. The contestants clapped and the audience chanted. A woman in a yellow robe with a head of disheveled gray hair sat on the sofa. Her eyes remained fixed on the TV as Morris came in behind her husband, and Rogers kept going past her in the direction of the kitchen.

"Is Anna out there?" the woman asked, her voice barely reaching them through the TV noise.

"Just watch your program, okay?"

The woman's eyes trailed from the TV to the two of them. They fixed on Morris, and she looked puzzled. "Who is this man?"

"He's a cop. From Breckville. I told you he was coming to ask me questions. God knows about what, though."

Morris nodded. "Ma'am. I'm sorry to disturb you."

Her eyes trailed down his body to his shoes and then back up. When they'd seen everything of him they wanted to see, she said, "Cops always want to disturb people, don't they?"

"Well, I'm sorry about that—"

"Just ignore her," Rogers said. "Come on. There's a show I want to watch later."

His wife turned back to the TV, and the two men entered the kitchen, then took chairs on opposite ends of the cluttered table. Rogers kept his cane nearby.

"I'd offer you something, but that's not really my thing. If you want some water . . ."

"I'm okay." An empty pint bottle of Jim Beam sat near the sink, and the room smelled like burned pork. "Like I said on the phone, it's just a few questions."

Rogers shook his head. "Hey, you're talking to another cop, okay? There's no such thing as a few questions. So just ask whatever you came to ask."

"I wanted to tell you I'm happy we know Anna is safe. I'm sure that's a relief to you and your family."

"She's not that safe. She's running around in Louisville, apparently. And she hasn't talked to us. My other daughter is trying to find her."

"Avery."

"The one who used to be a cop. Emphasis on 'used to.' I wanted to go up there myself and look, but my wife needs my attention. I'd find Anna pretty quickly if I went. She'd be back here before you knew it."

"As you know, we're working on the murder of Anna's roommate, Kayla Garvey."

"You don't think it's the Midnight Rambler?"

"Do you?" Morris asked.

"No."

"I like to consider everyone a suspect until they aren't."

Rogers looked pleased by the statement. He nodded. "Agreed."

"You've indicated you think it could be the work of someone you arrested."

"I put a lot of guys away over the years. A lot of them are out—or getting out. Wouldn't you worry about that?"

"I do."

The TV volume increased, but Rogers ignored it.

"Do you have a specific person in mind who might have done this? Someone recently released or harboring a longtime grudge against you?"

"How long a list do you want?" Rogers shifted his weight and stuck his leg out. "The guy who did this has never been caught. Have you ever been shot?"

"No, sir."

"I wouldn't recommend it." His eyes focused someplace else, someplace beyond the room and the house they sat in. "It takes something away when it happens. That's for sure. There's some darkness. . . ." His eyes snapped back into focus. "But I guess that's what we signed up for. What's that old song say? 'I never promised you a rose garden'?"

"I spoke to Lieutenant Paulson of the KSP. Do you know him?"

"I know who he is. Did he wear his jacket with the patches on the elbow?"

"I don't think so."

"The guy drinks tea. *Tea*. My daughters drink tea."

"He did drink tea."

"Told you."

"Beverage choices aside, he mentioned a few cases. Actually, two in particular."

"Which ones?"

"He mentioned your unsolved ambush. And he also mentioned the Douglas family killing. You remember that, of course."

"Of course."

"Three members of the Douglas family were killed in their home. All shot, execution-style. He said you were on the task force that was investigating them—"

"And our task force was pulled off of them three months before the shooting. Surely, Mr. Chamomile mentioned that."

"He did. But that crime remains unsolved despite KSP and even the FBI devoting a lot of resources to it. The Douglas family has a lot of connections to crime in this state. Since you were closely involved with the case at one time, and it's never been solved . . ."

"We didn't have anything on the Douglas family. We weren't close to making an arrest. That's why the task force was pulled back.

We weren't getting anywhere. They cover their tracks well. Very well. And it's true maybe one of their whack-job relatives decided to go out on his own and take a shot at me." He pointed to his leg again. "Fair enough. That thought crossed my mind a time or two. But why show up in Breckville? Now? And go after my daughter? When we never arrested them, and, as far as I know, KSP has backed off them ever since then? I don't see it."

"It's true, according to Paulson, that KSP has backed off them. But it's also true that members of the family are likely still involved in some illegal activity."

"Of course they are. People like that don't change. We know that. We're cops." He straightened his leg, grimacing. "Shit. Why would someone who has never been charged with a crime want to come after me? They'd have to get in line behind all the people we did arrest."

"It's possible the activities of that task force led to whatever happened to the Douglas family. And they haven't forgotten."

"We *know* what happened to the Douglas family. They screwed the wrong person. Or owed them money. Or stepped into the wrong territory. It happens every day. You're barking up the wrong tree."

"What we know is that there were two shooters. Two different weapons. Of course, they've proven to be untraceable. Never used in any other crimes that we know of. But two shooters. A pretty clean job. Someone who knew what they were doing."

"Are you implying something? Just say it."

"Maybe Lieutenant Ballard would have some insights."

"He might. If you can get him away from his goats."

"I guess that's worth trying. But you don't have anything you want to say about it? No insights?"

"Good riddance to bad garbage. It wasn't my case. And it wasn't Charlie's either. Why don't I give you a list of the guys I *did* arrest? I remember most of them."

"I have access to those records. I was really just here because I thought there might be something that doesn't show up in the records."

"Take it from me: Quit chasing shadows. The most obvious thing is usually the right thing."

"You think this Douglas killing was a turf war. Or a money thing. It was pretty vicious, you have to admit. Wiping out a family. Personal, in a way."

"Everything is personal, isn't it?"

An odd comment. Morris let it go.

Captain Rogers said, "Look, I'm a father. I have three girls. And two grandkids. I've spent my whole life worrying about them. I don't want to think about a family getting killed. Okay? Kids should be off-limits. Right?"

"Right."

"So we agree on something."

"I'll keep you posted on our investigation." Morris stood up. "We've called Anna repeatedly. I do hope at some point she gets in touch with us. She can be helpful to our investigation since she was living with Ms. Garvey. Maybe she saw something."

"Do you have children?"

"Two daughters. They're eight and eleven."

"Well, good fucking luck to you when they get older. Only one of mine treats me well."

"I'm sorry to hear that."

"It's fine. I'm kind of a son of a bitch. I know that."

"Some cops are."

"And some fathers."

"Fair enough."

"One more thing, Detective." Rogers sat at the table, not meeting his eye. His leg was still extended, the cane within easy reach. "I hate to ask you this. I do."

"I think we can be frank with each other."

"Yeah. Look, I need that damn walker. It's in the other room there, by the TV. Can you go get it and bring it here so I don't have to bother Jane? She doesn't always . . . Well, as the day goes on, she gets more tired. She works hard. You see?"

"No problem."

Morris went into the other room. *Wheel of Fortune* was over, and Jane sat on the couch channel surfing. She went through the channels so fast, Morris didn't know how she could decide on what to watch.

The walker sat folded next to the TV. He retrieved it and started back.

Jane Rogers appeared to be ignoring him, but then she said, "He gets upset when people ask him about the past."

"I don't know him well, but I don't think he's upset."

"He is. He hates being asked questions."

"Cops prefer to do the asking."

"I don't like these questions either. The past should stay in the past." She kept her eyes on the TV. *Zip zip zip* went the remote. "Are you going to find Anna and bring her home?"

"No, ma'am. That's not my task. Your daughter Avery is doing that."

"She's my stepdaughter. Anna is my only child."

"Right."

"I'm worried about Anna. No one can reach her. Not us. Not her sisters. Not even my cousin Libby."

"Is she close to them?"

"She's always been fond of Libby."

"What does Libby want to talk to her about?"

Jane's glassy eyes remained fixed on the TV.

Rogers yelled from the kitchen, "Detective? I need that walker."

"What are they going to talk about?" Morris asked.

"I don't think I can find the show I want," Jane said.

"What are you looking for? Maybe I can help."

"Hey, Morris? The walker, please? I have to go to the pisser. Then I'll help Jane. And ignore her talk about Libby. Her cousin is a crank. A shit stirrer. She's one of those artistic types. You know the kind. Alternative medicine. Yoga."

Morris brought the walker to the kitchen. He unfolded it and placed it in front of Captain Rogers. "Okay." He held out his hand to assist. "You ready?"

Rogers waved off Morris' help. It was a struggle, but he pushed himself up, breathing heavily once he had both hands on the walker and his body out of the chair. "Okay, you can go."

"Do you need anything else?" Morris asked.

"Yeah, stop bugging my wife. If you have questions, just ask me. She's not herself. Okay?"

"Sure thing, Captain. Thanks for your time."

Morris went to the door. Jane Rogers had changed the channel to a professional wrestling match. As he pulled the door shut, her eyes left the screen for a moment and watched him go.

31

Charlie stopped in front of the building so Avery could go up to the door.

"There's nowhere to park anyway," he said. "Not in this neighborhood on a Friday evening."

"Okay, I'll try. She may slam the door in my face. If she's even there."

"You may be surprised. I do think your sister admires you and probably would love to have a relationship with you."

"Have you been talking to Alisha?"

"Just my own observation. I have an older brother. He went into the army when I was little, so I never really knew him. I get what it's like to feel that distance from a sibling."

"Are you trying to make me feel worse?"

"I'm going to call my friend Mike while you're up there. The FBI agent."

Avery stepped out of the truck, felt the cooling night air on her face. With her hands in the pockets of her jacket, she walked to the building entrance. She moved slowly, not sure what she would say to Anna if they came face-to-face. And what would she do if Anna refused to come along?

She should've stayed in the truck. Charlie was better equipped for this mission. He possessed the ability to get along with anybody, to put everybody at ease. It made him the perfect foil for her dad at work—one partner everybody hated and one everybody loved. Together they struck the right note. . . .

Avery climbed to the third floor, regretting all the days she skipped the gym. She thought back to her time in the KSP, when she had been in the best shape of her life. She had run a marathon with Hank, after training alongside him and a group of fellow officers for weeks and weeks. They had started the training program as friends. They ended it in love, moving in together after only two months of dating. Only a fool lived in the past. So she must be the biggest fool in the world. She tried to look forward to her future—finishing the master's, maybe starting a PhD. A whole new career, likely in a new place. But would anything ever feel as vital as being a cop?

Even almost dying in the pond that day had made her feel more alive than anything else in her life. . . .

Avery knocked on the door. Reluctantly.

She wasn't just worried about facing Anna—she remembered that morning and the surprise she had found in the apartment in Breckville. Could it be true that the person who killed Kayla intended to hurt Anna? And was it possible that person had tracked Anna here?

Avery knocked again. With much more force, trying to guarantee anyone inside would hear her.

But nobody answered. And no sleepy-eyed bro came out of a neighboring apartment to help.

She went all the way back down. As she slid into the truck again, Charlie was ending a call.

"Okay, man. See you in a few. Good. Yeah."

He put the phone into his coat pocket.

"No answer."

"Maybe she thought you were selling magazines."

"Anna's too smart to sit around and wait for me to arrive. I'm sure she took off."

"Probably. She was never the predictable type."

"You're saying she's impulsive? I'd say she's spoiled. So, what now?"

"We're meeting Mike at a coffee shop up the way. He has stuff to tell us about this protest tomorrow. Stuff he really doesn't want to say on the phone or via text."

"Okay, then."

They drove for a few blocks in silence, in and out of the glow of streetlights. Then Charlie said, "You're speaking from the perspective of the oldest child. About the child of your dad's second marriage."

"What are you saying?"

"Calling Anna spoiled."

"She was."

"From your perspective. She lived in the shadow of two older sisters, both pretty great in their own way."

Avery's face flushed in the darkened truck.

"And," Charlie continued, "she lived with the knowledge that her mom broke up her dad's first marriage. She probably carried some weight there. Her existence was a daily reminder of that."

"Hey, I was a good sister to Anna when we were in the same house together."

"I never said you weren't."

"And maybe her two older sisters lived under a cloud too. Our parents split up. Then our mother died."

"Fair enough."

Charlie guided the truck onto a main road, in a business district. Restaurants and shops and pedestrians. Glowing lights and energy. Avery and Charlie remained quiet. Even the radio was off. The silence pressed against Avery like a force.

"Look, I know I could have been a better sister to Anna lately. I know that."

"Okay."

"Is there anything else to say about that?"

"Not from me."

"Alisha brought something up. Shit, I wish I'd handled it better."

"What's that?"

"Dad. And Jane. They asked me to be Anna's guardian. Like they were making a will. This was when I was about twenty. Anna was little."

"Twenty is kind of young."

"Fuck. I said no. I said I wouldn't do it. So they made Alisha the guardian. She said yes. Of course. Alisha the Good."

"Hey, you were young."

"Okay, but here's the thing, Charlie. Weren't *you* our guardian? When I was little, Dad always told us you were going to take care of us if anything happened to them. Dad always said to call you if something bad went down. That's what he said. Why did that change?"

Charlie kept his eyes on the road.

"Charlie?"

"I heard you."

"And they seemed so adamant. Jane was almost crazed about it. She acted like it was life-or-death."

"It was. Anna's life. Their deaths."

"Yeah, I know. People can die at any time. But . . . they acted like someone was after them. Like they were crossing items off a list. It was strange. Intense."

"I'm not sure, okay? Cops get spooked. Like anyone else. In fact, cops lead dangerous lives. Maybe that happened with your dad."

"He would have told you."

"Maybe. And maybe I wasn't the best choice to raise three girls. Once you and Alisha were old enough, it made sense for you to take care of Anna. If the worst happened. Right?"

"I don't know. . . ."

Charlie turned the truck to the right. They jounced over a speed bump and into a parking lot. He found a spot facing a brick wall, the side of the coffee shop with the name painted in giant script. The Beanery.

He put the truck in park but left it running.

He looked thoughtful in profile. "I wish for nothing more than that you would have knocked on that door and come back to the truck with Anna. Ready to go home and have everything be right." He sighed. "I just don't think anything is going to go easy this weekend. In many ways. Come on. Let's go talk to Mike."

32

The rich scent of roasted beans hit Avery as she and Charlie went through the door.

Nearly every table was occupied. An eclectic crowd of old and young. Couples and groups. A few played board games supplied by the Beanery. Somebody groaned as a Jenga tower collapsed.

Acoustic music played over the sound system. Don McLean. "Castles in the Air."

Across the room, a guy with dark hair that touched his collar nodded at Charlie, who led the way, Avery in his wake. They sat across from Mike, who reached out and shook Avery's hand. He looked to be in his forties. His Fu Manchu mustache was flecked with gray. Charlie never mentioned a last name. Just: "This is Mike."

"You getting coffee?" Mike asked.

"I'll get some."

Charlie left, and Avery was alone with Mike. A mug steamed in front of him, and next to the mug sat a novel about an FBI agent. Mike saw Avery's eyes track to it.

"Sad, isn't it? I can't get enough of this stuff. It's pretty good. Accurate too."

"Don't you want a break? You could read a book about the War of the Roses or something. Outer space."

"That would probably be healthy. So you're Russ Rogers' daughter."

"One of three."

"Right. The youngest one is on the lam in Louisville."

"She is."

"I'll fill you both in when Charlie gets back. What do you do?"

"I'm in graduate school. History."

"I see. So, you didn't follow in the old man's footsteps?"

"Well . . ."

"That's wise. You could end up like me, taking a break from work by reading a novel about an FBI agent."

Charlie came back holding two mugs. "You didn't want cream or anything, did you?"

"I'm good."

"So, Mr. Mike, what have you got for us?" Charlie asked.

For the first time, Mike acted like an FBI agent. He looked at the nearby tables. On one side, two teenagers talked awkwardly. A first date. From the bored look on the girl's face, likely the last. On the other, a couple in their mid-sixties shared a dessert and talked. It was disgusting how happy they looked in their long-term relationship. What could they still have to say to each other after all those years? How could they stand the sight of each other? Still?

Mike spoke in a lower voice. "I'm sure you both know there have been a lot of marches and rallies over the past few weeks, ever since the Burns shooting."

"Even some property damage, right? Looting?"

"Some businesses have been trashed. Cars burned. A few cops have been hurt. Protestors too. Nothing major, but it's been close to lighting up. A lot of miscreants around. The whole town is a tinderbox. If you'll pardon my use of a predictable cliché."

"You've been reading too many trashy novels," Avery said.

"Could be."

"I think I see where you're going with this," Charlie said.

Avery looked between the two men, waiting. The older couple laughed. The man said, "Oh, we need to get back to Cape Cod. And with the grandchildren this time."

Mike said, "Remember there's an election in a few weeks. Politicians *hate* it when stuff gets broken and burned right before an election." He lowered his voice even more. "This march tomorrow . . . I know for a fact the federal authorities have come in to help. And the state police. And agencies from surrounding counties. There's going to be a large police presence. And they're not going to tolerate any crap."

"Lovely," Avery said.

"And then . . ." Mike trailed off.

Charlie and Avery looked at each other and then back at Mike. Avery asked, "And then what?"

"We're picking up a lot of chatter. White supremacist groups."

"You've got to be kidding," Avery said.

"I'm not. There's no way to tell how serious any of them are. Sometimes it's just a keyboard warrior who pops off online while his mom makes him tuna salad in the next room. But sometimes, as we've seen in other places, they mean business. And they like nothing more than to sow a little chaos. When they see those marchers—young, woke, diverse—it gets their juices flowing."

"They want to get in there and take some cheap shots at these kids," Charlie said.

"It's not very sporting, but they do."

"How likely is it?" Avery asked.

"I'm not a betting man, but I think it's greater than fifty percent. There could be a three-way convergence here. Cops, protestors, and extremists."

Avery felt cold. She pictured Anna getting in the way of some overgrown thug with a baseball bat or a gun. "This is shitty."

"If you can get your sister out of here before all the hooligans show up, that would be great. Once it starts . . . it's going to be chaos."

"Thanks," Charlie said.

"Can you warn your sister off?" Mike asked.

"She currently isn't speaking to me. Or anyone in the family. Other than that, I have a great chance at getting her out."

Mike rubbed his chin. His knuckles looked like a fighter's. "There are a lot of different groups marching. They assemble in Baxter Park. But the young people tend to congregate just east of there. There's a chance your sister will be there. And you can try to find her. But . . ."

"Needle-in-a-haystack time," Avery said.

"I was going to say like picking fly shit out of pepper," Mike said. "But the same idea."

"Okay," Avery said, "if I don't find her beforehand, and she doesn't answer my calls, then what choice do I have? She's an adult. She'll come home when she wants to."

Mike drank from his mug and wiped a drop of coffee off his mustache. "Maybe I wasn't explicit enough. They are going to crack down. Hard. It's going to be real easy to get swept up in something tomorrow. And end up in jail."

"They're not going to hurt people protesting the police shooting of an innocent, unarmed woman."

Charlie's hand came over and rested on her arm.

"What?"

Mike looked like he'd been slapped. He wiped his mustache again. "What's so innocent about Tanya Burns? She had a record a mile long. What is this shit, Charlie? Is this what you brought me here for?"

"Hold on, now—"

Mike raised his voice. So much so that the Cape Cod–loving couple at the next table looked over. "I just don't want to hear cops getting run down. Again."

"Nobody's running down cops—"

"Maybe I am," Avery said. "It wasn't a good shooting. Anyone can tell that."

Mike looked at her with his mouth half open. His hand rested on the paperback, his fingers riffling the pages. *Scrack scrack scrack.* "Didn't you tell me you were Russ Rogers' daughter? Didn't you tell me that, Charlie?"

"Mike, can we not go there? Please?"

"I'm not *going* anywhere."

"Why do you want to defend someone who makes you look bad?" Avery asked. "He's a shitty cop. Get rid of him. Hold him accountable so everybody stops hating us."

Mike reacted to the word just as Avery realized she'd spoken it.

"*Us?* Who is this *us?*"

Avery was in too far to back down. "I was a cop. I know."

"*Was* a cop? Are you hearing this, Charlie?"

"Mike, everybody is looking at us. Like we're in a zoo."

Mike looked around and laughed. A bitter smile filled his face, and the other patrons who had turned their way averted their gazes. Mike stared at Avery but addressed his words to Charlie. "Your friend here said she's in grad school. Maybe she knows what the word 'irony' means."

"Mike—"

He stood up. "I helped you, okay? You got the tip. All accounts are cleared between us now." He waited. "Did you hear me, Charlie? It's all clear."

"I hear you."

Mike left the table as soon as Charlie answered.

When he was gone, Avery said, "Well, he seemed nice."

"Forget him."

"What's he mean about irony? And Dad? And all accounts being cleared?"

"It's cop talk. Old news."

"Charlie. What is it?"

"Come on. Let's get out of here."

33

Kayla stood on the edge of the balcony of her apartment in Breck-ville. Even though the apartment didn't have a balcony.

She leaned back against the railing, and the railing gave way. Anna ran across the apartment, reaching out for Kayla. Anna ran and ran. She ran for what felt like days. Then she reached her room-mate, held out her hand. Kayla took it—and then she slipped right through Anna's grip and fell out of sight.

When Anna looked down, there was no sign of Kayla.

She was gone.

Anna's eyes opened. She gasped like someone emerging from deep, cold water.

It all came back, landing on her like a load of scrap metal. Kayla was dead. Gone. Murdered in her bed.

Possibly because of Anna. Who she was. Who her family was.

At the very least, Anna should have been there. She should have been fighting alongside Kayla. She wiped the tears off her cheeks.

Voices reached her from the other room. Muffled conversation between two people. She recognized the messy room. Clothes on the floor. A comforter with a rip in it. Venetian blinds hanging lopsid-edly. A broken cord dangled over the desk. The mattress and box springs rested on the floor without benefit of a bed frame.

Anna pushed the covers back. She wore a pair of shorts and a T-shirt, neither of which belonged to her. Her feet were bare. She found her discarded socks on the floor and pulled them on before shuffling out of the bedroom.

When she opened the door, the conversation stopped. Eric and Rachel sat at the small dining room table. Both turned to look at her.

"Hey."

"Hey."

"I'm awake," she said. The smell of brewing coffee perked her up.

Rachel came over, arms open. She hugged Anna, pulled her tight. "Do you want to sleep longer?"

"Thanks, no. Sleep isn't . . ." The images came back. Kayla slipping through her hand. Kayla falling—

"What?"

"Nothing. It was good to sleep a little."

Rachel led her to the table like she was a child. Eric stood up, the kind of gesture Anna saw only in old movies. She recognized the look on his face—he had no idea what to say or do. He never did in a crisis. He tended to freeze, to stumble over his words or go completely silent. He didn't say anything but moved out of the way, letting Anna take his seat. He went out to the kitchen and came back with coffee and put it in front of Anna.

"Do you want toast? I have some bread I can scrape the mold off of. And I think there's some cheese. It might be a little moldy, but it's cheese, you know?"

"I'm okay." Anna sipped the hot coffee. Usually she needed it to calm a hangover, but she had drunk very little the night before. Her body had remained roiled and unbalanced all night, and she'd made the wise choice not to add alcohol to the mix. "Thanks. And thanks for the clothes."

"Sure. You've slept in my clothes before, I guess." Eric wore a long-underwear shirt. He'd cut his hair short. It made him look older, almost mature. "I think it's smart you guys didn't go back to Rachel's. Who knows what's going on, right?"

"Right," Rachel said. "Exactly."

Anna's parents did that. She'd come into the room and see her mom and dad sitting together, clearly in the middle of talking about her, and they'd try to act all casual, give off the vibe of *No, honey, we weren't talking about you.* But Anna would know they had been because they'd awkwardly launch into saying what they wanted her to do based on what they'd been talking about. She was sure Rachel and Eric were about to do the same thing.

Rachel would be taking the lead because Eric couldn't.

"So, we thought, you know, maybe you'd want to head back home today. Eric's off work and so am I, so one of us could drive your car and the other could follow, so you wouldn't be on your own. And then you could see your parents or talk to the cops or whatever you have to do now that you're rested and everything."

Anna swallowed more coffee, felt the warmth move through her body.

"That is, if you don't want to get in touch with Avery. Which I totally get if you don't want to, but that's an option too."

Rachel looked at Eric and shrugged—a gesture that seemed intended to appear totally casual but looked as convincing as a cat walking on its hind legs.

"Yeah," Eric said. "Avery. I know the two of you aren't always cool, but she's pretty good in a crisis. Remember that time I fell off my bike when I was ten, and Avery came out of the house and administered first aid to me even though I was all scared and crying? I'll never forget that about her." He looked at Rachel and pointed to his hairline. "I still have the scar."

"I really do appreciate the help both of you have given me," Anna said. "I know I wasn't in the best frame of mind last night. I'm still not. And I'm sorry you had to leave your house, Rachel."

"It's okay."

Anna rubbed her forehead. "I think I was pretty upset last night. I think I asked you to sleep in the bed with me, didn't I?"

"You did," Rachel said. "I didn't mind."

"And I didn't mind sleeping on the couch," Eric said. "I mean, I figured . . . you know, with everything going on . . . and I certainly never intended to ask . . ."

"Thanks, Eric." Anna moved the mug around, first one way and then another. "I want to go to the march. That's what I'm here for, and that's what I'm doing."

An uncomfortable silence settled. Anna waited for someone else to speak, while a clock ticked somewhere in the apartment.

"My friend Bonita works for a lawyer here in town." Rachel spoke gently, like she was addressing a spooked child. "And she says it could get ugly out there. The police aren't going to put up with anything."

"I don't care about the police. That's why I want to go to the march. That's the point. Somebody has to be held accountable for what they've done."

"And not just cops," Rachel said. "There are likely to be counterprotestors. You know, the guys who show up with guns and pretend like they're running around in Iraq because they never joined the army for real."

"I don't *care*," Anna said.

"Plenty of people will be marching," Eric said. "Good people. It doesn't just have to fall on you, after all you've been through. We thought if you don't want to go home, we could do something else. We could drive down to Bernheim Forest or go to a distillery. The day is young."

Anna's hands dropped to the table with a thwack. Her calm demeanor departed. "Do something touristy? Today?"

"We thought—" Rachel said.

"You thought what? You two had a nice time sitting out here making a plan for me. Thanks for that. And thanks for finally including me and asking me what I wanted to do."

"We wanted to let you sleep, Anna," Eric said.

"Well, I'm awake, okay? I don't know about the two of you, but I'm awake. And I'm going to the march. You can come with me or not. Really. I know where the park is. I can walk there if I have to."

"Anna, you don't have to—"

"And by the way, thanks for not asking for sex last night, Eric. What do you want? A medal?"

"Well, I—"

She stood up and left the room to get dressed, while he still sputtered.

34

Avery and Charlie had taken adjoining hotel rooms, and when she finally woke up and knocked on his door, he didn't answer. She found him downstairs in the dining room. A crumb-filled plate and a mug of coffee sat on the table before him. He scanned the local paper with a pair of store-bought readers perched on the end of his nose. When Avery sat with her plate of food, he folded the paper and tossed it onto an empty chair. He removed the glasses.

"Good morning, Starshine."

"What's so good about it?"

"There's free coffee and food."

"I'm sure the cost is slipped into the bill somewhere."

"I'm just trying to look on the bright side."

Avery started eating her rubbery eggs. "Sorry. I didn't sleep well."

"I get it. You're worried about Anna. And everything Mike told us."

"What is his deal?" She poured the cheap creamer into her coffee. "Why are you friends with him? And is Dad friends with him?"

Charlie held the glasses between his thumb and index finger. The frames were dark purple, and he bounced them against his thigh. "We're not friends. We had to work together from time to time. He's a source."

"Of aggravation? Of misconceptions about cops?"

"Just a source. I used to be idealistic when I was young, but that passed a long time ago. Mike provides what I need."

"And now some old debt is clear?"

"Don't concern yourself with what a couple of old farts talk about. Just war stories, that's all."

Avery drank coffee. The creamer did nothing. Less than nothing, since it might have been expired and it added a crappy taste to the coffee.

Charlie smiled about something.

"What?"

"I just remembered when you were little, very little, and I'd come over and sit around with Russ. We'd be out in the backyard having a beer or two, talking about work. And what would you do?"

"These eggs need ketchup. Do you see any?"

"You'd go out the front door and then sneak around. And you'd crawl up alongside the porch, so we couldn't see you. And you'd listen. To every word we said."

"I thought being a child was boring."

"And hearing cops talk wasn't. Right?"

"One night the two of you talked about an accident you'd seen. The driver was decapitated. I went inside to find the dictionary to look that word up. When I understood what it meant, I went back out to hear more. But you were done talking about it."

"I don't even remember that accident. I saw somebody with their head sliced off and I don't remember."

"I'm sure you saw that stuff more than once."

"I did." He stood up and grabbed a ketchup bottle off another table and brought it back. "Here."

"Thanks."

"Maybe I've repressed it all. Maybe that's why my blood pressure is so high. My lady friend says I stuff my emotions. Placid exterior. Churning interior."

Avery squeezed the ketchup, and the plastic bottle made a squirting sound. The condiment didn't help much, but it did enough. "Speaking of that . . ."

"My emotions?"

"I don't think you need to go today. The chances of finding Anna in the massive crowd are slim. She doesn't want to be located. And if a lot of trouble is going to come down . . ."

"You think I'm too old."

"I didn't say that."

"I appreciate it. I do." He folded the glasses and slid them into his shirt pocket. He patted the pocket once. "You girls are about the closest to having kids I'll ever come. My nieces and nephews live far away. They don't really know me."

Charlie spoke without looking at her. She sensed some sort of honest and open expression of emotion coming. And that always made her nervous and uncomfortable.

"I feel that close to all three of you," he said. "I hope you know that."

Something caught in Avery's throat. And it wasn't the rubbery eggs. "I do."

"What I'm saying is your dad can't do this. He's not well enough. So I *have* to do it for him. You know? Have to."

"Okay. I get it. I'm happy to have the company. Besides, I think it's a fruitless mission."

"Even a fruitless mission sounds interesting. It's no fun being retired."

"Really? You look like you're having a good time on the farm."

"I might be having a good time." He grappled for the right words. "It's just . . . it's not quite the same *purpose* I had when I worked. The feeling I was waking up every day to do something that mattered."

"And chasing down a pissed-off college student is on that level?"

"Come on, Avery. You know what I mean."

She did. Her comment was a defense, pushback to avoid really engaging with what he'd said. But she'd known even before Charlie said it. She felt the same way. She loved school. She loved what she had to look forward to.

But had any of it ever mattered as much as her time as a cop?

Had anything ever felt as big?

"I know." She pushed her nearly empty plate away. She went

across the room and refilled her coffee. When she came back, Charlie was still staring off into the distance. "Do you want to get going?"

"Your dad didn't have anything else noteworthy to say when you were at his house?" he asked.

It seemed like an odd question. Avery's dad never had anything noteworthy to say to her.

"He gave me the usual ungrateful-daughter speech, something right out of *King Lear*. He reminded me of what a disappointment I am. How I could have been a captain like him. He needed help finding a bottle. He complained about Jane's cousin Libby because she wanted to talk to Anna for some reason."

"Oh, yeah, Libby. Shit, Jane set me up with her. Remember?"

"She did?"

"We went on a few dates. I managed to sidestep further entanglements. She wasn't right for me."

"I hear you. Libby's pretty close to Jane. But she's really close to Anna. I think when Alisha and I were out of the house, Anna could turn to Libby for help or advice. You know, someone who wasn't her parents."

"Everybody needs that."

"Yeah. Kids are lucky if they find someone like that."

"They are. But you don't know why Libby was calling."

"No idea. She couldn't get ahold of Anna, so maybe she was just worried. Dad acted more irritated by the call than he should have, but that's par for the course. He randomly gets pissed about little shit."

"True enough."

"You ready to get out of here? We have a date with either angry cops, pissed-off racists, or super-woke social justice warriors. I, for one, can't wait."

"Hold on a minute." He shifted his body so he faced her. "I hope all that's going on with Anna is she's pissed off about the shooting. I hope we find her, or she just decides to return on her own. That's probably what this is about."

"What else would it be about?" Avery studied him. "You mean a scenario where the roommate's murder was some sort of revenge for something Dad did in the past? Is that it? And not just a random crime?"

"Right."

"That's always been a possibility."

Charlie nodded, as if confirming something to himself. "Okay."

"Okay."

Avery waited. Across the room, a hotel employee pulled a bulging trash bag out of a can and dragged it back to the kitchen.

"Do you want to go now? I think they're cleaning up."

"I just want you to know that we don't really know what's going on with Anna. And I think it's important for us to find her and make sure she's safe."

"And that's also why you wanted to come? In addition to liking to have a purpose and a mission."

"That's right."

"And there's nothing else I need to know?" Avery asked.

Charlie really seemed to think the question over. Then he nodded again and stood up. "No, I think we're good to go."

35

Yates' neck burned.

He'd spent the night in his car, keeping an eye on the apartment building. He'd allowed himself the indulgence of going to the back seat, and even closed his eyes and slept for about four hours, figuring the kids wouldn't be up at dawn after being out so late. The march started at nine.

Still, he didn't want to miss them. Not after he had spent the whole night before following them around. Not after he had come all that way.

Not when he needed to make this work so he could get back in the good graces of the man he worked for. And the family Hogan worked for.

Yates climbed out of the car into the cold morning air. Condensation covered the windows, and he shivered as he looked around. He needed to piss, needed to get coffee and something to eat. He'd seen a crappy little bakery on the corner—the kind of place that looked like it had been there since before World War Two. That meant either their products would be the best he ever had—or the worst. No in-between with a place like that.

He decided to risk it.

He started by going down an alley and taking a leak behind a dumpster while he scratched his stubbly face with his free hand. Sweet relief. He'd stayed in the car so long, holding it in, that the pee just kept coming and coming. Like being on a carnival ride, it felt so good.

He'd followed the two girls to a bar last night. A place with a brick-walled courtyard, white lights on a strand over everybody's heads. He'd watched from a distance, drinking club soda with a lime in it to keep his head clear. Anna didn't drink either, but her friend sure did. The friend ordered drink after drink—and talked a lot—while Anna stared off into the distance, like the friend wasn't even there.

Yates couldn't know for certain if Anna would recognize him. That night they had come face-to-face outside the apartment had been dark, the moon hidden by clouds, and based on the way Anna had stumbled out of the car, then fallen on the stairs, her head hadn't been exactly clear.

But Yates couldn't risk it. He'd stayed back, out of sight. Just another lonely guy in a bar on a Friday night, trying to pretend the baseball playoff game on the TV interested him.

He finished peeing and zipped up. He started down the street for the bakery. At some point the night before, the two girls had met up with a dude. Not a bad-looking guy but a little overweight. Clearly he was into Anna. He stared at her with puppy eyes even as she continued to look off into space, like a movie that nobody else could see was playing in her mind.

Yates had followed them from one bar to another, keeping his distance. Anna must have known her roommate had been killed—that must have been why she was so mopey—but even armed with that knowledge, the three of them took no special precautions. They walked right down the streets of Louisville, never looking behind them, never changing sides of the street, never splitting up or taking an unpredictable route. Yates grew bored with them. It was like tracking little kids just learning to play hide-and-seek.

At the end of the night, they had done one thing correctly. Rather than going back to the other girl's apartment, they went to the guy's place. That was where Yates spent the night in the car, outside the dude's building, which appeared to be a pretty decent place. Yates guessed there was a trust fund involved or some serious financial help from mommy and daddy.

Inside the bakery he ordered a giant coffee and a couple of donuts. The woman behind the counter, who wore a spot of flour on her nose and looked to have been working there since the place had opened, spoke to him in an accent so thick, he couldn't understand a word she said. That increased Yates' confidence that the place was the real deal, that the donuts were made on the spot and would deliver real taste.

And he was right.

He bit into the first one as he walked back to his car, and the sweet taste exploded in his mouth.

"Mmmm."

He drilled the rest of it, not minding at all that crumbs stuck to his stubble and fingers. By the time he reached the car, the donut was gone, and he told himself to hold off on the second one, to delay the gratification as long as he could. He anticipated climbing back into the car and wolfing it down, with the coffee chasing it.

But a cop stood next to his car with his ticket book in hand.

Yates spoke up without thinking. "Whoa, whoa."

He ran up to the car. The cop turned to him, acted utterly disinterested in Yates' arrival on the scene.

"Is there a problem, Officer? It's a Saturday. I'm here now."

The cop didn't look up. "You need a permit to park on this street."

"I do. A permit?"

"Yes, sir. I could have the vehicle towed."

"No, no. Not that. Look, I'm from out of town."

The cop nodded. "I see on the plate you're from Manchester County."

"That's right."

"Breckville?"

"Near there. I live in Hancock."

The cop studied Yates. He was a young guy, likely a rookie. He took Yates in like he thought the two of them had gone to high school together and the cop just couldn't place the name that went with the face.

Yates had to assume his description was out. Hopefully vague, but maybe the cops had found security footage or something? Maybe some nosy neighbor had taken a video?

"Are you here for the march?" the cop asked.

"No, sir. I'm a big supporter of the police."

"Then what are you here for? It kind of looks like you slept in your clothes. And in your car."

"Right. I just came up here to party. Go to some bars. That's what I was doing last night. And I didn't want to drive while I might be impaired, so . . ."

The cop stared at Yates.

"If you could just cut me a break on the ticket, I'm going to get out of here soon. And I promise to never park here again."

The cop kept looking. "They had a murder down in Breckville."

Everything inside Yates froze. His grip on the cup of coffee grew loose, like it might slip through his fingers and hit the ground. What was the right thing to say?

"Yes, I heard that. Terrible news."

"Maybe you didn't hear this part, but they caught the guy. Just this morning. Found him trying to get into another girl's apartment."

Yates' mouth didn't work. He struggled to form words. It felt like he stood there, dumb and silent, for five straight minutes. But it was just a few seconds.

"That's good. I'm glad to hear that."

The cop nodded.

Yates went on. "You know, I'm not going to that march because I support the cops. Totally. And see, I was right. The cops got their man down in Breckville."

The cop stared at him. He held a pen and used it to scratch the side of his neck. "If you get this vehicle out of here, I'll forget about the ticket. Especially since you were being responsible by not driving drunk."

"Yes, sir. Of course."

Yates scrambled for his keys, taking care not to spill his coffee. The cop backed away a few steps, looked like he wasn't going to leave.

Shit. He'd have to drive around the block, try to keep an eye on the apartment somehow without being staked out in the car. But it was far better to do that than to have the cop check him out, maybe run his name and find out about his record.

He unlocked the car and got inside while the cop watched him. He placed the coffee in the cup holder and started the engine, leaving sticky residue on the door handles and the steering wheel.

He prepared to pull away, and when he looked up, he saw them.

The three kids coming out of the building.

"Okay. Let's go. Let's go."

36

Morris met the lawyer in the hallway outside the interrogation room. The space smelled like floor polish and shattered dreams.

Rita Benitez had come to Breckville after three years in the state's attorney's office. She'd started there right out of law school but decided it was better to help those accused of crimes stand up to the full weight of the state than to try to send them away.

Rita checked something on her phone, then looked up at Morris. "You ready to set the terms?"

"I'd like to hear what he says first. Our guys caught him trying to go through a window, into a woman's apartment. And I bet if we fingerprint him, we can tie him to a few other crime scenes around town."

"But not the one you want to tie him to."

"I don't have a preference. I just love to catch criminals."

"Bullshit." Rita looked down at her phone again, then flicked the ringer off with her thumb. "We all know you want to arrest a murderer. And you don't really care that much about a pervert called the Midnight Rambler."

"Is that the public defender's office official policy? We don't care about guys who break into apartments and watch young women sleep? Come on, Rita."

Rita tilted her head from one side to the other like she was working a kink out of her neck. "Look, you've got him on the Midnight Rambler stuff. Dead to rights. He's willing to admit to all that. He's sick, Morris. He needs help. And he wants to get it."

"Okay, I'm listening."

"He's not a murderer. He was never in that apartment where Kayla Garvey died. You won't find his prints there."

"Maybe he wore gloves."

"You won't find hair, fiber, DNA, prints. Nothing. He wasn't there. I mean . . . Well, if you can, offer him a deal."

"You mean what?"

Rita watched Morris for a moment. Lips pursed, thoughts racing behind her eyes. "He wasn't *inside* the apartment."

"You're saying . . . he was outside? And he saw something?"

"I might be saying that."

Morris tried not to reveal anything. He didn't want to commit to any deal that would bite him in the ass later. "Can I just go in and talk to him?"

"I'm going to be there the whole time."

"I wouldn't expect anything less, Rita."

They went into the interrogation room. The Midnight Rambler, otherwise known as Jesse Stuben, sat at the small table with a Coke can and a candy bar wrapper in front of him. He looked up when they came in but showed little emotion. He looked tired, like a man who hadn't had a good night's sleep in a few days.

Morris sat in one empty chair and Rita took the other.

"Jesse," Rita said, "it's okay for you to talk to this officer and to tell him the things you told me. If there's something I don't want you to answer, I'll let you know. Okay?"

"Yeah, sure." Stuben seemed bored. Like a man waiting for a bus.

"Jesse, you understand what we want to talk about, right?" Morris asked.

"You want to know what I saw outside that apartment."

Stuben was a tall guy, taller than Morris. His body looked doughy, like he'd spent his entire life eating carbs and drinking soda. His fingers were thick like sausages.

"Which apartment would that be, Jesse?"

"The one where the girl got killed. Come on, you know what we're talking about."

"And you didn't kill her?"

Jesse looked offended by the question. His delicate sensibilities had been ruffled. "No. Not at all." He leaned forward, placed his clammy-looking hands on the table. "Look, I have my problems, but killing isn't one of them. I can't even ask a girl on a date, let alone kill one. Okay?"

"That's why you have to sneak into their apartments and watch them sleep? Because you don't know how to ask them out?"

"I'm not saying it's normal, man. But it's what I do."

"Morris, can we get to the point?" Rita asked.

Morris tried to give her a look that told her to stay out of his interrogation. He doubted the look would work on Rita, so he turned back to Jesse Stuben.

"So, what did you see on the night Kayla Garvey was killed?"

"Okay, I was there. In the parking lot. I admit that." As he spoke, his eyes moved back and forth from Morris to Rita. "I'd never been there before. I mean, I'd never, you know, tried it there before. I was running out of places to go. Apartments with students are the best because they tend not to lock their doors and stuff. They come and go and they forget. So I went out there that night, but not to do anything. Not yet. I like to check it out first, get the lay of the land before I try anything."

"You're a craftsman," Morris said. Jokingly.

But Jesse accepted the compliment like it was serious. "Exactly. So when I was looking, I saw a guy hanging around outside one of the buildings. Like he was waiting for somebody. I thought maybe he was a cop, but, really, he didn't look quite right for that. He wasn't clean-cut enough or something."

"So what happened?" Morris asked.

"I watched him. I couldn't really check out any doors or windows or anything if this guy was hanging around. I mean, he might have been a cop. I didn't know."

"He might have been competition."

"Exactly. A copycat. So I just waited. He didn't move. He stayed in the same spot, by the one building. For a long time. I was ready to just leave. There are other apartments I could try. Not many but a few. But then a car pulled up and the girl got out."

Morris shifted his weight a little, sat up straighter. The chair squeaked. Jesse finally had his attention. "Okay, what girl would this be?"

"I don't know the girl. I didn't recognize her. Like I said, I don't really know too many young women. But when the girl reached the stairs, the guy said something to her and then she ran inside, sort of like the dude freaked her out."

"And what did you do?"

"I left. And I didn't go back to that complex. It didn't seem right somehow. The vibe was off."

"Because you saw this guy?" Morris asked.

"Yeah. Yeah, I think so. He gave me a bad feeling."

"Bad enough that you didn't feel right creeping into women's apartments there?"

"Easy, Morris," Rita said.

"Hey," Jesse said, "I know I'm not a saint. Okay? I want to stop doing this too. But that doesn't mean I can't get a bad vibe off someone." He stabbed the table with his pudgy index finger for emphasis as he went on. "The key thing is, Detective, that's the building where Kayla Garvey was killed. The guy was hanging around outside of there, and then the next night, the woman inside ends up dead. See? It wasn't me. It was this other guy."

"See, Morris?" Rita gave him a slap on the biceps. "This is real."

Morris held his hands out, palms up. A giant shrug. "What's real? I've got a guy sitting here who we caught going through a woman's bedroom window, one of about thirty he's gone through, and he says he saw a guy staking out the place where a murder victim lived. How am I supposed to believe a word he says?"

Rita didn't answer. She unclasped her briefcase and reached inside. She brought out a phone. Not the one she had been holding in the hallway.

"What's this?" Morris asked.

"Tell him, Jesse."

"I bet you want a description of the guy I saw."

"It would help."

"I can do one better. I filmed him standing outside the apartment where the murder occurred."

37

Avery and Charlie took Jefferson Street and approached Baxter Park from the west.

Charlie drove, the radio playing bluegrass, while Avery rode in the passenger seat, staring out the window as traffic increased the deeper into the city they went. They struck a bottleneck near Western Cemetery. Everybody stopped ahead of them, and cops were re-routing people off Jefferson and onto side roads.

"We should park anywhere we can," Charlie said.

He made a right, drove around for a few minutes, and found parking in the lot of a high school football stadium. Others had had the same idea, and the area quickly filled up with cars.

They got out and started walking side by side. The morning sky was slightly overcast, making it difficult to tell where cloud ended and sky began. The crisp air made Avery wish they were there to see a game and not to search for someone they'd likely never find.

The crowd around them swelled. Avery had to admit that it felt good to be in the midst of such a diverse group. Young and old. All different colors. Breckville could be so plain, so homogenous. Students and professors, and that was about it. She'd leave in a couple of years, she often fantasized, and go for her PhD someplace far away— someplace she'd never been. California or Oregon, maybe. Sometimes she wanted to go someplace totally random—like Idaho. Or Wyoming. Wear a cowboy hat and boots, drive around in a Jeep.

Sure, it would be real diverse in those places.

"If we don't find her, Charlie, she'll be okay. Right? I mean, she's just going to go back to Breckville eventually. She'll cool off and go see Dad and Jane."

"Probably."

"And she's not likely to get hurt here, is she? There will be a lot of people, and Anna isn't a troublemaker."

"They don't always hurt the troublemakers," he said. "Isn't that why this march is happening?"

They walked east on Cedar Street, with Western Cemetery on their left. A beautiful spot inside the city. Graves dating back more than two hundred years, one of the first places people had been buried when Louisville was becoming a city. Faded flowers and tiny American flags rustled in the breeze.

Avery thought of Alisha's words, her desire for Avery to have a relationship with Anna, to be more accommodating with their dad and Jane. Avery had pushed them away, staved them off like they were diseased. She marched through life in the old man's footsteps, alone and prideful. In the end, what would remain? Likely just the alone part. She'd opt for cremation or donate her body to science. There wouldn't even be a grave to visit.

"You look serious," Charlie said.

"Just thinking."

"That's dangerous."

"It is." She forced herself to smile. "I was just thinking about . . . my family."

"That's one thing about family—everybody has one."

"Whether you want one or not." They walked farther in silence. Something was on Avery's mind. "Back at the hotel, you started— you acted like you might know something about Anna. Something you weren't sure you wanted to tell me."

"Did I?"

"Yeah. Was I just imagining things?"

The murmur of voices around them continued. Many shoes

stomped against pavement. Somebody pounded on a drum, an echoing *thwock thwock thwock*.

"There are some things only your dad can tell you," Charlie said.

"Like what?"

"Only your dad can—and Jane."

"Jane? She and I don't really connect."

"What's this?"

Avery looked up. Six men came down the street toward them. College-age guys who all looked alike. They turned to the right, then headed down Sixteenth Street. They wore stiff jeans and polo shirts, and walked with a swaggering confidence. Something about them jabbed a barb into Avery's mind.

"Shit, Charlie. I know that guy."

She jogged forward, not bothering to see if Charlie kept up. When she reached Sixteenth, she saw they'd stopped half a block down, gathered in a small cluster.

The face that had initially grabbed her attention belonged to the one guy who towered over the rest of the group.

Avery moved closer. They were in a huddle, looking down at a phone held in the center, and unaware of her approach. They seemed to all be talking at once.

"Avery?" Charlie kept up behind her. "This isn't the way."

"Hey," Avery said, ignoring Charlie.

Six heads turned her way. The tallest one, the one Avery recognized, cracked into a smirk.

"Oh, what is this ridiculous bullshit . . . ?"

"What are you guys doing here?" Avery asked.

The huddle broke, and the six guys formed a line spread out across the sidewalk. They were in an area of small homes, some newly built as an effort to reinvigorate the neighborhood. The six college guys in their country club outfits didn't belong.

"It's Stephen, isn't it?" She knew the smug, entitled face. "Why are you here?"

They all started talking.

"Why are you? It's a free country. For now."

"Who is this?"

"What's the deal?"

"She's a cop—I mean, a rent-a-cop—from campus. She tried to bust me the other day, but the real cops let me go."

Avery ignored the jabs. It happened—the Breckville cops sometimes let small infractions on and around campus slide. "Are you here because you support Tanya Burns and her family?"

"Don't answer that," one of them said.

"Yeah," Stephen said, "we're here to support the Burns family. Now, can you let us alone?"

"Avery . . ." Charlie placed his hand on her arm.

"Who's this?" Stephen asked. "Your boyfriend? He's a little old."

Avery lunged forward. Charlie held on to her arm, increasing his grip. Avery stopped.

"You're not a cop on campus," Stephen said, "and you're not even on campus anymore. So I don't know what you expect to do to us. Both of you, go cry your eyes out at the march. We'll be watching. . . ."

Charlie stepped forward. He brought out a leather billfold and flipped it open. His KSP badge, gold and shiny, glistened in the stunted daylight. "Maybe you all should disperse and let the march go on peacefully."

Stephen started to speak, but a guy on his left leaned forward, squinting. "That's the real deal, boys. This guy is a cop."

"Bullshit."

"He's KSP. I can tell."

"Come on, let's go."

Some of the guys started backing away. Stephen held his ground for a moment, doing his best to stare Charlie down. Charlie didn't move or blink. He looked like a statue dedicated to the enduring virtues of toughness and discipline.

"Okay," Stephen said, "you'll hear from us."

All six turned to go. As they walked away, Avery saw the outline of a gun under one of the men's shirts. She nudged Charlie and pointed.

"See that?"

"We have no authority in this city. And half the state carries something. Let's go. We came here for something else."

Stephen looked back once, a sneer of contempt on his face.

Avery felt a burning in her chest, a pounding in her temples.

But she let Charlie guide her back to Cedar and in the direction of the march.

38

Anna led the way.

They approached Baxter Park from the south after parking half a mile away and then walking, with Rachel and Eric scuffling along behind her. Anna felt a lot better being outside, doing something in the cool morning air. Having a clear purpose. They were going to join like-minded people and express themselves, do whatever they could to make sure no one else died the way Tanya Burns died.

If that went against everything her father and her sister believed in and stood for, all the better. She hoped they found out where she was, hoped they could see her two raised middle fingers from wherever they were.

It looked like they were late. A large crowd filled the park, pushing all the way out to the edges, across the sidewalk, and into the street. A voice echoed across the area, amplified by a bullhorn, the words rolling so far across the vast space that by the time it reached them it was hard to tell what was actually being said.

"Anna, slow down," Rachel said.

She kept going, not breaking stride. If Rachel and Eric couldn't keep up—

Cop cars lined the street. City of Louisville and some KSP. Officers stood outside their cars, thumbs hooked in belts, and scanned the area with their dead cop eyes. They were likely out in force, not just there, around the perimeter of the crowd, but along the entire route of the march, from Baxter Park to city hall. Anna assumed most of the cops' efforts would be concentrated on city hall. If some houses and businesses along the way got trashed, they could live with that. But the politicians up for reelection wouldn't want any of the city's pretty buildings to get messed up for social media or be shown on the evening news.

Anna reached the back of the crowd. A number of signs and banners were held aloft. A news van drove by, the camera guy filming the crowd through the open sliding door. People used their phones to record the day's events. Those accounts would be more reliable, Anna thought.

The voice through the bullhorn grew louder, and the crowd cheered.

"What did they say?" Rachel asked.

"I don't know."

"I wish I could—"

"Shh."

". . . because some people want to prevent us from marching, to silence our voices . . ."

An eruption of cheers. Rachel and Eric stood next to Anna. Eric looked around, seemed to be checking out the cops. He kept his head lowered, like he was afraid someone would come along and smack him one. Or maybe he just feared being recorded, his face popping up somewhere so that everyone would know that he was at the protest.

"We could move back farther," Eric said. "Stand in the next block or something."

"Stand where? We're at the back," Anna said.

"I don't know. Away from the crowd."

"If you want to go—"

". . . don't listen to all the chatter and rumormongering about other groups showing up and stopping our march. We have the right to march. The city has given us the right to march. And we will march . . . and be heard. . . ."

The crowd went wild. Anna felt the cheers inside her body like a shot of electricity. The noise passed from the others in the crowd—the hundreds and hundreds of people cheering and chanting along-side her. And she was a conduit, a way station for the energy as it went through her and then on to others, including—she hoped—her friends. Whether they cared as passionately about the cause as she did or not.

She belonged. She was part of something.

A new chant started on the far side of the park. An aggressive cadence, the sound rising above the noise of the crowd.

"What's that?" Rachel asked.

"I don't know."

The chanting grew louder. And louder. The voices barked, the tone deep and animallike.

"What are they saying?" Eric asked.

The crowd in the park started booing and hissing. Their collec-tive attention turned toward the far side of the park, away from where Anna and her friends stood.

"Easy now . . ." the voice said through the bullhorn. "We have to respect everyone. . . ."

"It's a counterprotest," Anna said. Anger gripped her heart like an iron fist. She wanted to push through the crowd, shove everyone aside, and go nose to nose with the other group. The voices of the counterprotestors sounded masculine, a group of dudes showing up to try to intimidate and harass. Typical.

"What are they saying?" Eric asked again.

The voices rose louder and the words became clearer. Sharp and bitter.

"Go home now. Blue lives matter."

"Oh, damn," Rachel said.

The crowd in the park chanted more and more, their voices rising above the counterprotestors. *"Say her name. Say her name."*

"Anna, do you want to go?" Eric asked.

"Why?" Anna turned away from him, joined the crowd. She screamed as loud as she could, "Say her name! Say her name!"

The volume of the crowd in the park rose so high, the counter-protestors were drowned out. Or they gave up. Either way, the sound of their chants faded away and disappeared, and all that could be heard in the park were the cheers and shouts of the group ready to depart for city hall.

The voice through the bullhorn returned. ". . . Yes, yes . . . our words are stronger, our voices louder. . . ."

"Yeah!" Anna raised a fist, felt spittle fly out of her mouth as she screamed, "Yeah!"

She caught a glimpse of Eric out of the corner of her eye. He looked like he didn't recognize her.

She didn't care.

". . . It's time for us to go, as one group, with one voice. . . ."

The cheering grew even louder. A police siren whooped behind the protestors. The crowd started moving east, in the direction of city hall, thousands of feet turning in one direction, the bodies pressed together in a mass.

The cops who had lined the perimeter turned as well. Some of them climbed back into their cruisers, while others walked, faces turned in profile, posture rigid and erect like a military guard.

The group bottlenecked leaving the park, everyone slowing like cars trying to merge in a traffic jam. They pretty much came to a standstill as the front of the crowd reached Jefferson Street. Anna and her friends were way back, so far back that they had to be patient.

She didn't care. They were starting. They—she, all of them—were *doing* something.

Her phone vibrated in her back pocket. She ignored it.

It vibrated again. Someone was calling.

Anna checked the screen. Libby again.

Libby.

Libby would *love* this.

Anna answered. "Libby, you'll never guess where I am."

Libby couldn't be heard over the noise of the crowd.

"Did you hear me? Do you know where I am?"

"I think I do. Anna, can we talk? I've been trying to get ahold of you."

"I don't want to talk about them. Okay? I don't want to hear about my parents."

"Anna, we *do* need to talk about them. But I can barely hear you. Can you get to someplace quiet?"

"No, I can't. There is nowhere quiet. Call me later."

"Anna, we need to talk about your birthday gift—"

"Later."

Anna hung up. The crowd started to move.

"Who was it?" Eric asked. "Your dad?"

"My cousin Libby."

"Did she want you to go home?"

"No, it was random. She wanted to talk about my birthday present. She might be high."

"Your birthday's not until April."

"I don't know, Eric. Let's just go—"

Crack.

The moment immediately after the noise felt like it lasted a year.

Almost a thousand people held their breath, wishing—hoping—someone had decided to set off firecrackers.

Crack-crack-crack.

Every voice screamed. Everybody moved in a different direction.

The crowd came toward Anna and her friends and knocked Anna to the ground. She disappeared in the tangle of bodies, beneath the thundering storm of pumping legs and stomping feet.

39

The park appeared in the distance.

The trees were in the process of changing to red and orange, bursting with color. A massive crowd huddled close together on the wide lawn.

"Sheesh," Charlie said. "I didn't think there'd be so many."

"People are pissed," Avery said.

"And if they called nine-one-one and no cops were there to answer, would they still be pissed?"

"You know it's more complicated than that."

They approached the park, moving down the sidewalk alongside people carrying signs and banners, their talk excited and energetic. An amplified voice came their way, rolling through the streets like thunder. The words were indistinct, but it didn't matter. The tone said it all—someone was exhorting the crowd to greater heights. Calling them to action.

"I don't know how we'll find her here," Charlie said. "I thought, you know, maybe a few hundred people to sort through."

"Then we can go somewhere else and you can buy me lunch."

"And tell Russ Rogers we failed him?"

Avery groaned. *Been there, done that.*

They drew closer. The amplified voice and the cheers of the crowd grew louder. Avery tried to analyze the crowd, categorize them, but they didn't fit into any one box. She spotted someone from every walk of life. And plenty of people who looked like college students, so Anna would be able to disappear like a scent on a windy day.

"Should we split up?" Charlie asked. "I can go around the perimeter to the north and then east. You can go along the south side that way. We can meet on the far edge. If one of us finds her, call or text. We'll cover more ground."

"Good plan."

"If trouble comes down in any form, get out of the way. Protect yourself."

"What about you? Are you going to do the same?"

"I've been doing that for years," he said. "Mostly with success."

"Okay, see you on the other side of the park. Maybe—and I say, maybe—with an unhappy college student in tow."

Charlie smiled but didn't leave.

"What?"

"You know, Alisha's right: Anna really does look up to you. You *are* her sister. You know?"

"Yeah, I know."

He still didn't go.

"What?"

"Let's talk after this, okay? I'll buy you lunch."

"Sure. Or maybe Anna can pick up the tab since she made us come here."

"Okay."

He started off in his direction, and she went in hers.

Avery navigated along the edge of the crowd. As she walked, she shook her head. She was on a fool's errand. Unless Anna stood right in her path, she wouldn't be found. She could be standing ten feet inside the park and Avery would never see her. And if she did find her sister, then what?

Anna refused to answer calls, refused to go home.

So why would she listen to Avery?

But something small and diamond-hard glowed inside Avery's chest. As much as she'd have liked to deny it, to push it away, she couldn't ignore the presence inside her. She wanted to find Anna and take her back home. Or to Breckville. She wanted to do something for the family, to ease whatever pain or anxiety the old man felt. She hated that it was true, but her family tugged on her like the tides, an ancient force she didn't fully understand but had to reckon with.

The crowd started cheering more. A chant erupted in the distance, some sort of call-and-response. One group said one thing, and the other said something else. Avery struggled to make out the words. But the chant triggered a memory in her mind. Anna used to sing when she was little. Once—and just once—Avery had helped her take a bath. Anna must have been about five, and she played with a plastic boat in the water. Anna sang a song she'd heard on a kiddie recording. *"Fish are swimming, fish are swimming, look and see, look and see...."*

Watching Anna splash in the water, bubbles in her hair, a goofy smile on her face, Avery had felt . . . what? Tenderness. A sense of vulnerability—both hers and her sister's. An intense desire to protect . . .

The feeling had failed to carry through to the rest of their lives. Or it had washed away with everything else as Avery allowed herself to feel more and more alienated from her family.

Like Anna felt now. They weren't that different—

The crowd started to move. The chanting stopped. Only the megaphone voice boomed over everyone, urging them on. The mood felt charged but peaceful. Avery would get a stroll on a beautiful fall morning out of the deal. That was about it.

Her phone rang. Charlie.

No way he already—

"What's up?"

"Any sign of our lost pup?"

"None. If I had another twenty years to wade through the crowd, I might find her. Or if they were all willing to freeze in place while I wandered past them."

"There is some good news to report. I just saw this on Twitter. They caught that creep in Breckville. The Midnight Rambler guy."

"Are you kidding?"

"Nope. They found him with his ass hanging out of a window about two miles from Anna's apartment. He's being questioned now."

"Okay, maybe he's the one who killed Kayla. Maybe that's taken care of."

Charlie's voice sounded distant. "Yeah, maybe."

"Let's think positive."

"Okay. Look, did you hear that fracas over here?"

"No."

"Some counterprotestors showed up. Started chanting. Things got pretty tense. They went away, but I don't think they're done."

Avery weaved around a group of elderly women holding a banner made from a bedsheet. "It's like Woodstock over here. In fact, I think some of these people were at Woodstock."

"Okay, be safe."

"Charlie?"

"Yeah."

"About Anna. I know . . . I know I can be a better sister. But . . . you know . . ."

"It's hard. I get it. Now that the two of you—"

He suddenly stopped talking. Had the call dropped?

"Charlie? Are you there?"

For a moment, nothing. Silence.

Then shouts through the line. Voices raised in anger.

"Charlie?"

"Avery . . ." Four sharp cracks. Gunshots. "Avery, run. . . ."

40

Feet kicked Anna. Knees banged against her.

She rolled over, tucked into a ball. Someone stepped on her hair.

She turned her body, managed to get to her knees. Just as she did, and felt a sliver of hope she'd get up, a body slammed into her, knocking her back to the ground. She felt grit and dirt against the palms of her hands, stabbing needle points against the soft flesh.

More bodies pressed against her. She covered her head again, but she received so many blows, struggled so much to get up, she started to lose hope. She might get trampled there. She might not be able to breathe soon. . . .

A woman fell to her knees in front of Anna. The woman's face looked blank, her eyes staring straight ahead. Anna heard the report—another shot fired. Something red bloomed on the woman's chest.

"Oh, God." Anna reached for the woman.

Blood came from the woman's nose. Eyes wide open, she tipped all the way over like a falling building.

Hands grabbed at Anna. They slid under her armpits.

"Anna, get up. Come on . . ."

Someone lifted her. She managed to get her feet underneath her body and stand.

Eric. It was Eric.

He took her by the hand, started working through the crowd. He pulled her close, kept her body against his. He was taller, and his frame provided shelter. Someone bumped against them, and Eric pushed the man away.

"Watch it," Eric said.

"Fuck you."

So much for peace and brotherhood. Everybody for themselves.

"Rachel?" Anna asked.

"She's okay. She left the park. I came back for you."

"Wow."

"Were those shots?"

"They were. Some idiot started firing on the crowd, I guess."

"Stay low, Anna."

"That girl back there . . . she was shot. I think she's dead."

They moved toward Jefferson Street, trying to get out of the park. The crowd thinned, parted like a river around a rock.

"Shit," Eric said.

Anna saw them too.

Cops. A row of them in riot gear. Shields over their faces and bodies. Batons raised. Each of them looked to be seven feet tall.

A few people got in their way, and the cops knocked them aside like plastic bowling pins.

"Fuck them," Anna said.

"Anna . . ."

Eric led them to the right, away from the line of cops. He looked like he wanted to get around them, swing around their edge and flank them. But the cops moved fast, and Anna and he couldn't get around the edge quickly enough.

The cop on the end, a guy taller than the others, if that was even possible, swiveled his head in their direction. He wore aviator sunglasses behind his face shield, and he looked like a creature from a science fiction movie. Part man, part bug, part cyborg.

His baton was raised, filling the sky.

Eric pulled Anna closer, pushed her head down against his chest. She smelled his sweat, felt dampness on his shirt. His grip was strong, like iron. Like he'd never let go.

"Hang on," Eric said.

A dull thudding noise was followed by a grunt. Like a baseball bat hitting a pillow.

Then they were past the line of cops.

Eric's weight shifted. He leaned more on Anna than she leaned on him. She realized she was holding him up.

They reached the street, limping along like they were in a three-legged race at day camp. Eric breathed more heavily, moved slower.

"Are you okay?" Anna asked.

"Keep going. Let's get . . . across the street. . . ."

They crossed Jefferson, and when they reached the other side, Rachel appeared. Her face was white as printer paper. She raised her hands to her cheeks.

"Help me, Rachel," Anna said.

"Did he get shot? People are fucking getting shot."

"No, but a cop whacked him."

Together, they eased him to the sidewalk. Eric groaned as they did.

"Why did he hit you?" Rachel asked.

"Because I was there," he said.

"He protected me." Anna ran her hand through Eric's hair. "I'm impressed."

"You didn't know I was so brave." He winced.

"I didn't."

"Those were shots," Rachel said. "Actual gunshots. Not fireworks. Not a car backfiring. Shots."

"They were." Anna looked back at the park. The crowd had thinned considerably. The line of cops moved across the open space, a blue line of men. Their presence no doubt drove more people away. Past the cops, on the far side of the park, Anna saw people lying in the grass. Sirens wailed in the distance, drawing closer. "A woman . . . she got shot right in front of me. . . . I saw her chest bleeding. . . . I think she's dead. . . ."

"Let's get out of here," Rachel said. "Can you stand?"

"I think so." Eric winced again. "I don't think anything is broken."

"Anna, we have to get him back to the car. He needs to be checked by a doctor."

"It's not too bad. . . . I don't think he broke too many of my ribs. . . ."

"Anna? What are you looking at?"

One of the cops swung his baton at someone on the ground, someone who already appeared to be hurt.

Anna didn't think. Her body acted without her brain. She jumped up, started across Jefferson back toward the park.

"Anna?"

"Get him home. I think he can walk. I'll see you there."

"Anna, don't do that. . . . They're shooting. . . ."

Anna didn't look back. She crossed the street and went back into the park.

41

The shots echoed through Avery's mind.

Four of them. Four shots fired into a crowd.

Since Avery was moving along the south side of the park, along Jefferson Street, the shots drove a lot of people—*a lot*—toward her. They screamed and fled, dashing out of the park and onto Jefferson, heading south toward the perceived safety of the surrounding streets and buildings.

The shots had come from the area of the park where Charlie was headed.

Run, he'd said. He must have seen something, maybe even the shooter brandishing the gun before all hell broke loose.

The cops who ringed the south side of the park moved north, heading toward the trouble. Guns were drawn, orders and information shouted into radios. Bodies came past her, jostled her, bumped against her. Avery moved like a ninja. She dodged most of the contact, stayed on her feet as she headed into the park.

Avery's phone screen showed that the call from Charlie was still active.

"Charlie? Charlie?"

It was nearly impossible to hear what was unfolding on his end of the line. Was she hearing shouts, voices raised in anger and panic?

People screamed around her. People screamed everywhere. She tried to listen and talk as she moved.

Charlie said nothing. But if Avery knew Charlie, he'd be helping, trying to subdue the shooter if he was close enough. . . .

Fuck, Charlie. Be careful. Just be careful. . . .

A woman approached, her hand held to her head. Blood ran down her face. Her mouth hung open, contorted with terror. Someone walked by her side, helping her.

Anna?

But, no. It wasn't. Yet it could have been. The bleeding woman looked to be Anna's age. If Anna were somewhere in the park, perhaps near where shots were fired or in the path of stampeding protestors . . .

The bleeding woman wept. "They're killing people. . . ."

Avery gave up on the phone. She slid it into her back pocket. She didn't want to drop it or have it knocked out of her hand and have no way to communicate with anybody. She moved forward slowly, a boat against the current.

A middle-aged man looked at her like she was crazy. "Get out of here. There's been a shooting."

As if on cue, another shot cracked. Avery flinched, crouched low to the ground. She'd never fired a weapon in the line of duty. Never been fired at. But there, in a peaceful park, shots whistled all around.

Avery continued forward. The press of bodies brought an odor to her nostrils. Fear and sweat seeping out of millions of human pores. She felt it in her own body. Adrenaline surging, heart pounding. Like approaching a car late at night on a traffic stop, uncertain of what waited inside. Like wrestling a suspect to the ground.

Like being in a pond on the side of the interstate . . .

Her head started to ache. She felt nauseated.

Ahead and to the right, a young woman lay in the grass. Her friends gathered around her, screaming and crying. The woman wasn't moving. Her white T-shirt was soaked with blood.

Soaked. She was ashen and pale, the life draining out of her.

"Fuck."

A line of cops in riot gear appeared in Avery's peripheral vision.

They moved to the center of the park, toward the spot where the young woman lay on the ground. The cops marched in lockstep, shields raised, batons gripped in their hands. Equipment rattling and squeaking. Louisville PD. Their presence relieved Avery. They'd clear the park, help the injured.

Avery turned away, scanned the crowd again. She looked for Anna. Looked for Charlie. Thousands of feet had churned the ground, dug up the earth with their marching and running, releasing a loamy scent into the air. Avery stumbled once, kept her balance.

The crowd seemed to be clearing. The swirling red light of an ambulance approached in the distance. When she looked to the right again, the line of cops was moving past the injured—*dying*—woman on the ground.

One of her friends reached out, tried to catch the attention of the marching cops.

A cop on the left end of the line lifted his baton and swung, clubbing the injured woman's friend on the side of the head.

"Hey!"

Avery sprinted forward, weaving through the crowd in the direction of the kid on the ground and the cop who had swung at her. One of the injured woman's friends sprang to his feet and used both hands to shove the cop backward.

The other cops turned back. Several of them waded in, helping their comrade who'd been pushed. More batons went up and came down.

Avery didn't break stride. She ran until she dove into the middle of the scrum.

42

As Anna ran toward the scuffle, more people approached.

A guy pushed a cop, and then some other cops started beating him. And a few protestors flew in from the left, trying to protect the girl on the ground. The closer Anna got, the more she questioned her judgment. But she couldn't stop.

She was in too far, going too fast. She was committed.

What did her dad always say? *Don't do anything halfway.*

People started grabbing at the cops, trying to pull them back. And the cops swung their batons and shoved with their hands. They swung the batons so wildly, she figured they must have hit other cops with them. But they wore so much gear, maybe the blows didn't matter.

And all of it was happening over the body of the girl who had been shot.

Dead.

Another dead girl. First Kayla, now this woman. Was Anna the problem? Was she haunted by murdered young women?

Anna's heart pounded in her ears. Her palms burned from the grit and dirt.

Anna reached the crowd. She extended her hand, grabbed hold of a cop's riot vest. She'd kept her eye on him—he was the one who had hit the kid and started all of this. She yanked as hard as she could, knowing as she did that a line had been crossed. She'd put her hands on a cop, opened herself up to being arrested.

She pulled and pulled. It was like trying to drag a car backward. The cop didn't budge. For all Anna knew, the cop didn't even know she was there. She had as much effect as a gnat landing on the hindquarters of a bull.

But then the cop stumbled back a little. Anna continued to lean in.

The cop's baton went into the air. His head turned. He knew she was there.

For sure.

He turned his whole body, one way and then the other, like a horse trying to buck an unwanted rider.

Anna's grip on the vest stretched to its limit. Her fingernails were going to be torn out. She let go and thumped to the ground, the air whooshing out of her lungs.

The cop rose above her, loomed like some armored figure from a futuristic battlefield. The baton looked as large as a baseball bat silhouetted against the gray sky. Anna's feet were tangled in the pile of humanity. She couldn't move. She braced herself for the baton to smash against her face. It started its downward arc toward her head—

Hands grabbed her again, pulled her body back. Like she'd been taken hold of by an unseen force.

The cop swung and the baton whistled through the air, missing her body by inches. The baton embedded itself in the soft grass, sending a chunk of mud flying up. The cop grunted with a combination of frustration and anger.

Eric? Again?

The voice in her ear sounded familiar. "Back off. Watch it, will you?"

The cop, teeth clenched in rage, lifted the baton to swing again. A chunk of mud clung to the end of it. That could easily have been her skull and hair stuck to the tip of the stick.

Anna didn't need an invitation. She dug her feet into the ground, propelled her body backward, out of range of the cop's swing. He missed again.

Anna continued to dig against the cool earth, scuttling like a crab. Then hands were on her again, helping her to her feet. Strong hands.

Familiar hands. *Is it . . . ? Could it be . . . ?*

She tried to catch a glimpse of the face, but the woman who had rescued her turned away, back toward the cop, who took a step forward and swung at her. She managed to dance out of the way like a graceful fighter, avoiding the baton, which would have crushed her ribs.

It *was*. It was Avery. Fucking Avery was right there, and she'd pulled Anna from harm's way.

The cop came forward, and Avery danced farther away.

The cop turned, took a step toward Anna. His mouth was still twisted into the hateful grimace. His forearms were corded with muscle, rippling with the power he could bring down.

"Anna, *go*. Get."

Paramedics came running up to the scene. Another cop placed his arm against the hateful cop's chest, trying to cool him down, guiding him back toward the crowd gathered around the injured girl.

"Back off, Anna," Avery said. "Go."

Anna locked eyes with the cop. She wanted to go forward again, try to see if anyone else needed help. But help was there. She'd distracted the cop enough. Why risk more trouble? Why get arrested?

Anna brushed her clothes off. She walked backward, keeping her eye on the proceedings. Watching her sister. "Come on, Avery."

"You go, Anna. Meet me at—"

When Avery turned to glance at Anna, a cop with a baton made a sudden lurch forward. He grabbed Avery by the arm, yanked her toward him, pulling Avery off her feet. She fell to the ground with a dull thud.

"Avery!"

Before Anna could move, another cop stepped in the way. He placed his hand on Anna's chest and shoved, sending Anna stumbling back out of the way. He extended his black-gloved hand, pointing over Anna's head. "Go."

The first cop held Avery with one hand and brought out a set of handcuffs with the other. They glinted dully in the gray morning light.

He started reading Avery her rights, his voice thin and high, and while he did, a police van came rolling across the grass and stopped right next to them.

Avery ignored the cop, looked right at Anna. "Go, Anna. I'm fine."

"You're not fine."

"Go."

The cop in front of Anna shoved her back again.

The other cop used the handcuffs to pull Avery to her feet, her arms wrenched behind her back. Her shoulders almost popping out of joint.

It looked painful.

Avery didn't grunt or cry out. She just kept saying, "I want a lawyer. You can't do this. I want a lawyer."

The cop said, "You can call one. Later."

They turned Avery, guiding her to the van.

"Avery, be careful."

"Go. Get the hell out of here."

But Anna took a step toward Avery instead. A different cop grabbed her, took her by the arm, and spun her away from the wagon.

"Easy now, little lady."

"That's my sister."

"Get out of here or you can ride with her." He shoved Anna in the direction she'd left Rachel and Eric.

Just before they got Avery in the wagon, she called to Anna one more time. "Get out of here. Find Charlie. He's here. Okay? Charlie Ballard. He'll help you."

The cops pushed her inside and slammed the door.

The paramedics tended to the injured girl. They compressed her chest, their gloved hands touching the blood-soaked shirt. The girl's eyes stared at nothing.

Blank. Dead.

Gone.

The cops were shooing everyone away.

For the first time in a long time, Anna listened to her oldest sister. She backed away and left the park, looking for Rachel and Eric.

43

Downtown Rydell, Kentucky, looked abandoned in the morning light. It was thirty miles east of Louisville but it might as well have been in the middle of a desert.

Scattered vehicles were parked up and down the street. Muscular pickups mostly, with giant tires and stickers in the windows extolling the hunting life or else showing support for UK basketball. A few businesses still operated. A laundromat, a secondhand clothing store. A pizzeria that opened only on the weekends. And Hutch's Hideaway, a bar on the corner of Main Street and Highway 78. A rusted wire grate covered Hutch's lone window, and a neon Budweiser side blinked on and off, barely visible.

Hogan parked his sedan and entered Hutch's. It felt like stepping into a cave. The lights were dim, the TV playing on the wall in the corner without sound. He waited while his eyes adjusted to the gloom. The place smelled like stale beer, and his feet stuck to the concrete floor.

The bartender stood behind the bar with a vaping pen in his mouth, one foot propped on the well of liquor bottles. His head was shaved and his sleeves rolled up, revealing tattoos up and down his arms. The whites of his eyes flashed in the dark. He didn't move or speak when Hogan came in.

Hogan nodded, started toward the rear of the room. One table was occupied by two old-timers in feed caps who nursed beers and stopped speaking as Hogan walked by. They made no attempt to hide their curiosity about his presence. They likely didn't see many people dressed as well as Hogan—clean jeans, button-down shirt, dark jacket. Hogan nodded at them, acknowledging their existence, and they nodded back, a combination of suspicion and respect on their faces.

In the rear corner of the bar, he found Taylor Combs sitting with his back to the wall, allowing him a clear line of sight in the room and toward anyone who entered. A glass of club soda with a slice o lime bobbing at the top sat before him. Hogan pulled out a chair and sat down.

"You don't want anything?" Combs asked. He sat with his arms crossed over his chest. He was trim, mid-forties, but looked younger. He wore a bright blue UK hoodie and had his hair cropped close to his head.

"I'm okay. It's a little early for me."

"The club soda is excellent here."

"Maybe some other time."

Combs leaned back, uncrossed his arms. He considered Hogan from across the table, his face a blank screen. "You've seen it, then?"

"Sure. It's all over."

"What's our risk on this?"

The question wasn't unexpected. "Minimal. The video isn't of the best quality. And just because a person was standing outside the building where a murder occurred doesn't mean that person committed the murder. But I'm not going to try to sugarcoat things. Someone could recognize him. And if he's brought into custody and offered some sort of deal . . ."

"Have you talked to him?"

"I don't know where he is."

Combs reached out, swallowed from his glass. The ice cubes rattled. "You do understand how unhappy we are about this. We asked you to carry out a relatively simple task, our reasons for which are our own. Now not only is an innocent girl dead, but the guy you sent to do this job has been captured on video. His image is going all over the state, maybe even the country. And as you so accurately pointed out, if our friend ends up in custody of some kind, it could make us all look bad. Very bad. So I guess my question remains. What is our risk on this?"

Hogan's hands rested on the table. His mouth was dry. He wished he had asked for a drink from the vaping bartender—even some shitty Rydell tap water, likely laced with who knew what carcinogen—so his mouth wouldn't be so dry.

"I have to find him before the police do," Hogan said.

"And are you able to do that?"

"I don't think I have a choice."

Combs nodded in agreement. He didn't need to add or clarify a thing. They both knew what Hogan needed to do.

"Then I guess you'll get on that," Combs said. His words carried a finality. They were not an invitation to further discussion.

Hogan was supposed to leave, push his chair back and depart through the gloom he had entered through. But he stayed in place.

"What is it?" Combs asked.

"Is this about that cop Rogers? The one who got shot in the leg?"

"Why do you ask?"

"It's just—if you want to get at the cop, then there are ways to do that. Maybe take a more direct approach."

Combs shook his head. "This is much more complicated than you're making it sound. More complicated than you know. It's getting into family business." Combs pointed his finger at Hogan's chest. "You just take care of your end of things. And we'll take care of ours."

"Okay. But if you ever want someone to—"

Combs waved his hand over the table like a magician. The gesture shut down the conversation and made everything go away. "I need to get back to the farm. You need to find your man."

"And the girl?"

Combs nodded. "I fully expect you to find her too."

44

Anna left the park.

She crossed Jefferson, heading back in the direction of where she had left Rachel and Eric. To her relief, she found them quickly. Her two friends walked side by side, Rachel supporting Eric as he shuffled along like a ninety-year-old man. He moved by half steps, his right arm holding his left side.

"There you are," Rachel said when Anna reached them. "Were you out of your mind, running back in there? Somebody was shooting."

"Yeah, nice Wonder Woman impersonation," Eric said.

"Nice old-man impersonation," Anna said.

Eric shook his head. "Sheesh, after I took a hit intended for you."

"What happened out there?" Rachel asked. "It looks so chaotic. And Eric is in pain, so we started walking. If you can call it walking."

"I saw my sister. Avery."

"Avery?" Eric perked up. "Can she give us a ride?"

"No. She got arrested. They threw her in the back of a police wagon."

"Arrested? For what?"

"For getting in the middle of the shit over there. She protected me. She took the heat for me."

"Wow," Rachel said. "So what are you going to do?" They'd all stopped on the sidewalk, forming a little triangle. People streamed around them, and more sirens sounded in the distance. "I'd like to get out of here in case another idiot starts shooting."

"The police station isn't far from here," Eric said. "In fact, it's right up ahead. You can go in and try to bail her out."

"Do you know how many people they're going to be arresting?" Anna asked. "It's going to be a zoo. Avery told me to call our family friend Charlie Ballard. He's here somewhere, and he was a cop with my dad. I guess he and Avery both came to look for me."

"A cop friend of your dad's?" Eric said. "He must have started the shooting."

"No, Charlie's not like that."

Anna stood still for a moment. The adrenaline of the incident in the park slowed inside her body. She'd been moving around and feeling like she was floating, but for the first time in a while she felt like her feet were on the ground. The rush of the adrenaline gave way to warmth, something that seeped through her body and calmed her. It replaced the image of the woman on the ground, her lifeless eyes staring straight ahead. . . .

"What's the matter?" Eric asked. "You're just standing there."

"Nothing. It's just . . . Avery really did come to look for me. And she found me. You know, like a real sister would."

"Maybe it's the other way around," Rachel said. "You found her."

"Still, we ended up in the same place at the same time. She was trying to help other people too, and so was I."

"I told you Avery was a badass," Eric said.

"All you've ever done is complain about her," Rachel said. "Are you changing your tune just because she helped you run away from an active-shooter situation? Anybody could do that. A stranger could."

"That's harsh, Rachel," Anna said.

"I'm sorry. But you've never acted like you gave a shit about her. And she didn't seem to give a shit about you. And all you've said for years is how much she hurts your feelings."

"I'm going to call Charlie. . . . Maybe you all should go on home. . . ."

"But it's still not safe at my place, right?" Rachel asked. "I mean, we haven't really dealt with any of this, have we? We don't know what's going on."

"Just go to Eric's for now."

"For now. But for how long? I'm sorry, Anna, and I'm sorry about Kayla, but . . . I don't know what to do if someone might be looking for you and they come to my place. Are we all in danger?"

Anna couldn't think of what to say. Rachel was right—they hadn't solved any of the larger problems. Anna had allowed the protest and all the chaos to distract her, to take her mind away from all the things she was running from. But eventually they would catch up with her. And they could catch up with deadly consequences—as they had for Kayla.

"Why don't you call this Charlie guy?" Eric said. "If he's a cop, maybe he knows something. Maybe he can help you get Avery out of jail. Or maybe he can tell us what to do."

"Yeah, good." Anna pulled her phone out but immediately felt defeated. "I'm sure I don't have his number. I've never called him. Who calls their dad's friends?"

"I do," Eric said.

"Call your dad and get the number," Rachel said.

"I'm not doing that," Anna said. "I'm going to call my mom's cousin. Libby. She called me earlier. And she knows Charlie. They used to date or hook up or something. . . ."

"Weird," Rachel said.

"Old people go on dates," Eric said. "My aunt's divorced, and my mom is always trying to set her up with somebody. She got her to go to dinner with the guy next door about two weeks after his wife died."

The call rang and rang. Libby finally answered. She sounded anxious. "Oh, Anna, thank goodness. I was talking to your mom."

"Libby, I don't want to talk about them, okay? I mean— They are okay, right?"

"They're fine, honey. As fine as they can be. But we do need to talk."

"Can you just do me a favor? I'm in Louisville, at this protest, and Avery is here."

"Avery? Are you with her?"

"No. It's a long story. Look, don't tell Dad, but Avery just got hauled away by the cops."

"Oh, shit."

"She said Charlie Ballard's here, and I need to call him. To help me get Avery out of jail. And other stuff. Things are kind of crazy here."

"What's Charlie doing there? Okay, never mind. Anna, we need to talk. Before you do anything else, we need to talk. Especially if Charlie is there. Especially if you're in that part of the state. And I heard about your roommate, and I'm so, so sorry about that. Okay? I really am. But you need to know what's going on, if you don't already. But I guess you don't know."

"Don't know what?"

"That's why I asked about the birthday gift."

"Libby, what the fuck is it with the birthday gift? You got me a pair of Adidas sneakers. Do you want another thank-you note or something? Can you just tell me if you have Charlie's number so I can get ahold of him?"

"I don't mean *my* gift, Anna. I mean *Trevor's* gift. You told me what he got you for your birthday. . . ."

"Trevor's gift?" Anna looked over at her friends. Eric was still clutching the side of his body. He looked like he'd been hit by a truck. And Rachel looked eager to get the hell out of there. "What are you talking about, Libby?"

45

Avery couldn't believe how long the police had held her.

At the park, she sat in the rear of the van for a good twenty minutes while the police rounded up more and more protestors and stuffed them in alongside her. The more people they put into the rear of the van, the hotter it grew. By the time the van finally pulled away, with about twenty people crammed inside, sitting thigh to thigh on the unforgiving bench seats, sweat dripped down the side of her face and down her neck. She remained cuffed, so she could do little to wipe it away. It had been a hell of a morning.

The motion of the van jerked the passengers from side to side. Few words were spoken. Mostly her fellow passengers muttered and cursed every time the van took a sharp turn or jounced over a bump, the combined body odors forcing Avery to breathe through her mouth. At one point, someone—a guy who looked to be about fifty, with a gray beard and a baseball cap on his head—asked, "Do you know if anyone was hurt by those shots?"

"Yes," Avery said. "A young woman was hit."

"Bad?"

Avery nodded and thought of Charlie, who seemed to have been in the vicinity of the shooting when they were speaking on the phone. She imagined a best-case scenario, one in which they'd pull up to the city jail—which she knew faced Jefferson Street, not far from the park—and Charlie would be waiting there, having already spoken to his law enforcement contacts and arranged for Avery's release. Her stomach grumbled, and she found that option most appealing because she wanted something to eat.

But Charlie wasn't there at the station.

The police herded the crowd into the jail, through a labyrinth of concrete hallways under the watchful eyes of more cops in riot gear. They quickly processed the group from her van, making them all surrender their personal effects, provide some basic information, and then pose for mug shots. Avery went along, her upper and lower teeth grinding against one another. She asked for a lawyer, and the cop who took her information said in a bored voice, "All in good time, my friend, all in good time. We've got a lot of folks to deal with here."

The holding cell smelled like a combination of a locker room and a portable toilet at a giant outdoor concert. The accumulated scents of years of human misery and bodily fluids permeated the cramped space. The police packed too many people into the room, the same cross section she'd observed at the rally. A few lucky protestors managed to snag seats on the benches bolted to the walls. Most, including Avery, stood. Men and women were mixed in together, which was not the typical practice, so Avery tried to stay alert. She found a space on the side of the cell closest to the iron-barred door and watched everything that went on around her.

But danger failed to come in the form of a physical threat. The enemy was boredom. Everybody stood around. And stood and stood and sat and stood. Voices murmured, and a young woman across the room cried on her boyfriend's shoulder, her teary words reaching Avery at one point. "What is my dad going to say about this?"

Same, Avery thought. *Same.*

Except Avery suspected her dad would be even more disappointed in her. He had sent her to find Anna, and she had come tantalizingly close. Only to let her sister slip away at the last moment. But it had been more important that Anna wasn't arrested—at least as far as Avery could tell. It was better that way, better to have Anna gone from the park and the vicinity of the shooting.

Anna.

What the hell was Anna doing? Out of the corner of her eye, Avery had caught a glimpse of her sister trying to drag a cop in full riot gear away from the protestors before he could inflict more damage on anyone. Feeling pride over Anna's bravery and shock at her stupidity, Avery shook her head at the image, which was now emblazoned in her mind. *My God, you* never *put your hands on a cop.*

But hadn't Avery done the same thing? Hadn't she thrown herself into the mix because one cop seemed to want to use protestors' heads for batting practice?

At least it looked like Anna had escaped. And when Avery managed to get her ass out of the city jail, she planned on going right to Rachel's apartment. She just couldn't be certain whether she was going to hug Anna or wring her neck when she saw her.

An hour passed. Then another. From time to time, the cops showed up and stuffed more people into the cell. At some point it seemed like the human mass jammed inside was going to ooze through the bars, like dough spilling over the edges of a pie pan.

Avery started to smell herself. She needed a shower, a change of clothes. She needed to get out so she could breathe. She wanted something to eat for lunch.

"Hey, I know you."

The voice rose above the low, murmuring din. Avery was conditioned to ignore random voices, to pretend shouts and taunts had nothing to do with her. Besides, no one in the cell actually knew who she was.

But the voice said it again. "I know you."

Avery ignored it.

She sensed a person moving through the crowd. A young guy weaving his way through the mass of people, coming her way.

She risked a glance, and her heart clenched. Yes, the guy was coming for her. And, yes, she recognized him.

46

Avery tensed.

The guy drew closer. He wore an untucked polo shirt with the Gracewood logo stitched on the left breast, jeans with a giant mud stain on the right knee, and white sneakers. He reached her, and Avery remained in fight-or-flight mode, despite the fact that he appeared to be four inches shorter than she was. His brown eyes looked soft behind long lashes. Nothing about him made him seem in any way dangerous.

"Remember?" he asked. "In the street earlier today, when you were with the cop? And also at that fight Stephen started on campus?"

It came back to Avery. That dude had been the target, the one almost on the receiving end of a beating the day she rolled up to the frat house and broke things up. Avery remembered walking away from the scene after the Breckville cops arrived, and that guy chose not to thank her but instead defended the much larger guy who wanted to beat his brains in.

Nice.

"It's coming back to me now," Avery said. "I need something to talk to my therapist about."

The guy flushed. He broke off eye contact. "Yeah, I'm sorry about that. When we drink, it can make for some bad outcomes."

"What's your name?"

"Cliff. Cliff Patton."

"What about today's outcomes? Drinking and guns?"

Cliff's head jerked up. "I didn't have a gun. And I didn't know Stephen was bringing one. I swear." He raised his hands in surrender. "In fact, right after we saw you in the street, I left those guys. I didn't want to have anything to do with whatever they were going to do."

"Why were you frat bros even there in the first place?"

"We're here for a regional meeting. It just so happened the march was going on. Stephen heard about it, and he got everybody worked up about going by. Stephen, you know, he's a shit stirrer. He likes to fuck with people."

"And then, once you got there, you decided it would be fun to start chanting, maybe fire a few shots into the crowd."

Cliff shook his head. Vigorously. "That wasn't my brothers. They just wanted to troll the protestors. I wasn't with them, but I saw them later. Right before I got arrested. They said it was some gang of biker-type guys. They were the ones chanting, and they were the ones who started shooting."

"Okay, whatever. I'm not sure what you want from me. I'm stuck in here with everybody else."

"I came over to thank you. For what you did for me the other day with Stephen. He was going to beat the crap out of me, and you stepped in. And I realize I didn't thank you the way I should have. It's kind of a lucky thing I ran into you here. See, I can thank you, right? So, thanks for saving my ass."

Avery relaxed. The muscles and tendons that had tightened like wire cables lost some of their tension. "Okay, you're welcome. Let's hope I don't get called to the frat house again."

"No doubt. None of us want that, do we?"

"We don't."

Avery figured that was the end of their business. They'd had their tender reconciliation and, with that out of the way, they could go on with the rest of their lives. The young guy to a middle-management position or law school. Avery back to wearing her tin badge and patrolling in a Hyundai.

"What are *you* doing here, anyway?" Cliff asked. "You're kind of like a cop, but you're marching against the cops?"

"I'm not on anybody's side. I'm looking for— As a matter of fact, maybe you can help me. I'm looking for my sister, and she's a student at Gracewood. It's a small enough place, so maybe you know her. Anna Rogers? Do you know her?"

"Anna Rogers?" His forehead wrinkled. "Which sorority is she in?"

"None. I mean, I don't think she's in one. If she is, I don't know which it is."

"She's your sister and you don't know if she's in a sorority?"

"Look, I don't have time for that. Do you know her?"

"What's she look like?"

Avery reached for her phone, then realized it currently sat in an envelope in an evidence locker along with all of her other belongings. "What does she look like? Well, I guess a little like me. We have the same dad. She's a criminology major."

"Hmmm. I don't know, man. It doesn't ring a bell, but I'm bad with names." His forehead remained wrinkled, and he stared at the grimy floor of the cell. "I did . . . I did see a girl I know from Gracewood here. Right before I got busted. But I don't know her name. We took a class together last year. Folklore. It was boring as shit. But this girl was really outspoken in class. She liked to argue with the professor and the other students, even."

"That runs in the family. Are you saying you saw her here today?"

"I did. When all hell was breaking loose. I went down a side street to get out of the way, which didn't end up doing me any good, since I got busted after all. But this girl was coming toward me, and I thought she looked familiar. This was on the south side of the park, right where the cops started busting people and smacking them around."

Avery remained silent, but that was where she had seen Anna. And where she'd told Anna to run.

"She kind of looked like you, I guess. In a general sense."

"But it could have been anybody from Gracewood. Right?"

"It could have." Cliff shrugged. "The only reason I remember this girl is because she wasn't hurt or anything, not that I could see, but—"

"She wasn't hurt, okay, good—"

"Yeah, she walked by me with a couple other people, and even though she didn't look hurt, she was crying. I mean, really, *really* crying."

47

Yates vacated the park as quickly as he could. The whole time he jogged away, he expected to be dragged down from behind, some giant cop the linebacker and Yates the running back trying to break away in the open field.

But the tackle never came. The baton never met his skull.

The cops must have had bigger fish to fry in the park. Someone firing shots into the crowd, people getting trampled like it was the running of the bulls. Ambulances and paramedics everywhere trying to help the injured. Yates—he was unimportant apparently. Just the way he liked it. All the better to blend in. And stay free.

He took side streets, far from the crowds of scattering protestors and, more important, cops. After the cop chased him earlier that morning, he'd moved his car a few blocks and chosen to walk to the protest. He managed to pick up the trail of the three kids on the way there and stayed close the whole time. But when the shots started flying and bodies started dropping, when cops started thumping skulls, Yates opted to leave.

It had looked to Yates like Anna was about to get her skull smashed by that cop who was swinging his baton at anything that moved. Yates' whole plan seemed to be about to implode. If Anna ended up in jail, then Yates would lose his chance to get her for God knew how long. The other woman had helped him out—the one who stepped in and protected Anna.

His plan was still alive.

He walked in the direction of the apartment the kids had started from earlier, the one they'd all crashed at the night before. Yates tried to imagine what had gone on in there overnight, one guy going home with two girls. Everybody buzzed or even drunk. They must have had a good time while he slept in the car and woke up behind fogged windows, being hassled by the police. Such was life. He'd never gone to college, never had rich parents to help him out. He told himself not to dwell on the things that had gone wrong in the past. There was only today—a chance to right the wrongs and make a name for himself.

But his roundabout route slowed him down, and when he reached the apartment building, there was no way to tell if the kids were inside.

What if the girl never left alone again?

He decided to give it time. To wait. Just wait and see. He didn't have anywhere better to go, and making this happen was the best thing he had going for him.

His phone rang. He checked the screen—Hogan.

Yates felt something clench his heart. Hogan always had that effect on him. But now, after the fuckup in Breckville, he really worried about what Hogan had in mind. He'd expressed his displeasure on behalf of the family, and the family had a lot of power. They felt no need to explain things to Yates. He was a piece on the chessboard they controlled. Like his dad always said, "You're on a need-to-know basis. And you don't need to know *shit*."

Yates decided it was better to answer Hogan's call than to duck the man forever.

If he even could—

"Where are you?" Hogan asked instead of any greeting.

"Why do you want to know?"

"Because," Hogan said. "Just tell me."

"Maybe I'm working on our little project."

Breath came through the line. "You need to be very careful."

"I think you'll be satisfied with the progress I've made."

"Are you in Louisville?"

"Yes. In fact, I have eyes on—"

"You have to understand something, Yates. Things are different now. Something pretty big has changed."

"What's that?"

"It's *you*. Have you not been checking the news?"

"I know they caught the Midnight Rambler in Breckville. That's good news for our little project, isn't it?"

More breathing. "Maybe not. I think you need to stand down. Okay? Maybe we can meet if you're in Louisville. I'm not far from there."

"What's changed?" The crick in Yates' neck started irritating him once again, like someone was pressing on it with a bony knuckle.

"This guy they arrested, the Midnight Rambler. He's providing certain information to the police. Something he witnessed and filmed the night you were doing work for us in Breckville."

The clouds that had lingered most of the morning were starting to break up. Sunlight leaked through the leaves overhead. But Yates felt a chill. "Are you fucking with me?"

"Why don't we talk, you and I? We can figure out the next step for you. For our little endeavor. It's probably best if you took a break from it, seeing as things are starting to warm up around you. In a big way."

"Okay . . . sure . . . maybe . . ."

But there were no maybes about it. If Yates had been seen—witnessed and . . . what, filmed?—then things were bad for him. Very bad. He'd be the one on the hook for murder—even though the family had sent him there in the first place.

"So, what do you say? Do you want to meet and figure out a plan?"

Yates wasn't the brightest or most educated guy in the world, but he knew one thing—and it tingled through his body like adrenaline. Hogan didn't want to have a friendly chat. Hogan wanted to do something to Yates. Something to keep him quiet forever.

"Well, sure, but I'm . . . I'm trying to think of the best place to do that."

"You tell me where you are, and I'll make it work. Maybe you can get a hotel room, camp out, have a nice meal. I'll pick up the tab."

The front door of the apartment building swung open. The girl—Anna Rogers—came sweeping out with her girlfriend in tow. Anna looked like she'd been crying, and she bull-rushed down the street, heading in the direction of the other girl's apartment.

"Anna, wait. Will you just wait so we can talk about this? So I can help you?"

"I'm getting my stuff. I'm taking care of this myself. I can't believe how fucking fucked-up my family is. . . ."

"Let's talk later," Yates said, rising to follow them.

"No. Wait—"

"We'll be in touch. Okay?"

He was taking matters into his own hands, even if it meant the girl turned into collateral damage. He ended the call and followed the two girls down the street.

48

Avery felt trapped. Helpless.

Avery asked Cliff the same question maybe ten different ways but always received the same answer: He simply had no idea why Anna had been crying. If it had even been Anna he'd passed on the street in the first place.

After ten tries, she gave up. Cliff didn't really know anything that could help her. Avery couldn't do anything unless she got out. If doctors made the worst patients, did former cops make the worst prisoners?

She turned one way in the cramped cell and then another and thought of Anna. Was she hurt or scared? Or both?

Cliff squeezed back into the crowd, no doubt relieved to be freed from any further interrogation. Tension grew in Avery's chest, a swelling tide pushing against her rib cage. She wanted to know how Anna was. She wanted to get in touch with Charlie.

Her watch ticked past noon, and then movement started to happen. Cops came back to the holding cell and started dismissing the rounded-up troublemakers in groups of ten. There was no rhyme or reason to who they let go or in what order. A cop would come to the door, open it, and wave a group of ten or fifteen out. Everyone, including Avery, pushed toward the door. But most of the people in the cell were men, and they displayed no hesitation about elbowing their compatriots out of their way, so it took four rounds of releases before Avery was processed. Her belongings were returned to her by a bored-looking desk sergeant who informed her that she was being released with no charges pressed.

"So that's it?" Avery asked. "I spent almost three hours in a holding cell for nothing?"

"Would you rather be charged with something? We can arrange it."

Avery signed the release and left. Outside, the clouds were breaking up, and she squinted. She checked her phone. No messages or calls. Nothing even from Charlie.

"What the fuck?"

Standing on the weedy sidewalk outside the station, she called him. Cop cars came and went, and released protestors streamed past her, chattering with nervous relief, heading off to whatever came next for them. Brunch? Drinks? A party?

He didn't answer, and the call went to voice mail. She redialed, waiting and waiting. Finally, Charlie answered. His voice sounded hoarse, and a lot of noise filled the background.

"Where are you?" Avery asked.

"I could ask you the same thing."

"I just got out of jail. They swept me up at the park."

"Oh, shit. I hoped maybe you'd found our girl and were with her."

"I *did* find her." Avery's frustration rose as she recounted the events right before her arrest. "I saw her, Charlie. I had my hands on her. But the cops came down on us, and I got dragged away. I told Anna to run, and she did. But I don't know where the hell she went. It was bad out there, Charlie. I saw a girl who had been shot in the chest."

Charlie didn't respond. A voice came over the line, one that didn't belong to him. And then Charlie said thanks.

"Charlie? Where are you?"

"Okay, I'm in the hospital. But I don't want you to worry."

"What are you doing in the hospital? What happened?"

"When all that chaos broke out at the park, I got caught up in the crowd. Everybody was pushing and shoving, and I got knocked down. Somebody put their foot right in my back and used me like a welcome mat. It knocked the wind out of me."

"Did you break something?"

"I don't think so. But when the paramedics came by, I was struggling to catch my breath. I told you I have a little high blood pressure. Anyway, they were worried about that, probably because I'm starting to look like an old man. So they said they wanted to bring me in and check me over. I agreed."

"Okay, what hospital are you in? I'm going to come down."

"You said you don't know where Anna is?"

A few young women came out of the police station. One of them, who looked to be Anna's age, talked on a phone. She sniffled and wiped at her eyes. "No, Mom, really, we weren't doing anything. I swear."

Was she the woman Cliff had seen?

"I don't know. A guy from Gracewood might have seen her. And she might have been crying. But I don't know much more than that. Look, I'm coming to the hospital and then we can figure out the next step."

"Where would you go if you were Anna? I mean, if you were at the protest and it got busted up like that?"

"I'd get the hell out. I'd go back to my friend's apartment where I was staying."

"Why don't you go check for her there and let me know?"

"No. You're all alone in the hospital."

"Avery, I'm a big boy. They took some blood, and they're waiting for the results. They x-rayed my leg and chest, gave me an EKG. When those come back, they'll let me go. See if you can find Anna at the friend's house. By the time you have that wrapped up, I'll be released. Okay?"

"If you're sure."

"Use me as an excuse. Tell her I'm in the hospital, and I want to see her. Play the pity card."

"That's good, Charlie, but it doesn't work to get her all the way home to Dad and Jane."

"Those are her parents. I'm her uncle Charlie." Someone said something in the background of the call again. "Avery, I have to go. I'm at Presbyterian Hospital. Okay? Come find me, and maybe you'll have Anna with you."

"Okay, are you sure—"

He hung up before she finished the question.

49

Avery knocked on the door, and a muffled voice from the other side asked, "Who is it?"

The person sounded shaky and uncertain, like they thought that whoever was knocking intended to burst through and do them harm.

"Rachel? This is Avery Rogers. Anna's sister. You remember me, right?"

A chain rattled, and then the lock was unlatched. The door swung in with a squeak, and a woman in her early twenties stood there, her red hair pulled back off her face, an oversized sweater covering her body. She held a phone in her hand, no doubt ready to dial the police if Avery turned out to be some iteration of the boogeyman.

"Oh, hi, Avery."

"Can I come in?"

"Sure." Rachel stepped out of the way, and Avery followed her inside. Before Avery could say anything or even attempt to ask a question, Rachel started explaining. "Look, Avery. I don't know what's going on with Anna. And I don't know why she's doing what she's doing. She's acting really weird, and she won't accept any help from me or Eric."

"Eric's here?"

"He's at his place. We were all together this morning. At the march. I really didn't want to go. Neither of us did. But Anna wanted to, so we went along with her. She's pretty upset about her roommate."

"Sure, I understand. Where is Anna now? She isn't here?"

"No, she left. And I couldn't stop her."

Rachel sounded defensive, like she thought Avery had shown up looking for someone to blame. And the blame was going to land on her.

"Do you want to sit down?" Avery asked.

"Oh, yeah. Sure. Sorry." Rachel sat on the end of the couch. She wore fuzzy slippers that made her look younger than she was.

Avery sat in an upholstered chair that looked like it had come from Rachel's grandmother's house.

"Rachel, I saw Anna today at the park, before the cops started hauling people away."

"Yeah, she told me. Did you really get arrested?"

"I got taken in. Not arrested. There's a difference."

"Two people got shot. One's in critical condition. It's on Twitter."

"I didn't know that." The news made Avery nauseated. A peaceful protest, and people end up hurt. "I was in the jail for almost three hours."

"I'm sorry." Rachel seemed to have settled down. She showed that by remembering her manners. "Would you like something? I can make some tea or whatever. I know your family, especially Alisha, thinks I just drink all the time. But I don't."

"It's okay, Rachel. I don't want to bother you. I just want to know where Anna is. I thought she might be here. Is she with Eric?"

Rachel shook her head. "No. That's what I'm saying. We don't know what's going on with her. Eric's really worried."

"Well, he's been in love with her since they were kids."

"I know. It's kind of sweet. And kind of sad. Anna kind of uses him. Whenever she's in town to see me, she sees Eric. You know. *Sees* him. But that's about all she does. It's been that way since she broke up with Trevor."

Avery wasn't sure how much she needed to know about her half sister's sex life. "Right. The ex-boyfriend from Gracewood."

"Yeah, Anna was upset when they broke up. But then everything's been making her upset lately." Rachel's eyebrows went up. "I think that's what started all of this. Or at least it contributed."

"What did?"

"Trevor."

"Trevor? What does he have to do with it? Was he here?"

"No." Rachel lifted her hand and nibbled on her thumbnail. "Your cousin called. Libby? Is that her name? She kept trying to call Anna, and finally Anna answered after the march. No, Anna called her. Libby's your cousin, right?"

"She's Anna's cousin. We have different mothers. Remember?"

"Sure, I know that. Yeah, Anna used to talk about that. How you— Well, anyway, Anna talked to Libby, and Libby said something to Anna about the birthday gift Trevor got her. Anna looked at something on her phone, and then she started crying. She got all upset about it. But she wouldn't tell us what it was. Anna can be like that. If she was angry or unhappy about something, she might not tell you for weeks. If ever. You know Anna can be like that."

"I understand."

"So, we came back here, and Anna grabbed her stuff. She said she needed to leave. I tried to get her to calm down or talk to me, but she wouldn't hear of it. She said she needed to go and figure some things out."

"And you don't know what?"

"No, I don't." Rachel nibbled on the nail again.

"And what was this gift?"

Rachel shook her head. "I don't know that either. Anna wouldn't say. But she kept checking stuff on her phone. And she was crying. But I couldn't get anything else out of her."

"So, she left? And you let her leave when she was crying?"

"Have you ever tried to stop Anna when she wanted to do something?"

Avery remembered Anna as a child. Her willfulness. Her stubbornness. Her refusal to accept help.

Something they all shared in common with their dad.

"Okay, can you at least tell me where she was going?"

Rachel lifted her hands in a shrug. "She didn't say anything specific. Just that she had to go somewhere *right away*."

"Where?"

"She wouldn't tell me."

"Damn it."

"She can be really private, you know."

"Yeah, I know."

Rachel's mouth contorted. She looked away from Avery and then back at her. Then away again.

"What is it, Rachel?"

"Well . . . it's . . ."

"Rachel. We're dealing with serious stuff. Okay? This isn't like getting in trouble for spiking the punch."

"I totally did not do that."

"Okay. Tell me anything else you know, and I'll never mention the punch again."

"Okay. So, I was worried about Anna. And whatever she was up to. So when she went to the bathroom, I looked at her phone. I snooped. It's awful, but she had a map called up. Directions to some random town. A place called Rydell."

"Rydell? Why was she going there?"

"I have no idea. Don't tell Anna I snooped. She'll be so pissed."

"Rydell." Avery wanted to shrug as well. "What's out that way?"

"Well," Rachel said, "I know Dead River Cave is. It's supposed to be haunted by the ghosts of Native Americans and Union soldiers and stuff."

"Yeah, I've heard that. I also know that it's the part of the state that grows the most marijuana." Avery stood to go, muttering under her breath, "Maybe Anna just has a craving for some good Kentucky weed before she goes home."

50

Avery's footsteps echoed down the hallway of the hospital.

Charlie's room was on the third floor of the east wing, the cardiac care center. Everything felt hushed in that section of the hospital. Less chaos, fewer beeping machines and monitors. It was as if the hospital staff tried to keep everything still and calm so as not to startle the patients with the weakest hearts.

Charlie rested in a private room, a thin blanket pulled up to his chin. The TV, which was bolted to the wall above the closet, played a news program. A rehash of the events in the park with special emphasis given to the shots fired. Charlie's hands rested on top of the blanket, holding the remote control.

He looked over when she stopped in the open doorway. "Hey, champ. I'm scanning the crowd, but I don't see you."

Avery hadn't thought about what it would be like to see Charlie in a hospital bed. On the way over, she had worried about Charlie's health, felt her pulse rate increase when he said he wasn't able to leave yet but needed to be held overnight for observation.

When she saw him in the bed, with the hospital gown on and the monitors hooked up to his body, emotion surged inside of her. It caught in her throat, and she stayed in the doorway, swallowing a time or two in order to be able to get any words out.

"What is it?" he asked. "You can come in."

Avery cleared her throat. She'd grown used to having a hobbling, aging, and distant father. She'd moved on—as best as she could—

from her mother's death. But she wasn't ready to see Charlie in a hospital bed, the color drained from his face, looking weaker than she'd ever imagined he could look.

"I'm okay," she said, coming farther into the room. "I just— I didn't think you'd be staying. I thought they just wanted to run some tests."

He muted the TV and waved her over, gesturing toward a wooden chair with a faux-leather cushion that sat next to his bed. "They did. But tests always find shit. Some of my levels are up, so they want to do more tests. Tomorrow. You know how it is."

She did know. That was the problem. As her mom's illness had progressed, she went to the hospital over and over. Infections. Trouble breathing. Anemia. Avery's hands shook as she sat down.

"What did they say is wrong with you?" Avery asked. "Besides the fact you're getting old."

"Nice. They don't know. The tests showed the possibility of a heart attack. Likely a mild one. Some enzyme popped up on the bloodwork. So they need to look around more. Hey, I don't care about that. It's nothing."

"A heart attack isn't nothing."

"What did you find out about our lost pup? You said you'd learned something."

"It's not important. I'll come back tomorrow."

Charlie lifted his left hand off the blanket. "You say it's not important. But I can hear in your voice that you have something on your mind. What is it?"

"Do you want me to call someone? You said you had a new woman in your life."

"What's the question on the table?"

He was right. Avery wanted to see the light he might shed on things. If he could. She even found her concern for his health dipping as the possibility of answers drew closer.

"Okay," she said. "Anna has run off again. She talked to Libby. And Libby brought up something about a birthday gift Anna's ex-boyfriend got her. And then Anna was crying and making plans to go to Rydell. But she wouldn't say what was wrong."

The expression on Charlie's face changed slightly. A tensing of the muscles around his mouth and eyes. "What's she going to Rydell for?"

"I thought maybe you'd have a guess."

"And what's this gift they're talking about?"

"I don't know that either. But we can call Libby and ask if you want. I was ready to do it, but then I thought I'd talk to you first. I really can't stand talking to Libby, so I hoped maybe I could get out of it."

Charlie stared at the TV, which was now showing a football game. The sound remained muted.

"Charlie? Rydell?"

"Yeah, Rydell."

"I know they grow a lot of weed there. And there's a river and a cave that's supposed to be haunted. Those are the two facts I know from my time in the KSP."

"And Jesse James hid in the cave once," Charlie said.

"Every town in this state has a Jesse James story. One percent of them are true. Or less. Helps tourism, though. Otherwise, I always heard the town was kind of a dump."

"It is. I'd call it a one-horse town, but that would be insulting to actual one-horse towns."

"Then why is Anna going there?" Avery asked. "Any guesses?"

He paused, thinking about his answer. "She must know someone there."

"Who would Anna know in some little town like that?"

"She goes to school with kids from all over the state."

"Then why not just say that? Why not tell her friend Rachel who she was going to see?"

He lifted his hands off the blanket again and let them fall back down. "You said Anna can be a mysterious little cat. Maybe she has a guy there. Or a girl."

Avery leaned forward, resting her elbows on her knees. She tilted her head to get a better look at Charlie. "Her roommate was murdered. They can say it was this Midnight Rambler guy, just your average everyday perv. But Anna's running off in tears to a town where she has no apparent connections, and she's not telling anyone why she's going. And the only thing I know about the place is they grow a lot of weed there. And, oh, my dad and his best friend just happen to be retired cops who worked on a drug task force years earlier. Charlie, I don't know which thread to pull, but there are a lot of them to choose from."

"Okay, okay." He laughed a little. "Sometimes I think I'm talking to your dad when you get wound up like that."

"Are you trying to piss me off?"

"I'm trying to compliment you. Believe it or not." He shifted in the bed a little, grimacing as he adjusted his weight.

"Are you okay? Should I shut up?"

"I'm okay." The volume of his voice had gone down. "You need to hear this."

"Hear what?"

"I can tell you some things and make some guesses, okay? That's it. Maybe I can clip some of those threads."

Avery's hands clenched into fists and unclenched. "Okay. If you're up for it."

"You might want to ask yourself that question."

"What are you saying?"

"There's a lot of history in Rydell."

"What kind of history? You mean of the town, or something personal?"

"Both."

"Okay. You've got my attention."

"Look, I know you want to go running off there and look for Anna. But even in a small town, it's hard to find somebody if they don't want to be found."

"It sounds like you don't want me to go."

"I want you to take your time. We can go when I get out, okay?"

A nurse came breezing into the room. She checked the monitor on the side of the bed, and then announced she needed to draw more blood. "But you're welcome to stay."

"Wait," Charlie said. "Can you go get me a candy bar or something? Maybe a Coke? I haven't had any lunch."

"Sure," Avery said. "I hate needles almost as much as I hate water."

"It will just be a few minutes," the nurse said. "And there's a vending machine at the end of the hallway. Although maybe you shouldn't be having any candy right now."

"Just a taste," Charlie said, winking at the nurse, who smiled back.

"Okay," Avery said. "I'll carry out my mission." She pushed herself up and started for the door while the nurse arranged her equipment.

Charlie's voice stopped Avery before she left. "Hey, do me a favor. Don't call Libby yet, okay?"

Avery looked back. "Didn't you hear me? I can't stand Libby."

Charlie gave her a thumbs-up, and she left, heading for the vending machines.

51

Morris sat at his desk, finishing a report. He'd recently closed a case involving a large-scale theft of electronics. A group of guys in Breckville had ripped off a Best Buy delivery truck and started reselling the stuff. Computers, phones, iPads. When one of the guys sold an iPhone to a high school student for a hundred dollars, a parent reported it. The whole thing came tumbling down. Each guy they picked up identified two others who were involved. No honor among thieves indeed.

Morris had come in to finish the report because the station was relatively quiet early on a Saturday afternoon. Most of the students from Gracewood were hibernating, saving up their energy for a night of partying and mayhem. A Saturday before the chaos made him think he could continue working as a detective indefinitely, as opposed to every other day of the week, when he found himself calculating how many more months until he was eligible to retire.

The front desk officer called back, told him he had a visitor.

"Who?"

"Lieutenant Paulson. KSP."

Morris' eyebrows went up, even though no one was there to see him do so. "Send him back."

When Paulson came into his office, he looked like he was wearing the same thing he had worn at the diner. Except his fleece pullover was decorated with the logo of a local Catholic grade school. They shook hands, and Paulson took a seat. As he did, his eyes roamed around the small room, taking it in.

"Spartan," Paulson said.

"I'm going to have to move out someday, right?"

"Why move anything in that you have to move out?"

"Exactly."

"That's one approach."

"Did you come by just to analyze my decor, or lack thereof?"

"You know better than that," Paulson said, rubbing his chin. He hadn't shaved, which was the only thing remotely imperfect in the man's appearance. "I've been thinking about this guy you got the pictures of outside your murder scene. I think I have some ideas on that."

Morris saved his work and closed the window on his computer. He swiveled his chair to better face the KSP lieutenant and rested his hands on top of the desk. "I'm all ears."

Paulson took his time speaking. Finally, he said, "You've been getting a lot of tips, I'm guessing, ever since you made the photos public?"

"True. Mostly garbage tips. You know, 'I think that's my brother-in-law. I always suspected he was a murderer. He lives in California, but maybe he was in Breckville outside that poor girl's apartment that night.' That kind of high-quality thing. I'm hoping, maybe, you're here to deliver an upgrade."

"Maybe I am."

But Morris could tell Paulson was going to take his sweet time filling him in. So he waited. He reminded himself not to tap his fingers on the desk or start whistling, as those things could cause Paulson to think twice or clam up. The best course of action was to remain still, to let the information flow to him in its own time.

Finally, Paulson said, "Has anybody given you the name Nicholas Yates?"

"No."

Paulson nodded. "About a year ago, we investigated an assault case. This Nicholas Yates beat the daylights out of some other guy. We always thought there was more to it. We never found out what the beef was about. The victim wouldn't really say, just that the two guys had a 'misunderstanding.' If that was the case, it was a hell of a misunderstanding. Guy was in the hospital for a week."

"He owed somebody money. That's what you thought, right?"

"Right."

"Drugs?"

"Likely. But no one admitted anything. Yates did a month in county for it. He's still on probation, I would imagine. But that was the end of it. Until I saw those images you all released. The images of the guy outside Kayla Garvey's apartment."

"They're not great. They're grainy and dark. And taken by a Peeping Tom."

"Maybe more Peeping Toms need to go to film school."

"I'm sure some would be happy to. I'm sure some of the best directors are just washed-out Peeping Toms. So you think it looks like this Yates. And you think there was more to the story on this assault he got busted for. Like maybe he's a low-level enforcer for somebody. And I'm guessing there's a little more you have to say about this. Right?"

Paulson rubbed his stubbly cheek. "I'm drawing a line between two things that may not be related. But I'm willing to step out onto that limb."

"I wish you would. And I think I know where you're going with this."

"I'm sure you do. If we suspect Yates is some kind of enforcer for those involved in the pharmaceutical industry in the state, and it's possible Anna Rogers was the intended victim of what happened in that apartment and not Kayla Garvey, and Ms. Rogers might have been targeted as some form of revenge against her father, who used to be the head of a drug task force for KSP . . ."

"Yeah." Morris lifted his index finger and tapped it against his dry lips. "Here's the thing, though—if Captain Rogers has been out of the game for five years, why take revenge on him now? Why not then? And that's assuming somebody shooting him and crippling him for life wasn't enough revenge."

"I don't know," Paulson said, "unless the person was locked up. They went away for years and just got out. And decided to go after Rogers now."

"And why the daughter and not him?"

"What would hurt you more? Somebody doing something to you or to one of your kids?"

"And let me go a step further," Morris said. "Maybe Kayla Garvey *was* really the target. Maybe she's involved in something sketchy, or her family is. Or maybe it's not about Russ Rogers' career as a cop, but he has gambling debts or a drug problem. People with injuries like his get hooked on stuff."

"We've looked all over the Garvey family. They're so clean, they squeak. The worst thing I can say about Kayla's dad is he's a workaholic. There's no sign Russ Rogers is a pillhead or a gambler."

"I guess you're right. It's a bold enough move to go after a cop, even if he's retired. But to go after a family member . . . That's *Godfather* kind of shit."

"I wanted to share the information with you," Paulson said. "If you can find Yates, maybe you can find out who he works for. The assault wasn't a big-deal charge, but we're talking murder now. He's looking at a long sentence, maybe life. Maybe he's more willing to deal this time."

"Yeah, maybe he is."

"Yates' records are all in the system, so you can read up on him. Of course, I am just guessing. I don't know if it's him. But something about it kind of makes sense." Paulson stood up, extended his hand. "Let me know if I can do anything else."

Morris rose as well, and the men shook hands. "You've done quite a bit. The cynical part of me wants to know why you'd hand this information to me at all. You could run it down, get the arrest for yourself."

"I believe in cooperating. Besides, you gave me some fries the other day."

Morris laughed. "If this works out, I'll buy you a steak dinner."

"Deal."

Once Paulson was gone, Morris jumped back on the computer. He started to read about Nicholas Yates.

52

The whole way down the hall, Avery thought about calling Libby. Yes, Charlie had told her not to—but what objection could he have to her trying to find out more?

Clearly, Libby knew something—something that not only made Anna cry but sent her running off. And to Rydell? What the fuck did she want to go to Rydell for?

Was Anna mixed up in drugs? Did that explain her troubles in school, her detachment from the family? Was that why whoever had gone into the apartment and killed Kayla was looking for her?

But Anna? Was it even possible?

Avery slid dollar bills into the vending machine in the lounge at the end of the hall, listened to the satisfying whirr, and then pressed the buttons for Charlie's Coke. She studied the other options, clueless as to what kind of candy bar he might want, so she opted for something reliable that she might want a bite of as well. A Milky Way. Perfect for a heart patient.

No one else was in the lounge. Avery stepped over to the partially curtained window, which provided a nice view of the Louisville skyline. Avery looked west, could even see the park where the march had started and the chaos descended. The park where she—briefly—had seen Anna and pulled her free. She wished she'd done more. Hung on to Anna no matter what, clutched her tight and tried to get the answers they all needed.

But it was a fool's game to replay a moment like that.

She decided to ignore Charlie, and pulled out her phone. She placed the call, listening to the chirring ring on the other end. Disappointment took over quickly as the phone continued to ring. And ring. She'd never anticipated Libby wouldn't answer. She'd pictured Libby waiting for any call about Anna's whereabouts. Instead, Avery heard the robotic voice mail recording and failed to hide her frustration when she left a message imploring Libby to call her back as soon as she could.

She waited thirty seconds, in case Libby called right back, but she didn't.

Then she thought of Trevor, the ex-boyfriend who had given the gift in question. What on earth had he given Anna for her birthday? A pound of grass?

Alisha might have his phone number.

She held off on calling her sister. Charlie had said there was more to say, and the nurse must have finished doing her Dracula routine on him by now. Avery started back, still hoping for Libby to call.

It took only a couple of minutes to get back to Charlie's room, and as she neared, she saw two nurses standing in the doorway. Then a third nurse came running up, pushed past the other two, and entered. The two in the hallway wheeled around and went inside as well.

"What the fuck . . . ?"

Avery felt cold. Everywhere on her body. As though the temperature of the soda had spread from her hand to each of her cells.

She started running.

It was as if one of the nurses possessed X-ray vision. She came out when Avery reached the doorway and placed her hand gently on Avery's shoulder. "You can't come in now."

"What's wrong?"

"You just can't come in."

The nurse guided Avery into the hall, but Avery heard frantic voices. Commands being given. *"Vital signs—"*

"BP dropping. Do you have the Epi?"

"I'm going in."

"You can't," the nurse said. "Now, can I ask you—are you his daughter?"

"I might as well be."

"Are you authorized to make medical decisions for him?"

"Just do whatever you have to—"

"Do you know who is authorized to do that?"

"I don't— Can I just see him?"

"No, you can't. Please just wait here."

The nurse went back into the room, and Avery waited only a beat before following her.

Charlie lay on the bed, eyes half open, surrounded by six people performing various tasks. Charlie's body moved, but not of its own volition. Their movements shook him, and his head flopped and lolled from one side to the other like nothing controlled it.

"Clear."

"Charlie?"

The same nurse peeled away from the bed and used more force in pushing Avery out into the hall. "You can't be in there."

"But I have to be in there. He's family. . . ."

"Let us do our jobs. Just sit in this chair here."

Avery sank into the chair, her body suddenly limp. Everything inside her felt like Jell-O. As loose and disjointed as Charlie's flopping, dangling head . . .

"Clear."

"Clear."

They shouted that call-and-response two more times before they stopped saying it.

53

Yates parked on the west end of Main Street in Rydell.

He stayed in the car and shook his head. Twenty minutes earlier, he'd stopped picking up anything but country and religious stations on the radio. He couldn't believe places like that town still existed. The land that time forgot.

A few cars sat along the street. A few businesses were open.

More than anything, the town was the Combs family. Big business, the kind of thing Yates only dreamed about.

Ahead, through the dusty windshield, Yates watched Anna Rogers step out of her car. Yates had been following her since she left her friend's place in Louisville. At first he'd assumed Anna was heading back to school. Returning to Breckville and her life as a college student. Who wouldn't want that? With the way colleges catered to kids today, her dead roommate would be her ticket to easy street. The professors would probably let her retake all her classes. Provide plenty of counseling and emotional support, maybe a break on tuition. Anna Rogers didn't know it, but Yates had done her a favor. All she had to do was turn around and take advantage of it.

But the kid had headed east, out of Louisville and into the countryside. Headed toward Rydell. Yates figured her destination out pretty quickly. He couldn't connect all the dots—not yet—but the Combs family operated there. Hogan had brought him on board to find out what Anna knew about the Combs family, to bring her to them if he could. And now she was heading right to the source. Toward the belly of the beast.

Opportunity. That was what Yates saw through that dusty windshield. Opportunity.

He gave the girl a moment to get her bearings. For all he knew, she might have a plan in place. She might have somebody meeting her. But when she stood looking up and down Main Street, no doubt experiencing her own feeling of having driven through a wormhole back into the pioneer days, he figured out there was no plan. She was just there. In Rydell.

And she had no idea what to do or where to go next.

She looked at the storefronts, most of which were empty. She checked her phone. Probably no or spotty service.

Yates considered the girl. Not bad-looking, not bad-looking at all. Kind of short but solid-looking. Maybe a soccer player growing up? She possessed that look. She had grown up with a cop for a father, so she'd probably acquired her toughness there. In the park, he'd seen her throw her body into the pile like a pro wrestler, take hold of a cop and try to drag him off the girl he was pounding.

So the daughter of a cop who liked to rough up cops. Daddy issues much?

Anna made a choice. And there wasn't much to choose from. She started down the block, stepping lightly over the crumbling sidewalk, and went inside a little dive with a sign above the door marking it as Hutch's Hideaway.

Yates pushed his car door open, stepped out into the warming afternoon. It was a risk. If he followed her inside, he was taking a big risk. But no balls, no babies. And what else did he have? If he stayed outside and hoped everything worked out, he'd find himself on the wrong end of things. Maybe dead. Better to seize the moment when it presented itself. If the girl recognized him from outside her apartment the other night, then he'd have to punt. But he hoped for something more. A touchdown or at least a field goal . . .

He went down the street, seeing no one. He passed the dingy windows of a laundromat and peeked inside. One overweight man, wearing sweatpants and Crocs, folded a pair of giant briefs. It was the most depressing sight Yates had ever seen.

He moved on and entered the gloom of Hutch's.

He paused just inside while his eyes adjusted. A TV above the bar played a college football game. It looked like two SEC teams, and Yates couldn't have cared less about it. The bartender watched the game with his foot resting on the bar rail. The room smelled like an accumulation of cigarette smoke and stale alcohol, like it hadn't been aired out since the 1960s. A couple of old farts sat at a table looking like they'd been there for decades, glasses of draft beer in front of them alongside an empty bag of pretzels. He saw no one else. Not even Anna.

Maybe she'd hit the head?

Yates took a seat, waited while the bartender took his sweet time peeling his eyes off the TV and came over to him. "Help you?"

"Kentucky Common."

The bartender turned without saying anything and brought back a can, then placed it on the bar in front of Yates. "Want a glass?"

"I'm good."

They were done conversing because the bartender turned away. He didn't even ask for payment. The can made a satisfying *pffft* when Yates opened it, and the first swallow stung the back of his throat and tasted great. He usually preferred to hold off on drinking until the evening, but this was a special occasion. And he needed to try to blend in a little bit, act like a guy without a care in the world.

He checked the back of the room, where the bathrooms would be. Maybe Anna had spotted him and given him the slip out the back. The chatty bartender could have told her where to go. Yates contemplated other plans, things that might help him get out from under whatever the Combs family and Hogan might have in store for him. He could get back in his car and drive. And just keep driving. End up someplace warm and sunny, someplace to blend in. And start over.

He lacked any real skills and carried little money. But he was young and healthy. He could make a new start.

Anna emerged from the bathroom and headed toward the far end of the bar, away from where Yates sat with his can of beer. She looked a little frazzled. She seemed out of breath, not quite able to fix her eyes on any one thing in the room. She played with her hair, pulled it back off her face into a tight knot, then waved at the bartender, who reluctantly walked down and asked her the same question he'd asked Yates.

"Help you?" He looked like a man awaiting his own execution.

"Maybe," Anna said. "I don't know."

Her eyes made a circuit of the room again, passing over the old-timers, who seemed to be ignoring the pretty girl in their midst. Her eyes briefly settled on Yates before they passed by, and he tried not to flinch, kept what he hoped was a casual look on his face as he took another swallow from his beer and looked around for a bowl of peanuts.

Anna said, "I'm trying to find some people."

The bartender craned his head around, taking in the room. He wore a long beard, and his head was shaved. His sleeves were rolled up, revealing an extensive array of tattoos. He turned back to Anna. "I think you can pretty much see the whole cast of characters here."

"Right. This is a small town."

"Do you not like small towns?"

His question knocked Anna off her stride a little. "No, it's not that. I meant that in a town like this everybody pretty much knows everybody else."

The bartender remained silent. Someone scored a touchdown on the TV. Guys in blue uniforms jumped around like they'd just taken over the world.

"I'm looking for members of the Combs family. I understand they live here, but I'm not sure where."

If they were all in a movie, the sound of a record scratching would have played over everything.

The bartender's entire body tensed, the muscles in his exposed arms locking into place like guy wires. One of the old-timers at the table paused as he lifted his beer, the half-full glass hovering between the table and his mouth. The other guy's eyes widened beneath his trucker cap, but neither spoke.

Yates waited, a hand resting on the frigid beer can.

"Do you know them?" Anna asked. "Any of you?"

The bartender shook his head. "No, ma'am. I sure don't. Never heard of them."

"Never? You don't know one person around here by the last name of Combs? I know they're here, but I don't have an address."

"I don't know everybody in town. And I don't know anybody named Combs."

Anne turned her attention to the two old farts. "What about you guys? Do you know them?"

The two guys ignored her. They stared into their beers.

Anna took a step toward them. "Did you hear me?"

"No, ma'am, we don't know them," one finally said. "Can we get two more here?"

The bartender moved away from Anna and carried out the old-timer's request by grabbing two glasses and filling them with beer. While he did that, Anna took yet another step forward, fixed her eyes on Yates, and raised her index finger, aiming it right at him.

"What about you? Do you know them?"

The question hovered in the stale air of the bar. The other three men went about their business, but Yates knew they were listening.

And as Anna waited for his answer, her eyes narrowed. She studied his face. She tried to place him from . . . somewhere. . . .

It was on Yates now. Time to make the bold move or to run away.

He drank from his cold can. "Yes, I know them. And I can take you if you want to go."

54

The nurse, the one who had tried to keep Avery out of Charlie's room like she was the bouncer in a nightclub, brought her a box of tissues.

Avery stood in the hallway, wiping her face and sniffling.

"Are you sure? I mean, he was just talking to me. Are you sure?"

The nurse rubbed Avery's upper arm and spoke in a soothing voice. "He had heart disease. Apparently, a history of it. Didn't you know that?"

"No, I didn't."

"How are you related to him?"

"He's a family friend. Like my second dad." She sniffed and wiped. "So much better than my dad in a lot of ways."

"Well, I'm sorry. I really am. Is there someone you'd like to call? Does he have children or a partner?"

"No children. He talked about a girlfriend, but I don't know her. I hadn't seen him in a couple of years."

"And the two of you were here for the march?"

Avery understood the nurse wasn't asking questions in any official capacity. She was just curious. Avery and Charlie made something of an odd pair, and the nurse wanted to crack the code. "Can I see him?"

"Sure. Just give us a minute."

The nurse disappeared, and Avery sank back down into the chair, the box of tissues balanced on her lap. She tried to comprehend the enormity of what had just happened, but her brain couldn't stretch far enough to make the information fit. Charlie dead. Gone forever. Fine one minute, gone the next.

Her dad's and Jane's health seemed so much more tenuous, their ability to function in the world so much more limited, and yet it was Charlie who was gone. Erased. Evaporated from the world as if by magic.

Avery wanted to call someone. To share the news.

But who would she call? Alisha was the only one who would understand. Avery and Alisha felt the same way about Charlie.

Their mom was gone. Now Charlie. Anna was who knew where. And Anna's roommate . . .

Avery wasn't ready to let go of anyone else.

"Ma'am?" The nurse stood in the doorway to Charlie's room. She wore a ridiculously garish smock, one decorated with pumpkins and black cats for Halloween. A much more benevolent representation of death than the one Avery was about to see through the doorway. "You can come on in."

Avery pushed herself up, grabbed a wad of tissues from the box, and carried them in her fist.

"You can have as much time as you want," the nurse said. "And if you need anything, just holler for me."

"Okay. Thanks."

"He looks very peaceful."

"Yeah, great." Avery didn't know why the nurse had said that. Didn't know why it mattered if he looked peaceful or not.

When her mom had died, after a year of fighting cancer, the funeral home had gone to great lengths to make her look presentable for the open-casket service. Avery couldn't count the number of people who had told her how lifelike and beautiful her mom looked that evening, and Avery had wondered if that was supposed to have made her feel better. Because it hadn't. Wasn't her mother supposed to look sick and dead?

She stepped into the room.

Charlie lay in the same position he had been in when Avery first showed up, no more than an hour ago. The blanket was up to his chin. His hands rested one on top of the other. His eyes were closed, his lips turned down slightly.

It felt like it took twenty minutes to cross the room to his bedside. When she got there, she reached out, placed her hand on his. It was still warm. She took a deep breath, trying to steady herself. It shuddered as it passed from her lungs through her mouth. She thought of his girlfriend. His dogs and who would take care of them.

She'd have to tell Alisha and her dad and Jane. . . .

"Oh, Charlie . . . shit . . ."

She closed her eyes, tried to find calm. When she opened them, she removed her hand from his, wiped a lone tear off her cheek. Dealing with Anna seemed suddenly so unimportant. Everything did.

Something on the floor caught her eye. Next to the nightstand. A folded piece of paper.

Avery bent down. She opened it. Stationery with the hospital logo across the top. Charlie's shaky scrawl covered the page:

Rydell
Combs family
Russ Jane
~~Dont~~

Don't. But "Dont" was crossed out.

So then, do, Charlie? Do what?

And why were her dad's and Jane's names on there?

Had he written the note between the time Avery stepped out of the room and his death? What was he trying to tell her? If the note was for her at all . . .

"Are you okay, hon?"

Avery put the note down by her thigh, out of sight. "Yes. Thanks. Just a few more minutes, okay?"

"Sure thing."

When the nurse was gone, Avery looked at the note again. *Rydell.*
Combs family. Dont.

Don't. Don't what? Don't go? Don't tell? Don't look for Anna?
Why not go?

She slid open the nightstand drawer, saw Charlie's wallet and
loose change and other personal effects. She grabbed the keys to his
truck and slid them into her pocket.

Fuck yes, she was going to Rydell.

PART III

55

Avery walked the six blocks back to Charlie's truck

The walk helped.

She tried to focus on the warm breeze on her face, the sun bright. She tried to focus on life, not death. Not Charlie in the bed with his cooling hands folded on top of his body . . .

It felt strange to slide into the driver's seat. The truck smelled like Charlie. Coffee and aftershave and sweat. His sunglasses sat on the dashboard. His dogs' hair covered the seats. A tiny Gideons New Testament sat in the center console, well thumbed. Avery hadn't noticed it before.

She had to call her dad.

She didn't want to call him. And tell him. As complicated as her feelings were for the old man, she hated bringing him more bad news. For a moment, her mind flashed on a scheme to call Alisha and ask her to do it. But that was a chickenshit approach, the most cowardly thing possible. She was the oldest. She'd been with Charlie when he died. She needed to call.

So she did. She sucked in a deep breath like she was inhaling from a joint. She held it and she called.

Jane answered. "Oh, Avery, did you find her?"

"No, I didn't. I need to talk to Dad. Can you put him on?"

"Avery, can you just tell me the truth? I don't want to be lied to. I know Anna's dead. Will you just tell me? We saw all the trouble there. It's been on the news—"

"Anna's not dead. I saw her. She's alive and well."

"Are you sure?"

"I'm sure, Jane. Okay?" She reminded herself of her stepmother's fragility. She didn't want to add any stress or pain to the woman's life. It was enough being married to her dad. "Jane, I promise I'm not lying to you. But I do need to talk to Dad."

"Okay, honey . . . Are you okay? You sound upset."

Jane. She was so sweet. It was always difficult for Avery to blame the dissolution of her family on someone she liked so much. "I'm okay. Thank you for asking."

"Okay, I'll get Dad for you—"

"Wait, Jane."

"What?"

"Have you talked to Libby? She's been trying to talk to Anna about this birthday gift her ex-boyfriend got her. Do you know anything about that?"

Silence filled the line. Avery imagined Jane standing there, phone in her hand, robe clutched tight.

"Jane?"

"Oh, Avery. Maybe you should talk to Dad about that. This whole thing is so very complicated. It always has been. I don't understand it all. . . . He's here. . . . Russ, it's Avery."

Rustling sounds, the clumsiness of the phone being passed over to the old man. His voice gravelly and sharp. "Did she find her?"

Then into the phone: "Did you find her?"

"No, I didn't, Dad."

"Jesus."

"But I saw her. In the park at the protest. She was okay. And I believe I know where she's going."

"Where?"

"Hold on, Dad. I have to tell you something. Okay?" She tried to speak as calmly as possible to mitigate the shock of what was to come. "Are you sitting down?"

"No, I'm standing here with my stupid walker. Why do you want me to sit down?"

"Is Jane right there?"

"Of course. She watches me like I'm a newborn. What are you trying to tell me?"

Avery took another deep breath. Sucked the air into her lungs as deeply as she could.

"Dad, I met up with Charlie. And we went to the protest together to look for Anna. There was trouble there. The cops cracked down, and there were counterprotestors. It was chaotic and crazy. And we got swept up in it. There was a shooting—"

"I know." Her dad's voice lost some of its edge, as if it were a sharp knife rubbed dull by use. "Are you trying to tell me . . . ?"

He was still a cop. His instincts weren't dull. He sensed trouble when it drew near.

"Dad, it's Charlie. He had some kind of episode when the trouble came down. His heart . . ."

"He has a bad heart. I know that."

"Dad, he didn't make it. Charlie died in the hospital after the protest."

Avery listened for something—anything—from the other end of the line.

A long silence drew out. She didn't even hear breathing.

"Dad?"

"I'm here."

"Are you okay?"

She waited again. Then her dad said, "No. No, I'm not. I'm too old for this bullshit."

"Okay. I'm sorry. I know how close you and Charlie were."

"Were you with him when it happened?"

Avery decided to lie. Better than saying she had been down the hall getting a Milky Way. "Yes, I was. He went peacefully. I was holding his hand."

"I'm glad he wasn't alone."

"He wasn't. And he was happy. Happy doing something and trying to find Anna."

Her dad blew his nose, a loud, wet honking. Like a goose being
tortured. Finally, he asked, "I don't understand—did you find Anna?
Is she with you?"

"No, but I saw her. We came very close to each other right before
the march got broken up."

"She was okay?"

"She was. The cops grabbed me and dragged me away. But Anna
got away."

"Shit."

"I think I know where she's headed. And we need to talk about
that, because I'm ready to go find her. And I don't want to waste any
more time. She's ahead of me by a little bit."

"Where is she?"

Some of the eagerness and desperation had left his voice. He no
longer sounded as curious as he had before. He sounded more re-
signed, like a man anticipating a fate he couldn't avoid.

"She's going to Rydell, Kentucky. I'm sure you've heard of it. And
when Charlie . . . died, he left behind a note. He'd written down
'Rydell,' and the name 'Combs family.' Charlie acted like he knew
something about this. In fact, he said he was going to tell me about
it. So you must know something too. Right? I know they grow weed
there. Why is Anna going to Rydell? Does she have dealings with
this family? Do you know them?"

"Avery, this is all a misunderstanding. But it's also very dangerous.
Is Anna in Rydell yet?"

"I don't know. But she had a few hours' head start if she left right
after the protest. Maybe more."

"Avery, you need to go get her. I don't know what she thinks she's
doing, but you have to get her out."

"Dad, I can't just keep chasing Anna across the state without knowing what's going on. Is this about your job? Can you just tell me?"

He cleared his throat. "Yes, it is related to my job. The Combs family is a dangerous group. They're involved in a lot of criminal activities. Okay? And it's not safe for Anna to be going up there alone. You need to step in."

"If it's not safe or if something illegal is going on, then call the police. Lord knows you have enough contacts. Get them on it."

Her dad sounded much calmer than usual. "Avery, I'd like to keep this inside the family. Okay? It's a family matter. For us. Anna is just confused. She's young, and a young person can get that way. I need you to bring her back here, to our house, and then we can all talk to her. That's what I've wanted all along."

"But you're not going to—"

"Avery, I need you. You're the only one I can count on. You and Charlie, of course. But he's gone. Okay? Can you just do that for me?"

The old man was smart. He knew exactly which buttons to push. She wanted to tell him to screw off, to deal with his own problems. She wanted to say she was going to hang up the phone and call the police herself, send them into Rydell to drag Anna out by the scruff of her neck. If they could even find her.

But she didn't.

Her dad had showed faith in her. Placed all his chips on her.

Was she supposed to say no to that?

"What does Libby have to do with this? She won't call me back."

"Libby's confused as well. I'll talk to her. You go find Anna."

"Dad, I want to ask you something?"

"What?" He sounded irritable. Impatient.

"Why *did* you ask me to be Anna's guardian ten years ago? I know you're pissed about me saying no, but why did you need me to do it? Charlie was our guardian, wasn't he?"

"And see, he ended up dead."

"Dad."

"Ten years ago"—he breathed into the phone—"somebody threatened us. Somebody from the past. Okay? And we were worried we could get hurt. Charlie and me. So we needed a plan. Your sister is a lot younger than you are. We had to make sure she was okay."

"So you thought you and Charlie could get hurt, because this was someone you put away."

"More or less. Yes."

"And you thought Jane was in danger as well?"

"Absolutely. Jane could have been taken away."

"Do you think the same people came after Anna and killed her roommate?"

"I—I don't know."

"Are those people in Rydell?"

"Could be. Yes."

"So these people are pretty dangerous, right?" Avery asked.

"That's what I've been saying. Did you bring something with you?"

"No. But I'm driving Charlie's truck."

"Check under the seat."

She reached down, fumbled around. She felt grit and dirt against her skin. Then she felt the grip of a weapon. She slid it out and lifted it into her lap. "An M and P Nine."

"That a girl."

"Dad, if it's this dangerous . . ."

"You can handle it. Okay? Just get there and get Anna before she goes too far. Then bring her back here. And we'll talk. We will." It sounded like he'd wanted to say something else and reconsidered. Then he said, "Just take care of yourself, champ. And your sister."

He hung up.

56

The girl refused to get into the car with Yates. He offered to drive her and take just one car out into the countryside to the Combs farm, but the girl refused.

Yates couldn't blame her. She had brains. And guts. A dangerous combination.

They stood on the street outside of Hutch's with the girl studying his face. Yates held his breath, expecting at any moment for Anna to scream or cry, to run back inside and call the police, because she recognized him from that gloomy night outside her apartment building when she had come home and found Yates standing there in the dark, scouting the place. Looking for her. It was a short jump from that to saying he killed her roommate.

"What are *you* doing here," she asked, "out where Christ lost his shoes?"

Yates looked at the building they'd just left, where the bartender practically had his giant face pressed against the grimy window. The only thing the dude had acted interested in all day.

Yates said, "I do some work for the Combs family, and you want to know where they are. I can show you. We can help each other out."

"How can I help you?" she asked. She stood with her hands on her hips, her head slightly cocked to one side. She gave him a bit of the side-eye, like someone who was wiser than her twenty-one years.

"I'm just trying to do a good job. I think the family will be happy to see you."

"Okay. But I'm keeping my distance from you. I don't trust you."

"I don't trust me either."

So he told her to follow him, which she did, and he led them outside of Rydell and onto a county road that initially cut through fields of harvested corn and soybeans and then into a stretch of trees that grew over the road like a canopy and blocked out the light.

Yates checked the rearview every mile or so. He expected at any moment for the girl—Anna—to peel off, take her car off the road, execute a three-sixty turn, and go in another direction. Back toward Breckville or where her parents lived. Anything but out into the remote countryside with Yates leading the way. A guy she didn't know who she'd met in a bar. A guy she apparently didn't recognize from the night he'd stood outside her building.

But Anna hung with him. She stayed close, made every turn he made. Traffic was light. At one point they passed a farmer rolling his combine down the road going in the opposite direction. A couple of other cars passed, but it was mostly quiet and still. It felt like a pleasant drive, like they were tourists out to look at the changing leaves. Find a roadside stand and buy a pumpkin or some cider. But they passed no such stands. They were too far out, away from the heavily trafficked roads where the weekend drivers might have wandered.

Yates made sure to keep his eyes on the road. He'd been to the Combs farm once, six months or so earlier. It was hard to find—and he couldn't just search on Google Maps. He had a pretty good eye for landmarks, though, and a pretty good brain for directions once he'd been somewhere. The turnoff was coming up, so he kept his eyes forward more than he worried about what Anna was doing behind him. She'd hung with him so far, so she seemed to be in it for the long haul.

Yates' heart surprised him by beating faster and faster. He'd see Hogan soon. And the Combs family. How many big chances did someone get? Not many. Not many at all. Yates knew one rode behind him right then, an opportunity to take a step up in the world. He didn't intend to blow it.

The road dipped and rose again. They passed over a bridge that spanned a small creek. No, not a creek. Dead River. That was it. Dead River. What a name. Called that as long as anyone could remember because two early settlers had drowned there, trying to cross. Their bodies never found. The river meant Anna and he were getting close to Combs land. Very close.

Yates slowed, trained his eyes on the right side of the road. The trees were thick, growing close together, twining into one another like capillaries and veins. The undergrowth was thick as well—vines and weeds and bushes. Thick enough to lose oneself. Thick enough to disappear.

He slowed. Ahead a narrow opening in the trees. Not even a mailbox or a sign to mark the spot.

"That's it. That has to be it."

He put on his turn signal, eased almost to a stop before he guided the car onto the gravel drive. He watched, saw Anna slowing as well, her turn signal on. The car jounced over a small rut. The drive ahead disappeared into the trees. He might be in the wrong place, might find himself face-to-face with an angry farmer, an old guy in overalls with a shotgun crooked in his arm. Didn't matter. Yates couldn't turn back now.

He drove into the trees. It felt as if they were swallowing him rather than he was entering them. The road hooked to the left, and quickly his car would be out of sight from the road. But Anna stayed with him as the road straightened again.

A few hundred feet farther along, he saw the cattle gate. It was padlocked shut, and on either side hung a no-trespassing sign. He stopped, the tires kicking up dust. Past the gate, nothing was visible. More of the gravel road disappearing into the trees. He turned the car off and climbed out.

Anna stayed in her car, which was still running. Her hands gripped the wheel. The bunny might have been spooked. If she wanted to slam the car into reverse and go, she could. It wouldn't be easy to back down the gravel road, and there weren't any places to turn around. But it wouldn't be easy to stop her. Still, if she went, so would he. He'd follow her back out to the road and bring her back again. In a very real sense, their fates were joined. He wanted things to keep moving in the right direction.

Finally, Anna pushed her door open and stepped out. She remained behind the door like it was a shield. "This is it?" she asked.

"It is."

"How do we get in? Is there a bell?"

Yates shook his head. "They'll be here."

"How?"

"Nothing happens in these woods without them knowing. Besides, I can guarantee you, as soon as we left that dive bar, the bartender called and told them company was on the way."

"For real?"

"Sure. That's how these things work."

Anna looked around. Late-season crickets chirped in the tall grass. A squirrel scurried away from them. Alice had landed in Wonderland. "They all acted sketchy in the bar when I said the family name."

"That's right. You said the magic word in this county."

"And is that because they're doing something illegal here?"

"Illegal?" Yates shrugged. "You could call it stimulating the local economy." He watched her continue to look around. "You planning on staying? Because you don't have much time to decide."

Anna cut her eyes to him. "I'm staying. I promise."

"Okay. Are you going to tell me what you want from them?"

"Are you related to them?"

"No. I'm just a worker bee."

"Then you don't need to know what I'm here for, do you?"

"I don't. But maybe I could help."

A crow cawed overhead and beat its wings.

"Okay, I'm not trying to be a dick," Anna said. "Do you know what they're like?"

Yates considered the question. "Tough," he said finally. "Tough and hard."

Anna kept a poker face, but some fear seeped through. She looked very young. Maybe—no, strike that—she *definitely* didn't know what she was getting into. How could she?

And it wasn't his problem, he reminded himself. His ass had fallen into the fryer. He needed to lift it out—and there had only ever been one person who could do that for him: her.

Anna tapped her fingers against the top of the door, but she didn't say anything. Even Yates grew impatient. He tapped his foot, kicked at the gravel.

A figure came down the drive. A man alone. He puffed a cigarette while he walked, a stream of smoke trailing from his nose as he moved along. He wore a tan blazer and jeans, with dress shoes crunching the gravel.

Hogan spotted Yates, and his face creased. As he approached, he no doubt prepared the words he wanted to use to chew Yates' ass, give him an earful for showing up at the Combs farm without an invitation. After being told to stay in Breckville, Yates had gone to Louisville and then to Rydell, improvising like a guy who didn't understand his place in the pecking order.

Hogan's eyes trailed past Yates, to the second car. And the girl standing there, waiting.

"Mr. Hogan," Yates said, "can I introduce you to a friend of mine? This is—"

Hogan cut him off. "Yes, I know who this is. Anna Rogers. It's good to see you here. We've been hoping you would come by."

57

Avery parked on Main Street.

She looked around. She saw no one. Nothing.

It looked like the town was abandoned, like everyone had packed up their stuff and moved away, leaving behind the buildings and sidewalks and the one stoplight that blinked yellow and might just continue to blink until long after the world ended.

What the fuck would Anna want here?

The police station, a redbrick building slightly newer than everything else around it, sat on the corner of Main and Lincoln. One cruiser sat out front, and in the light breeze, the American flag rustled, flapping against the pole.

Avery went to the door, pushed her way through. No one sat at the large wooden desk just inside, but her entrance set off an electronic tone that notified everyone in the building she'd come in. Everything smelled like floor polish. It took a minute, but a middle-aged man in a Rydell PD uniform emerged from the back. His dark hair was slicked down against his head, and his neatly pressed clothes hung loose on his trim body.

"How are you today? Did you need something?"

Avery introduced herself as a former cop, and they shook hands. The man's hand was warm, his skin soft.

"I'm Ted Hardeman. Chief of police here in Rydell. Do you want to come back and sit?"

She followed him to a small office. Hardeman sat behind his

desk, which was strangely uncluttered, and Avery took a seat across from him. He leaned back in his chair, which squeaked like a small animal.

He waited for Avery to speak, so she did. She told Hardeman who she was and where she was from. And she explained that she was looking for her sister, Anna, who, she had reason to believe, was in Rydell. Perhaps with the Combs family.

"Do you know them?" Avery asked.

Hardeman took his time answering. "Well, yes, I do know the Combs family. They've lived here a long time, much longer than I've been alive. I went to school with Taylor Combs."

Avery read between the lines of the answer. Hardeman knew the Combs family, and they were good people, the kind who wouldn't cause anybody any harm.

"I guess I'm coming to you as a courtesy. I'm planning on going out to their property, because I want to see if my sister is there."

"Oh, you know where the Combs family lives?"

"No," Avery said.

"Let me ask you something else—how old is your sister?"

"She's twenty-one."

Hardeman picked up a paper clip and started twisting it in his fingers. "She's old enough to do whatever she wants. She's not a child."

"My father wants her to come home. He's worried about her."

"Fathers worry about their daughters. He might be worried about you coming out here."

"I think he is." Her dad had said the Combs family was dangerous. Those were his words. But Avery sensed that Hardeman might not be receptive to that message. As chief of police, he must know it. And might be willfully ignoring it. "See, Anna's parents are having health problems. They want their daughter home. They fought, like parents and kids do. I just want to talk to Anna and try to convince her to come home."

Hardeman tossed the paper clip onto the desk. "Well, it's a free country. For now. You can say whatever you want to your sister. Or any other family member. That's not a police matter, so I'll stay out of it. I appreciate your courtesy. And I wish you luck. But, as a public servant, I do feel compelled to offer you some free advice."

"Let me guess. You want to tell me to go home and forget about this little mission."

"I do." His chair squeaked again. "You may not understand what it's like to live out in this part of the state, but I do. People out here don't like other people sniffing around. There's a reason they live way out in the country. If you go rolling up on them, they get nervous."

"Do they have other reasons to be nervous, maybe based on a certain crop they grow?"

"That crop you're referencing is a lucrative one for the people around here. We don't have factories in this county. No manufacturing to speak of. Farmers are having a tough go of it all over the country, not just here. I'm not a prude. Like a lot of people, I've tried that crop a time or two in my life. So long as they're not cooking meth or trafficking in heroin, well, I'm inclined to live and let live. Do you feel the same way?"

"I'm not really worried about the crop they grow."

"See? We're all on the same page. And here's the truth. Sometimes people get the notion to come through here—sometimes it's reporters, sometimes it's immigration. But they all stir the pot and then go away. And we all still have to live here. So I guess what I'm saying is—do you really have to stir this pot?"

"I'm not interested in anything but my sister. . . . I just want to talk to her."

"Why'd she want to visit with the Combs family?"

"I'm not really sure," Avery said. "She's been through a trauma. Her roommate was killed by a creep in Breckville. I'm worried about her. We all are."

Hardeman considered it all, his lips pressed tight. "We were talking about crops, and now we're talking about murder. Shouldn't your sister be home grieving for her roommate?"

"I don't know what she's thinking."

"And neither do I. But I'd be wondering about it."

"The only way I can find out is to talk to Anna. So if you can just tell me where they are . . ."

Hardeman shook his head. "Once you're on that property, I can't really protect you."

"It's strange that a police officer would say that to a citizen, isn't it?"

"I'm a city official, not county. When you get out there, things are a little different. That's all. People come and go, and I never see them. Farmworkers, they're transient. I can't keep track of or help everyone."

"Are you saying people are in danger, or have been hurt?"

"I never said that. I don't know what goes on out there. But no one's filed any charges."

"I hear you. And I guess you know what you're talking about, since you went to school with this Taylor Combs and all."

Hardeman picked up the paper clip, started twisting it again. "I'll give them a call, see if they're accepting visitors."

Avery sighed. "Chief, I guess I could start calling some of my dad's KSP colleagues, maybe get them out here to help me look around."

Hardeman leaned back, bit down on his lower lip. "You're determined to be a thorn in my side, aren't you?"

"It's not about you at all, Chief. I promise."

Hardeman let out a sigh of his own. He told Avery how to get to the farm.

58

Avery missed the turnoff the first time. Even though she'd slowed like she was driving through a school zone, she still managed to miss the turn, which was obscured by trees and brush. She went down the county road about half a mile, found another turnoff, and then back-tracked. That time, as she approached from the east, she saw it more clearly and turned in, brush on either side of the gravel road thwack-ing at the front of Charlie's truck.

She realized she'd quickly disappeared from anyone's view, and then just as quickly came to a cattle gate, where she stopped the truck but left the engine running. The air-conditioning ran on low, and the tightly sealed cabin of the truck blocked all the noise from the woods. Chief Hardeman had been right: In a way she felt like she'd crossed into another world out there. If she opened the door and stepped out of the truck, she'd be crossing an even more perilous line.

And all for a sister she barely knew and who didn't want to be found.

But she couldn't forget the old man hobbling on his walker. Cry-ing, yes, *crying* at the house because he feared for Anna's safety. And Anna herself, that silly little girl splashing in the bathtub. Who did Avery think she was? The king's horseman and the king's man who was going to put all the family pieces back together again?

Avery sure as hell was out there to try.

She stepped out of the truck. The day was still warm in the late afternoon. Birds called to one another above her, and the woods crackled with life. She reached into the cab, pulled the gun from under the seat. She slipped it into the waistband of her jeans, then pulled her shirt down to cover it. She wasn't sure how to make contact with whoever lived there. She could honk or shout. Or wait.

She checked her phone. One bar.

She'd expected service to be spotty out there, and it was. She took the chance that a call would go through and dialed Alisha.

"Hey. Where are you?"

"Working as an extra on the sequel to *Deliverance*. I don't have much time to talk."

"Dad said . . . find Anna . . ."

"Alisha, the call's breaking up. Can you hear me?"

"I can. Yes. Dad said you were finding Anna."

"I think I know where she is. If anything happens, or you don't hear from me in a day or so—"

"I can't hear you."

"I said if you don't hear from me in a few days, tell Dad I'm at the Combs farm outside Rydell. Okay? Did you get that?"

"Yeah. . . . Who are they?"

"Dad knows about them."

"Oh."

"Let's just say they're organic farmers."

"I see."

"So if you don't hear from me . . ."

"I'm on it. Will you be careful? Please?"

"I will."

Avery looked beyond the gate, saw movement in the distance. But nothing came into focus.

"Look, Al, I get what you're saying about the way I've been with Anna. Can you hear me?"

"I can. Barely, but I can."

"When she was born, Mom had taken us to Florida and it just felt like a hole had been ripped in our lives. And then we were supposed to fill that hole with this new person. And Dad's new marriage. Do you see what I'm saying?"

"What you're saying is . . . feel about . . . Dad . . ."

"I don't know." Avery turned her back to the gate and moved closer to the road. "You're breaking up."

"You're there now . . . matters . . ."

"If it does any good."

"And you . . . love . . ."

"Keep an eye on Dad for me too. I know you will."

". . . will . . ."

"Okay. Take care."

"You . . . care. Okay?"

"Okay. Bye."

Avery ended the call. She turned around. Two men stood on the other side of the cattle gate, staring back at her.

59

Avery remained in place.

She studied the two men who stood on the far side of the cattle gate. The man on the left had soft facial features—slightly puffy cheeks and heavy-lidded eyes. She guessed he was about her age. His eyes were hard and flat and fixed on her.

The middle-aged man on the right wore a suit coat over a button-down shirt and no tie. His hair was neatly combed in place, and one corner of his mouth went up in an attempt at a smile. He lifted a cigarette and fitted it neatly into that side of his mouth like it belonged there.

Avery felt the bulk of Charlie's pistol against the front of her body, a cold, comforting presence against her skin. But if any trouble started, she'd have to draw like someone in an old Western movie, and she doubted her ability to do that. Then she told herself not to breathe too deeply, to project calm. Nothing had happened yet. She was just looking for her sister.

"Did you need something?" the older man asked. The cigarette barely moved while he talked.

"I'm looking for the Combs farm."

"That wasn't the question," the younger guy said.

The middle-aged guy's eyes bounced to his companion and back, and Avery read disapproval there. The older guy wanted to ask the questions. He wanted to be a solo act.

"Okay," Avery said, directing her comments to the middle-aged guy. "I'm looking for the Combs farm, because I have reason to believe my sister is here. That's who I'm looking for. My sister. Her name is Anna Rogers."

"And you have the feeling she's at the Combs place?" the middle-aged guy asked.

"I do. You haven't told me I'm wrong about this being the Combs place. I think I followed the directions the police chief gave me properly."

"Oh, he gave you directions." The man removed his cigarette and studied the ash like he expected to see something fascinating there. He tossed the butt into the grass. "I didn't know he worked as a guide in his spare time."

Avery kept her face a mask, kept her body still. She reminded herself to remain poised and calm and not give these guys any reason to feel edgy. She wanted to keep the temperature low. "So, is my sister here by chance?"

"Maybe your sister doesn't want to see you. Maybe she's with the right kind of people now." The younger guy spoke with an odd certitude, like someone who'd just won a large bet and was basking in the afterglow.

Avery decided she hated him. It was an easy decision to make.

She took a step forward, remaining alongside Charlie's truck. "If you know my sister as well as I do, you'll know that's a distinct possibility. She may very well want to tell me to fuck off. And since she's an adult for the most part, I'd have to respect that. But sometimes it's best to hear that 'Fuck off' straight from the horse's mouth. It carries more weight that way. So, if Anna's here . . ."

The older guy reached into the inside pocket of his suit coat.

Avery tensed, her own hand sliding ever so slightly in the direction of the gun butt near her belly button.

The older guy might have noticed her movement because his half smirk grew slightly as he brought out his pack of cigarettes and shook one loose. He placed it in his mouth, then held the pack out toward Avery, even though she was a good thirty feet away. "Want one?"

"No, thanks."

He put the pack away. "I guess I'm a bit of a dinosaur, still smoking. You don't smoke, do you, Nick?"

The other man shook his head, eyes still on Avery. "Bad habit, Hogan."

Hogan lit his cigarette with a nickel-plated lighter and took a long draw. When he exhaled, the smoke rushed away on the breeze. "There aren't any hotels left in Rydell, and phone reception is spotty, but I'm guessing your sister has your number. I'll tell her you came by, and she can call you when she's ready. She's getting acquainted with some folks back at the house, so she could be busy for a while. If you're looking for a place to stay, there's a motel back in Hinesville. You likely came through there on your way to Rydell."

"I want to talk to my sister now. I don't think that's a big ask."

The younger guy—Nick—made a snorting noise. "Didn't you hear the man? She's busy getting to know some folks up at the house. You can't just show up here uninvited and expect to get in and see her. This is a family matter."

"A family matter? *I'm* her family. Her parents sent me."

Hogan waved his hand at Nick, trying to calm him down. As he did, Avery recognized the position she was in. She stood in the middle of nowhere, facing off against two men who radiated danger, and insisted on seeing the sister she'd been ignoring at best and denying at worst. She couldn't blame Anna if she refused to see her. But what about the march when she'd saved Anna's bacon? Wouldn't Anna remember how Avery had helped her get away?

Anyway, she couldn't forgive herself if she left without making sure Anna was okay.

"What my young friend is trying to say," Hogan said, "is that Anna is occupied right now. And she's doing rather a lot of catching up. But, like I said, I'll pass the message along." He puffed on the cigarette, then said, "As I understand it, you and Anna have not been particularly close. So perhaps she won't be in a hurry to get back in touch, and you'll just have to be patient."

"Are you serious right now?"

Avery's body moved forward without her mind being in full command of the action. She walked toward the gate, her shoes scuffing over the gravel. The two men held their ground. They didn't move or flinch, and Avery stopped ten feet away from them.

"Her father—*our* father—is retired KSP. Do you want *him* sending people out here to find Anna? Do you want that attention on this . . . *farm*?"

"We know about your father," Hogan said. "All about him."

"Besides," Nick said, "that's not relevant anymore. That's all yesterday's news."

Avery turned her head his way. "KSP isn't yesterday's news."

"Yeah, are you going to—"

"Avery?"

The single word—her name—cut through the bickering. Avery looked past the men and up the gravel drive to where her sister had emerged from around the bend. She came walking down the middle of the road, about thirty feet away and getting closer. Her hair had slipped free from its ponytail and bounced around her shoulders. As she drew closer, Avery saw her skin was blotchy, her eyes red like she'd been crying.

"Anna, are you okay? What is it?"

"What are you doing here, Avery? I came down here to see what was going on, and it's you?"

"I'm looking for you. Dad and Jane, they're worried about you. They want to talk to you—they want you to come back."

Anna studied her sister, suspicion etched on her face. She looked young and wary, a kid waking up from a nightmare. "What do they care?"

"Anna, can we just talk? I don't know what you're doing here or who you're with, but if we can just talk, maybe we can figure something out. Whatever it is, you don't have to deal with it alone."

"She's not alone," Nick said.

"Quiet," Hogan said.

"I don't understand you, Avery. We lived in the same town for three years and you wouldn't even talk to me. Now that I've left, you've come all the way across the state because you want to help me." Anna wiped at her eyes with one hand and then the other. "I don't know what the fuck is going on with that family. I really don't. But you of all people . . ."

Anna turned on her heel, kicking up gravel, and started off.

Nick laughed.

"*Anna*. Anna, please." Her sister kept walking, so Avery moved closer. She walked all the way over to the gate. "Anna, look—okay, you're right. You're right about everything. I've been a shit. I have. Okay? And I'm sorry. Do you hear me? I'm sorry."

Anna stopped. She didn't turn around, keeping her back to Avery. But she did stop.

"Anna, I'm here. Okay? My life hasn't exactly worked out the way I wanted it to, so maybe I took it out on you. Because you were there. And you had two parents. My dad. And . . . look, this is a lot of Freudian bullshit. Okay? I was a jerk, and I'm sorry. But I'm here now, so can you just talk to me for, like, five minutes, so I don't have to go back and tell Dad I couldn't even get to talk to you? Can you just give me that? And, hell, don't do it for me. Do it for Jane. All right? She's worried about you."

Anna stood still for a long time. Avery forgot about the two men flanking her.

A train whistle sounded in the distance, and the trees rustled.

Anna turned to Hogan. She didn't look at Avery, but she said, "Do me a favor and let her in."

She walked off up the drive without looking back while Nick came over and unlatched the gate.

60

As the gate swung open, Avery stepped toward the truck.

"Hold it," Hogan said.

Both men came through the gate toward Avery.

"Nick, you drive the truck. Are the keys in there?"

"It's running," Avery said.

Nick stepped past her without meeting her eye. He slid into the truck cab and pulled the door shut.

"You can walk with me," Hogan said. "We can talk."

It wasn't an invitation but a command. Hogan punctuated the command by coming close to Avery. He reached out and lifted her shirt enough to reveal the gun, which he removed and tucked into his own pants. He held out his hand again. "Phone."

"I can't keep my phone?"

"Service is shit out here anyway. It works about one out of every ten days." He tilted his head back toward the road. "Or you can go and not see your sister. That's fine with me too."

Avery waited. Her spine tingled. It wasn't smart to go on. Everything was flipped. The farther she went, the less control she had. But since she'd reached this point . . . and had little to go back to except arresting drunk college kids who doubled as white supremacist rabble-rousers on the weekend . . .

If she crossed the line, stepped onto their property, she'd be playing by their rules. She might not come back out.

She backed up, moved out of Hogan's reach. "I do need to check in with my contacts in the KSP. They need to know where I am and that I'm okay."

"No one wants any trouble, *Officer*." Hogan stepped forward, grabbed the phone from her hand. "This is for everyone's safety. Right?"

Nick dropped the truck into gear and drove through the gate, the giant tires scrunching the gravel.

"Shall we?" Hogan said, sweeping his arm in the direction of Charlie's retreating truck. And watching Charlie's truck being driven by another man made Avery realize Anna was inside that place and help was far away and Avery had no idea what she was stepping into.

Hogan locked the gate once they were through, and side by side they started up the drive. Hogan stood over six feet tall and looked to be around fifty. His stride was steady and quick, and Avery moved briskly to keep up with him.

"I think you need to understand some things about the Combs family before you get up there," he said. While they walked, he tossed away one cigarette and lit another. "The family has lived here a long time. They like to keep to themselves, like a lot of folks who live out in this area. What I want you to understand is it's not comfortable for them to have people just show up. Especially people who used to be cops."

"'Used to' is the operative phrase there. I'm not here in that capacity. I'm here to see my sister. Besides, cops or ex-cops shouldn't make people nervous just by showing up. I'm not interested in their crop."

Hogan laughed. "Fair enough."

"What do you do for the Combs family, Mr. Hogan? Are you a relative?"

"I'm an employee. I've worked for them for a number of years. If they have a problem, something not directly related to the management of the farm, then I try to help them with it. I used to work in law enforcement myself. Up in Ohio. City of Cincinnati."

"Really? You found this work more lucrative?"

"I find it a little less restrictive."

"Interesting choice of words."

"Your sister is the one who can tell you why she's here. And, of course, it's going to be her choice to decide how long she wants to remain. All I can say is, she's welcome to stay as long as she likes. And we simply ask that you respect that decision when she makes it. Families are complicated things, aren't they?"

"They are."

"I've fallen out of touch with my own family. But I've found a place for myself here. With the Combses."

Avery saw a break in the trees ahead. The road opened on a clearing, and in the distance stood a large two-story log home with a green metal roof. It looked like it belonged in a magazine devoted to elegant rural living. But the windows seemed unusually small and failed to take advantage of the natural views around it. She didn't see Charlie's truck.

"Well, I'm glad you found a place here. It looks pretty nice." Avery continued walking in the direction of the house, assuming that to be their destination.

Hogan's voice redirected her. "Oh, we're not going there." He pointed off to the right. The road forked, and one side went to the big house as a kind of driveway. The other fork went across the clearing toward another opening in the trees. "Your sister is in the house, yes. But it's not time for you to talk to her. There's a place you can stay over this way."

Avery stopped. Hogan took a few steps and then said, "Avery?" Hogan tossed his cigarette down and ground it under his shoe. When he spoke, his voice remained patient. Annoyingly so. "I told you, it's not time for you to see her. Like I said, Avery, if you're here, then you're agreeing to operate on our terms. That's the only way it can be. We insist on that."

Avery looked at the house. Behind one of the windows, someone moved while looking down on them. Was it Anna?

The figure was obscured behind the glass and a sheer curtain.

"How soon before I talk to her?" Avery asked, turning to Hogan.

"I don't know."

She felt boxed in, without many choices.

"I'd like to talk to her soon," she said. "Like I said—"

"I know. Daddy's cop friends will be upset," Hogan said. "You're playing by a different set of rules out here. Come on. This way."

She followed along behind him.

61

They continued on, through the opening in the trees and down a hill. A cluster of four tiny cabins lay ahead, the kind of dwellings you might have seen in a campground. They were arranged in a square, with a firepit and stone benches in the center.

"You came at the right time of year," Hogan said as they reached the buildings. "Some of our farmhands moved on at the end of the summer, so there's a cabin empty. You can have it to yourself. I think you'll find it comfortable."

Avery kept her mouth shut, but she hated camping. Hank liked to go, so she'd agreed to spend weekends in the woods with him, sleeping in a tent and pooping in the bushes, waking up each day smelling like a fire.

"These are the south cabins. A few more workers stay in the north cabins, down the continuation of this path about a quarter of a mile from here. Beyond that runs Dead River, which is closer to a fat creek, but I didn't name it. The water is murky and cold and flows into the cave, eventually dropping off into . . . well, who knows what. There have always been stories about it being haunted. That people have gone down the river in there and never come back."

"I've heard about that." Avery shivered, felt her throat close tighter. "Lovely."

"All in all, the family owns hundreds of acres, so you can walk a long way and still be on Combs land. And that includes the entrance to the cave, which has been a bone of contention with the government.

They want access to it. You know, for research purposes. Study the cave and the rocks and the water. It's possible soldiers from both armies quartered there during the Civil War. And the family has found arrowheads. Lord only knows how old those are. But, like I said, the family has been here a long time. It's theirs. There are more caves in Kentucky than just about anywhere else, so those eggheads can study other places. And we don't really like outsiders poking around."

The air was cooling in the late afternoon. The charred logs in the firepit were still smoking. A stack of kindling and logs sat off to the side, leading Avery to believe she'd have to channel her inner Girl Scout to stay warm.

"So I'm just supposed to hang out around here until . . . when?"

Hogan shrugged. "Like I said, you're on the family's timetable now. Now, if you're interested in working, we might be able to find something for you to do. Would you like that? Get your hands dirty a little bit? Help the family out with their harvest?"

"I didn't come here for that."

"We'll see what happens. You know what they say about idle hands."

"Can you assure me Anna is okay?"

"You saw her."

"She was crying."

"She's having an emotional time here."

"Why? Can you tell me that?"

"I'll make sure some food is sent down here to you. The workers who stay here will be coming back soon. They can help get a fire going."

He walked off without saying anything else, presumably heading back to the house, where Anna remained out of Avery's sight. Avery groaned about the paper she was supposed to write that weekend. Not one line. Not one word.

She sat on the stone bench and stared at the cold fire. Within fifteen minutes, four people emerged from the trees and approached the cabins. They froze when they spotted Avery.

Avery stood and offered a friendly wave, trying to appear as non-threatening as possible. They must have been the farmhands Hogan had talked about, the ones who stayed in that cluster of cabins. And they were no doubt wondering about the stranger waiting for them.

"Hello," Avery said. "I'm just . . . visiting." She pointed in the direction of the big house, but how could she explain Anna? They likely didn't know Anna was there. So Avery tried a different approach. "I was wondering if any of you had a match or a lighter. This is ready to go, but I don't have anything to ignite it with. If you do, we can get it going." She rubbed her arms. "The sun's going down, and it's going to get cool."

The four people stared at her, unmoving.

Then Avery heard a noise come from the group. Was someone holding a cat?

Avery craned her head, tried to look more closely. One of the women shifted her weight and hefted the bundle in her hands. A baby. The woman was holding a baby.

"Would you like to come over and get warm?" Avery asked.

They remained in place, studying her. It started to feel like no one would ever move, and they'd all stand there in the woods until the sun rose the next morning.

One of the men nodded and came forward. He dug around in the pocket of his stained pants as he approached. He withdrew his hand, holding up a book of matches.

"Aquí," he said.

And he handed it to Avery, who lit the fire while the rest of the group came over and sat down.

62

The flames grew.

The others came closer as Avery handed the matches back to the man. He nodded at her, and she said, "Thanks. *Gracias.*"

The workers all sat, but they looked uneasy. They arranged themselves on the benches on the far side of the fire, away from Avery. She felt like an intruder. After all, what would you think if you came back from harvesting an illegal crop and a stranger was standing outside your house?

"My name's Avery." She waved at them. "I'm just— Well, my sister is here. Up at the big house. And I'm waiting for her. I think."

Four blank looks. Did they speak or understand English? Since Avery could fall back only on her two years of high school Spanish, they might all be spending a lot of time staring at one another across the fire.

The woman holding the baby pointed at herself and said, "Camila. I'm Camila." She nodded at the man who had handed over the matches. "He is Gilberto. She is Celina. And he is Vladimir."

Avery nodded at each person as they were introduced. And smiled. Then she said, "And what is the baby's name?" Avery pointed. "The baby. *El niño?*"

"Oh, Alexa. She has— She is six months old."

Avery wished she knew what to say about somebody's child. She couldn't even manage to do it for Alisha, but she decided to try with this stranger. "She's lovely." Avery couldn't even see the baby's face because of the blanket, but her statement sounded pretty good. "*Bonita.* Right? *Bonita.*"

"Yes, thank you," Camila said. "Your sister—does she work here?"

"No. At least I don't think so." Avery was reminded of how she hadn't known the names of her sister's ex-boyfriend or her roommate. How was she supposed to convince Anna to place her trust in Avery when they barely knew each other? "To be honest, I don't know what my sister is doing here. Do you know who lives in the big house? I think she's here to see them."

Camila shook her head quickly, dismissing the notion she knew any of the goings-on inside the big house. Gilberto said something to her in Spanish, and Camila answered. Avery caught the word *casa*, and before Camila was finished, Gilberto was shaking his head.

"No, no. No sé. No sé."

"That's okay. I understand." Avery pointed to her temple. *"Comprendo.* I do." She craned her head around, trying to look in the direction of the big house, hoping Anna might even at that moment be strolling down the hillside toward them. But no one was there, and Avery turned back to the warmth of the fire. "I guess I'm just going to wait. If you don't mind. I don't know the word— 'Wait'? 'Hang out'?"

"Yes, please," Camila said. "Hang out. They'll bring food. Soon."

"Thank you. *Gracias.*"

The silence again grew awkward. They were like a bunch of kids waiting for an assignment from a substitute teacher.

The heat against Avery's face felt comforting. The sky darkened, and birds, black shapes against the clouds, swept overhead. "So you all work here? On the farm? Work here? *Trabajo?*"

"Sí," Camila said.

"How long have you worked here? *Cuantos . . . tiempo?*"

Camila nodded. "Since summer. We've been here since summer." Camila shifted her weight on the bench. She looked at her coworkers, who were studying the fire.

Avery felt like she'd exhausted all the small talk. The ex-cop curiosity came to the forefront. "And there's a cave, right?" Avery asked. "The river runs into the cave somewhere, doesn't it? *El río . . .*"

Camila shook her head. The others shook their heads as well—they didn't want to talk about it.

"*No sé,*" Camila said. "*No sé.*"

Avery let it go. Caves made ideal locations for drying marijuana. Constant cool temperature, lots of space.

"I guess I can look for it tomorrow," Avery said. "I'm sleeping here—*aquí*—tonight."

"We don't know the cave," Camila said, shaking her head. "Not the cave."

"Are you not allowed? Or you just don't want to go?"

"We don't go in the cave. *Nunca.* Never."

"I see. Is Mr. Hogan in charge? Is he the boss here?"

Gilberto spoke to Camila in Spanish, and she answered. He shook his head.

"*No, no,*" he said. "*Solo trabajamos aquí. Solo trabajamos aquí.*"

"Yes, we just work," Camila said. "Just work. That's all."

"Okay, I'm sorry. I was being nosy. *Lo siento.*"

Avery directed her apology to Gilberto, but he looked away from her. He lit a cigarette with a match from the book he'd loaned to her. While he puffed he stared off into the distance, watching the darkening tree line. Camila bounced her baby, and the other couple spoke to each other in Spanish in low voices, then stopped.

For fifteen minutes, they all sat in silence. Avery tended the fire, adding new wood when needed. Poking it with a large stick she'd found. The sky grew darker, the air cooler. Avery pulled her jacket tighter around her body. She thought of Charlie as the sparks went up into the sky and disappeared. Stars came out, faint pinpricks of light. She tried to think of anything she could have done, anything that would have changed the outcome for Charlie.

They shouldn't have split up. If she'd stayed with him as they searched the park, maybe she could have protected him. But she wouldn't have seen Anna. She wouldn't have protected Anna. And she wouldn't be there now, waiting to see her.

If she ever saw her sister . . .

Footsteps approached from the direction of the house. Avery's heart surprised her by jumping. Did she want to see Anna that much? Their roles had become reversed. She was sitting around, hoping for a scrap of recognition from her sister.

A man approached the fire. Avery recognized him—the one named Nick. He carried a basket in each hand and moved steadily with the weight evenly distributed. He reached the fire and set the baskets down without comment. Avery's companions stood and started opening the baskets and removing items from inside. It looked like a routine they'd been through many times.

Nick stood back, watching, hands on hips. He seemed to be waiting for something.

Avery wanted to remain silent, but she couldn't stop herself. "Is my sister coming down here soon?"

Nick shrugged. "You should go ahead and eat. There's plenty. Everybody gets treated well here."

"And Anna?"

"You might not see her until tomorrow. I don't know."

"Where's my truck?"

"It's safe. Don't worry. But it's not your truck, is it? Unless your name is Charles Ballard. KSP, retired." Nick smirked like he'd scored a big victory. "My condolences, by the way. He got a mention on the news."

He turned and started back for the house.

Avery wanted to pick up a rock and aim for the back of his head. Her hands clenched at her sides, and she calculated the odds of her taking him if they fought with fists only.

But she let it go. She let it go for Anna's sake.

She turned back and watched the fire flicker over four anxious faces.

Avery shook her head, jerked her thumb over her shoulder. *"Pendejo,"* she said, using a word her high school classmates had liked to use.

Camila smiled, but nobody laughed. Avery sat down and started eating.

63

The food was surprisingly good.

Avery realized she hadn't eaten since the morning, and the sandwiches and potato salad and milk that came in the basket tasted like one of the best meals she'd ever had.

While they ate, Avery tried to make small talk. She told the others where she was from and where she went to school. She asked them where they were from.

"Mexico," Camila said. "All of us."

"It can't be easy to work on a farm with a baby," Avery said.

Camila shrugged. "I make do. Always."

Having eaten a meal with the workers—and feeling a little more desperate—Avery decided to push a little harder.

"Do you like working here?"

Camila didn't answer.

"Do you know that man who brought the food?"

Gilberto spoke to Camila in Spanish, and she shook her head.

"I don't know him. I have never seen him."

"And did you see a young woman? Twenty-one years old?"

Gilberto spoke again, and Camila shushed him. She said something, and Avery caught the word *"hermana."*

Camila turned back to Avery. "I didn't see a girl. We don't go to the house. Do you mean your sister?"

"Yes."

"Why is she here?"

"I don't know. But I'm trying to find out."

They stayed around the fire for a couple more hours. When Alexa started to cry, Camila took her into one of the cabins, and Gilberto followed. The other couple went into their cabin, and for a while Avery sat outside by herself. The fire kept her warm, but she faced a cold night in the cabin. She sat outside as long as she could, feeding the fire. She tried not to keep looking over her shoulder to see if Anna was approaching. And she tried not to jump every time a twig snapped or a leaf crunched. The more time passed, the less hopeful she grew that she'd see Anna.

When her eyelids felt heavy, she went into a cabin. It was, one could say, rustic. In one corner sat a cot with a rough-looking army blanket and a single pillow. On the nightstand next to the bed were two candles in mason jars. But she could see no matches. A rickety card table was pushed against a wall with one folding chair sitting at an angle to it.

Avery shivered. She considered sleeping outside by the fire, where it would be warmer.

She went over and inspected the cot, aided by the firelight that leaked in through the open door. She didn't know what she was looking for. Bedbugs? Fleas? A snake?

How would she see it in the dim light?

"Hello?"

Avery turned. Camila stood in the doorway, a bundle in her arms. Was it the baby? She extended the bundle to Avery. A blanket.

"Here. It's extra. It gets cold. And matches. For the candles."

"Oh, no, I couldn't—"

"Take it. Please. It's okay."

"You need the extra. It's so cold, you need everything you can get your hands on."

But Camila didn't back down. She stood there, the blanket extended. Avery didn't like to accept help, and even though it rubbed against her grain, she did it. Somehow, Camila's generosity seemed tolerable.

"Okay. *Gracias.* That's very nice. I'll see if my sister can get me another blanket or something."

"*Sí*, maybe."

Camila remained in the cabin. Avery assumed the baby was asleep under Gilberto's watchful eye.

"Do you have brothers and sisters?" Avery asked.

"A sister. But"—Camila shook her head—"not for a long time."

"You haven't seen her for a long time?"

"Yes. She's in Mexico."

"You must miss her."

"I do. It's dangerous there."

"I'm sorry."

"*Cómo se dice . . . ?* It is what it is? Right?"

"Yeah, right."

Camila stepped out and said one more thing before leaving. "If I did see my sister . . . I would . . ."

"You would what? Hug her?"

Camila shook her head. "I would . . . get her out of there." She mimed throwing a punch. "I would fight. For her."

Avery understood. Loud and clear.

64

The extra blanket helped. But Avery still shivered as she tried to fall asleep.

The blankets scratched like sandpaper. The thin mattress, which smelled like a damp sock, barely kept the metal springs of the cot from pressing into her back. She wore her clothes, including her shoes. And every few minutes she thought a spider was crawling on her neck.

Avery couldn't say how long it took her to fall asleep. It felt like hours that she tossed and turned. But at some point she fell asleep, because she dreamed about her mom. The first time in months, maybe years, she'd dreamed about her. And her mother was saying her name, and Avery tried to call out to her and might have—

"Mom. Mom."

Someone was shaking Avery awake. She bolted up, forcing the person to step back from the cot.

"Camila?"

"Avery? It's me. It's Anna."

Avery squinted into the dark. A figure was silhouetted in the middle of the cabin, backlit by the faint light coming in through the open door. "Anna?"

"Yes, it's me."

"What time is it?"

"After midnight."

"Are you okay? Did anybody hurt you?"

"No, of course not. I'm fine."

Avery swung her legs off the cot. She was still tangled in the coarse blankets, and the air was chilly. Anna wore a down coat that looked two sizes too large for her.

"How did you find me?" Avery asked.

"I knocked on one of the other cabins. The woman told me where you were. She didn't want to, but I kept asking. I told her you were my sister. I can't believe you're sleeping in here. I thought you hated camping."

"Well, I wasn't offered other accommodations. I guess there's no room at the inn."

"I didn't ask you to come out here."

"You're welcome."

"Jesus, Avery . . . Okay, thanks for checking up on me. I appreciate it. Okay? Are you doing it just because Russell and Jane asked you to?"

Russell and Jane? Avery shivered again. "It started with them asking."

"Started that way? What did it become?"

"Someone who knows you from Gracewood saw you at the protest. Walking away from the protest, actually. And he said you were crying. Hard. And then your friend Rachel told me you just took off for Rydell without saying why you were going or who you were going to see. So I am kind of curious as to why you're out here in the middle of nowhere staying on a giant marijuana farm. And why the people who greeted me at the gate acted like they didn't want me to come close to you. Any answers would be appreciated."

"You should just go home, Avery. I'll talk to Russell and Jane eventually, but I'm not ready to now. I'm still making sense of all of this."

"Anna, take it from me, if you're in trouble or need help with something, it's better to reach out to someone. I've always tried to go it alone, and it doesn't really work. Okay? So if you can just tell me what's going on, we can figure it out. We can leave, and you don't have to go back to Dad's house if you don't want. We can go back to Breckville. You can stay at my place. We can do all the stupid sisterly things we've never—I mean, *I've* never—done with you."

"Avery . . ."

"What?"

"We're not sisters."

Avery sighed. "Anna, saying we're stepsisters, it was shitty. And I'm really sorry. It's not about you. It's about me, and I won't—"

"No, we're *not* sisters. You and me *and* Alisha. We're not. I'm not sisters with you. And Dad and Mom . . ." Something caught in Anna's voice, a small yelp in the dark. "I took one of those online DNA tests. And . . . and . . . fuck, Avery . . . I'm not related to *anyone* in our family. I'm related to *this* family. The people who own this farm."

65

Even in the darkness of the cramped, musty cabin, Anna saw Avery's face change.

Avery cocked her head to one side, and her mouth moved around like she was working on a wad of peanut butter. Then she finally started talking. "Anna, what you're saying doesn't make sense. Can you tell me what you're talking about—"

Anna waved her hands in the air like an umpire signaling a runner safe. She knew she'd get the older-sister attitude, the whole *You're too young and inexperienced to understand anything.* And if Anna would just keep her mouth shut and listen, her older siblings would make sense of the situation for her.

Avery did that less—mainly because they rarely saw each other or talked about anything real. But Alisha did it. Alisha, who was so much more understanding than Avery or her dad. If Anna complained about anything or asked for advice, Alisha listened and tried to help—but always with a little sliver of *I know better than you because I'm older.*

But none of it was real anyway. Alisha wasn't her sister. Avery wasn't.

Anna's mom and dad weren't . . .

"I don't want to talk about this here," Anna said. "There are people in the other cabins, and . . . it's none of their business. Avery, just go home tomorrow. We'll talk another time."

Avery stood up, the springs squeaking as she moved. The dingy blanket around her body fell to the cabin floor. She went closer to Anna, reached out, and placed her hands on Anna's upper arms. Avery was four inches taller than Anna and much stronger. Anna had always been a little afraid of Avery. No, not fear. She had always respected Avery for being bigger and stronger and older. Kind of like having a second mother around when she was little.

"Anna, I want to hear whatever you have to say. I have a lot of questions. I'm sure this is some kind of misunderstanding. I want to talk to you about it *right now*. Not tomorrow. Or next week or whenever. Do you want to go for a walk? I have to tell you something too."

Anna remembered the scene in the park. Bodies falling to the ground. The shots being fired. The giant cop swinging his baton at anyone who moved.

The dead girl's face. The blood . . .

And Avery's voice cutting through it, calling her name.

Anna.

The way Avery had said it, the emotion she'd invested in saying the name. Anna tried to remember if anyone had ever said her name that way. Not Trevor. Nor Eric or Rachel.

Maybe her— No, not her mom. Jane. Maybe Jane had. When Anna was little, and Anna had done something that surprised or pleased or even angered her. Jane would say her name.

Anna.

And she'd invest it with such emotion, such care, such energy, that Anna could still hear it ringing across the years.

Anna.

But was she the same Anna anymore? Was she Anna at all?

Sure. But she was also alone. Caught between two families she didn't belong to. No-man's-land.

Avery's hands felt warm through Anna's thick jacket. The touch felt real, even if everything else was a mistake. Or a lie.

"Okay, we can go for a little walk. It's dark, and I don't really know where anything is."

Avery nodded, but she didn't let go. "Anna, did someone say you couldn't see me or talk to me? Did they tell you not to leave that house?"

No, no one in the house had explicitly told her not to leave. No one had told her not to speak to Avery. And Hogan had told her she could talk to Avery at some point, but he did act a little vague about when. He also asked a lot of questions about Avery, a low-key interrogation, like Hogan wanted to write a book about Avery and needed to know a lot of details about her. Most of them relating to her career as a cop and how many people in law enforcement she remained in contact with.

"No, not really. But . . ."

"But what?"

"They didn't exactly say I *could* leave the house. I didn't ask when I came down here. I just did because . . . because I wanted to tell you why I was here and what was going on, I guess. Maybe if you hear it all, you'll decide to go away and let me handle this."

"Anna, if Dad or Jane heard you say these things, that you're not really related to them, that they're not your family . . . my God, do you know how much that would hurt them? Do you know how much it would hurt Alisha?"

Anna pulled back, slipped out of Avery's grip. "It's always about them, isn't it? Even now it's about how *they* might feel. I would think you'd take my side, Avery. You're the one who tried to break away. You're the one who had to put up with so much of Dad's bullshit." She backed out of the cabin, smelled the smoking remnants of the fire. "We can walk down here and talk. There's a path. But not far. It's been a long day."

66

As they moved past the area of the firepit and out of the small cluster of cabins, Avery hurried to keep up with Anna.

When Avery came alongside her, Anna kept her eyes forward, and the two of them headed toward an opening in the trees.

Their shoes crunched the gravel, and when the path turned to packed dirt, their footfalls made soft padding sounds. Night birds called in the trees, and the farther they went, the more Avery became aware of a faint rushing sound. She tried to identify it, then realized it was running water. Dead River, which ran through the property owned by the Combs family.

The trees overhead blocked out the stars and the moon. Even though they were side by side, Anna was a shadow in the dark. Avery tried to process what Anna had told her, tried to understand what she had been saying about their family, and could make no sense of any of it.

After they'd been walking for a while and were plenty far from the cabins and the big house, Anna said, "We can just sit here." She pointed to a large fallen tree that ran parallel to the path and looked to have been placed there for the sole purpose of giving people a place to sit and talk.

They sat down, and Avery wasted no time in asking questions. "Are you saying you did one of these online tests? The thing that tells you your ethnicity?"

"Yes, that's right. Trevor got me one for my birthday, and then we broke up, so I never checked the results. I was so pissed about him breaking up with me. Hurt by it, really. So I just pretended the gift didn't exist. I wasn't that curious about my ethnic makeup. I mean, look at me. I didn't think there were any surprises to be found there. I figured I was a European white girl. Like you. And Alisha and Mom."

"But . . ."

"But Libby had her DNA tested a month ago or so. She got a full report. And she knew Trevor had gotten me on there as a birthday gift, so she looked for me. But we weren't matched. At all. And she looked to see if I'm matched with some cousins we have on there, but I'm not matched to them either.

"So I looked, and I was matched to the Combs family and a bunch of other people in this part of the state. Brittany Combs' name and the town where she lives—Rydell—are on there for me to see. It said she was my aunt or cousin. I came here and asked around and found this farm."

"Okay, so it's a mistake. They mixed up the samples. Do you know how many times labs fuck stuff up?"

"It's not a fuckup, Avery. There are too many points that agree."

Avery's hands rested in her lap. She didn't know what to do with them. She didn't know what to do with the information coming at her. "What are you trying to say? That Dad . . . Jane . . . I don't get it. . . . Are you saying you're adopted, and they decided not to tell you? That's the kind of thing that happened in the 1950s. Not today."

"Do you remember when I was born? You and Alisha are both old enough to remember. You're nine years older than I am. And Alisha's eight years older. So what do you remember about it?"

"I wasn't in the delivery room."

"What do you remember about it, Avery?"

"I don't know. We weren't in town. Dad—he and my mom were on very bad terms, as you know, because of—"

"Because he had an affair with my mom."

"Right. And Mom always said, 'Watch, girls, he's going to have a new baby with his new wife, and you'll be cast aside.'"

"She said that?"

"She wasn't the happiest person."

What portion of Avery's feelings toward her sister were the product of actual experience and what part could be laid at the feet of her mother's bitterness and hurt? The repeated messages that Avery and Alisha were going to be forgotten and replaced.

"We were in Florida when you were born. My mom had a new boyfriend, and she moved us down there to be with him. It didn't last. Dad wasn't in contact with us, and Mom didn't want to have anything to do with him. But they must have talked. One day, Mom told Alisha and me that Jane had had a baby. A girl. Anna. An A name, like Alisha's and mine. That was it. When we came back home, we saw you. "

"And conveniently there aren't any pictures of Mom pregnant, right? No picture of me in the hospital or right after I came home?"

"They had that fire . . ." Avery's words sounded weak to her, even as she said them.

"That destroyed all the photos. What? They'd never sent a newborn photo of me to anyone? Every photo of me under a certain age disappeared? There are photos when I'm a little older but none as a newborn."

"Okay . . . okay . . . let's say it's all true. Let's say the DNA test is right, and you aren't Dad and Jane's kid. And you aren't related to Libby or our cousins or anyone else. You were adopted. Why keep that a secret? Why?"

"I don't know. Except Mom—Jane—"

"You can't start calling her Jane. She raised you—"

"Don't lecture me, Avery. This is my fucking life and my fucking feelings."

"Okay. Call her whatever you want. Lord knows I've called Dad some things over the years."

"Okay. Thank you. But Jane . . . Jane . . . all she wanted to do was have a baby. She always told me how much she wanted to be a mom. She still complained about how much she wishes you would accept her as a mother figure of some kind. Especially since your mom died."

"Yeah . . . okay . . ."

"So they pretended I was theirs all those years, so their perfect little narrative all hung together. They fell in love. Who cares that Big Russ was already married and had kids with his current wife? Russ and Jane were so in love, they had to be together at all costs. And how could that perfect union not produce a child if they wanted one?"

"I always thought we looked alike."

"You used to go around saying we *didn't* look alike. If we were in a store, the three of us, or at a family function or whatever, and someone would comment on how much we three girls looked alike, Alisha would take the compliment and agree. But not you. No. You'd go out of your way to say that we didn't look alike, that we were just stepsisters and not related. You said that all the time."

"Okay, I'm an asshole. Guilty as charged."

"It's true, though. Why am I so much shorter than the rest of the family?"

"Okay, you're a smaller person. Grandma Ava was short. She died before you were born, but she was about four-eleven."

"Nice try."

"Anna, I just talked to Dad. You should see how worried he is."

Anna made a huffing noise.

"I'm just saying Dad and Jane really care for you. And they see Al and me as your sisters."

"Jesus, Avery, did you know? You're the oldest. Did you know? Is that why you never accepted me? Did you know I wasn't really your sister? Does Alisha know too, and nobody fucking bothered to tell me?"

"No. *No*, Anna. I didn't know any of this. And, again, I'm sorry about the stepsister shit. It's an awful thing to say—"

"No, don't apologize. You were right. Clearly. You knew something and I didn't."

"Anna, it doesn't mean—"

Anna stood up. She dusted off the back of her jeans. "Avery, don't." She held her hand up in the dark. "Just don't. Dad—Russ—and I, we never understood each other. And you didn't ever give a shit about me. Alisha and Jane . . ." She lifted her hands, shrugging to the heavens. "Maybe they're just good people. You know? Better than you or me. Whatever shittiness exists inside Dad—I mean, *Russ*—the bitterness and the anger, we have it. It must be in the air and not genetic. But Alisha and Jane are better than you and me. That explains that."

Avery stood up, and Anna backed away like she feared Avery would wrestle her to the ground and force her to listen. "I came all this way for you. For you, Anna. For the little girl who played with her boats in the bathtub while I watched over her. The one who crawled in bed with me when she got scared. That's you and that's real."

Anna backed farther away. "No, don't do that manipulative shit on me, Avery. Don't play the childhood-memory card. We were in the same house by chance. Sometimes. By accident. And that was a long time ago." Anna's voice caught, just like it had down at the gate when Avery arrived. "Don't push me on this, Avery."

"Okay, I won't."

"You said you had to tell me something. What is it?"

"Oh, shit." Avery wished she didn't have to say it, but she had no choice. "Oh, Anna, you know I came to Louisville with Charlie. To use his contacts to help find you."

"Yeah, you told me."

"There was all that shooting and chaos in the park. And Charlie, I didn't really know this, but he had some health problems."

Anna listened, her head tilted forward. "He has a bad heart. I knew that."

"I guess I didn't know how bad it was." Avery looked at the dirt, her right shoe resting on a twig. "He had an episode of some kind and went to the hospital."

"Don't say it, Avery. I don't want any more bad news."

"I'm sorry. He died in the hospital."

Anna turned away, showing Avery her back. Her shoulders shook.

Avery took a step toward Anna. She placed her hand on her sister's back.

"I'm fine." Anna sniffled and huffed. "I'm fine, Avery."

"I'm sorry to tell you that on top of everything else. Maybe I shouldn't have."

"No, I want to know. I'm tired of shit being kept from me."

"Well, I'm still sorry. He really cared about our family. He wanted to find you."

"I know. . . ." Anna's sniffling slowed. She ran her sleeve across her face. "Jesus, Avery. Kayla. And Charlie. And that girl in the park—did you see her?"

"I did."

"She's dead too, right?"

"I believe she is. Yes."

"What the fuck, Avery?"

"Anna, if you want to talk more—"

"Just leave in the morning. Go home. You can tell . . . those people whatever you want. I'm so fucking mad at them, I don't know if I can ever talk to either one of them again." She jabbed her index finger against her chest, sinking it into the deep down of the coat. "It's my decision to tell them what I want to tell them. Or maybe I'll decide never to speak to them again. Okay?"

"Okay. I'm not trying to convince you of anything, Anna."

Anna wiped at her eyes and sniffled. "Fucking right." She started off, kicking over twigs and stones as she went in the dark. "Just go. And don't try to come and say good-bye. You'll hear from me when you hear from me. Or you won't. I'm here because—because I want to see if this is where I belong. If these are the people I connect with. Okay? Can you let me have that?"

Avery watched her go, disappearing into the darkness.

67

Morris was in the passenger seat as Hardeman pulled his Rydell cruiser up to the gate of the Combs property. It was morning, the sun climbing.

Hardeman had insisted on going along and insisted on driving, which hadn't bothered Morris at all. He'd figured Hardeman would want to go to great lengths to make sure the Combs family was treated as fairly as possible. They had the biggest business in the county, and Hardeman's future as chief of police likely rode on their approval.

Hardeman dropped the car into park but made no move to get out. Morris looked over, impressed by how sharply pressed the man's uniform was. Like he lived in a dry cleaner's shop.

"Are you going to call?" Morris asked. "How do they know we're here?"

"Oh, they know. Just wait."

Morris looked around. The gravel road continued on past the cattle gate and disappeared into the thick trees. There was no way to tell what lay beyond the gate, back on the property, which was exactly the way the Combs family preferred it. And Morris didn't really care what they did. He was investigating a murder, not trying to bust someone for growing and distributing weed. Sure, if a drug charge provided leverage on a murder charge, he'd be happy to explore that option. But something told him the Combs family was well versed in avoiding trouble and keeping their business contained inside the boundaries of their property.

"Here we go," Hardeman said.

Two men came down the gravel road, heading for the gate. Taking their time.

"Do you know these gentlemen?" Morris asked.

"Sure. The one on the left is Taylor Combs. He's the current patriarch of the family. Not a bad guy. I grew up with him. The other is Colby Hogan. He works for the Combs family."

"Doing what?"

Hardeman rubbed his clean-shaven chin. "Well, I guess whatever needs to be done. Let's get out."

They reached the gate at the same time the two men on the other side did. Taylor Combs wore a bright blue UK sweatshirt and a matching hat. His cargo pants were clean, but mud was caked to the soles of his work boots. He looked like any number of men in the state who worked as farmers or contractors or builders. A combination of businessman and laborer.

Colby Hogan rested his left arm on the top of the gate. He wore a suit coat over a sweater, like he was about to step into an important meeting. "Howdy. What could the law possibly want with us on such a fine fall morning?"

Taylor Combs remained silent, hands stuffed into his sweatshirt pockets. A flock of geese in an arrow formation swept by overhead, honking.

It was Hardeman's show, so Morris let him run it.

"Well, we sure are sorry to bother you so early in the day," Hardeman said as though he were seeking favors from a king. "But this is Detective Vic Morris, from down in Breckville. He's up here investigating a case, and he just wanted to ask a few questions."

"That's a long way from home," Hogan said.

"We had a young woman murdered in her apartment near Gracewood's campus," Morris said. "Kayla Garvey. She was just twenty-one. Her parents are devastated, as I'm sure you understand."

"I heard about that," Hogan said, shaking his head. "Terrible."

"Anytime a young life is snuffed out that way, it's terrible," Hardeman said.

"I think we can all agree on that," Morris said. "We're here because we've identified a potential witness. A man named Nicholas Yates. We were hoping to speak with him, but he's proving to be a tough man to track down."

"And you think he's here?" Hogan asked.

Morris addressed his comments to Taylor Combs even though he hadn't yet spoken. "We hoped maybe you'd seen or heard from him."

Taylor Combs kept his eyes locked on Morris. "Do you know anybody named Nicholas Yates, Hogan?"

"I don't seem to recall anyone by that name. You have to understand, Detective, the nature of farmwork is seasonal. And transient. We hire folks for short periods of time, and then they move on to the next place when their work here is done. If this Yates worked here for a short period of time, we may not have known him very well. Or even remember his name."

"I don't think he worked as a field hand," Morris said, moving his eyes from Combs to Hogan and then back again. "He likely did more specialized work."

Hogan laughed. "Most of the specialized work here is done by the family. They do their own books, file their own taxes—which they pay on time, as the chief can tell you. The county sheriff could tell you the same thing. It's a quiet, simple business. If this Mr. Yates is mixed up in something unsavory, we don't like that. And he wouldn't be around here for long."

"Well, we thank you for—"

Morris cut Hardeman off. "This Mr. Yates was seen by a witness outside Kayla Garvey's apartment right before she was killed. And then a police officer spotted Mr. Yates—and started to issue him a parking citation—outside another apartment in Louisville."

"A parking citation? Wow. Dangerous."

"This parking citation, Mr. Hogan, was almost issued outside an apartment where we believe another young woman was staying.

Kayla Garvey's roommate, who may have been the actual target that night. Maybe you know her. Anna Rogers?"

"Anna Rogers?"

"Her father is a retired captain with the Kentucky State Police."

Hogan looked over at Combs, who continued to stare straight ahead at Morris. "I don't believe I know this Anna Rogers you're talking about either. Or her father. Do you, Taylor?"

"No, I don't," Combs said, his lips barely moving as the words came out.

The sun rose higher, grew hot against the back of Morris' neck. "So no Nicholas Yates and no Anna Rogers? You don't know either one."

"We sure don't."

"Well, then—"

Morris cut Hardeman off again. "Would you have any objection to me coming through the gate and looking around? It's possible, as you said, that one of these folks is working for you on a seasonal or temporary basis and you just don't know who they are. But if I could come and have a look, maybe I'll recognize one of them."

"Do you have a warrant for that?" Hogan asked. "Either one of you?"

"No, we sure don't," Morris said.

"It's generally our policy that if someone from law enforcement wants to come onto the property here and start looking around, they need to have a warrant. It's just a policy we follow. I'm sure you understand. We try to follow the law and to limit government overreach."

"I see."

"Is that all you wanted?" Combs asked.

"I think that's it," Morris said.

"Then have a good day," Combs said, already backing up and turning around.

Hogan nodded and fired off a salute in their direction as he followed along behind Taylor Combs.

When Morris and he were back in the car, Hardeman jerked it

into reverse, backed up until they came out onto the county road, and started back for town.

"I didn't know you were going to push them so hard," he said. The muscles in his jaw were clenched.

"You think that was pushing hard?" Morris asked.

"Yes, I do."

"Interesting. To me, that was just a little tap on the shoulder to get their attention."

68

Avery managed to sleep at some point.

She had spent hours on the miserable cot, staring at the rough boards of the cabin, listening to the sounds of the night. Crickets and birds, the haunting call of an owl. Something scurried across the roof of the cabin at one point, and Avery jumped, adrenaline surging through her body.

She guessed she fell asleep around four or five. Until then, she replayed the conversation with Anna. Over and over. No matter how many times she did, it made no more sense. Anna had been adopted but no one had told her. Why not?

Was it possible Alisha knew? Avery and Alisha told each other everything—or so she thought. But had her sister kept this from her?

Avery's mind went to even darker places. Was Alisha really her sister? But Avery pushed those thoughts aside quickly. Avery had seen the photos in her mom's album. Photos of their mom pregnant and Avery just a baby. Photos of their mom and dad bringing Alisha home from the hospital—and Avery was there. Photos of Avery and Alisha at every stage of growing up.

That was real—*wasn't it?*

Avery woke after dreaming of the old man. He was young and able-bodied, and they were in the house they'd lived in before he and her mom split up. And her dad was running around the house, locking the windows and doors, telling them someone was outside trying to get in, and he had to stop them.

Avery looked out the window in the dream, and it was Anna in the yard. The person her dad was trying to keep out of the house—

She sat up on the cot and checked her watch. Eight thirty.

"Shit."

She hadn't slept that late in years. Something about tossing and turning half the night while running over devastating and shocking family news had made it possible for her to sleep late.

She walked out into the bright sun. The day was warm, clear. The fire was cold, the logs reduced to ash. No one was around—the workers all away. Even on a Sunday. She reminded herself not to complain about her job. Ever again. Even arresting drunk frat boys looked pretty good.

Her bladder was full, so she stepped into the woods and found a large tree, then squatted over the loamy dirt. When she came out and looked around, she knew she needed to decide what to do next. Anna had told her to leave—to get lost, essentially. And Avery figured it would accomplish nothing to push her sister—*sister?*—at that point. She needed to get Charlie's truck and keys back, along with her phone. And Charlie's gun.

Anna was on her own journey, and Avery could offer little help.

Except to try to make sure Anna was safe there. On the pot farm run by her biological family.

Avery walked in the direction she'd gone with Anna the night before—down the path she guessed led in the direction of the river and the cave. Soon she came alongside the fallen tree that she and Anna had sat on the night before. How odd that such a nondescript spot had been the site of one of the most puzzling and consequential conversations of her entire life.

Avery kept walking, and the sound of running water increased in volume. As far as Avery could tell, she was the only person in the area. She might as well have been the only person on Combs land.

But that wasn't true. Just as the family watched the front gate and knew when anyone pulled up there, they had to have eyes on every part of the property. She remembered Camila saying she and the other workers never went into the cave. Guess where the Combs family really, *really* wouldn't want Avery to go.

The path angled to the left and led to a small wooden footbridge. The ground sloped down sharply, and the sound of running water increased even more. Avery continued to walk, and the river came into view.

More of a large creek than a river. About fifteen feet across, with the water moving swiftly. The eroded banks showed exposed tree roots and limestone rocks. Avery stepped out onto the worn and weathered boards of the bridge. It looked like it had been there for years. She stopped in the middle, leaned against the top of the railing, and stared down the length of Dead River. It disappeared around a bend one hundred yards away, and Avery guessed that somewhere farther on it ran into the cave.

The water below was muddy, opaque. A small fish jumped, then hit the surface, looking for something to eat. Avery's stomach rumbled. She must have missed whatever food—if any—had been brought to the cabins that morning. Or maybe food was carried out to the fields, directly to the workers.

Avery went across the bridge the rest of the way, to where the trail rose. River birch and pin oak crowded the sides of the path, and when she reached the top of the rise, she could see crops stretched out below her, the farmworkers moving among them. Harvesting.

She tried to guess at the size of the field. Seventy acres or more. Nearly half of it had been harvested already, leaving the land there covered with stubbled stalks cut close to the ground. The workers moved among the remaining stalks, hunched over, cutting off branches by hand. It looked like backbreaking work.

She spotted Camila, with the baby strapped to her back. Gilberto worked nearby, as did the other couple Avery had met at the fire. Working near them were two more men, who looked younger, like teenagers. A swarm of gnats circled in the air.

As Avery went down the hill, moving closer, the smell of the maturing plants reached her. The distinctive odor like skunk that told the grower it was time to take down his plants, cure them, and dry them. It worked its way into her nostrils, almost making her gag. How did the workers breathe that stink all day?

The farmhands didn't seem to notice her. They snipped away at the branches, removing them from the stems, and then carried the harvested crop to a large farm truck that sat off to the side. Its bed already looked to be half full.

Avery tried to do the math but couldn't. Simply put, she was staring at a lot of money in the form of the marijuana crop. A massive amount waiting to be distributed and sold. And other crimes to accompany that process.

The breeze blew lightly across the bottom, where the crop grew. The workers continued at their steady pace. Camila looked up, her baby on her back. It was like she felt Avery's eyes on her. She locked her gaze on Avery for a long moment. Avery lifted her hand, waved.

Camila showed no recognition. She bent to her task and kept harvesting like Avery wasn't there.

One of the others—a guy Avery hadn't seen before—did look at her. He wore a large floppy hat and a baggy long-sleeved T-shirt.

Something squeaked. A door of the truck swinging open.

From the driver's side, a man emerged, wearing sunglasses and a ball cap pulled low on his forehead. He looked to be about thirty, and he wore a puffy vest over a flannel shirt. He looked at the workers, his jaw moving as he chewed gum.

"Hey." He directed the word at all of them among the crops. "Let's pick up the pace a little here. Okay? No looking around."

The guy in the floppy hat said something, a smirk on his face.

The man from the truck stepped forward. His hand came out and swung, a quick, sudden blow. He punched the young guy in the face, knocking him down. The guy rolled on the ground, rubbing his jaw.

Avery felt her heart twist. She expected someone to spring to the guy's defense.

But the migrant workers ignored the violence. They continued to work while the young guy gathered himself.

The man from the truck kicked the guy while he was down. Not hard, but still . . . The guy finally pushed himself to his feet. While he did, the man from the truck stood there, arms crossed. He looked like a general inspecting his troops.

Nothing else happened. The guy went back to work, cowed by the blow to his face, the follow-up kick.

Avery felt sick.

The man from the truck turned, arms still crossed. He spotted Avery and started walking toward her. His face remained stony. Avery spotted the pistol strapped to his hip. A Glock that bounced against his thigh as he came closer.

Avery remained in place.

"Did you need something?" He didn't seem embarrassed or concerned that she might have seen him smack one of the farmworkers.

"Just taking a walk."

"You can't walk here. In fact—" He stopped about ten feet away from her, arms still crossed. "Wait. Are you the sister I'm hearing about?"

"That's right."

"I heard you might be around."

"And you are?"

"Collins. Not that it's any of your business."

"Have you seen Anna this morning, Mr. Collins?"

"You shouldn't be here," he said. "These folks have work to do. And it's best if no one distracts them from that work. They get easily distracted, as you can see. And they can't get distracted. We need them to keep moving."

"I'm not distracting anyone."

Collins' head jerked back slightly. Like a rock had spoken to him. "No one's allowed down here unless they're working." He made a shooing gesture with his hand. "You should head back."

Avery knew Collins wasn't as likely to take his frustration out on her as on the workers. Even though she wanted to say more, wanted to ask him where his horse and whip were, she kept her mouth shut.

"That sounds like good advice," she said. "My cot is so comfortable, I can't wait to get back to it."

One side of Collins' mouth went up in a disapproving half smirk. "Most people who show up here unannounced get worse than that." He jerked his thumb over his shoulder. "Or worse than what he just got. That's nothing."

Before Avery turned to go, a different man, harvesting on the far side of the row of crops, straightened up, shading his eyes with his hand. She couldn't tell from that distance if he was looking at her or trying to get her attention.

But he stared at her—intently. And Collins, with his back to the man, couldn't see what he was doing. That the other man was standing up and not working. He was putting himself in danger from that Collins thug.

Did the man need help? He wore dirty jeans and work boots. He was thin. Almost scarecrowlike in his baggy clothes.

Something about him struck Avery as familiar. His posture, the way he stood with his weight shifted slightly to his left side.

She took a step forward without realizing she was moving. The man's hair was longer than she remembered and he'd grown a thin, patchy beard. If it was . . . He'd tried to grow a beard once before, years earlier. And it had also come in thin and patchy then. As he'd put it, "Not like a man's beard at all."

His name moved to the tip of her tongue. She might have said it out loud, except his eyes shifted, indicating Collins, and Avery knew she couldn't give the man away. That he'd stopped working, even for a moment.

That he'd recognized her. Knew her.

He bent down to work again, slicing away at the plant in front of him.

Collins cocked his head as if he might have seen Avery notice the other man. So Avery quickly backed away.

No, she didn't speak the man's name, but it lingered in her mouth. And in her mind.

It was him. She knew it.

Hank.

69

Avery stumbled slightly as she started up the hill. She hated to think of Collins seeing her wobble, the full-on smirk it likely brought to his face.

But getting out of there was the right thing to do.

Clearly, the migrant workers were in jeopardy. She couldn't put them more at risk.

She would also put Hank in jeopardy if anyone learned he was a cop.

She continued up the hill, toward the river and the cabins. As she walked, her calves groaning as she climbed the slope, she thought about Hank. It *was* him. Scruffier and scragglier. But him. Working on the farm. Having infiltrated for KSP.

It explained the unanswered texts. The evasiveness about his whereabouts. She tried to make her concern for his safety the dominant emotion—not relief that she hadn't come off as a clinging, needy ex-girlfriend who couldn't get her texts answered. Hank was risking a lot to be there. It was better if she left—not only the fields but the whole farm as well.

The river rushed by. Someone stood on the bridge, in almost exactly the same spot Avery had paused just a few minutes earlier. The man stared into the water and didn't look her way until she stepped onto the bridge, the boards creaking beneath her shoes.

"Mr. Yates," she said.

"So formal. You can call me Nick, *Ms.* Rogers."

"I don't think we're going to grow to be friends. But in a way you're just the man I wanted to see."

"Oh?"

"It looks like my sister intends to stay, and I'm not sure I can do anything about that even if I wanted to. And it's possible my being here will only crowd her and make her journey more difficult."

Yates nodded. "That's very enlightened of you."

"I don't know about that. But sometimes being in a family means knowing when to step aside, even if you don't want to."

Yates adjusted his stance on the bridge, looked down into the water again. "My understanding is the two of you aren't family. Not the way you thought you were."

"Is everybody talking about that around here?"

"It's a small farm."

"I know my dad and her mom are still going to think of Anna as their daughter. Nothing is going to change that for them."

"Does it change anything for you?" he asked, looking back at her.

Avery had been thinking about that question all night. "No, it doesn't. It's complicated, but it's always been complicated with Anna and me and our family. A second marriage. A stepmother."

"And your father, the former cop? I guess your dad and stepmother are the ones who are going to have the answers, right? If you went back and told them about all of this, then they'd likely have to say how Anna came to be raised by them and why they never told any of you. Right?"

Yates' attitude had shifted. They were connecting. Commiserating. Now he seemed to know something he was enjoying not telling her.

"I think that sounds about right," she said. Cautious. "That's why I wanted to see you. Last I knew, the truck keys and the truck were in your possession. Along with my other belongings. If I'm going to leave, then I need those back."

"Indeed you do."

"So . . . can you make that happen for me?"

"Perhaps you misunderstand my position at this outfit," Yates said. "I'm not really one of the people who make the decisions around here. I do what I'm told. When I'm told. But I can tell you this—I can't give you your keys or your truck or your phone or your gun back. I can't do anything like that at all."

He turned his attention to the water again like he might be ready to take a header off the bridge.

"How do you think the workers are treated here?" Avery asked.

He continued to stare straight ahead. "Shit flows downhill."

"Seriously, though."

"Seriously, though. You should drop it."

Avery couldn't say for sure what was going on with the man, but she'd hit a dead end with him. She brushed past him without saying anything else and started for the main house.

"Oh, Avery?"

She stopped and looked back.

Yates lifted his eyebrows. "I know it gets cold in these cabins at night. And the blankets aren't the best. If you need someone to keep you warm during those long hours, I'm available. Maybe I'll come by. . . ."

Bitterness rose in the back of Avery's throat. She felt sick.

She shook her head and walked off, her hands shaking.

70

Anna came downstairs and went into the dining room, where she heard voices chattering.

At the long, smoothly varnished barn table, two kids, the son and daughter of Taylor and Brittany Combs, sat before plates of pancakes. The kids seemed every bit as intent on staring at their iPads and arguing with each other as they did on eating.

But they looked up when she came in.

"Anna."

The smile spread across her face. "Hey, guys." She came into the room and stopped on the opposite side of the table without sitting. The kids were twelve and ten, Cash and Carrie-Ann. Both blond haired and blue eyed.

"You slept late," Carrie-Ann said.

"I was tired."

"Are you going to eat now?" Cash asked.

"Where's your mom?"

"She's in the kitchen. Are you going to eat with us?"

"You look more interested in those screens," Anna said.

"We're allowed to have them at the table during Sunday breakfast. That's the only time."

"Really? My roommate and I—well, we used to always have our phones out when we ate together. I guess that's what happens when you're in college."

"Lucky," Cash said.

The thought of Kayla made Anna both sick and sad. "Yeah, I was lucky."

"What's the matter?" Carrie-Ann asked. "Are you hungry?"

"No, just thinking about my roommate. I'm going to go talk to your mom for a minute."

"She'll make you a pancake if you ask," Cash said.

"I'll be sure to say 'please.'"

"You have to. Or she won't."

Anna went through the swinging door that led from the dining room to the kitchen. As it whooshed shut behind her, she imagined—and not for the first time—that that was what it had been like for Avery and Alisha growing up so close in age. The bickering, the shared language and experience. Meals and baths and beds side by side. Those two—Cash and Carrie-Ann—were her . . . what? Cousins? She couldn't say—and no one had really told her. But her sisters sat on one side of her, and those two kids sat on the other. Pairs of close siblings—and Anna in the middle, alone.

"Hey," Brittany said. "You hungry?"

"I heard a rumor there are pancakes."

"You can hear those two all over the county. I practically had to tie them to their chairs so they'd let you sleep."

"Thanks. I was tired."

"I bet. Was the bed comfortable?"

"Oh my gosh, Brittany, it was the most comfortable bed I've ever slept in."

"Wow, that's good to hear. It cost us enough." She started pouring batter onto a skillet, her back to Anna. Brittany wore her blond hair in a long ponytail, and her robe—which looked like it might have been cashmere—accentuated her curves perfectly. She was barefoot, and moved around the kitchen with the easy grace of a dancer. Anna guessed she was about forty. "I heard you go out last night. Late."

Anna felt like a schoolkid who had been caught doing something wrong. "Oh, did I wake you?"

"No, I was up reading." The batter started to sizzle. "I always stay up late. It's the only time the house is quiet. I imagine you went out to see your sister. Avery, right?"

"Right."

"I'll just tell you—somebody always knows what you're doing on this farm. That's the way it is around here. If I heard you, then Hogan heard you. Or Collins. You met him, right?"

"Briefly. Was I not supposed to go talk to Avery?"

"I didn't say that," Brittany said. "Just . . . you know . . . Do you want to sit? Do you want juice or coffee?"

"Coffee. I think the kids want me out there."

"Those boogers will be okay."

Anna sat at the breakfast bar while Brittany poured coffee and placed the steaming mug in front of her. Anna wanted to inhale it, but she sipped because it was so hot.

Brittany returned her attention to the giant gas stove, with its gleaming subway-tile backsplash. She gently moved the pancakes around with a spatula. Anna watched her back, watched her ponytail swish around as she worked.

"Is Taylor around?" Anna asked.

Brittany shook her head. "He and Colby went out early this morning. There's a bee in their bonnets about something. Always is."

Anna felt relief even as the caffeine made her heart beat faster. "I wanted to ask you something. And it seems like Taylor didn't really want to talk about it last night."

"Oh?" Brittany seemed to be feigning nonchalance. Maybe Anna imagined it, but Brittany's body looked like it had tensed under the robe. "What's that?" She turned with a plate, two fluffy pancakes on top. She put the plate in front of Anna and then handed over a fork, a cloth napkin, and a bottle of syrup. "Butter?"

"No, thanks."

Brittany pushed her robe sleeves up and leaned against the other side of the breakfast bar. A tattoo of a tai chi symbol decorated the pale flesh on the inside of her left forearm. "What do you want to know?"

Anna cut into the pancake stack, forked a piece into her mouth. "Mmmm. Wow."

"Thanks."

"Damn, you should open a restaurant."

"Weekends are the only time I really get to cook. Someone helps out during the week. You know, there's food to be made for everyone who works here. It's a lot."

Anna ate another bite, chased it with coffee. She suppressed another moan over the taste of the food. "I'm sure you understand that I'm trying to figure out what's going on and how I'm related to you all."

"Well, yeah, of course."

Brittany was the picture of Kentucky hospitality and wholesomeness. Open, inviting, warm. But—

"Last night, during dinner, when I tried to talk about it, well, no one really seemed to want to go there. Especially Taylor and Mr. Hogan."

"Really? Did you think that?"

"They seemed to want to steer the conversation in other directions. Politely, I guess. But still . . ."

"Hmm." Brittany straightened up. Again her nonchalance seemed forced. "Well, they're men. What do you expect? They don't like to talk about anything. I'm lucky if I get a grunt out of Taylor."

"Sure. My ex-boyfriend was like that too. My friend Eric isn't, but Trevor was." Anna ate another bite and then another. "But since it's just us now, and since you and I are the ones who are related, right? You came up as my match on the DNA site. It says we might be cousins. Or we might be half-siblings. Or maybe I'm your niece. I don't know anything, but you must. So can you tell me anything you know?"

Brittany scratched her head. The kitchen door swung open, and the two kids burst through and slid to a stop on socked feet. "Is Anna going to eat with us?"

"She's eating here. Look." Cash pointed, like they'd caught Anna breaking the law.

"Hey," Brittany said, "I'm talking to Anna, okay? Grown-up talk. You two go upstairs."

"Really?" Cash asked.

"Yes. Really. Leave your dishes out there and go."

Carrie-Ann looked suspicious. "You're letting us leave our dirty dishes on the table?"

"Yes, because I'm the best mother ever. Now go on, get upstairs. You can bother Anna later."

The kids turned and went out through the door as fast as they had come in.

"They're too cute," Anna said.

"They are. You can have some of your own someday."

"Oh, no. I don't know about that."

"You might change your mind," Brittany said. "You have time. We waited awhile before we had ours. I was thirty. Most of my friends from growing up had kids when they were twenty."

"That's too young."

"It is."

"So, what can you tell me about how we're related?"

Brittany scratched her head again. "Taylor doesn't like to talk about this. That's why he was so closed off last night." She looked around the kitchen. "It's times like these I wish I still smoked."

Anna finished eating, placed her silverware on the plate, and moved it away. Brittany noticed. She removed the plate and refilled Anna's coffee mug.

"Here's the thing, Anna. This is difficult for me too." She swallowed hard, and her eyes filled. "I think you're my brother's baby. My brother, Danny."

71

Anna scooted forward on her stool.

If she had gone another inch farther, she'd have fallen off. Her curiosity had spiked, hitting her body like a surge of adrenaline.

"So you think I'm your niece? Did—did something happen to your brother?"

"He's passed," Brittany said. "That's why it's tough for me to talk about."

"I'm sorry, Brittany." The impulse struck Anna to say that they didn't need to keep talking if the subject was too painful, that they could steer clear of it, pretend like it wasn't hovering there between them.

But she couldn't. This was *her* identity. And she hadn't come all that way not to find out what was really going on with the DNA test and everything else. They were talking about her family as well. Her parents.

"It's okay," Brittany said.

"Why do you think he might be my father?" The words sounded so strange. For her entire life, those words had meant something—*someone*—very specific. They had meant her dad. Captain Russ Rogers. Big Russ. But now . . .

"We were estranged from him when he died," Brittany said. "Taylor and I weren't even married yet, but Danny and Taylor were good friends. They worked together too. You know"—she waved her hand in the air, indicating the farm and its business—"my and Danny's papaw bought this land. Years ago. The family farmed it. Not the same crop as now . . . Our dad started that line of work, and Danny and Taylor continued with it. My dad died when I was eighteen, and my mom didn't want to run the place. Taylor stepped up and bought the property. He always dreamed big. He built things here, maybe took more risks. I guess Danny wasn't as enthusiastic about the direction of things. That happens, you know. So we all had a falling-out, and for about a year we didn't speak."

Brittany's words stopped. Shut off like someone had quickly turned the knob on a spigot, shutting off the flow. Her eyes filled again, but no tears spilled down her cheeks. She sniffled, wiped the back of her hand across her nose.

"What happened to him?" Anna asked.

"Them," Brittany said.

"'Them'?"

"Danny was married. And he had a little daughter. Somebody killed them. All three of them. The murders have never been solved."

"Oh, God. All of them. The child—their daughter too?"

"Yes. All of them. Shot to death in their home. Not far from here."

Brittany turned her back to Anna. She dug around in the sink, pretending to wash a dish. But Anna didn't believe she was really doing anything. She was just collecting herself, turning away from Anna until she was sure she wouldn't cry.

Anna let Brittany take her time even though the questions surged through her body faster than adrenaline. When Brittany turned around again, she apologized.

"It's just—with you here, after all this time, it's bringing everything up in a way I thought it wouldn't. And you—you look like him. Like Danny. And, really, like me. When I saw you . . ."

"I didn't mean to cause any problems for you, Brittany."

"Oh, no, honey. Don't feel that way. Please. I want you to be here. I do. See, that's why I took the test in the first place. I wanted to know if maybe you were out there."

"Why did you think I was? Wait—how could I be out there if they were all killed, including the daughter?"

Brittany reached up, placed her hand on her forehead. "I think . . . I think Danny's wife, Shelby, was pregnant in the time leading up to the murders. I knew she wanted to have more kids. We weren't talking then—none of us were talking then—but I ran into a mutual friend about two months before they died. She was careful about what she said. . . . She knew all of us weren't on the best terms, but she hinted . . . she hinted that maybe Shelby was pregnant. And far along. I didn't know anything for sure, but like I said, it was a feeling I had."

"So you're saying . . . that if I was there then . . . what? They let me live?"

"Who could shoot a baby? An infant? And I'm guessing the cops found you and handed you over to the state. You were put up for adoption and here you are now. We found each other."

"Yeah . . ."

"Taylor didn't want me to take the DNA test. I talked about it, and he said it was a bad idea. He doesn't trust the government, doesn't want his information in some database somewhere. For obvious reasons. I get that. I do. I have the same fears. But I always had that nagging question, so I went ahead and did it. Just to see. It was a long shot, like buying a lottery ticket. My information was up there for almost two years before there was a match as close as yours. I didn't tell Taylor until after I saw we matched. And even then, he was angry I had done it. He was worried. He didn't know who you might be. . . . He wanted to—"

Her words shut off again. Like she was about to say something she shouldn't.

"He wanted to what?"

"He was just worried, that's all. Protective. That's how men are."

Anna suspected there was something more, something that wasn't being said. But maybe it wasn't time to push. Not yet.

Instead, she said, "But all of this is speculation. You don't know anything for sure about your sister-in-law or there being a baby. Right?"

"I feel it."

Anna decided to let it go. Brittany seemed convinced, and who was she to argue with Brittany's feelings? She had more questions anyway.

One more. A big one.

"Who killed your brother and his family, then? You must have a guess. The police must have suspects."

Brittany shook her head. "They never told us anything, except it's an ongoing investigation. And that there were two guns, two different shooters. And they always said that, given Danny's line of work . . . And that's true. It's a dangerous business to be in. Maybe that's why Danny wanted to get out. It's always possible Danny cheated somebody. Or owed somebody money. Maybe something happened after we all stopped speaking. But I always thought . . . maybe it was closer to home. . . ."

"Meaning what?"

"I don't know. That's just another feeling. Look, just do me a favor. Don't bring this up with Taylor. Or with Hogan. Okay? If you want to talk about this with me, it's okay. We can talk about anything. But those guys . . . they do their own thing."

"When I go home, I can ask my parents—or whoever they are. I guess . . ."

"They're your parents. They raised you."

"Yeah, I guess so." What did these words even mean: parents, family, sisters? Did this news about the DNA wipe away the previous twenty-one years? "I can ask them. Maybe they'll tell me now. . . ."

"They might. And you should go see them. But I do hope you stay with us for a while. And get to know us. If you're Danny's girl, you're part of this family. I want to know you."

Anna was willing to stay, because she had a lot more questions.

"Brittany, can you please tell me . . . what do you mean the killer might be close to home?"

Brittany started to say something, then stopped. She stared past Anna and shook her head. "Oh, it's nothing. Just silly things I think about sometimes."

72

Hogan walked back up the drive and toward the house with Taylor at his side.

The two men remained quiet.

Hogan knew that Taylor would speak when he wanted to, that his mind was turning over the visit from the two cops—Hardeman from town and Morris from Breckville. Hogan took one sidelong glance at his boss, saw Taylor's jaw muscles working under the skin. The unexpected visitors and rediscovered family connections were cranking up the tension.

It was Brittany who had submitted her DNA to the website—without Taylor knowing—and Hogan suspected Taylor was as steamed at his wife as at anyone else. The problems reaching the farm extended into the Combses' marital bed. Only a fool would have meddled in that. Brittany wasn't the kind of woman who could be told what to do. She carried herself with confidence and possessed her own mind. The couple rarely talked for real in front of Hogan, but he suspected Brittany was included in a lot of decisions Taylor had to make about the farm.

For all Hogan knew, Brittany was the brains behind the whole operation.

But submitting her DNA to a website and bringing a flesh-and-blood ghost to her front gate wasn't the smartest play.

The house came into view. The wide porch was empty, most of the curtains behind the front windows open. The trees rustled around them, and Hogan squinted against the morning light. He puffed on his cigarette and wished for more coffee. He'd been about to have a cup when the cops showed up at the gate.

"This is because of Yates," Taylor said. "You did tell him to stay put?"

"Of course."

Even though Taylor was ten years younger than Hogan, they both knew who was in charge. Hogan drew hard on his cigarette. He wanted at least to clarify that Brittany submitting her DNA had precipitated everything, but he couldn't say that. The man with the most money possessed the most power and authority. It was a simple way to understand that world.

Where the gravel drive reached what served as the open front yard, Taylor stopped and let his eyes wander up to the house. He wore his usual outfit—a zip-up UK fleece and a UK hat. He took his time before saying anything. Hogan tossed his cigarette down and ground it out.

"Where is he?" Taylor asked. He meant Yates.

"I'm not sure. He slept down in the north cabins. I know that."

Taylor took a deep breath through his nostrils and let it back out. "He knows a lot."

"He does."

"He seems . . . unpredictable. If you told him to stay, and he didn't . . ."

"You're right."

"We need to be very careful. If someone comes around thinking we're involved in a murder . . ."

"I agree."

"My children are here. I can't have them around this."

Hogan understood what Taylor meant. He wasn't referring to the cops coming to the gate, although he didn't want that happening with his family around either. No, Taylor meant something else. And Hogan got it. That was a big part of Hogan's job—to infer things that were only implied. To proceed with certainty when Taylor supplied none.

When Taylor had asked Hogan to find someone in Breckville to locate the girl—Anna—from the DNA test, to keep an eye on her and see what she was all about, he made the request directly. There was nothing to hide—Yates was just supposed to watch. To report. To talk to her only if it was safe.

But now Yates was a problem.

A big problem.

"I can talk to him. After dark."

Taylor nodded. They were both about to start for the house when Avery Rogers appeared on the far side of the clearing, coming from the direction of the cabins and the fields. She looked very much like a woman on a mission.

73

Avery saw the two men—Hogan and Combs—and altered her course.

They stood next to each other at the edge of the yard, looking very much like two neighbors having a chat on a pleasant fall morning. As she walked toward them, she looked at the house, where light reflected off the many small windows. Anna was in there, maybe even looking out and watching her.

Had she really come so far and so close to her sister only to leave without her?

It felt like Anna was far out of reach, like she'd moved into another orbit, one that didn't include Avery.

She reached the two men. Combs' face remained neutral, stoic, the same mask Collins had worn down by the crops. But Hogan offered a used-car salesman's smile as he dug out his pack of cigarettes and lit one.

"Ms. Rogers," he said, "did you have a restful night?"

"Not really. And the morning hasn't been any better."

"I'm sorry to hear that. We do our best to provide decent accommodations for the farmworkers, but there's a lot of turnover in this business. We can't always know who is staying in the cabins or if they're likely to take good care of them."

"That must be why you have an overseer watching them, a guy with a gun who looked like he just wandered out of *Cool Hand Luke.*"

Avery hadn't planned to say anything, but the words rolled out. And once they were in the air, Combs and Hogan exchanged a look.

"Did you go for a morning stroll?" Hogan asked. He tried to keep the used-car salesman vibe going, but the skin on his face stretched tight while he talked.

"I did. Down by the river."

Combs studied her. Avery tried to decide which one of the two men she trusted less. Sure, Hogan looked like the epitome of trouble, his hail-fellow-well-met bullshit disguising contempt and likely a capacity for violence.

But only one thing emanated from Combs—coldness. Like a fire gave off heat, the man exuded cold, a chill that nearly made Avery shiver even as she stood in the midmorning sun.

"We offer employment in a depressed part of the state," Combs said. "We give jobs to people who might not ordinarily find them."

Avery decided it was time to back off. "Look, I'm not a labor lawyer. Okay? I came to talk to you because—"

"Anna says you were a police officer for a few years," Combs said, "and you still work in security down in Breckville."

"That's right. But I'm not here in any official capacity. I'm here because of my—because of Anna." She thought of Hank toiling in the fields under the watchful eye of Collins. She had no idea how long he'd been there, how close he was to making a move with KSP. "I was looking for you because I'm ready to leave. Anna doesn't seem to want to have anything to do with me, so I'm giving her space. When I showed up here, you all took my keys and phone and all that. I need to get back to Breckville. My job and school."

"Anna indicated the two of you aren't really that close," Combs said.

Avery looked at the house again. "You got a lot of information out of Anna in one evening."

"My wife is good at making people feel comfortable."

"Anna and I haven't always been close, that's true. I'm trying to do right by her now and get out of her way. She wants me to leave, so . . . I'm leaving. I don't have any luggage. I just need my keys and things."

Avery addressed her comments to Combs, figuring it was his land, his house, his rules. But it was Hogan who answered, acting like he was the mouthpiece for Combs.

"We were hoping you would stay a little longer," he said. "You just got here, and we don't want you running off so soon."

He spoke the words calmly and without any real inflection, which made them only seem more menacing.

"Maybe you didn't understand me. I'm ready to leave now. I just need to know where Yates parked the truck, and then somebody has to give me the keys. And the phone and the gun. And then I'll be out of here."

"You said you went down by the crops and you saw Collins down there. Right?"

"I did see him. And we chatted. He's an . . . interesting guy."

"You didn't like what you saw?"

"Was I supposed to?"

Hogan drew on his cigarette and then studied the tip, like there might be something interesting there. Combs stood by, listening but not saying or doing anything.

"We have people like Collins working here," Hogan said, "just to keep everything as secure as possible. And we're going to let everyone know you'll be staying with us a little longer."

The two men stood between her and the gate. With no keys and no phone, even if she did get past them—which seemed unlikely—what would she do out there? Flag down a passing car, when it seemed like no cars passed? Walk back to Rydell and find the chief of police, who seemed to be a master of turning a blind eye?

Or wait—and . . . hope something else came to mind to get her out of there?

Her recent conversation with Yates ran through her head. The bitter taste rose inside her throat. She nearly gagged.

She remembered sinking below the water that day on the side of the interstate. She felt like she was sinking now. Options being closed off, doors closing.

The murky dark even in the bright sun.

"Why don't you go back to your cabin?" Hogan said.

"Are you serious?"

Hogan made one small gesture. He placed his hand on his waist, and the movement caused his suit coat to pull back, revealing the shoulder holster and the gun attached to the side of his chest.

He might as well have whipped his dick out and waved it in the air.

"Are you threatening me? You can't just—"

Hogan's hand came out, gripped Avery's forearm like a giant clamp. It seemed like little effort on his part, but he pushed at her, and she stumbled in the direction of the cabins. She almost went down but caught herself.

Anger flooded her chest. She started back toward them, felt her hand rising in a fist.

But the two men stood still, unflinching. Unyielding.

She looked at the house one more time, wondered if there was any chance Anna had seen what was happening.

Would she even care?

Avery's heart thumped. The walls were closing in.

She felt powerless. She hated feeling powerless.

Hogan took a step toward her. "Go on. Go."

Avery backed away, retreating to her cabin. She was out of options. For now.

PART IV

By the middle of the afternoon, Yates started to worry.

He had been on thin ice before he showed up at the farm. Bringing Anna Rogers right to their door was supposed to erase the sin from his record. Namely, the way he had squeezed the life out of the girl in Breckville. Rather than run, he'd taken his best shot with Hogan and the Combs family, hoping he'd so impressed them that they'd see the value he could bring to the operation.

And for a while it had looked like his plan had worked.

They were all so happy to see the girl they'd been looking for. They welcomed her in like she was the prodigal daughter, which, in a way, maybe she was. Hogan had shaken his hand and told him he'd done well for himself. Even Taylor Combs, who had never spoken one word to Yates, had nodded his way and said one word. "Thanks."

But today felt different.

Colder.

Yates figured he'd be sleeping in the house, but late last night Hogan had directed him out to the north cluster of cabins, where a few of the migrant workers stayed. Yates slept on a musty cot with a threadbare blanket to keep him warm. He shat in the woods like a homeless person and borrowed toilet paper from one of the others—James? Joseph?—in order to wipe himself.

Then that morning . . . nothing.

Yates started up to the house, expecting to get something to eat. Instead, on the trail, he ran into the guard Collins, the guy who looked like a graduate of the Blackwater school of intimidation. Collins carried a basket of food for all the workers, who were already up and preparing to go out to harvest weed all day. For a moment, Yates thought Collins would send him on up to the house, but Collins told him his food was in the basket too. So Yates sat around with the laborers and ate breakfast sandwiches and drank coffee, while Collins stood nearby with his hand resting in the vicinity of the Glock on his hip. Yates started to worry that Collins was going to order him out to the fields with the workers. He didn't. But he told Yates to stay close to the cabins and to wait until someone told him what to do.

What was he? A child?

He refused to sit like he was in a time-out. So he spent the day wandering around, even though there was little to see. He watched the workers harvest. He stared into the murky depths of the river.

And saw the sister—Avery Rogers—walking by.

She didn't see him, since he was still on the side path that led down to the cave. He stayed still, like a predator stalking prey in the woods, and watched her heading toward the fields.

He followed quietly behind her on the chance that he could learn something that might help his cause. Or, short of that, he could be distracted for a little bit since he was in the woods with no phone and no one to talk to.

She went down by the fields and watched as Collins came out of his truck and smacked around the punk field hand. The woman cop seemed to give him a little grief—good for her—but not enough to change anything. And before she turned around to come back up to the river, Yates decided to turn around as well, so she didn't know he'd been watching her.

But before he turned, he saw one of the guys working in the field—the very one who'd loaned him toilet paper that morning—staring intently at the sister while Collins' back was to him.

Like he thought he knew her. Like this James or Joseph dude wanted to say something to her but couldn't.

Yates filed that away, didn't say anything about the other man when she came walking past him again on the bridge. She wanted to know about her truck and her keys, and he told her the truth—all of that was out of his hands. He possessed very little power there. Maybe he pushed too hard, suggesting he might come by her cabin during the night. But she wasn't bad-looking, not by a long shot, and what else was there to do with them all stuck out in the woods? He couldn't touch the younger sister—she was way off-limits. But the older one, the one who had shown up and stirred the pot? Did anybody care what happened to her?

Combs and Hogan weren't just going to let her leave free and clear, were they?

She stormed off toward the house like she was going to give somebody a piece of her mind, like she was going to chew out the manager in a store. Did she really think that would work with Hogan or Combs or anybody else here?

She was jumping up and down on thin ice.

He didn't see her after that.

He didn't see anyone until late in the day, when the workers returned to their cabins, with the air of exhaustion you had only when you'd been doing hard work. Real work. The kind of physical labor Yates had done one summer for a landscaping service. That was also the summer he'd decided he didn't want to do physical labor the rest of his life.

Somebody built a fire as the sun went down. Collins brought more food, and they all sat around eating. No one bothered to ask Yates why he was there. He assumed that meant they were used to people passing through from time to time without anyone really knowing what they were doing. Or that the workers, mostly young people and immigrants, knew that they should keep their heads down, that not asking questions or knowing too much was a solid policy for making it on the Combs farm.

Conversation during the meal was light. He figured the workers were all too tired and hungry, and with Yates—a guy they knew nothing at all about—sitting there in the middle of them, they focused on eating and not talking. Everyone chewed and stared into the flickering and popping fire like it held the secrets of the universe. The night grew colder once the sun was gone, and the only thing that seemed to exist was the circle of light created by the flames.

Yates wanted to believe that was the whole world as well. He wanted to believe things were that simple and focused. But they weren't. He might be fighting for survival. He needed any advantage he could get.

Then James or Joseph stood up, brushing crumbs off his work pants, and moved out of the firelight and back into the trees, likely to go to the bathroom. Yates gave him a few minutes and let him find a private place to do his business. Then he rose and followed.

75

Yates moved through the dark woods. Insects chirped in the tall grass.

He managed to discern a small path, worn to dirt by who knew how many pairs of feet trudging over it. Maybe it had been there since Native people roamed the land. It gave him a nice sense of epic purpose to walk that way. Like he was doing more than just trying to save his own skin from a bunch of rural criminals. He was fitting into a long line of warriors who fought for survival.

Something rustled in the brush ahead of him. It had to be the guy.

Yates kept going, moving slowly, making sure he didn't trip over a tree root or a rock. Soon enough the guy came into view ahead of him. A skinny dude with a patchy beard. Dirty clothes and a drawn face. He carried a small flashlight that provided faint illumination in the dark. He tilted it down so it didn't blind Yates.

"Hey, man," Yates said. "Hitting the head?"

"Exactly. You too?"

"Yeah." Yates didn't have to pee, but it sounded like a good cover for why he was back there, following the dude around in the dark. "They had you all put in a long day, huh?"

"Harvesttime."

The guy smiled, but he couldn't cover how exhausted he was. Yates saw it in his drawn cheeks, his red-rimmed eyes. The slump of his shoulders.

Yates gambled with his fifty-fifty chance. "It's James, right?"

"Yeah, James. And you're Nick, right?"

"Right on."

The two men stood there for an awkward moment. Two guys with not much to say to each other, which was pretty much any two guys Yates had ever known. An owl hooted in a distant tree, lonely as a train whistle.

"Well," James said, "I'll let you get—"

"Hold up, though," Yates said.

"Yeah?"

"I wanted to ask you something."

James looked guarded. It was the same look everyone on the farm wore. Yates understood. In his line of work—doing jobs for people like the Combses—he needed to keep his guard up. All the time. There was no way to know when trouble, real trouble, might be coming down. Or who would be bringing it.

Something flapped its wings in the tree overhead, shaking the remaining leaves. Yates asked, "Did you see that chick hanging around the crops this morning? The one who just showed up out of nowhere but doesn't seem to be working here or anything?"

James scratched at the scraggly little beard he wore. The kind a high school or college kid would grow on summer break. But, up close, Yates could see James was older than that. Much closer to thirty than twenty.

"I didn't see her," he said. "Who is she?"

Yates' spine tingled. The guy was lying. Flat-out lying. He didn't know Yates had seen him giving the chick the eye, and now for some reason he wanted to pretend that he hadn't even seen her.

Why?

"I don't know who she is," Yates said. A light wind kicked up. "But she's poking around. I thought maybe she knew you, since she was kind of looking your way."

"She was? Weird."

Yates had to hand it to the guy. He was a good liar. He didn't flinch or stammer or shift his weight from one foot to the other. He maintained eye contact with Yates the whole time. He never wavered.

"I don't know who she is," Yates said. "I mean, her sister's here, and then she showed up as well. They have some ties to the family. You know?"

"No, I don't. I just keep my head down and work. I don't want any trouble. I'm trying to finish this harvest and then get out West. I've got a buddy in California who can put me up. Harvest some shit out there. In the sunshine."

"Hmm. Sounds good."

"Yeah, I'm looking forward to it." James stretched a little, looking tired. Trying to be casual. "What about you? You working here?"

"I do some work for the family. Just usually not on the farm. I had to deliver a package here."

"I see. A courier."

"Right. I'm just chilling for a couple of days and then moving on."

"Sweet. I guess I'm going to turn in. We'll be up early again tomorrow. They want to finish the harvest in the next week."

James started to go, but Yates reached out, placed his hand on the guy's scrawny arm. When he touched it, he felt the corded muscle there. The guy wasn't a weakling. Maybe working in the fields had sharpened his muscles. Or maybe the guy had been fit before he showed up here to wield his pruning shears.

"This chick I'm telling you about," Yates said. "The one who gave you the eye?"

James looked down where Yates' hand touched—held—his arm. Something passed across the guy's eyes, a blankness that undercut his chill-hippie vibe. This was a dude who didn't like—or wasn't used to—people grabbing hold of his arm. He was a guy used to being in control of interactions.

James looked back up. His voice was flat. "What about her?"

"She used to be a cop, man. Can you believe that? She used to be a cop."

The blankness remained in his eyes, and he hesitated before answering. "That sounds like a problem," he said finally. "What's she doing here?"

"Snooping around. Making trouble."

Yates let that hang in the air for a moment, and then he slid his hand off the guy's arm.

"Well," James said, "she ought to mind her own business."

"Yeah. Okay, man. I got to take a leak myself."

"Cool."

James started to walk away, brushing past Yates up the path and back toward the cabins and the fire.

As he walked away, Yates said, "James?"

The man stopped, looked back. The flashlight pointed at the ground, showed a dark centipede scurrying across the path and into the weeds. "Yeah?"

Yates wanted to ask the man why he had been staring at Avery so hard. Did he know her?

Did he know her because she was a cop?

But Yates decided not to ask. He'd see if he could use what he knew at some other time to help preserve his own hide. Some things were better left unsaid. Some cards better held until later in the game.

"Nothing, man," Yates said. "I just never really thanked you for the poop paper this morning."

James smiled, still guarded. "You're welcome."

And he walked off into the dark.

76

Avery was sitting outside when the farmhands came back at sundown.

She'd gone ahead and built a fire, making sure it was waiting for them when they returned from work. It seemed like the least she could do, since they were harvesting crops all day under the abusive attention of the man named Collins. She wished she could do more.

She replayed the encounter with Hogan and Combs over and over. The one with Yates too. And whenever she did, she felt anger grow inside her chest, felt her arm burn where Hogan had grabbed her. Felt sick when she thought of Yates threatening her. But she pushed her anger down, reminded herself not to let that become the dominant emotion she felt as she sat around waiting and staring at the wooden walls. She told herself to be smart, to make a plan and figure out the best way to leave. Too many times she jumped without looking, let her emotions rule the day, whether it was dealing with drunken frat boys or belligerent cops in the park.

And to leave without jeopardizing anyone else—Anna, Hank, the migrant workers.

If it was even possible to do that . . .

When the workers came back and sat around the crackling fire, there was tension there that hadn't existed before. Everyone stared forward, lips pressed tight. Vladimir kept his head down, but the light caught marks on the side of his neck.

Bruises.

More of Collins' handiwork?

Celina sat next to him, her eyes wide and fearful.

Avery wanted to ask, felt the words leap into her mouth, but she held them back. She shivered.

Camila tended to the baby in her arms. Avery remembered waving at her that morning—and the stony look she received in return. She considered apologizing but thought that might make it worse. She pretended nothing had happened, nodding her greeting to them as the farmhands sat and mostly remained silent. The fire chased away the descending chill.

Collins arrived not long after the workers, carrying a basket of food. He refused to make eye contact with Avery or anyone else, but when he put the basket on the ground, dropping it there like it was a bag of garbage, he said, "The boss says eat and then go inside. He doesn't want to see anyone outside of these cabins tonight. If you have to go to the bathroom, go fast and get back inside. Hear me?"

Everyone nodded. Even Vladimir.

Collins turned and left.

Avery tried to gauge whether Collins' order was typical or something that had never happened before. Again the others kept their faces blank, avoiding eye contact with Avery as they all ate in silence.

Near the end of the meal, Vladimir and Celina went into their cabin. Gilberto nudged Camila and said something, his jaw taut, his words harsh. Camila responded in an equally sharp tone. When Gilberto spoke again, he nodded his head toward Avery, who understood what was going on. Avery spoke in a low voice.

"I'm sorry about earlier," she said. "I won't come near the fields again. I understand now. *Lo siento.*"

Gilberto heard the words but remained stone-faced. Camila nodded. "Okay," she said. "It's okay. We just want to finish. It's almost over. If not, they threaten. ICE. Immigration. We want no trouble."

"I know. Neither do I. Not for you."

Gilberto stood up, waved his hand for Camila to go to the cabin with him. Camila ignored him and said to Avery, "But you want trouble? For the others here?"

"Possibly."

"You should leave. People get hurt here if they make trouble."

Gilberto spoke again, and Camila ignored him.

"I can't leave," Avery said. "They won't let me."

Camila nodded. Gilberto came over and placed his hand on her arm. He helped her up while she held the baby. They stepped out of the circle of firelight, heeding Collins' warning. As Avery had expected them to.

But Camila stopped and turned back, Gilberto's hand still on her arm. "You should leave. *Seriamente.* Leave."

Then Camila allowed herself to be led away.

Avery watched the fire awhile longer. She didn't feed it anymore, and it slowly died out while Camila's words turned over in her mind. They reminded her that she needed a way to protect herself in case Yates followed through on his threat. She went into her cabin and lay staring at the ceiling, the blanket up to her chin. She wondered what Anna was doing over in the big house. It was hard not knowing whether she was happy to be getting to know her new family or sad about losing her mom and dad—and Alisha. Avery couldn't even be sure Anna was safe.

Could she leave without Anna, no matter who she was related to?

There was no lock on Avery's cabin door, nothing to stop someone from coming in. She had brought in a rock from outside, wedged it against the door as a measure of security. But she decided to stay awake as long as she could, to avoid being blindsided by someone like Yates pushing into her cabin.

Her eyes grew heavy, eventually. She needed sleep to be at her best. If she stayed up all night, she'd be worthless tomorrow. A little sleep . . . a little rest . . .

She drifted away.

She didn't hear the rock move, didn't hear the cabin door open.

She felt the hand over her mouth, large and clammy. Damp skin against her face, cutting off her ability to cry out.

To breathe.

She tried to sit up, tried to fight back. Her body thrashed.

They wouldn't take her. No one would take her—

"Shhhh," the voice said. "Avery, shhhh. It's me."

77

Yates was awake when they came for him.

It was late, past midnight, and Yates and all the workers were shut up in their cabins. When Collins had dropped off food earlier, he'd issued a warning to stay inside after they ate. Yates knew the others were so intimidated, so afraid of making even one wrong move, they'd do whatever Collins told them. Even if their bladders burst.

The fire had died long ago, leaving just a few glowing embers in the dark. Night sounds swelled.

Yates lay on his cot, listening.

He heard what he expected to hear. One of the cabin doors opened and closed. Then someone walked off into the night. Yates liked being right, liked the warm, satisfying glow that spread through him when he made a call and saw it come true. He was on something of a streak. He had known Anna Rogers would be heading to Rydell, knew she could be his ticket onto the farm and out of trouble.

And then he guessed something was up with his new pal, James. The guy was connected to Avery Rogers, the one who used to be a cop. And when that cabin door opened and someone walked away— in direct defiance of Collins' order—Yates knew he was right.

He made the decision to wait, to listen for the return of the foot-steps. When James—or whatever his name really was—came back, Yates would have him by the short ones and could do whatever he pleased. If the guy was a narc and Yates exposed him to Combs and Hogan, that would surely cement Yates' place as a member of the family's crew. He smiled in the dark, loving it when a plan came together so well.

Two sets of footsteps returned. Not what he'd expected.

Yates sat up, his body tense. He swung his feet to the grungy floor of the cabin.

Had James brought Avery Rogers back with him? Were they trying to get out of there together?

Yates stood up, moved closer to the door of his cabin. He listened for voices, but nothing reached him.

But the footsteps drew closer and closer. And they seemed to be coming right to his cabin. Right to his door, which was yanked open.

In the dim light, Hogan stood there, a cigarette dangling from the corner of his mouth. He wore the same suit coat, the same collared shirt that he'd worn earlier. He looked like a guy who had just returned from dinner at a decent restaurant, not a guy who was wandering around a weed farm in the middle of the night.

Collins appeared behind him, wearing a ball cap pulled low over his eyes. So low, Yates wondered how the man could see in the dark. Behind them the embers of the fire glowed a faint red, a small curl of smoke rising toward the inky sky.

"What's this?" Yates asked. He managed to keep his voice level. Even though his heart raced, almost like it was separate from the calming thoughts he tried to play in his mind. His heart galloped away on its own. "It's kind of late for a social call."

"We think it's time you left," Hogan said. "And we think it's best you left while it's dark."

Yates moved his eyes from Hogan to the other man and then back to Hogan. "Why?"

Hogan jerked his head in the direction of the river. "Let's talk somewhere else. People are sleeping, and we don't want to wake them," Hogan said. "They have a long day ahead. And, see, we got a visitor earlier. An unexpected *police* visitor. Somebody who wanted to know about something that happened down in Breckville. And they think we might have had something to do with it."

"Oh, I see."

Yates considered his options. He held no gun, no weapon of any kind. He didn't know the area, couldn't have guessed how to get off the farm even if he wanted to. And certainly not in the dark. And he didn't even know how many guards were out there watching the perimeter.

He could try to fight, bull his way past the two men—and then what? Stumble around in the dark. Take a bullet in the back.

Fall in the river. Get swallowed up by the cave. How many bodies had the family disposed of down there in the cold, murky water? A person could be dumped there and rot away alongside the bones of ancient people.

Yates suspected they didn't want to just let him go. The two of them wouldn't have shown up in the middle of the night just to wish him Godspeed.

Yates tried to play the hand he held.

"We should talk," he said. "I need to tell you both something." He nodded toward James' empty cabin. "I need to tell you something about a guy who works here."

"Good," Collins said. "Good." He stepped back, clearing a path for Yates to walk out.

"We can mutually benefit one another," Hogan said. "There can be a symbiosis."

Yates had heard the word before but wasn't sure what it meant. He stepped out of the cabin and started walking down the path to the river, with the two men behind him.

78

Collins had a flashlight, and he shined it on the path, illuminating the way as they progressed. Yates remained quiet most of the way, perhaps plotting an escape. Perhaps trying to figure out what he could say to change the course of things.

At the cabin, he'd said something about information he had to share. It was a dodge, of course, an attempt to save his own bacon. And it worked. Hogan was curious. He was a man who liked to know everything and anything he could. He could never tell which piece of information from which source might prove beneficial in the future. So he intended to let Yates speak. And he could speak as long as what he was saying was helpful to Hogan and the family.

When they were about halfway to the river, Yates said, "Are you sending me out through the cave? One of the farmworkers told me there's a way out through there. The river flows underground and comes out the other side. I guess that would keep anyone from seeing me go."

"That's a rumor," Collins said. "There's no way out through the cave."

"Really?"

"You can try it," Collins said. "I hope you can hold your breath a long time."

When they reached the footbridge over the river, Yates stopped in the middle of it.

"Come on," Collins said.

"Wait," Yates said. "I told you I have information for you. You need to hear it now that we're away from the cabins."

"You can tell us," Hogan said, "but we're going to go farther."

"No." Yates froze on the bridge. He held his hands out, palms facing toward the other men, like he wanted to charge forward and shove them both down. He didn't make a move because he was outgunned. But he wanted to express his defiance, make some kind of stand and try to even gain a piece of control over the situation again. "Now," he said.

Collins stepped toward Yates, ready to move him along with physical force. Or a gun if need be. Hogan held out his hand, not touching Collins but letting him know he should stop. There was no reason to escalate yet. The bridge was as good a place as any to get whatever information they needed.

Hogan reached into his coat pocket and extracted a cigarette. He stuck it in his mouth and spun the wheel of his lighter with his thumb until it ignited in the dark night. When the cigarette was lit—and Yates had been forced to wait longer—Hogan said, "Okay, Yates. What have you got for us?"

In the glow from Collins' flashlight, Yates' eyes bounced from one man to the other. He nodded his head slowly, certainty returning to his posture. He thought exactly what Hogan wanted him to think— that he'd taken control of the situation. Hogan puffed away, the end of the cigarette glowing in the dark. The wind picked up, carrying the smoke away. He wished he'd worn a heavier coat.

"This guy James. The skinny guy with the half-assed beard. I think there's something going on with him."

"Like what?"

"He saw the Rogers girl, the older one. Avery. And the two of them were staring at each other like they knew each other. Out at the crops. You were there, Collins, but your back was turned, so you couldn't see him."

Hogan looked at Collins, who said, "Yeah, she was down there this morning. I chased her off, told her not to come back and disrupt the harvest again." He turned back to Yates. "Are you saying the two of them are friendly?"

"Yes," Yates said. "And she used to be a cop. How does she know him? It seems like kind of a coincidence, doesn't it? And you said a cop came out to the farm today, and that must be what you two are all stirred up about. Right? You're saying it's about that girl down in Breckville. But maybe it isn't. Not entirely. Maybe they have a guy in here who went undercover. A narc. And he's right now plotting with that Rogers girl. You see, just before you came down to wake me up, James left his cabin. How much do you want to bet he's with that Avery Rogers right now? On the same day she was sniffing around the crop. Once a cop, always a cop."

Hogan had to hand it to Yates. The guy was smarter than he appeared. Made some connections that would help Hogan and the family.

Hogan turned to Collins. "This James—that the guy you were worried about?"

"It is."

"See, Yates, sometimes people show up here looking to work, and we know there might be something funny about them. They're trying really hard to look scraggly or down on their luck, but you can look past the superficial grime and tell they aren't. Maybe their socks are too clean. Or their teeth are in too good a shape. There are ways to tell. And this James guy—he might be one of those. It's the risk of being in business the way we are." He flicked an ash off the bridge and into the river. "But you've helped us—you really have. Now that we know about him and Avery Rogers, we'll be sure to check on that."

"Okay. Good." Yates lowered his hands for the first time, let them drop to his side. "See? I brought you Anna Rogers. And I told you about this James and Avery Rogers. I can do a lot more for you. This thing in Breckville, it will blow over."

Hogan shook his head. "No, it won't, I'm sorry to say. They know it was you. And they traced you here. So you have to go. Now."

Yates started backing up, his shoes clunking against the weathered wooden boards.

"We'll get you out of here," Hogan said, moving forward. "Quick and easy."

"No."

Yates spun away, started to run. Hogan would have waited, would have handled it all differently, but Collins jumped into action. His gun was out, and the muzzle flash illuminated the night.

Yates grunted and fell, too far away for them to see him.

"Damn it." Hogan threw his cigarette away. "You'll wake the whole damn county."

"He ran."

"Where the fuck was he going to go?"

They moved across the bridge, Collins sweeping the night with his flashlight and his gun.

Yates lay twenty feet up the path. Facedown. A bullet hole in his jacket on the upper-right side of his back. He was moaning. Using his arms to try to drag his body forward, he looked like a turtle laying eggs on a beach.

"No," Yates said, his voice choked. "I can help you . . . more. . . ."

Hogan looked at Collins. "Well, you started it."

The second shot ended it.

79

Avery nodded, and Hank removed his hand from her mouth.

Her heart raced, and she took in big gulps of air. When she could speak, she said, "Shit, I thought you were here to kill me. Or worse."

"Sorry. But I didn't want you to yell."

Hank settled on the edge of her cot, his back just barely touching her thighs. They hadn't been that close to each other, hadn't made contact with each other since . . . It had been over two years.

Even in the dark, beneath the beard and the grime, he was the same man. His eyes were bright and alert. His muscles tense. His body was even more wiry beneath his ragged flannel coat.

"Do you want to talk here?" she asked in a very low voice.

"It's safest. And I can't stay here long."

"Collins told us all to stay inside. What time is it?"

"About one. He told our crew the same thing."

"Has he ever done that before?"

"Yes. Once."

"And?"

"It was right after I got here. One of the workers, a young guy who'd dropped out of college and was hitchhiking across the country, he liked to mouth off to Collins. You can't mouth off to Collins. You just can't. This guy threatened to report the family to the law when he left. That night, Collins told us all to stay inside like this. Next day, the guy was gone. Collins said he decided to leave and hitchhike away. I don't know if that's what went down or not."

"You think he's going after that guy he decked today?"

"His name is Tommy. I don't know. They're kind of low on workers, and they want to finish the harvest soon."

"Shit. We should get out of here."

Hank shook his head. "*You* should. Not me. Not yet, anyway. But I think— Well, we can get to that in a minute. What the fuck are you doing here, Avery?"

So she told him, giving him the CliffsNotes version of Anna running off and the DNA test that had brought her there, the one that Anna said showed she was related to the Combs family and not Jane or Big Russ.

"Anna told me to get lost when I talked to her," Avery said. "But then those guys, Hogan and Combs, told me I had to stay. And not politely. They have the keys to Charlie's truck and the truck itself. And my phone and gun."

"Charlie really died?"

"Yes."

"I'm sorry, Avery. Damn. I know how much he meant to you. He was a good cop too."

"He was."

Hank reached out and rubbed her arm. His touch hit Avery with the force of an electric shock, just as it always did. Hank waited a respectful amount of time, and then he returned to business. "We're in some trouble here, Avery. I don't think it matters what they told you to do. You should get out of here."

"And you?"

He shook his head. "I have a couple more weeks of work to do. There's a lot going on. I need to stick it out no matter what."

"What do you mean, 'no matter what'?"

He remained quiet, like he didn't want to say, sitting there in the dark, his body giving off a strong odor of sweat and dirt.

"Hank?"

"I think I got made today. When you came down to the field, we locked eyes. For just a moment. I couldn't help it. I was so shocked to see you there. And I haven't seen you in so long. I should have played it cooler, but Collins had his back to me, so I looked at you. . . ."

"So what's the problem?"

Hank blew on his hands, rubbed them together. Avery's eyes were adjusted to the dark. She saw the dirt under his nails, the scrapes on the backs of his hands from the labor.

"There's a guy here. Yates. I think he knows you."

"Oh, yeah."

"Who is he?"

"I don't know. One of their low-level enforcers. I think he brought Anna here. I don't know how. He's dangerous because he's trying to prove himself. What does he have to do with us?"

"He picked up on us looking at each other, and he told me so tonight. Or he hinted about it. Right after I'd taken a piss in the woods. He followed me out there, snuck up on me. He brought up you being a former cop. He wondered how we knew each other. Maybe I'm being paranoid and he's just fucking with me. But it's too risky for you."

"Then it's too risky for you too. I've seen the way Collins treats the farmworkers. What would they do to you?"

"It wouldn't be pretty, but I'm almost done. Avery, there's a lot more wrong here than just the weed growing, okay? The local cops are getting paid off."

"And the migrant workers?"

"That too. Labor trafficking. My understanding is the family is relying more on the undocumented workers, thinking they'll talk less and be more easily controlled. Easier to abuse. They're transient. They show up with a small bag of personal items and that's about it. Collins likes to threaten them with ICE. It keeps them too scared to make any move. It's ugly." Hank shook his head. "You need to go. Just get out."

"How? Run really fast? Do you have a jet pack I can use? They're guarding the perimeter, right?"

"They keep a close eye on things. Collins is the most dangerous."

He shook his head. "Look, there's a trail out of here. I've seen it. It's tough to find in the dark, but—"

"It has to be guarded."

"It is. But that's not a concern tonight. I stopped by there already."

"You did?"

"Avery, you'll just have to hoof it through the woods and get out."

"What about Anna? If she's not safe here, I'm not leaving without her."

Hank sighed. "You said she's related to these people. Maybe she belongs here."

"Have you seen her since she's been here?"

"No. But I don't get anywhere near the big house. None of us do. I don't know how you're going to get her out of here. I don't even know if *you're* going to get out. Two people make it a lot more complicated."

"Then I'll wait too. If you and Anna are here and in danger—"

"Avery, you can't worry about me. Okay?"

Avery's face flushed. "Don't flatter yourself, okay? I'm worried about you as a human being. Not because I'm in love with you." Avery hoped she'd sounded convincing. She was worried about him just because he was a person in an unsafe environment. But she still loved him. Enough to send that text when she had been in Breckville. Enough to wonder why he hadn't written back. Enough to worry about him. *A lot.* "I'm worried about everybody here who might be innocent."

He rubbed her arm again. "I've thought about you too. I've wondered how you were doing in Breckville. In school. I should have been in better touch, but . . ."

"It's okay."

"No, it's not. I regret— Well, I wish I'd listened better. You went through a real trauma at the pond. I should have been there more."

"Just get us all out of here alive, and I'll forgive you."

Despite the tension and the stakes, Hank laughed. "Right. If only we did have that jet pack. That might be our best bet. Short of that . . . we'll have to sneak out just before first light. And I don't know what to do about Anna—"

A gunshot split the night.

Both Avery and Hank jumped.

"Is that normal?" Avery asked.

"No. Not in the middle of the night."

Another shot cracked the silence. And Hank was off the cot and moving out of the cabin.

80

A noise woke Anna.

A door slamming somewhere in the house. Or a firework being shot off outside.

Or maybe she'd been dreaming and her own dream, her own mind, had woken her up.

She sat upright in the large bed, the fluffy covers pooling around her waist. She wore clothes borrowed from Brittany and slept in a guest room down the hall from the family. The family? *Her* family.

So it seemed. Brittany was her aunt, her father's sister. A man who had died violently years earlier, someone Anna would never know. Had she dreamed of the gunshots that killed her family? Her mother and her sibling?

The room was dark, the curtains opened, but little light came through them. All the shapes in the room were vague and unfamiliar. It was like waking up in a hotel or a strange guy's bedroom. Except she really belonged here—they were all linked by blood.

But she felt like she didn't belong anywhere. And, strangely, as she had lain in bed trying to fall asleep earlier, images of her parents—the people who'd *raised* her—had run through her head on a loop. She saw them over and over again. She missed them—an absence that seemed inextricably linked to their own vulnerability and aging. What would they think if they heard the news? If they knew she'd found out about it from strangers—and might never go back?

She'd gone from being angry at them to feeling a sliver of pity for them. Her mind felt like a tangled cord.

The second shot told her it was all real. Very, very real.

She threw the covers off, swung her legs around, and stepped into her sneakers. She grabbed a hoodie from the end of the bed and pulled it on, struggling to get her hands through the sleeves as she moved. Before she reached the bedroom door, voices came from another part of the house. Raised voices. Had the shots woken the kids?

Anna pulled the door open and stepped out into the hallway.

To her right, the carpeted staircase went down to the foyer. The sound of voices came up, reaching her where she stood. Brittany and Taylor were arguing down there. They stood near the front door.

Anna started down the stairs. The carpet muffled her steps, so they didn't hear her coming.

"My children are asleep upstairs——"

"*Our* children."

"You promised me this would never happen here. *Never.* After what happened to my brother? And with his child upstairs . . ."

"I'm right here," Anna said.

They both whipped their heads in her direction. She was halfway down the stairs and felt like a child walking in on her parents having an argument. And since they were in her mind, she realized her mom and dad had almost never argued.

"It's okay, honey." Brittany wore her robe, and her feet were bare. Her hair was down and tumbling over her shoulders. "I'm sorry if we woke you."

"You didn't wake me. The gunshots did." Anna came the rest of the way down the stairs.

Taylor watched her. He was fully dressed, like he hadn't been asleep. And every muscle in his body looked tense beneath his clothes. "Those weren't gunshots. The neighbors set off some fireworks."

Anna felt her face flush. "I'm a cop's daughter. I've been to the range with him. I know what gunshots sound like. It sounded like a nine-millimeter. Two shots. Probably down by the river. What's going on?"

"It's nothing," Taylor said. "Just . . . It's nothing."

The house felt chilled, like the heat had been turned down for the night. Anna pulled the hoodie tighter around her body, zipped it up. The mood in the house had been bizarre all day. Tense. Anna had seen little of Taylor, even little of Brittany after the morning. A heavy quiet had filled the house like a fog.

"Gunshots aren't nothing," Anna said.

"You can go back to sleep, Anna," Taylor said.

Hogan wasn't there. If someone was firing a gun, it was likely Hogan. But why would he be doing that in the middle of the night? And what or who would he be shooting at? Anna couldn't guess, but Taylor had positioned himself between the two women and the door, as though he wanted to make sure they didn't go outside.

Could this be something to do with one of the farmworkers? Anna hadn't seen much of them, and even then only from a distance, but they all looked tired and worn-out. Food was taken to them at the cabins, but what kind of life was that? Working in the fields all day. Eating a meal at a campfire. Sleeping in a little shack and starting all over again the next day.

"I'd like to go look," Anna said. "And get some air."

Taylor remained in place.

"Anna," Brittany said, "it's best if you stay in here. Your sister is fine. This isn't about her."

Anna turned to Brittany. "What are you talking about? My sister? You told me she left."

Taylor groaned. He gave Brittany the stare down, his eyes boring in on her like lasers.

Color rose on Brittany's cheeks. "She stayed, Anna. She didn't leave yet. It was better for her to stay."

"Are you telling me Avery has been here all day? And she's out there where someone is shooting?"

Taylor's voice rose and sharpened. He spoke to Anna like she was one of his children. "She's fine, okay? None of this has anything to do with her. And you can just go on up to bed and forget about it."

"I'm going out there to check on her." Anna started for the door. Started for Taylor, who didn't look like he was going to move. "Please."

Taylor didn't budge. He gave her the same stare he'd given his wife, as if his eyes alone could push someone up the stairs. "This will be fine. Okay? You're here now. We're your family. And we'll take care of you. So trust me when I say whatever is happening out there doesn't concern you."

"Does it concern this family?" Anna asked. "If I'm part of it?"

"It's business," Taylor said.

"I'm going." Anna made a move to the left, trying to maneuver around him. He shifted one step to his right, blocking her path. "This is idiotic. Let me through."

Anna took another half step forward. Taylor still didn't move. He didn't flinch. He kept his eyes on her.

"Let her go," Brittany said. She sounded like a drill sergeant giving a command. Her voice carried through the house, louder and sharper than the gunshots. "Just let her go check on her sister or whoever she is."

Taylor looked like he wasn't going to move, like he hadn't heard his wife speak.

But then he slid slightly to the left and out of the way. Anna moved forward, reaching for the knob. She wasn't sure he would really let her pass or if he was going to reach out and grab her arm, preventing her from going.

He didn't.

But as she passed, he spoke to her through gritted teeth. "You're going to need to pick a side now. Us or them."

81

Avery left the cabin just a few steps behind Hank.

He ran so fast, he disappeared into the dark ahead of her, and she rushed to keep up with him.

As she went through the cluster of cabins and past the smoldering campfire, she took a quick look around. None of the cabin doors had opened. No one stuck their head out or made a sound, despite the gunshots and the pounding steps of Hank and Avery. They were completely intimidated by Collins' order to stay put.

As Avery followed along, increasing her speed to keep up, she tried to figure out what the shots meant. It was unlikely that any of the farmhands had a gun. Would Collins have shot one of them for leaving their cabin?

Anna. Could Anna be hurt or in trouble?

Or was it more likely someone else? She pictured Yates standing on the bridge the day before, telling her he had little power around the farm. Had he proven to be expendable for some reason?

The darkness smothered her. Trees and brush grew close on either side of the path, blotting out the sky and stars, and only occasionally did she catch a glimpse of Hank ahead of her. She expected at any moment to hook her foot on a tree root or a rock and go tumbling to the ground, then roll along the path like a loose wheel.

But she stayed upright as they passed the north set of cabins, where the workers also remained out of sight. Hank and she kept going, getting closer and closer to the river, where they'd heard the shots come from. Soon enough, Hank stopped, his body blocking the path.

Avery stopped running as well and came up behind him. Her heart pounded and her breath was gone. She bent over slightly, wanting to rest her hands on her knees and gulp air until she felt normal again. But she didn't.

Past Hank stood Hogan and Collins. Hogan had his hands on his hips, his suit coat rising a little in the light wind. He looked like he didn't have a care in the world, like he had just been waiting for them to show up. And now that everyone was assembled, one side of his mouth went up a little bit.

"Ah," he said, "I see the two of you are spending time together on this fine night." He gestured over his shoulder toward Collins. "We were just informed that the two of you might have a previous acquaintance, and it looks like we were informed correctly."

"Is somebody hurt down here?" Hank asked. "What was the shooting about?"

Hogan turned, looking over his shoulder toward the bridge, like he had no idea any shots had been fired. He turned back to face Hank and Avery. "It's really nothing to worry about. An internal security matter. We took care of it."

"If someone's hurt—"

Hogan held his hand out, shaking his head. "It's okay. We were just coming to talk to the two of you. We really didn't expect to find you out of your cabins against the wish expressed by Mr. Collins here. But maybe this has worked out for the best. We can talk someplace more private. Maybe we can step down the trail here."

Collins cleared his throat. "Remember, there's something in the path."

"Oh, right," Hogan said. He scratched his jaw. "Then I suppose your cabin is empty, James. Or whatever your name is. We'll keep our voices down, and the others know well enough to mind their own business."

"I want to know where my sister is," Avery said. "Is she hurt?"

"She's not your sister," Hogan said, pointing to the trail behind Avery and Hank, the way back to the cabins. "Shall we?"

Avery looked around, thought about running. But where would she go? Hogan and Collins were both armed. She could turn and run and catch a bullet in her back for her trouble.

Hank turned and walked past Avery, nodding, asking her to go along. So she turned as well, and they started back up the trail, Hogan and Collins behind them. Avery's arm brushed against Hank's, maybe the last touch they'd ever share. The last touch she'd ever share with anyone.

Behind them, Hogan's and Collins' feet tramped over the trail, crushing twigs and leaves. Hank moved faster. Not running, not making a break for it. But he pulled ahead, and it seemed intentional. Avery moved faster to keep up.

Hank lifted his hand to his mouth like he was stifling a cough. "If you get out," he said. His voice was so low, she could barely hear above the movement and the steps and the night sounds. "Trail. Out. Past crops."

"What are you saying up there?" Collins asked.

"Keep moving," Hogan said.

Avery thought that was it, that was all Hank wanted to say. The risk of speaking again was too great.

But in an even lower voice, he said, "North. Nine."

Nine?

Collins came up behind them. He swung his fist, landing a blow in the dead center of Hank's back. It knocked him forward, making him stumble and almost go to the ground.

Hank managed to stay upright. His body tensed. His fists clenched.

Avery expected him to spin around, to charge back at Collins. She hoped he wouldn't. And he didn't. He kept on going forward.

"You'll get your chance to talk when we're inside that cabin," Collins said.

They went the rest of the way in silence.

82

They went into the cabin with Collins and Hogan behind them. Collins shut the door once they were all inside the crowded space.

The air felt close and smelled musty, like the cabin had a years-long leak in the roof. Hogan lit a hurricane lamp that threw their flickering shadows against the rough-hewn walls.

"Sit down," Hogan said.

Avery and Hank sat on the edge of the cot, their bodies close to each other. Hank's hands rested on the edge of the mattress, his fingers hooked like he was holding on for dear life. Hogan and Collins remained standing, their bodies looming over Avery and Hank. There was simply no way out.

"We're in a tough spot here," Hogan said. He placed the lamp on a small table next to the cot. It lit his face from below. "We feel pretty certain you're a cop. And we know *you're* a former cop. From a line of cops. You'd have to understand that just about anybody would feel uncomfortable with the police sniffing around their business, not saying what they were doing there. Or even identifying themselves."

"He's not a cop," Avery said. "We met here."

"Is that so? Was it love at first sight?"

"Let Avery go," Hank said. "She came here only to find her sister. And she did. She didn't come here in any law enforcement capacity."

"Now, how do I know that?" Hogan asked. "Better yet, how do you know it? Now, tell me. What are you? FBI? KSP? DEA?"

"Just let her go, okay? I'll make a deal with you."

"Oh, he's making deals," Collins said from where he stood by the cabin door. He was farther from the lamp and harder to see in the half-light.

"Let her go and I'll tell you whatever you want to know. Okay? She has nothing to do with any of it. She's not a cop. And she wants nothing to do with the family."

"She's just going to leave her here, the one she thinks is her sister?" Collins said. "She came a long way to find her. She doesn't seem like the type to let go easily."

"I tried to leave, remember?" Avery asked. "You wouldn't let me."

"Things keep getting more complicated," Hogan said.

For the first time, Avery detected an undercurrent of uncertainty in his voice. It made her more nervous, more scared. If he wasn't sure what to do, then how might he react?

Hank moved slightly next to her, gripping the mattress with greater force. Why didn't he sit still?

Avery tried to stall.

"I just want to see my—see Anna. I haven't seen her in a day. I have to go back and talk to my parents, and they're going to want to know if she's okay. And I want to be able to tell them the truth. Since you kept me away from her, I'd like to make sure she's all right."

"That's not going to happen," Hogan said.

"Besides," Collins said, "she doesn't want to see you. I saw her up at the house earlier and told her you were still here, and she said she didn't want anything to do with you. Said the whole family lied to her and now she's moved on. So . . ." He shrugged like he was dismissing the most minor matter in the world.

Avery suspected he was lying. She couldn't imagine Anna would have shared her feelings with Collins. And it was easy for them to guess that telling her that Anna wanted nothing to do with her would be a sharp verbal slap.

On the other hand, Anna *had* told her to get lost. Avery wasn't going to win any sister-of-the-year prizes. Maybe Anna had really had enough? Maybe she was ready to push her family away once and for all?

How did a family ever come back from that?

They all heard a noise outside. Collins turned, stepped to the door, and placed his hand on it. Avery tilted her head, tried to listen. Had one of the others heard the shots and now the talk in Hank's cabin and stuck their head out to see what was going on?

"Avery?"

She knew the voice. Anna.

Collins pushed the cabin door open, moved halfway outside to see what was going on. Hogan turned toward the door as well.

Hank made his move. His hand slid farther under the mattress and came out, holding an object that flashed briefly as the lamp flame reflected off it.

Hank brought it down, striking a blow in the upper part of Hogan's back.

The man howled with pain, his body contorting. Hank brought his hand back, the blade bloody in his hand. He brought it down again, burying it in Hogan's back one more time.

Avery jumped off the cot and went for Collins.

83

Anna ran from the house and down the trail in the dark.

She had no phone, no light. Her hoodie barely protected her against the cool night air. Her heart pounded. She was in terrible shape for someone her age. She regretted all the nights drinking. The pot and the cigarettes in bars and the days sitting around the apartment instead of exercising like Kayla.

Oh, Kayla. Fuck.

But she ran on anyway, her sneakers slapping the trail. Avery was out there—where someone was shooting. The family hadn't let Avery leave the farm. Something was wrong.

She went through the first group of cabins. They were closed up, quiet. A fire smoldered, and as Anna passed, she thought she heard the crying of a baby from behind one of the closed doors.

She looked in Avery's cabin—and it was empty, the blankets dumped on the floor in a heap.

She ran farther down the trail, in the direction she and Avery had walked just the night before. She passed the log where they had sat when Anna told Avery the truth about their family.

The second set of cabins came into view, and she slowed. Her breath came in heaving gasps. In high school she could run the mile as fast as anybody. Now she felt like she was fifty.

Voices came from behind the closed doors of one of the cabins.

Anna could barely form words, but she tried. Her mouth was

cottony and dry. She swallowed, almost choked. Then the word came out.

"Avery?"

She waited. Something stirred behind the door.

"Avery? Is that you?"

The door opened, revealing Collins. The despicable guard. The guy who walked around acting like he owned the place, bullying the workers. He pushed the door open, sticking his head out cautiously like he might get shot. He spotted Anna, and a little grin spread across his face.

"Well, well, the princess of the castle."

He took one step her way, and then a commotion erupted behind him. Bodies slammed into each other. And a man grunted and then gasped in pain inside the cabin.

Collins stopped, turned his head back to look inside the cabin— and as he did, Avery came charging out. She lifted her arms to chest level like a football player throwing a block, and she plowed into Collins, taking him by surprise and knocking him to the ground. He tumbled like an out-of-control acrobat.

Avery stepped over him and extended her hand toward Anna.

Their hands clasped.

"Anna, let's go."

She let Avery lead her—and they ran. Down the path and in the direction of the river and the crops.

Anna didn't know why—they were moving too fast for her to think. But it felt right to trust Avery, to let her sister lead her someplace that—she hoped—was safe.

Avery was clearly in better shape, and Anna tried to keep up with her. Avery slowed to allow Anna to stay with her. And Avery kept looking back, making sure no one was gaining on them.

Anna ran with every muscle in her body tense. Her thighs and calves burned. She expected gunshots to go flying over their heads at any moment. How had her life come to that point?

They pounded across the crappy wooden bridge and kept on.

"Where are we going, Avery?"

"Out. I know the way."

Just past the bridge, Anna saw a man-sized lump off in the low weeds. They both stopped.

Anna was grateful for the break. She tried to catch her breath, knew she couldn't. Not without a good fifteen minutes of rest.

Avery went to the man. The body?

"Is that . . . ?" Anna huffed and puffed. "Who is that?"

"It's Yates."

"Is he . . . ?"

"He's dead, Anna. Somebody shot him. Let's get the fuck out of here before they do the same to us."

"But why?"

"Let's go, Anna."

Avery took her hand again. Grabbed it so tightly, it felt like she'd never let go.

It took Anna back to childhood, to the times Avery had grabbed her hand and guided her across a street or through a parking lot. It felt good to once again feel certain of something, to know the order of things. Big sister taking care of little sister. That was the way it was supposed to be.

Avery yanked Anna down the trail, and they kept going, leaving the dead man and everything else behind them.

84

The pain seared Hogan's body.

He stumbled forward, catching himself against the front wall of the cabin, the rough boards scraping his palm.

Then Avery Rogers rushed past him, plowing into Collins and then out into the night.

Hogan's immediate concerns were more pressing. Whatever he'd been stabbed with—knife, screwdriver, shank—remained buried in his back. He felt it there, a foreign object lighting up his nerves with pain that radiated down his arms to the tips of his fingers. Like he was on fire.

The fucking bastard had stabbed him in the back.

And if Hogan didn't do something, things would get worse.

Hogan lumbered through the cabin door. Like Frankenstein. An ungraceful parody of a man.

Collins lay on the ground, knocked over by Avery Rogers, who had hit him like a charging bull. The two women—the two Rogers women—had run off into the darkness, in the direction of Yates' body, which Collins and Hogan had failed to get out of sight in time.

"Get them," he said through pain-gritted teeth. "Get them, damn you."

Collins rose to his feet, started off.

Hogan managed to reach inside his coat. His hand shook as he wrapped it around the grip of his gun. He hoped he could manage to hold it steady with the pain and the impending loss of blood from the two wounds in his back. The man—James, the cop, whoever the fuck he was—came closer and closer. Ready with the finishing blow.

Hogan drew the gun, held on to it as best he could.

He turned, saw the man coming toward him. He aimed at the center of the man's chest and fired once and then again.

85

Avery led the way across the fields that lay between the end of the trail through the woods and the one on the far side that Hank had told her about.

She tried to balance moving quickly with being careful. The only light came from the distant moon and the faint stars. The ground was uneven, and the possibility of turning an ankle in a hole or falling hard was very real. Avery also knew Collins would be right behind them. And possibly Hogan, depending on how deep the knife Hank had driven into his back went.

Avery replayed *that* a few times. Hank off the cot. Wielding the knife he'd clearly hidden. Jamming it into Hogan's back once and then again, allowing her to escape.

"Fuck," she said out loud as the images replayed.

"What's wrong?" Anna kept up but breathed heavily.

"Nothing. I was just thinking about the cabin back there. And how I got out."

"How *did* you get out? Besides that baller move of running Collins over. It sounded like there was a fight. Did you have to kick somebody's ass?"

Avery watched the ground, picking her way carefully. "It wasn't me. It was Hank."

"Hank? You mean, *Hank* Hank? Your ex-boyfriend?"

"Yeah."

"What's he doing here? Is that why you came? To see him?"

"No, I came for you. But Hank was here. He's undercover, I guess. I didn't know about it." She considered not telling her sister any more but went ahead. Anna was old enough now, after everything they'd all been through. "He . . . stabbed Hogan in the back. Twice. And that's how I got out."

Anna remained quiet for a minute. "He did that? Fuck."

"He's a cop. Sometimes cops have to make life-and-death decisions. Dad had to. I did a few times. That's the job."

"Shit."

"Just watch your step."

"Avery, where are we going?"

"There's a way out on the far side of this bottomland. Hank told me to head this way. A trail that leads out to Highway Nine. And then help."

"Won't it be guarded?"

"Hank says he took care of it. Let's hope he did. . . ."

"How did this become our lives?"

"I don't know, Anna. I'm not sure what we're dealing with. But I just want to get out of here and then figure it all out."

Avery looked back a few times, making sure no one was following them. But it was so dark, the distance so great, she'd never have been able to see anyone unless they were right on top of her. The only thing they could do was keep moving. Avery worried about shots being fired their way. But if Anna was really related to the Combs family, and Hogan and Collins worked for them, she doubted they would fire randomly in her direction.

Anna's presence might keep them safe from that.

She *hoped*.

Ahead, she made out the tree line, the one that the path Hank told her about would cut through. She silently willed them on, holding on to a wish that they'd make it that far before Collins or Hogan—if he could—reached them.

She also carried a thought for those back on the farm. The migrant workers confined to their cabins. They had likely heard the shots, heard the scrum between her and Hank and Collins and Ho-gan. One man was already dead, killed by Hogan and Collins. Hank's time might be limited, if he wasn't dead already. She'd seen the treatment of the workers, Hank's concerns about them.

What was going to happen if everything blew up? If those who ran the farm feared exposure?

Avery and Anna reached the trees. But in the dark it wouldn't be easy to find the path. They couldn't just plunge into the pitch-dark woods without knowing the right way to go. It would be too easy to get lost, to wander in circles and end up right back on the farm and in deeper trouble than before.

If there really was a path that led to the highway, that was the only way to get out without a compass or a light or anything else.

"I'm so tired, Avery. I don't— You're in way better shape than I am."

"And I'm so much older, right?"

"I didn't say that. I'm just . . . I'm impressed . . . with you and Hank. . . ."

"That's the second time he saved my life."

They walked along, parallel to the trees, trying to find an open-ing. Avery kept one ear trained behind them in case someone came up. Sound would carry well across the open, flat bottomland. Unless Collins was good at sneaking up on people, they'd know he was coming.

Finally, they came to an opening.

Avery studied it, took a few steps into the trees with Anna behind her. Avery made sure it really was a path. And it was. Not too wide but clearly there. Easy to follow. And it headed north, through the Combs property and—hopefully—out onto Highway 9. From there it would be easy to flag down a passing car, find a driver with a phone that worked. Get into the nearest town.

"You're sure this is it?" Anna asked.

"I don't see any other options."

"Then let's go. I'm feeling better. I can make it."

Avery hesitated, stood in the middle of the path. She looked forward and then back.

"Avery?"

Something moved behind her. A rustling of the tall grass louder than the other night sounds. The crickets and the birds—

"Avery?"

"Shhh."

A man emerged from the left side of the trail, his arms extended. He lurched at them, and Anna screamed.

86

He was the guard. The one Hank was supposed to have taken out.

But he was on his feet, coming right toward them.

Avery had never seen him. His face was contorted with anger. His mouth snarled like an angry dog's. His giant hands groped the air before them.

Avery stepped forward, put herself between Anna and the man. She prepared to strike, to lash out with her fist and do whatever she could to stop the man and let Anna run away.

But before she swung, the man dropped to his knees. He stared straight ahead, eyes unfocused. His gnarled facial features relaxed. His mouth grew loose and slack, his chin falling to his chest. He tipped forward, going flat onto the ground, his face mashing into the dirt.

Avery saw the sticky mess on the back of his head. The blood where someone—Hank—had struck him.

He lay still. A single low moan escaped from his mouth, and then he grew silent.

"Oh, God, Avery. Is he dead?"

"I doubt it." Avery looked over, saw the hoodie Anna wore. She grabbed the drawstring and gave it a good yank, pulling it all the way free.

"*Ow.* Avery."

"Shhh."

Avery dropped to one knee next to the man and pulled his hands together behind his back. She quickly tied the man with a constrictor knot, making sure he couldn't do much even if he did manage to stand again.

"How do you know how to do that?" Anna asked.

"Dad taught me."

"Why bother with that? He can't catch us. Let's go."

"No." Avery stood up. "You're going on without me."

"What are you talking about?"

"I'm going back," she said. "There are too many people in danger. Look at this place. I can't just leave them."

"No, Avery. We're going to go out this trail. We'll get the police. *That* will help everybody."

Avery walked to her sister, placed her hands on her shoulders. "I can't. You go. Just follow the path. Get out to the highway and get ahold of the police. Tell them—tell them there's a KSP officer here and he's in danger. Probably hurt. And a man's been killed, and there's human trafficking and every kind of illegal activity. They won't be surprised. They know what goes on here—they're just turning a blind eye until they can't anymore."

"You're going to get hurt. Let's go—"

Avery wrapped her arms around Anna and pulled her tight. She held her sister for an extended moment, longer probably than she'd held her at any moment since they were children. Anna's body trembled. She sniffled.

Avery held her as long as she could, then released her.

"I love you, kiddo. Now go. Just go."

Avery turned, walked past the immobile man on the ground. The farmworkers needed help.

And Hank. Yes, Hank. She couldn't deny she was going back for him as well.

87

Hogan took a step toward the cabin and stopped.

If the two shots Collins had fired into Yates hadn't woken the whole place, his two shots into the cop—cop?—would have.

Hogan wanted to make sure the man was dead, but he didn't trust himself to stay on his feet. He shifted the gun to his left hand and reached with his right. His hand scrabbled around his back, trying to find the object buried in his flesh. He couldn't reach it or feel it, but it was there. Stuck like a giant thorn.

"Shit."

He needed to talk to Taylor, needed to let him know what was happening since all hell had broken loose.

Hogan turned, started up the trail to the house. It might be the last thing he was able to do, but he intended to carry out the mission and report to the boss. Taylor could decide what to do after that—send his family away. Dig in for a siege. Hogan would help him in any way he could. But he couldn't help Taylor if he didn't fill him in.

Hogan's steps up the trail were cautious ones. It required effort to move one foot in front of the other. And he wanted to be careful not to fall, since he wasn't sure he'd be able to push himself off the ground again if he did.

The house came into sight in the distance, all the windows lit up like the family was having a party. They'd heard the shots. Taylor would be inside reassuring his wife and kids. Anna Rogers had run out, looking for her sister. Somehow Taylor hadn't been able to keep her inside. Hogan knew Brittany wanted to get to know Anna better, already thought of her as a kind of kid sister or something. She wouldn't be happy if Anna never came back.

Hogan trusted Collins to find the girl—if only because there was nowhere for her to run. In the dark and without a phone or a light, it would be tough to get away. But she had her sister with her, and the sister was a tough nut. She'd knocked Collins down, led Anna away into the dark.

Hogan tried to focus on the task at hand. He crossed the yard, stumbled slightly on a rock, and moved toward the porch steps. As he did, Taylor came out of the house.

"What the hell is going on?" he asked through gritted teeth. He came down into the yard. When he drew close to Hogan, a look of surprise crossed his face. "You look like an ad for death. What happened to you?"

"It's not important. . . . What's important is the Rogers girls, both of them. They ran off. Collins is after them."

"What was the shooting?" Taylor asked.

Hogan looked past his boss, saw Brittany appear in the doorway of the house. She stood with her arms crossed. He could tell she wasn't going anywhere. She intended to hear whatever Hogan had to say. And Taylor wasn't going to tell her to leave.

"That farmworker we were worried about . . . the skinny guy . . ." Hogan took a deep breath. The yard swirled a little, like he was on a carnival ride. He took another deep breath, made sure his feet were planted on the ground. "He might be a cop. . . . Yates knew. . . . I had to shoot. . . ."

"Are you okay?" Taylor came closer, examined Hogan's face.

Hogan grimaced again, involuntarily reached for his back, trying again to grab whatever was planted there.

Taylor saw the movement and went behind him. "Oh, God," he said. "Somebody stabbed you. What is this?"

"The guy . . . the cop . . . he stuck me twice."

"It's still in you. I can see the handle."

"It's okay. It doesn't hurt that bad."

Brittany came down the porch steps and crossed to where the two men stood. She came right up into Hogan's face, her eyes flashing in the dark. "Where's Anna? Tell me."

"She ran off. With her sister."

"Ran off where?" she asked.

"I don't know. Toward the river. Collins went after them. To bring them back."

Brittany looked at Taylor. "He'd better not hurt her."

"He won't," Hogan said. "He knows better. But we can . . . we can go help. . . ."

"Hogan's right," Taylor said. "Why don't we get you inside and help you with this injury? Collins will bring them back."

"Taylor, so help me God, that girl had better not get hurt. And I mean not a scratch. She's my niece, not some random fieldworker you all treat like a dog."

Taylor stared at his wife. "Okay, I'll go make sure. You take Hogan inside."

"He's not coming in the house with a knife sticking out of his back. We have children."

"Then take him to the garage—"

"I'm okay," Hogan said. He blinked his eyes a few times, trying to focus. He felt steadier after standing still for a moment. Either he'd grown used to the pain or it was easing a little. "Really. I can go with you. I walked up here. It's downhill going back."

"Take him with you, Taylor. I want him away from the house. And he can control Collins better than you can."

"But his back—"

Brittany reached out and turned Hogan's body to the right.

"Wait," Taylor said. "You're not supposed to—"

Hogan didn't have time to think about what she was doing, but he felt something change in his back. A quick stab of pain that made him cry out. And then relief—like pressure had been removed.

He turned and looked. Brittany held a bloody steak knife with a four-inch blade in her hand.

"It's out," she said. "Okay? He's fine. Go find my niece and bring her back home. Go."

Hogan's back felt better. And he didn't see many other choices.

He turned, and with Taylor by his side, they started down the trail.

88

Avery started back across the fields and toward the trail.

Saying good-bye to Anna had made her more emotional than she'd expected.

She hoped like hell that Hank was right, and the trail through the woods led to Highway 9. And help. And that Anna would make it out.

As she trudged over the uneven ground, crunching leaves and pebbles, she realized she cared more for Anna's safety than for her own. She'd gotten her sister out. She'd made a difference for a change.

Maybe she could even do more. . . .

Her eyes were well-adjusted to the dark. She heard the river tumbling as she got closer. Something crested the ridge and moved at the top of the trail. Avery tried to see if it was an animal or a person.

But she knew quickly—Collins. Coming after her.

He moved down the grade slowly, watching every inch of ground ahead of him. But he thought that Avery had left with Anna and that they were together, either searching for the trail on the other side of the cropland or else wandering around in the dark, unsure of where to go.

He wouldn't expect one or both of them to turn around and come back to the farm after running away. So that gave Avery an advantage.

She slipped off the path. She found some tall weeds and nestled her body among them. She tried to regulate her breathing. In the quiet night, she started to gasp like a beached fish but suppressed the noise. The weeds and long grass tickled her arms and face. A buzzing insect landed on her ear, and she brushed it away.

Collins came closer. He was fifty feet away from her spot. He didn't appear to have a light, and in the darkness there was no way for him to see her unless he stepped off the path and really, really looked. He could lay his eyes directly on her in the dark and still miss her.

She could just let him pass. He was clearly going to go all the way across the cropland to the far side to see if Anna and Avery were over there looking for the trail out. Avery was more than happy to let him slip past, and then, when he was far enough away, she could continue on up the path to the camp. She could look for Hank—and help the others get out.

Her mind locked up like an engine without oil.

What good would it do to let Collins pass if he might somehow catch up to Anna? Or if Avery tried to lead the others out the same way Anna went—and Collins was down there ahead of them? Waiting. Blocking the way.

Her mouth was dry. Cold sweat ran down her neck and under her shirt. She couldn't let Collins pass freely. It was too risky to have him wandering around loose, able to do harm to everyone else.

She needed to stop him. For real.

But without a weapon of any kind—and him with a gun—how could she?

Collins was thirty feet away.

Avery felt around in the grass and weeds. She figured she'd end up being covered by every form of poison ivy that grew in the wild. And she imagined her hands closing on a snake or a frog as she groped in the dark.

Her hand bumped against something. A jagged shape in the darkness.

A rock. Almost twice the size of her hand, with sharp edges. She gripped it, and it fit her palm like a small basketball. She could hold on to it and take one good swing.

She needed to get close to Collins without him hearing. And then—

If she missed . . .

She couldn't think about missing.

Collins was twenty feet away.

Avery gripped the rock tighter, felt the edges dig into her flesh. Every muscle in her body tensed. She waited in a crouch, like a sprinter on the starting blocks. When Collins came by and moved a little past her, she could spring onto the path. She needed to move and swing the rock in one motion. With nothing wasted.

Ten feet and then five. He moved his head from side to side, checking the ground. She saw him. He was a man. He was flesh. When the rock made contact with his body, it would do damage and cause considerable pain.

It could kill him.

But she had no choice. Too many other lives, including Anna's, were at stake.

Collins drew even with her and then moved past her. Avery felt nauseated. Her mouth was bone-dry.

She needed to act.

She moved forward quickly. She raised the rock and went for Collins.

As she moved from the brush, she stepped on a twig she didn't see. It snapped, like a bone cracking in the quiet night.

Collins turned her way, his gun raised. Avery brought the rock down, but Collins' turn meant she struck him a glancing blow, against the side of his neck.

He cried out in pain, tried to work the gun around in Avery's direction. Avery grabbed for the gun with her left hand. With her right, she swung the rock again. She managed a better trajectory and slammed the rock against the side of his head. It made a sick thump, like a watermelon hitting the ground.

Collins' body went limp.

Avery backed up, let him fall to the ground. He lay there, not making a sound. The gun fell next to his hand, and Avery kicked it away. Then she bent down, fearing that she'd killed him. But when she leaned closer, she heard his breathing. Slightly shallow but there.

She felt relieved. Although she wasn't sure why she cared what happened to him. He'd have a hell of a headache once he woke up.

Avery picked up the gun, stuffed it into her pants. She grabbed his flashlight as well.

She took hold of Collins by one of his arms and dragged him off the trail and into the weeds where she had hidden. He moaned a little, a smear of blood in his hair. She wished she had something to tie him with, and if she took the time to look around, she might find something.

But it was more important to get moving. She hoped she'd hit him hard enough to keep him out of commission until she got off the farm.

She even thought about hitting him again just to make sure. But she decided to move on. She started up the trail toward the cabins and the farmworkers.

And Hank.

89

When Hogan was halfway to the first set of cabins, the pain came back.

Hogan felt the stickiness of the blood between his shirt and his skin. He started to sweat, even though the night was cool. He stopped on the trail.

Taylor looked his way. "What is it?"

"I'll be okay. . . ."

"Do you want to go back?"

"No. I just— I'm okay." Hogan blinked a few times, tried to keep his vision from swimming. "Just a second."

"You really think this guy is a cop?" Taylor asked.

"I do. . . ."

"And you shot him?"

"I did. Twice."

"Fuck. And Yates?"

"Yes." Hogan took a few breaths, straightened up. "I'm okay. I'm not sure your wife should have pulled that knife out. It might have been better to leave it in."

"She likes to solve problems when she sees them. You're supposed to do that too, not make more of them. Let's go before things get more out of hand."

Hogan's pain was replaced by a sliver of anger. Everything had started to go wrong when they let Anna Rogers onto the property. When Brittany quickly grew attached to her because they were supposedly related. They could have handled the cop. But Hogan wasn't sure they could handle the problems between a husband and wife. Who could? Family fucked up everything.

"I'm ready," Hogan said through gritted teeth.

They continued on in the dark. It helped Hogan to inventory his tasks, to list them and then cross them off as they were accomplished. So, first: They needed to dispose of two bodies. They needed to keep the farmworkers out of the way.

And they needed to find the two Rogers girls and bring them back before they made any more trouble. He felt better with the list in his head. Taylor and he could do it. Clean up and control.

He'd worry about his stab wounds later. The knife blade wasn't too long. It seemed not to have hit his lung or anything else too important. If it had, he'd have been in a lot worse shape. He'd seen knife wounds before. He knew what bad ones looked like.

The south set of cabins came into view. Hogan expected to find nothing there. Collins had warned the workers to stay inside, to keep their noses out of everything that was going on. They would. They'd seen what happened to others who got out of line. Collins had counted on that, used it to keep the operation running. It would only be at the north set of cabins, where the cop's dead or injured body waited, that they would have a mess to clean up.

As they passed through the center of the cabins, near the campfire, Taylor stopped.

"What?" Hogan asked.

"It's so quiet."

"It's always quiet here at night. They're scared. They heard the shots too."

Taylor went to the door of one of the cabins. Hogan tried to remember who lived in that one. One of the Hispanic couples, but Hogan wasn't sure which.

"They're asleep—"

Taylor knocked on the door. Hard. *"Hola? Hola?"*

He waited a moment, head cocked at the door. Listening. Taylor pulled the door open and went inside. Just as quickly, he came out. "Check the ones on your side."

Hogan did. The one where Avery had stayed was empty as he expected. But so was the other one.

"They're both empty," Hogan said.

Taylor turned away from the second one on his side.

"They're all empty," he said, teeth clenched. "They're all running away."

90

Anna felt like Little Red Riding Hood.

The darkness restricted her vision to about fifteen feet ahead. Would the trail soon reach a dead end or come to a creek or river she wouldn't be able to cross? She'd be screwed. Avery had told her to head north, but it seemed impossible to find a direction without a phone.

She wore shorts and the borrowed hoodie, and even though she kept moving steadily, the woods were cold. Sweat ran down her body, and weeds and vines whipped against her legs, scratching them. Her sneakers rubbed at her feet, because she wore no socks. She'd dressed perfectly for making a daring escape through the woods.

Unseen things moved in the trees. Once something large thrashed through the brush twenty feet off the trail, and Anna became convinced a bear was tracking her, waiting for the opportune time to spring out and sink its claws into her neck. Bears were spotted occasionally around the state. Why wouldn't one be out here in the middle of nothingness?

She kept putting one foot in front of the other because Avery had told her to. That was it. That was the only reason. *Avery.* Avery had told her to.

For so long Anna had hated being the youngest child, the one everyone could tell what to do. Even benevolent Alisha liked to give Anna unsolicited advice on life. When Alisha had had her kids, Anna felt relief—maybe someone else would fall below her in the pecking order. But everybody fawned over the grandkids and acted like they could do nothing wrong, so the shit that flowed downhill stopped with Anna.

But in the woods, with the night closing around her like a giant, dark fist, Anna felt grateful for Avery. Her sister—*sister?*—had grabbed her hand and led her away from Collins and Hogan. Avery had known the way to the trail. Anna wished only that Avery had come with her instead of leaving her on her own.

But Avery had gone back—to help the workers. To see if Hank was okay.

How could Anna argue with that?

Her pace slowed. Should she go back too? Did Avery need her help? Anna had seen the workers, knew they looked ragged and exhausted, beaten down by their shitty lives. At least one of them had a baby. Could Avery protect them or help them by herself, especially against men with guns?

Anna stopped and looked back. She could find her way out of the woods and back to the farm. The path led there. And what about Brittany and the kids? Weren't they innocent bystanders to whatever was happening at the farm? Would Avery know that?

Anna rubbed her hands up and down her arms, trying to stay warm. Her teeth chattered a little, as much from nerves and fear as from the chill.

She took one step back toward the farm. And stopped.

"No."

She said it out loud, her voice like a shout in the quiet night.

The guard was there. Avery had tied him up like a hog, but maybe he had worked his way loose.

A voice in her head said, *For once, listen to Avery. Listen to your family, if they can still be called that. Avery is in charge. Let her be.*

Anna reversed her course and started moving up the path again, hoping against all hope that Avery was right and eventually she'd find herself in a place where she could get help.

Before it was too late.

91

Avery passed Yates' body again and crossed the bridge.

As she moved toward the north set of cabins, she walked cautiously. She worried about Hogan. If Hank jamming a knife into him a couple of times hadn't disabled or killed the man, then he was going to be stomping around the farm like a bear with his paw in a trap. He'd be angrier and more dangerous than ever. And there was no way to know who he was going to take it out on.

Hank first. For sure. And Avery herself.

She wanted to find Hank and the others and get them out before any more harm came to them. If Anna found a way out and managed to reach help, then all the better. Someone might arrive to provide backup. Although Avery had her doubts about the local cops. She suspected Hardeman had been paid to look the other way, like a referee in a pro wrestling match.

As Avery approached the cabins, a group of people came toward her. She froze in the path, worried that it was Hogan and Collins coming to get her. But there were too many people—and unless they'd found reinforcements, it couldn't be them.

At the front of the group, one figure emerged. Avery recognized the slender body and the scraggly beard. He walked with his body canted to one side, his right arm applying pressure to his left biceps. Hank. Like the Pied Piper, he was leading a group of workers away from the cabins and down the path toward escape.

He came closer, blood on his arm, skin pale. Sweat beaded on his forehead like raindrops. He looked to be holding on by a narrow thread.

"My God, you've been shot," Avery said as they reached each other.

"Just once," he said, wincing, as if the words cost him effort. "I'm lucky I stabbed Hogan before he tried to shoot me. It messed up his aim."

"Still, this is a lot of blood. Too much."

"Why did you come back, Avery? I thought you were getting Anna out of here. Couldn't you find the trail? You need to go. Now."

"We found it. I put Anna on it. But I came back because—well, I was worried about you. And I thought other people needed help." She looked past Hank to the crowd of farmworkers. They looked scared, their eyes wide and haunted in the dark. Camila and Gilberto—and their baby. The guy Collins had beaten in the field. Tommy. Celina and Vladimir. She had made the right choice. "Let's get all of you out of here. Where's Hogan?"

"He's on his feet. I saw him walk away. I think he went to get help. Maybe Collins—"

"I took care of Collins. He's out of commission for a bit."

"Nice. Everyone's scared. They've always been told not to leave without permission."

"Come on. Hogan won't be far off. Let's get everyone to the trail."

Avery took a step that way and waved her hand at the crowd, who looked uncertain. Hank said something to them in Spanish. Avery understood one word. *Peligro.* Tommy nodded along, said, "Let's go, people. This is fucked."

"Easy, Tommy," Hank said. "They'll get moving."

"I'm ready to go," Tommy said, touching his bruised and swollen face. "Now."

They all started walking, but Hank remained in place, still clutching his arm. He started shaking his head.

"Hank?"

"I can't, Avery. If you hadn't shown up . . ."

"No. Come on. I'll carry you if I have to."

"I'll slow you down on the trail, and you have to move fast. And it's going to be hard enough to move quickly with this group. I'll make it worse."

"What are you saying?"

"You take them out. You know where the trail is, so go. I'll . . ." He looked behind him, in the direction of the other set of cabins and ultimately the big house. If Hogan was coming with reinforcements, he'd be coming that way. "I'm going to stay here. I'll slow them down and maybe . . . maybe Anna will have found help by then. Or else . . . I don't know."

"Let's all go. This is bullshit, Hank."

"This is the right way. And you know it. Get them out of here. Or at least hide them in the woods until help gets here. If I stay right here in this clearing, I can slow them down long enough to give you a chance. It isn't a big one, but it's something. Go."

"I won't—"

"Go. Okay? Please."

He was right. She could tell by looking at him that he might not make it very far. And if they hoped to get the ragtag group down to the trail and off the property, it would take every bit of good fortune they could find.

It ripped her heart in half to leave him behind.

She lifted her shirt and brought out the gun she had taken from Collins.

"This might help. Can you hold it?"

Hank took it. "I can hold it well enough to make some noise."

"Will you try to be careful?"

"We're a little past careful. Go."

"No, Hank . . . I—I'm going to stay with you."

"You're going to go. Now."

Avery waved the workers forward, and they started moving, heading down the path toward what she hoped was safety.

She said, "I'm sorry we didn't—I didn't handle things better.

Between us. I'm glad you dragged me out of that pond, but it also seems like everything started to go wrong then. You know?"

"There's nothing to be sorry for. Just go."

He turned his back and started past the firepit, toward the far side of the clearing. He moved slowly, like a man who was wiped out on his feet.

Avery wanted to say more but couldn't think of anything.

Besides, she was the Pied Piper now, and she needed to get her charges as far away from Hogan and the Combs family as she possibly could, as quickly as she could.

She fell in behind them as they moved down the path.

92

The north set of cabins came into view.

Hogan tried to breathe evenly, to keep his heart rate level. He gripped the pistol, hoped he'd be able to use it if he had to.

He hoped he didn't have to.

Taylor asked, "Where's the cop?"

"In his cabin, on the left."

When they reached the clearing, a voice called out from the far side.

"Hold it."

Both men froze in their tracks. Hogan cocked his head to one side, tried to figure out who'd spoken. The male voice rang with authority. Not like one of the farmhands speaking. They'd have known better.

He thought he knew—

"Who's that?" Taylor asked. "Collins?"

"Don't come any farther," the voice said. "Just stay there."

"It's the cop," Hogan said. "He's in the brush past the cabins."

"I thought you—"

"I don't know," Hogan said. "But it's him. Has to be."

Hogan had fired up close, but it had been dark and his arm and back had been burning. His shots could have missed, could have flown harmlessly over the cop's head and become embedded in the rear wall of the cabin.

But what could the cop do to them? His only weapon had ended up in Hogan's back. And now Brittany had it.

Hogan stepped forward. "Okay, cop. Whatever your name is. We're just trying to find out what's going on with our employees. They all seem to have flown the coop. See, that's taking money out of Mr. Combs' pockets. This is his land and his business. So we want those folks to just come on back, return to their cabins, and get back to work. That's it. We don't have a quarrel with you either, even though you put a knife in my back. Twice. Let's just all cool down and keep everybody safe."

"Your *employees* are leaving. You stay there and let them go."

"I imagine your girlfriend is trying to take them off the farm," Hogan said. "But Mr. Collins might have something to say about that."

"Mr. Collins is incapacitated."

Hogan felt a cold wave pass through him, a combination of anger and surprise. He stopped for a moment, then shook his head. "That's bullshit."

"Just stand there, both of you. Just wait. Everyone will be gone, and then you can do whatever you want with me."

Hogan started forward, his grip on the gun tightening.

"Be careful, Hogan—"

Hogan moved past the campfire, saw the open door of the cabin in which he had shot at the cop. As he moved, something whistled past his head, followed by the crack of a report.

"Get down," Taylor said.

The cop had a gun. And he was using it.

Another shot went past Hogan's head. He dove to the side, taking shelter behind the cabin wall. Taylor did the same across the way.

The cop had a gun. Collins' gun. Collins really was incapacitated. And they were pinned down, helpless to stop the workers getting out and blowing the lid off everything.

93

Avery and the workers crossed the wooden bridge over the river and moved on down the trail.

Avery led the group, knowing full well they were going to pass Yates' body. She suspected that the group could handle the sight, that they'd seen plenty in their lives, but she still felt protective. She wished none of them had to see anything like Yates' dead body, face-down in the dirt.

But when they reached it, the workers barely gave it a second look. They'd heard the shots, so they knew what they were dealing with. Avery found herself slightly sickened by the body, something in her core shaking as they walked past it. But the others kept their re-actions to themselves.

Once they were past Yates, and the trail started to make a slight downward slope toward the fields, Avery allowed herself to feel slightly better. She knew the way to the trail. She could get them all there. She could keep them safe.

She tried not to think about Hank. The bullet wound in his arm. Hogan and whoever else from the farm closing in on him. Hank putting himself between them and the workers so everyone could get away . . .

His actions didn't surprise her. And she tried to take comfort in believing in Hank's toughness and resourcefulness. If anyone could find a way out, he could.

A shot cracked.

Everyone froze and ducked, even though, Avery could tell, the shot had been fired back at the cabins. Back where Hank stood guard, protecting them.

"It's okay," she said. "Let's keep moving."

Then another shot cut through the night. The same gun.

Hank? Holding them off?

Or being gunned down?

"This is getting really bad," Tommy said.

"Keep moving," she said again, waving them forward.

The tension in Avery rose. If Hogan and the others managed to get past Hank, they could come down the trail behind the workers and her. Close in on them.

Something moved on the trail ahead of them.

Avery slowed her pace, squinted her eyes to stare into the dark. She tried to make out the movement on the trail.

The figure resolved into a man-sized shape. Stumbling up the trail toward the top of the hill. Stumbling but moving toward them.

Collins.

94

Avery froze.

The rest of the group saw Collins as well. Since they'd been living under his thumb, they knew what it meant to come across him in the dark. After he'd told them all to stay inside no matter what. They had defied his order.

When Collins spotted them, his posture stiffened. He wobbled a little, though, no doubt feeling the effects of the blow Avery had struck.

But he was on his feet, facing them.

And he was pissed.

"What the fuck is this?" he asked.

"Piece of shit," Tommy said, his voice low.

Even in the dark, Avery saw Collins' gaze fix on her.

"Who do you think you are?" he asked. His hand went to the back of his head, gingerly touched the spot where Avery had whacked him. "Do you know what you've done? Do you know how bad this is going to be for you? For all of you? *Todos ustedes.*"

Avery sensed the unease as it passed through the group. Some of the workers started to back away.

But where would they go? With Hogan and Combs behind and Collins ahead?

"A la cueva."

The voice was low. Avery recognized it. Camila.

She said it again, loud enough for the group to hear. But not Collins.

"*A la cueva.*"

It might be the best chance they had. They outnumbered Collins, but did Avery really want to stake everything on trying to physically overwhelm a man in the dark? She couldn't know what other weapons he might have. Even with an injured head and a likely concussion, he'd be a tough adversary. Angry and ready to fight—like Hogan with the knife in his back.

She didn't want to expose the farmworkers to attack or injury.

But if the group reached the cave, maybe they could hide there. Avery didn't know how big or deep it was, but maybe they could avoid the men until help arrived. The cave also offered a clear view of anyone approaching—and might enable them to defend themselves with anything available: rocks, sticks. *Anything.*

"Go," Avery said. "*A la cueva.*"

"Yeah, let's go," Tommy said.

They started to move that way.

"Fast," Avery said. "*Rápido. A la cueva.*"

The group moved down the path that paralleled the river, and headed for the cave.

Only Avery remained in place—face-to-face with Collins.

Collins came forward, his hands raised.

He looked like a wrestler getting ready to grapple.

Avery had taken him once, down by the crops. But she'd surprised him that time, come up behind him and gonged him with a rock.

In a direct confrontation, even with him hobbling because of the injury, she didn't think she could fight him off. Her only hope was to slow him down, give the workers a chance to get to the cave and hide.

But once Collins was past her, it would be easy for him to quickly catch up to the farmworkers. And how far behind were Hogan and Combs? How badly would they treat those who had defied them?

Avery's mind raced.

Collins approached. There were no rocks to grab. But Avery bent down, scooped her hand in the dirt. She brought up a handful and flung it, aiming for Collins' face. Some of the dirt struck him in the eyes, temporarily blinding him and knocking him off-balance.

He grunted, lifted his hands to brush at his face.

Avery could have run forward, tried to knock him down again and dash for freedom the same way Anna had gone. But she couldn't leave the workers to fend for themselves.

She turned to run down the path and toward the cave. She risked a look back, saw Collins lumbering her way.

Another shot was fired, that one in her direction.

Hogan?

"Avery, run."

It was Hank.

He had saved her ass once again.

95

Avery pounded down the path that ran parallel to the river.

As she went, the river grew wider and the force of the rushing water increased.

Another shot sounded behind her, but she kept running. She refused to look back. As she got closer to the cave, she felt the temperature drop dramatically. At least fifteen degrees.

She ran what must have been a thousand feet and finally caught up with the crowd of workers. The ones at the rear of the group, including Camila and her baby, turned to look back at her as she approached.

"Inside the cave," Avery said. "Quick, hide inside."

Whether they all understood her words or not, they understood her meaning. Avery urged them along, making pushing gestures with her hands. She hoped they could get inside there, press themselves back into some obscure corner and wait for help to arrive. Even if it took all night. Avery checked her watch—it was almost two. Four hours until sunrise. By then—surely by then—Anna would be back with help.

The cave mouth resolved into view in the dark. It was easily three stories high and as wide as a small house. The river ran through the left side of the cave opening. On the right was the cave floor, large enough for at least fifty people to crowd in comfortably. They all filed in, the sound of the river now so loud as it echoed off the rocky cave walls that they could barely hear anything they said to one another.

"Move back. Move to the back," Avery said.

"Come on, people," Tommy said.

They did. Avery smelled something familiar. Something that stung her nostrils.

She turned on the flashlight, used it to quickly scan the space, up and then over at the walls. Suspended in the air, from a series of ropes and cords, were hundreds and hundreds of marijuana plants. The Combs family used the cave to dry and cure their crop.

Avery's mind couldn't calculate fast enough how much the plants must be worth, but it was certainly an enormous amount of money—with more still in the field waiting to be harvested.

"Holy crap," she said as she continued to look around.

"Good temperature," Camila said loudly into her ear. "Cool."

"Right."

"Jesus," Tommy said. "This is worth . . . fuck, I don't know how much."

They continued to move back, entering darkness. Avery used the flashlight to show the way, although it didn't reveal much. And the risk of exposing the workers to their pursuers was too great. She needed to turn the flashlight off quickly.

The ground they stood on was shaped like a wedge of pie. They'd entered the cave at the crust, and the farther back they moved toward the point, the less room there was. Eventually, they were crowded against the edge of the rushing river with nowhere to go. The river flowed on into the cave, out of sight and into the distance. But they were out of land. All they could do was stand there, about three hundred feet from the mouth of the cave, their eyes adjusting to the gloom. And wait.

And hope.

Avery stared down at the water, then turned the light off. Her proximity to the river caused a reaction inside her, a shivering, cringing aversion that hit the reptilian portion of her brain and made her want to back away in fear. She couldn't control it. The feeling controlled her. Camila stood next to her, and Avery wanted to reach out and take her hand. Anything to steady herself, anything for reassurance that she wasn't about to get sucked into the dark, cold water.

Avery stepped back, looked over at Camila. "We'll just wait. My sister went to get help."

"Okay," Camila said. But her eyes showed greater concern. "They will leave us alone here?"

The tone of her voice told Avery what she thought the answer to the question was.

No.

Avery had attacked them. The workers were running from them.

And all that stood between them and the three men chasing them was Hank. Hank with his scrawny body and his one good arm. How many rounds remained in his gun?

The sound of two more shots reached them.

No, they weren't going to leave the workers alone.

Avery knew—*they were coming.*

And if she had any doubts, they were erased a few minutes later. As the group huddled together against the rear wall of the cave, waiting and waiting, something caught Avery's eye. Something light in the dark river heading toward them. She raised the flashlight for a moment.

It might have been an animal, something floating along on the top of the water. But it was flat. Light colored. Not an animal or a person.

A piece of paper? A note?

Not that either. But it *was* a message.

When it came abreast of them in the cave, she understood it.

A shirt. Hank's bloodstained shirt.

Hank was dead. And they were next.

96

Long minutes ticked by.

The baby started to cry, competing with the noise of the rushing water.

"We'll be okay," Avery said. "It's okay."

"I don't know, dude," Tommy said. "These guys play hard."

"They have guns," Camila said. "We have none."

"Protect your baby," Avery said. "Move back. Protect the baby."

"Podemos salir por la cueva," Gilberto shouted.

"What's that?" Avery asked.

"He says we can go . . . through the cave," Camila said.

"We can't. It ends."

"A través del río. El río al borde del bosque. Por el camino."

"He says through the river. The river comes out on the other side. By the road." Camila nodded, confirming what her husband said. "He says. Everybody says."

"Are you sure?"

"She's right," Tommy said. "The river runs underground. Some people say, anyway."

"Sí. Collins said it once. Very dangerous."

"Then we shouldn't do it," Avery said.

"Maybe they just want to keep us here," Camila said. "So they tell us this."

"Yeah, maybe we should wait," Tommy said. "Are the cops coming?"

"I don't know. Probably."

"Probably?"

Gilberto came over and started pointing at the water. *"Tenemos que irnos. Tenemos que irnos ahora. Ahora."*

Avery didn't need a translation. He wanted them to go—and go now.

"Is he going to swim?" Avery asked. "What's he going to do?"

Gilberto and Vladimir started having an intense discussion. Gilberto pointed at the rushing water. Vladimir pointed back toward the opening of the cave. Celina tried to say something and was shouted down.

They all stopped when a sound rose above the rushing water.

Avery recognized the voice.

Hogan.

"Listen down there," he said. "We don't want to see anyone get hurt. But you're going to have to come out of there and come back to camp. None of you have been listening to us very well. Especially you, Officer Rogers. We really want to talk to you about this situation. Now just come out—or we're going to have to come in."

Avery stepped forward. "Let these people out, okay? They haven't done anything. If you want me, that's fine. But not them."

"We might be open to that," Hogan said, his voice echoing through the cave. "But you all have to come out first."

Avery turned to the group. "Let me go out. I'll talk to them. They want—maybe they won't do anything to you if I go out and talk to them."

She stepped that way, and Camila reached out, put her hand on Avery's arm. "Don't go. Don't."

"They want *me*. Not you."

"Camila's right," Tommy said. "Listen to her."

"They have guns," Camila said. "They hurt people."

"Well?" Hogan said. His voice sounded closer. "It's time to decide."

A large splash echoed through the cave. Avery looked. Celina had jumped into the water. She flailed for a moment, her arms beating the surface. But the rushing water swept her away and out of sight, out the back of the cave.

"Oh my God," Avery said.

"Fuck it—I'm going." Tommy jumped in as well. As the current pulled him away, he said, "It's colllld."

Vladimir followed suit. He jumped into the water almost like a cannonball and let the rushing water sweep him away.

"Uno a la vez," Gilberto said. He waved at Camila. *"Vamos. Vamos."*

"One at a time," Camila said. "Very narrow."

"Vamos. Vamos."

"I can't go, Camila. I'm terrified of the water. I can't get in there. You go."

"You must."

"I can't. You don't understand. I can't."

"You *must.*"

As if to prove Camila right, Hogan shouted one more time. "We're coming in now."

A bullet whizzed over Avery's head, close enough for her to feel it pass, followed by the report, which echoed off the cave walls.

"Vamos." Gilberto pointed at the water. *"Vamos."*

"Vete, vete." Camila made shooing gestures with the hand that wasn't holding the baby. *"Estaré justo detrás de ti."*

"La bebé?"

"Vete. Vete."

Gilberto looked reluctant to go. Another shot was fired, and that decided him. He stepped toward the river, folded his arms across his chest, and said, *"Te quiero."*

"Te quiero."

He jumped in and was gone, leaving Avery and Camila alone by the river with the baby. Avery looked back once toward the mouth of the cave.

A shot whistled past her head. It thumped into flesh—and then Camila screamed.

Avery turned as Camila dropped to the cave floor. She held on to the baby with one hand. But Camila's groans echoed off the walls. The red stain on Camila's shoulder grew larger, her face contorted by searing pain.

"No, Camila. Shit."

Avery bent down, examined the wound. It looked like the bullet had gone through flesh, and flesh only. No bone or artery. That was the good news.

But Camila needed to get out immediately.

With a baby.

Avery helped Camila to her feet. The baby started to cry. "Camila, go."

Camila shook her head. "It hurts. *Mucho dolor.*"

"Can you just hold on with one arm?"

Avery sounded like an idiot making the suggestion. And Camila shook her head.

Another bullet whipped over them.

Camila moved forward, thrust the baby into Avery's arms.

"Wait, no . . ."

"You must."

"But I—"

"You must. You take her."

The baby settled into Avery's arms. She tried to think of the last time she'd held one. One of Alisha's kids? And even then, the babies had always felt unnatural in her hands, like someone had tossed a wild animal at her.

Camila leaned in, kissed the baby on the top of the head. She looked at Avery. "You're strong. *Fuerte.* You have two arms."

Camila jumped in as the others had and was swept away by the river.

Avery felt frozen in place. The baby started to squirm. She pulled it closer, whispered in her ear to calm her, felt the soft, downy hair against her lips. She turned her body so it was between the child and the men coming into the cave.

Firing into the cave.

Avery pulled the baby even tighter to her chest. Terror rose inside her, spreading to every cell in her body. Her muscles quaked. She broke out in a sweat, even in the cool cave.

No no no no no.

I can't I can't I can't I can't.

But she had no choice.

She moved to the edge of the river, placed her hand over the baby's head—the little protection she could offer.

And jumped in.

97

The stinging cold water took her breath away.

Needles digging into her skin.

Avery closed her eyes, squeezed them tight. She felt the water rise over her face as she bobbed. Panic spread like a wildfire along every nerve ending inside her.

The baby the baby.

She held the baby tight, pressed against her chest. She made sure the baby's head stayed above the water.

The current took her away. Like she was in a jet from a fire hose, she was shot forward, propelled into the darkness at the back of the cave.

Avery couldn't tell where the baby and she were going—if they were going to smash into a wall or a rock. If they'd find themselves crashing into the broken bodies of the workers. Or if some random movement of the river might kill Avery—and the baby—and the others would be left waiting outside, never knowing what had happened to them.

The river dropped down a small waterfall. Avery yelped.

They were flat for a while. Then the river dropped again, like an elevator quickly plunging, creating the feeling—briefly—of there being nothing beneath them.

But there was water. Always cold, dark water in the dark, dark cave.

Avery's eyes remained closed—and she found herself back in the pond on the side of I-65—below the surface of the water, her body sinking down to the bottom of the pond. Hands reaching her—Hank—pulling her up—

Hank.

He was dead. They had killed him. They had sent his shirt down the river to tell her.

She should have gone back—she should have done more.

He'd saved her at the pond, and he'd saved her today.

But she held the baby—*the baby the baby*—

Anna was the first baby Avery had ever held. She'd saved Anna. She'd saved the workers. She held the baby—was that enough?

Was it ever enough?

Then she was in the air, shooting over the water. The air changed—warmer. Avery splashed down into a pool. They briefly went under and came right back up. The water was warmer as well.

When she came to the surface, the baby was crying. Avery opened her eyes. She saw trees around them, stars above. They were outside.

Outside. Out of the cave.

Avery's feet dug, found purchase against the bottom of the pool of water. She straightened up, pulled the baby closer.

"Shhh. Shhh. It's okay. We're out."

But where were the others? Had something gone wrong?

Panic gripped Avery. Colder than anything else she'd felt. Were they hurt? Lost? Captured?

"Alexa!"

Someone waded into the water, splashing toward them. Camila and Gilberto.

"She's okay," Avery said. "She's okay."

Camila took the baby, folded her in her arms, ignoring her own pain. Kissed the baby all over her tiny head.

"She's okay," Avery said. "She's okay."

Was she talking about the baby? Or Anna?

Or herself?

"That was totally badass," Tommy said. "Fuck, yes."

Avery had never felt so tired in her life. They all sloshed to the bank, moving out of the water and onto the muddy shore. Avery's legs turned to rubber. They couldn't hold her. She simply let her body go and sat down on the ground. She waited for her breath to come back. Her entire body shivered.

She was out. Holy crap—she was out.

They were all out.

Avery looked up. The river flowed on, smaller and with less force. In the dark, she saw the outline of the small bridge, the one she'd driven across when she came looking for the Combs farm.

Then she heard them. Faint at first but growing closer.

Sirens. More than one. She heard the engines revving, saw the cruisers pass over the bridge, heading down the county road to the entrance of the Combs farm.

They were there. Anna got them. She must have. That was why the cops were coming, and that was why it was going to be—

Gilberto came over to her. He leaned down.

"Estás bien?"

She nodded her head in the dark.

"Sí, sí. I'm okay. I am okay."

98

It took hours to sort things out.

Avery led the farmworkers up a small hill, at the top of which they reached the county road. Avery flagged down one of the cruisers as it sped by, and quickly medical attention came for their group. Along with the KSP and the sheriff's office, who had questions.

A lot of questions.

Avery asked one of her own first. Was Anna okay?

A KSP officer told her that Anna was just fine. She'd managed to walk the trail all the way out to Highway 9, as Hank had promised. And once there, she had flagged down a passing motorist—a nurse returning from her shift in the ER—and they called the police. Anna was currently being questioned at the police station in Rydell. She'd said she didn't need any medical attention, but she was hungry.

Avery was cold. Wrapped in a blanket—and wishing for another one. She sat in the back of a KSP cruiser, shivering, even though the heat blasted out like someone had opened a portal to hell. But her heart glowed with pride when she heard about Anna making it. Help wouldn't have arrived without her.

Avery then asked about Hank. A KSP detective she didn't know, name of Cross, was handling her questioning. Cross said he couldn't say anything for sure about Hank but promised to find out.

"After all," Cross said, "he's one of our brothers."

"Right."

"In the meantime," Cross said, "I need you to tell me what went on in there."

Avery did, slowly and carefully, trying her best to leave nothing out. Once she thought they'd been through it thoroughly the first time, she was asked to go through it again. She did—she tried to—but as she did, she grew more tired, more hungry, more irritated by the process, even though she understood that was exactly how things were going to unfold with the police. That was likely to be the first of countless times she repeated the story in the coming weeks and months, and she tried very carefully to remember every detail, to relate things in the exact and necessary order. She took pride in being able to do so. She might not be a cop anymore, but she didn't want anyone to forget that she had once been one. She knew how to report the most important information. And report it accurately.

As she went through the story both times, emergency vehicles came and went from the Combs property. Police cruisers, ambulances. Any number of unmarked cars. She wondered each time if they were bringing Hank out. And if he was alive. The image of his shirt floating down the river, bloodstained. The shots that had rung out behind her.

Hope seemed foolish.

"Can we get out of here?" Avery asked. "I'm cold. And I have to use the bathroom."

"Sure," Cross said. "We can head back to the station in Rydell. We have enough to go on now. Let me just clear it."

Cross stepped out of the car and made a call. As Avery waited in the back, a white van went by. Even in the dark, she was able to read the word on the side of the van: CORONER.

The chill inside Avery gripped her harder. Like a claw hanging on to the back of her neck. Something large, like an animal, was ready to shake her and torment her.

She tried to shift her thoughts to something positive. Something she'd won. Anna was okay. The workers were okay. Alexa, the baby, was okay.

But was anything in the win column enough to offset the losses?

Cross climbed back in, turned the vehicle around, and drove back to Rydell. They rode in silence for a few miles. Avery stared out the window, the blanket pulled tight around her body. Once the questions about Hank swirled, others swirled as well. They encased her head like a whirlwind. How was Anna related to these people? And how had none of Avery's family known?

"What do you know about these people, Detective?" Avery asked. "What do you suspect about how my sister ended up here?"

Cross drove on, the tires humming over the pavement in the dark. Avery thought he was ignoring her. But then he said, "You understand I can't say much, right?"

"You don't have to say anything if you don't want."

"I'm going to say *something*," he said. "I just have to be discreet. But you're a former cop, so I know you understand."

It felt good to be referred to that way, to have Cross include her in a fraternity.

"These are bad people," he said. "Violent people. We've had our eye on them for a long time. Years. And there are bodies strewn along the way."

"I can imagine that now."

"If your sister is related to them, I hope she will make some peace with it," he said, "but it's a tough hand to be dealt. To find out your family has killers in it. But maybe your folks can help her. She was lucky to be raised in your family and not this one. She'll understand that someday."

They pulled into Rydell and stopped in front of the police station. Cross stepped out and opened the back door for Avery. She'd just started to feel warm as they drove along, and stepping out into the cold night made her shiver again. Would her body ever stop trembling? She'd felt the same way for days after the experience in the pond. Was she starting that all over again?

Outside the station, a couple of men stood on the sidewalk talking in low voices. They nodded to Cross as Avery and he passed. More cars were parked on the street in the middle of the night than Avery had seen in the daytime, and inside, the front room was full as well. Avery scanned the crowd, looking for Anna, but didn't see her. She did see Hardeman, who sat off to the side, looking like an extra appendage.

Cross spoke to an officer in a suit and hooked his thumb in Avery's direction. The guy in the suit nodded, and Cross led Avery through a closed door and down a short hallway, where bright fluorescent lights glowed off the dull linoleum floor. The glare gave Avery a headache. At the end of the hall, Cross knocked on a door and then stepped back.

"Go on," he said.

Avery turned the knob, the blanket still draped over her shoulders like a poncho, and went in. Anna sat alone in a small wooden chair. She wore a matching blanket over her shoulders, and the two of them looked like twins. The harsh light made Anna look younger, like a child waiting in a nurse's office. Her face brightened when Avery appeared. She stood up.

The two women went to each other. Anna collapsed into Avery's arms.

"Avery, you're here. You're okay."

"I'm okay. Don't worry. I'm glad to see you."

Avery pulled her tight. Like the baby she'd held a few hours earlier.

"I was terrified you were hurt." Anna started to sob, her body shuddering against Avery's. Avery held her, rubbed her sister's back. "It's okay. You're safe."

Tears filled Avery's eyes as well. A few ran out and down her face. She let them go. She didn't wipe them. She held on to Anna instead.

After a few minutes, Anna calmed down. She said, "They said you swam through an underground river or something. Is that right?"

Avery laughed a little. "I didn't really swim. I was swept by the current. I held on for dear life."

"You hate the water. You never swim. Alisha's always said— Well, never mind."

"I do hate the water. But I like living, so I did it."

"And you saved all those people? And a baby?"

Avery loosened her hold on Anna, took a step back so she could meet her sister's eyes. "I did what had to be done. That's all. Are you okay?"

Anna nodded. "I didn't get hurt. I just went through the woods like you said. I almost turned back . . . but you told me to go on, so I did."

"Good."

Anna looked at the floor.

"What?"

"I was able to call home. I talked to Dad for a minute. You know, just to let them know I was okay."

"Good. I'm sure they were worried."

"I guess. . . . I don't know what I'm supposed to make of all of this."

"I don't know either, Anna."

"They're saying . . ." She looked at Avery, looked down again. Her breath came in huffs. "My parents, my biological parents, were murdered . . . and they're saying maybe someone close to them did it . . . like maybe it was Taylor. Some beef over the drug business."

Someone knocked on the door.

"Hold on," Avery said. She turned back to Anna. "I'm so sorry. But we'll figure this out. Okay? Now that all of this has been broken open, the police can make some connections. They've arrested all of them, including Taylor Combs. They'll find out what's going on." Avery remembered what Cross had said in the car. The brutality of the family stretching back many years. "I think the Combs family must have threatened Dad and Charlie years ago. Dad was always paranoid, but maybe it was with good reason. It's not going to be easy, but we'll be there with you as this gets sorted out."

"Who will?"

"We will. Your family who loves you."

The knocking again. That time, someone pushed the door open. It was Cross. "We need to ask both of you a few more questions. Then you can go."

"Do you mind waiting a minute?" Avery asked. "We're talking."

"Okay," Cross said. "But we have a station full of people trying to work." He closed the door.

"Fucking cops," Avery said.

"It's okay." But Anna didn't sound convinced.

"What's the matter?"

"It's just— It's Dad. On the phone before."

"What did he do?"

"Can we just talk about it on the way home?"

Avery studied her sister's face. "Sure. Okay."

"I want to get out of here. Go get that cop so we can go."

"Are you sure?"

It took Anna a moment to answer. Then she said, "I'm not sure of anything. But I know I want to go."

"Okay."

Avery opened the door. Cross waited in the hall. And with him was Detective Morris from Breckville.

"Hey, Avery," he said. "When I heard about the excitement here, I just knew you had to be tied up in it in some way."

99

Avery and Morris went into another room. That one was smaller than the one she'd been in with Anna. A gunmetal gray desk took up most of the space, along with a bookshelf that held ancient copies of law enforcement manuals. The same deadly bright lights burned from the ceiling.

Morris sat behind the desk, leaving Avery in the uncomfortable chair on the other side.

"You okay?" Morris asked. "I hear you had quite an adventure."

"Can you answer a question for me?" Avery asked.

"I can try."

"Officer Hank Landry. He was inside the farm. Undercover. Do you have an update on his condition?"

"Hmm. They were talking about him out there. Said he's in surgery. Two gunshot wounds. They were cautiously optimistic."

Avery felt like fifty pounds had been lifted off her shoulders. "Thank you."

"Friend of yours?"

"Something like that."

"There's been plenty of excitement around these parts."

"Enough for the rest of my life."

"It looks like your sister's okay."

"She's safe. She has a lot to work through."

"Sure, I heard about that too." Morris ran his hand over the laminated top of the desk like he was brushing off dust only he could see.

"I know you want to get home. And get your sister back. I won't take much time."

"That's merciful."

"My only real interest here is the murder I'm investigating."

"Kayla Garvey."

"Right. This Nicholas Yates, who I understand is now deceased, is my prime suspect. Did you talk to him inside there? Did he say anything that could help me?"

Avery still wore the blanket, but her body temperature seemed to be returning to normal. She let the blanket slide off the top of her shoulders. "I talked to him only once, really, but not about Kayla. He went out of his way to tell me he didn't have any power in the Combs organization. That he couldn't make anything happen." She shrugged. "I was more concerned with getting out of there than with anything else. I suspect Hogan is the guy you want to talk to. I suspect that he sent Yates after Anna and that he killed Yates to shut him up."

"Hogan says they meant no harm to Anna. Yates was sent to her apartment merely to check her out, to see who this person was who was suddenly a genetic match to Brittany Combs. I guess Yates couldn't follow instructions. Somehow he ended up killing Kayla instead of learning who your sister is."

It felt like twenty years ago in some ways, but the memory of discovering Kayla's body burned fresh in her mind. The way the lamp glowed over her face. Avery shuddered.

"Cold?" Morris asked.

"Bad memories."

"Mmm. Sorry."

"Well, I've lived with those before," Avery said.

Morris nodded. "I don't want to be more of a pain. If you didn't hear anything else, I get it. We probably have enough on Yates as it stands. Now that he's gone, unfortunately. Thanks."

But Morris remained seated behind the desk. The swivel chair with green padding on the arms squeaked under his weight. He looked like a man in no hurry.

"Was there something else?" Avery asked.

Morris ran his fingers over the imaginary dust again. "I don't have a dog in this hunt, but I am curious. Do *you* have any idea how your sister was related to the Combs family and yet raised by your father and stepmother?"

Avery laughed. The release felt good. "Detective, I'm not omniscient. Anna heard some things from Brittany Combs indicating there was bad blood between her birth father and Taylor Combs. Nobody could have anticipated that twenty-some years later we'd have online DNA tests to dig up all the old bones. They're drug dealers. What do *you* know about it?"

"Not much. An execution-style killing. Three family members. Some in law enforcement are theorizing your sister was an infant at the time."

"And she was handed over to the state to be adopted?"

"That's a theory. We'd have to dig back into the records."

"Any suspects?"

"Two shooters. Untraceable weapons. No surprise there."

"They're drug dealers. What do you expect?"

"Right. Sure." He lifted his hand from the desk, rubbed the tips of his index and middle fingers with this thumb. "Did you know your father was on a KSP task force that was investigating the Combs and Douglas families?"

The rhythm of Avery's heart altered slightly. "No, I didn't know that."

"It's true. I learned that from Lieutenant Paulson. KSP. Do you know him?"

"I know the name."

"He said the task force stopped working on the family a few months before the shooting. But still . . ."

"But still what?"

"I know you lost Charlie Ballard in Louisville. And I'm sorry for that. I've looked into this a little bit, and he was on that task force as well. Maybe he mentioned something when you were together—"

"He didn't. And if you're only here to investigate Kayla's murder, and your suspect is dead, why are you hectoring me?"

"I want to find out if you know anything. This is your family. And it looks like your father was surveilling a drug ring. Members of the drug ring ended up dead. And your father ended up with their baby but never told anyone where she came from."

"My dad—he's not very open. Maybe he didn't want Anna to feel strange about being adopted."

"Yeah, maybe. Or . . ."

"Or what, Detective?"

Avery's voice had come out louder than she'd planned. But the late hour, the cold, her exhaustion, had all conspired to push her to the limit.

Morris raised his hands. "You're right. I'll back off. I'm a cop. I'm curious. And I'm just thinking out loud. I'm sorry to have pushed you on it. I know you had a very rough few days." He stood up from the squeaky chair and came around the desk. "I'll let you get on your way."

Avery remained in her chair. She felt like she couldn't get up, that to do so required energy and will that she couldn't summon.

"Are you okay?"

"Yeah."

"Maybe you want to crash in a hotel for a while. The pickings are slim, but I found a decent place over in Blanton. You and your sister could stay there."

"No, I want to get Anna home. People are worried about her."

"Sure." He lingered a moment longer. "Have a safe trip."

"When this shooting occurred, the murder of this family, the police talked to my dad, right? And Charlie?"

"I would think so."

"And?"

"I guess your dad and Charlie Ballard cooperated with the investigation. They probably provided some leads. Names of other lowlifes who might have wanted to harm the Douglas family."

"That's probably a long list."

"Undoubtedly."

"And they followed all those leads?"

"They probably tried. There may not have been a lot of tears shed over Danny Douglas. And if your dad, well, cut some corners to adopt the surviving baby, I don't think anyone would want to jam him up now."

There was a fire . . . all the pictures . . . and she and Alisha were gone. . . .

"Thank you, Detective."

"You're welcome."

He closed the door when he left, and Avery sat in the little room until Cross knocked on the door and told her she could take Anna home now.

100

Anna's hands still shook. She couldn't drive.

The sun was just about to come up, and they'd be on narrow back roads, so she let Avery do it. The cops said she could come back to Rydell and claim her car at any time—and if she didn't want to go back, she could ask someone else to go get it. Rachel and Eric could make an afternoon of it if they wanted.

They rode in Charlie's truck, which felt weird. It smelled like him, retained his presence, and Anna had trouble thinking of him being gone. She hadn't seen him in several years. And now she never would again.

Avery mentioned going by Charlie's house and getting her car. But she could do that another day as well. Anna got the feeling her sister wanted to get them home as soon as possible. Fulfill the promise she'd made to their dad to bring her back. Hell or high water, as the old man always said.

Hell or high water. Avery and she had found both.

Avery could tell their dad that she had swum through an underground river to save people. Alisha had always said that she traced the difficulties between their dad and Avery back to his tossing Avery into the deep end of the pool so she would learn how to swim. Maybe Avery was happy that his efforts had finally borne fruit.

The sky lightened as they drove. It turned salmon and coral while a few wisps of fog clung to the low-lying areas around the trees. The sisters rode mostly in silence. No radio. The tires hummed against the road, with the occasional bump. Anna tried not to think about what would come next. Walk in the door of the house. Her mom and dad fawning over her, telling her how glad they were she was safe. . . .

Then what?

Would she simply ask, *Where the hell did I come from?*

And what about school? She'd fucked up the semester by not going to class. No way on earth was she going back and living in the apartment where Kayla had died. Students could get a break from the college if they had a tragedy like a roommate dying. In Anna's freshman year, a woman in her dorm had died in a car accident. The school let her traumatized roommate take her classes over. But Anna couldn't ask for that. She'd bailed on school before Kayla died. Her trauma was self-inflicted. Or family inflicted, to be more precise.

"Do you mind if I ask you something?"

Avery's voice pulled Anna out of her own head. She felt relieved to hear it. She recognized the spiral she could head into, trying to anticipate everything that lay ahead of her. She could tell there were no easy answers—maybe no answers at all. Avery's voice brought her back to the present.

Anna turned from the window. She'd been staring out at the passing scenery, squinting as the sun got brighter.

"Sure."

"When we were talking at the police station, you mentioned something Dad said on the phone. You said we could talk about it on the way home."

"Oh, that." Anna had stopped thinking about it back at the police station. "Just Dad being . . . Well, I almost said stupid. But let's just say it was Dad being Dad."

"What did he say?"

"Dad—*Russ*—said, 'You know, this isn't easy for your mother and me to remember either.' What did he mean by that? Not easy for *them* to remember?"

"He said that?"

"I don't know what he's talking about. You and I are the ones who were here. What are *they* remembering?"

"I don't know...."

Anna studied Avery as she drove. Some energy seemed to have drained from her sister. Her shoulders slumped slightly. Her head hung low. Understandable, given how tired she must be.

But her grip on the steering wheel was so tight her knuckles bulged.

"Are you okay, Avery?"

"I'm okay," she said. "We'll have you back soon."

101

Avery pulled up in front of the house.

She left the engine on, and Anna let out a sigh.

"You're coming in, right?" Anna asked.

Avery replayed the events of the past few days in her head. She'd been doing that the whole way home from Rydell. It made for a complicated puzzle with a lot of jagged pieces. She'd figured out that she could fit them together in a certain way, and she couldn't stop seeing it.

"Avery?"

"Sure. I guess."

"Maybe you need to take a nap."

"Anna, it's just— Well, your parents do care for you. I know that."

"I know it too."

Avery looked ahead, down the familiar street. She felt Anna's eyes on her.

"Avery? Is something wrong?"

"When Brittany Combs talked to you about her brother and who she thought your family was, she said she worried the killer was someone close to the family. Right?"

"That's right. I thought she meant Taylor. Or Hogan, I guess."

"Yeah."

"That would make sense, wouldn't it? Since they were fighting about the business."

"What were they fighting over?"

"Jesus, Avery. Haven't we been through enough?"

"Do you know?"

Anna sighed. "Ugh. Brittany says Danny—that's my dad, I guess—wanted to get out of the business. And Taylor wanted to expand. I guess that was their beef."

"Hmm. Okay."

"Do you think it was someone else?"

Avery looked at the house. "Your mom's coming out. Alisha's here too."

Anna turned and looked as well. Jane came through the door. The wind picked up, making her untied robe lift up like wings, revealing the pink nightgown underneath. She tried to gather it down and then gave up. She came across the lawn toward the car.

"You'd better get out," Avery said. "You're the star of the show."

Avery climbed out too and walked around the front of the truck. She watched Jane pull Anna tight. Tears streamed down Jane's face, which rested on Anna's shoulder.

"Oh, honey, oh, baby, oh, I was so worried about you."

"I know. I'm okay, Mom."

Alisha came out the door and across the lawn as well. She bypassed the reunion between mother and daughter and jogged up to Avery.

"Wow, you really are a badass," Alisha said.

"Did you ever doubt it?"

Then her sister did something—and though Avery tried, she couldn't remember the last time it had happened. Alisha reached out and hugged Avery, pulling her close. She squeezed so hard, Avery thought her ribs would crack.

"Girl, I was so worried about both of you. I was so fucking worried. You're both a couple of lunatics. You know that?"

"We're safe, Al. We are."

"I'm so glad." Alisha let go and wiped her face. "Look at me—crying, of course. Just like when we were kids. You'd do something brave, and I'd cry."

"You have two children. You're braver than I am."

Alisha walked over and hugged Anna just as tightly. Jane belted her robe and came over to Avery.

"Thank you for getting her." She reached out and hugged Avery. "I'm so grateful for you."

"Thanks, Jane."

"We love you. We really do."

"I know."

The front door opened, and slowly, like a bear emerging from his den after hibernation, her dad came onto the porch, using the walker. He blinked in the sun but stayed on the stoop, watching the women cry and hug.

He surveyed the scene, and then his eyes locked on Avery's. He was too far away to say anything, so they stared at each other for a drawn-out moment. For the first time ever, Avery felt like she might have won his approval. She'd brought home the prize, in the person of Anna.

She wondered why she'd been chasing that prize all those years.

"Come on," Jane said, placing her hand on Avery's arm. "Let's all go see Daddy. He can't come down the steps."

Avery wanted to resist. Turn and get in the car and go.

It might be better that way.

But she couldn't. Maybe that was her problem. When push came to shove, she couldn't turn away from her family.

She allowed Jane to lead her across the lawn.

102

Alisha and Anna went inside the house first.

As Avery approached the porch, her dad kept his eyes on her. His eyes looked small and glassy, with pouches of flesh beneath. She could only imagine how much he'd been drinking while worried about Anna.

"Jane, do you mind going on in?" Avery asked. "I wanted to talk to Dad for a minute."

Jane kept her arm linked through Avery's. She no doubt feared leaving the two of them alone to talk. Not because of what Avery wanted to talk about. Only because she feared the combustible combination.

"Well . . . I . . . Can't we all be inside together as a family?" Jane asked. "Wouldn't that be nice?"

"It might only take a minute," Avery said. "I hope it does."

"I don't want to have us, you know, rehashing the past," Jane said. "All the time, rehashing the past. The distant past."

Her dad kept his eyes on Avery, but he nodded to the house. "Go on, Jane. It's fine."

Jane moved her gaze between the two of them. "Are you sure we shouldn't have something to eat first?"

"Go on in," he said.

Jane let her arm slide out of Avery's. Despite the years of bitter feelings, Avery felt moved as she looked at Jane. Had Jane ever been able to stand up to her dad? What could she have ever done with him? Especially once his leg had been shattered.

Jane went in, and the door closed behind her. Avery's dad remained six inches above her, the walker keeping him up on the porch.

"Well," he said, "you found her. And you brought her back."

"I did."

The next words came out like they cost him dearly. "Well . . . you did good." He cleared his throat. "I heard about . . . the river. The water. I know . . . that's tough for you. But you did it."

"I know you were on that task force watching the Douglas and the Combs families. And the Douglases ended up dead after the investigation ended."

"That's no secret."

"And you know Anna's related to them. The Douglas family and the Combses. She told you, right?"

The muscles in his neck corded. "Jane's right. We don't have to go over all of this. It's settled."

"It's not, Dad. Anna just found out she's adopted. That's a big thing to learn when you're twenty-one years old. And not only that, but she's from a family of drug dealers—people who were murdered. Executed. This isn't a small thing."

"Okay, we'll help her sort it out. We're her parents. That's our concern. You did your job and we'll do ours. Are you coming inside or not?"

"Dad . . ." Avery looked to the sky. "Dad, see this from my point of view, okay? You were on a task force investigating a bunch of drug dealers. They end up dead. And then a baby related to them becomes my sister. And nobody even knew she was adopted. When I was with Charlie—"

He looked down. "That's the end of a fine man."

"We agree about that, I think. Charlie was on the task force with you, right?"

"He was. Why?"

"He acted weird about everything. About Anna. About Rydell. He said there were some things only *you* could tell me. And he told me Rydell had a lot of history."

"He should have kept his mouth shut. Charlie always did have a soft spot for you girls. He should have had his own family and butted out of mine."

"What do you have to tell me? About Rydell. And our family."

Her dad shifted his position a little, moving the walker slightly forward. "All of a sudden it's *our* family? All this time we never heard from you. You don't even get in touch with Anna down in Breckville. . . . *Now* it's our family. I could have used that attitude when we were trying to raise a daughter. When Jane—my wife—starting having her memory problems, I could have used you."

Avery shook her head. "Don't turn it around on me now. I can beat myself up just fine. And I will. But this is about you. And the Douglas family. And Anna."

"Just leave it. Okay?"

Avery stepped forward, placing one foot on the porch. "Do you want me to go in and ask Jane? I can. She could tell me how Anna came to live with the two of you. But maybe she doesn't know the whole truth either."

"You stop." His voice rang out like hammerblows against stone. The old authority that froze Avery in her tracks. "Leave Jane out of it. Do you hear me? She's not well."

His invocation of Jane had the desired effect. Avery backed off. She had always intended to keep her floundering stepmother out of it. "Then tell me."

He remained silent, his jaw clenched tight.

"Are you going to tell me, or do I have to go talk to the cops in Rydell? Or Breckville or wherever they're looking into this."

"You'd like that, wouldn't you? To finally knock me off my perch?"

"I hope you know that's the last thing I want. But I really do want the truth, Dad. The whole way back from Rydell, I've been hoping the truth isn't what I think it is. So maybe you can tell me what really happened and put my mind at ease."

"Here . . ." He shifted his weight again, moved the walker closer to the edge of the porch.

"Be careful."

"Help me down, will you?"

He started moving. She reached her hands out, steadied him while he lowered the walker off the porch and then gently stepped down. First one foot and then the other. Avery held him up. When he was down, he shuffled along the front walk, heading toward the curb.

Avery walked beside him. "Where are you going?"

"Just away from the house. So no one else can hear."

When they were far enough away, he stopped. Sweat popped out on his forehead, even though it was early and the day wasn't that warm. His skin flushed. Avery worried he was sick. Or about to have a stroke.

"Are you okay?" she asked.

"Don't ask me that anymore. You want to hear something about the past, then don't ask me if I'm okay. I'm not okay talking about the past, but I'll do it. Maybe then you'll understand everything and keep your mouth shut."

103

Avery's dad wobbled a little, then tightened his grip on the walker. He expelled a deep breath.

"Listen to me. I wasn't necessarily looking to have another child. You older two, well, I wasn't always— I mean, being a dad—it wasn't exactly in my wheelhouse. But when I met Jane and we got married, well, she wanted a child of her own. You and your sister were with your mom most of the time. And I don't think either one of you wanted to have much to do with me."

"That's not true. We did. Desperately."

"Well, you sure acted like you didn't. You still do." He wiped the sweat off his forehead. It popped out again immediately. "When Jane wanted a child, it seemed like the natural course of things. Why shouldn't she have her own child if she wanted? And I was working a lot, so maybe she wouldn't have been so lonely."

"How does this relate to the task force?"

He kept his eyes from meeting Avery's. "I'm not the first cop to take a little money on the side. It happens. Hell, maybe you did when you were on the job."

"I never did. Nothing more than free coffee."

"Well, aren't you grand? You and fucking Charlie. He never took a goddamned dime either. I remember once—you must have been about twelve, a few years after the divorce—you told me you wished Charlie was your dad and not me."

"I said that out loud?"

"You did. Don't worry. I see it. I sometimes wished . . . I could be more like him."

He lifted his hand and rubbed at his eyes. Tears or sweat? Avery couldn't tell. She wasn't sure she wanted to know.

"Are you saying you were taking money on the task force? Money from the Douglas family?"

"For a while, yeah. It was mutually beneficial. They got some heat off of them. It was just fucking weed. It wasn't hurting anyone too bad. I can't stand the other shit. Heroin and meth. I draw the line there. But pot? Who cares? . . . And I . . . I had child support to pay. I was giving your mother money the whole time she was down in Florida."

"Dirty money."

"What other kind is there? I was supporting two households on a cop's salary. What was your mother doing in Florida, huh? Working? Going to church? Or what?"

Avery couldn't defend her mother's behavior down there, so she remained silent.

"Alisha told me when you all came back. The boyfriends she had. The partying. The two of you girls left alone a lot. Or with creeps coming in and out of the apartment. I paid for that."

"Okay, I hear you. Mom was hurt by your behavior, you know?"

"Yeah." He took a quick look back at the house. "Jane couldn't get pregnant. It was a problem with her uterus. We went to all the doctors. Paid a shit ton of money for the tests and procedures. None of it worked. Jane . . . Do you know how depressed a woman gets when she wants a baby and can't have one? Do you know what it's like to live with someone that heartbroken?"

"Mom was that heartbroken."

"Then you get it." His grip tightened on the walker. "You'd do anything to make that person happy."

"There would be a limit to what I'd do, Dad."

"Maybe you're better with limits than I am," he said. "Danny Douglas wasn't good with them either. He wanted to keep pushing, expand their business. Take more risks. He wanted to get into that other stuff. Pills and heroin and guns. Taylor Combs didn't want to do it."

"So Taylor killed his brother-in-law?"

Dad wiped his forehead again. "That's a theory."

"Is that your theory?"

"Avery, let's go inside. It's hot. Your sister's home."

"Anna has a lot of questions. And she deserves answers."

"The cops will find them."

"Dad, they're talking to Taylor Combs right now. What are they going to find out from him? Do you know?"

Some of the color left his face. He looked faint, but Avery wanted to keep talking.

"Dad? Taylor Combs is facing serious charges. Drugs. Murder. Labor trafficking. Now, if he killed his brother-in-law, then he might have reason to clam up about that along with everything else. But if someone else killed Danny Douglas and his family and Taylor knows who it was . . . he can talk. He can try to hand them somebody."

"There's no evidence."

"Of what, Dad? Say it."

"Danny was a loose cannon. He wanted more and more. He was going to bring more attention on anyone associated with him. He was risking everything. There'd be too much scrutiny, you see? Who could stand up to the scrutiny?"

"If he got caught . . ."

"Everyone would get tangled up in the net."

"The police who enabled him and turned a blind eye. His brother-in-law, Taylor Combs. Everybody." The air around them grew still. Avery couldn't hear anything. Not even the singing of a single bird. No trees moved. "What happened, Dad?"

"You're right. If he'd overstepped and been busted, a lot of people would have been hurt. A lot of things would have blown up. Even for his brother-in-law . . ."

"What did you do?"

"Someone was going to kill him at one time or another. His own brother-in-law might have. Combs was a young guy, just starting out. He didn't want Danny blowing up the whole operation. Maybe even getting him thrown into jail."

"What did you do?"

Her dad shook his head. Words were slow to form on his lips. The fumbling made him look older. "I was going to . . . take care of things. Quick and clean." He stared at Avery but seemed to be looking past her. Through her. To the moment that still lived vividly in his mind. "Danny was outside when we pulled up, and his family was inside. . . ."

"You and Charlie? There were two shooters."

"We'd seen the baby before. We knew about her. Just a tiny thing. A few weeks old at that point. Not many people knew about it. His wife gave birth at home. They were isolated, living away from every-one. They were paranoid. It was no environment for a baby. And Jane was so depressed, longing for a baby. . . ."

"They had another child as well. A toddler. Someone killed that child. And its mother." Avery took a couple of steps back. She looked at the sky. The puffy clouds. The robin's-egg blue. If a meteor had streaked down and landed on her head, it couldn't have stunned her any more than she already was. She managed one word. "Dad . . ."

"Jane lay low with her for a while. We didn't have a lot of friends. Nobody really came around to see. . . ."

"Dad . . ."

"If you have enough money—and know the right people—you can get documents. Every day, I expected someone to knock on the door. That's why we moved here, away from Louisville. I thought about mov-ing across the country, or to Mexico. But that would have looked even more suspicious. And I didn't want to be far from you girls. Neither did Jane. But I lived in fear. And I kept that fear locked away. Maybe it took a toll on me in ways I didn't realize. But with each passing day that the murder was unsolved . . . and Anna stayed with us. . . ." He pointed down at his shattered leg. "Maybe this is karma, or a piece of it. I accepted this as a down payment on what I owed the world. This pain."

"Jesus, Dad. You killed three people. A woman and a child . . ."

"I know," he said.

"You're going to go to jail. For the rest of your life."

"Only if you tell. And if you do that you—"

"They're going to investigate. The Combs family just learned about Anna, and it dredged up the past. They're going to want to know who—"

"Hell, Avery. Taylor Combs knew about it back then. He wanted Danny Douglas gone, same as me. Do you think he wants his wife to know that he knew who killed her brother? Do you think he wants that to come out? This has remained unsolved for over twenty years."

"I have an obligation to report a crime."

"You have an obligation to *us*."

The front door opened. Jane stepped onto the porch again and came down the walk toward them.

"What are you two talking about?" she asked.

"Go inside, Janie," Dad said.

Jane didn't move. She moved her eyes from her husband to Avery and back again. Her eyes were sharp and clear. "I know what you're talking about," she said. "Anna's asking questions inside. About the same thing."

"Tell her to stop," he said. "She should just be happy to be home and safe."

"Avery," Jane said, "I don't want you to think the worst of me. Or your dad. We weren't perfect, but we tried our best."

"Did you know, Jane, where your baby came from?"

"Avery," said her dad, "stop this right—"

"I'm sorry to tell you this—really sorry—but Dad stole Anna from her birth parents . . . and he killed them."

"Oh, Avery," Jane said, "you're so naive. . . ."

"My God, you knew. The three most important adults left in my life. Dad and Charlie killed a family and took their baby. Then you . . . you raised that child and kept quiet about it. I can't even—"

"Surely, Daddy told you—"

"Jane—" Russ said.

"—Charlie tried to talk us out of it. He told us not to go. Sometimes I think I should have listened to him, but then when I see my sweet Anna—"

"Janie, be quiet—"

"What do you mean, Charlie tried to talk *you* out of it?" Avery asked. "You mean he tried to talk *Dad* out of it?"

Jane lifted her hand to her chest, pressed it tight against her heart. "Avery, you're relentless, aren't you? Charlie wasn't there that night."

"Jane—" Russ said again.

"But there were two shooters," Avery said.

"I went because of the baby. To help take care of her and get her out of there. I didn't plan on doing anything else. But Russ made me keep a gun just in case . . . and that woman got past Russ. . . . Avery, she ran out of the house. She left her children inside instead of protecting them. A mother shouldn't do that."

"Jane—"

"I was there for my husband. And for Anna. I had to do what I had to do. Sometimes you have to do what you have to do in the moment. You see? And Anna had a good life with us. She had you and Alisha. I did the same as you when you got Anna off that farm and jumped into the river to help those people."

"It's not like that, not at all. . . ."

"Avery," Dad said, "if you go to the police, you'll be depriving Anna of both of her parents. Do you hear me? Are you going to do that to your sister? You know what it's like to lose a parent. That family she just found, they're going to jail no matter what, so why add to the girl's pain and confusion?"

Avery backed away, heading to the truck. As she did, Anna and Alisha came out onto the front porch.

"Where are you going?" Alisha asked.

"I have to go . . . back to Breckville. . . ."

"Avery?" Anna said.

Avery kept going. She climbed into Charlie's truck and drove off, leaving her family behind.

Epilogue

The weather turned cold early that week in Breckville.

Frost came during a few nights, and snow flurries fell one afternoon. Avery lost herself in work. Upon returning from Upton and Rydell—and everything that had unfolded there—she rededicated herself to school. She took a leave of absence from the security guard job with the end of the semester looming. She decided she could live on ramen noodles and peanut butter and jelly while she focused on school. And figure out what she wanted to do next.

Someone rapped lightly on the door. He'd texted earlier. But she still looked through the peephole cautiously, the chain still hooked. When she saw it was Hank—smiling in the porch light, his face clean-shaven, his hair shorter—she opened the door for him.

"Wow, you really did come to Breckville," Avery said.

"I was in the neighborhood."

Avery laughed. "I see. In the neighborhood."

"Sure. I have some time on my hands." He shrugged. "And I wanted to talk to you, since the last time we saw each other—you know, I had a bullet inside me."

"I remember that very well."

"Speaking of my bullet wound . . . are you going to let me come in? I need to sit."

"Oh, yeah. Sure. Sorry."

Avery moved out of the way. They went and sat on the couch.

Hank winced a little as he adjusted his body. Some of the color drained from his face.

"Are you in a lot of pain?"

"I get flashes of it. But it's a lot better. Still . . . sometimes . . ."

"Do you want me to get you anything?"

"I just need to sit."

He took a few deep breaths. After a minute or two, his color started to come back.

"Are you sure you're okay?" Avery asked.

"Right as rain. Whatever that means."

"Yeah, I don't know what that means either." Avery waited a little longer. Then she said, "You know, I never really thanked you for saving me out there. If you hadn't been there . . ."

"You're welcome. But you did pretty well for yourself. You got Anna out. And those farmworkers . . ."

"It seems like a dream, to be honest." Avery rubbed her cold hands together. "I dream about it all the time."

"Are you seeing someone about it?"

"Not now. Maybe. The dreams . . . they might help me work through it. I used to dream about the pond a lot. Now I'm dreaming about the river."

"If you want to talk about it—"

"Not really."

"Okay."

"I mean, thanks. Maybe I will. Soon."

"I get it." Hank smiled at her. "You know, maybe I will take some water."

Avery went to the kitchen and filled a glass. Water. Just plain old water. She brought it back and handed it to Hank. He gulped half of it down. "That's good," he said. "Thanks."

"There's more. There seems to be water everywhere. Ponds. Rivers."

"True enough." He emptied the glass. "Speaking of things we don't like to talk about . . . I keep hearing about your family. I know the investigation is still going on, and maybe you'd rather not say anything about it."

Avery let out a sigh. It seemed to be the only sound she could summon in relation to her family. A long, deflating sigh. "Yeah, my family."

"We can skip it."

"No, we probably shouldn't." She sighed again and slumped back against the couch. "What do you hear about the investigation?"

"All I know is Taylor Combs lawyered up. He's not saying anything about anything. Including Anna or his brother-in-law."

"Or my dad."

"Right. Have you talked to him? Your dad."

"Not since the day I drove away from their house. I've talked to my sisters, and they both have a *lot* to sort through. We all do. And Anna especially . . . I'm trying to be here for her. She's supposed to come visit soon. Other than that . . ."

"There's stuff you don't want to tell me. Or anyone."

"There's stuff . . . and I think it's going to come out, one way or another. . . ."

"But not now?"

Avery shook her head. "Someday we'll talk about it. We're probably going to have to."

Hank nodded, adjusted his body, and winced again. "It takes a toll, doesn't it? All the stuff we go through."

"It does, sure."

"You know, you and I, we understand each other in a different way. A real way. And I can't work right now. I'm on medical leave." He rubbed his smooth chin. "I don't know if I ever really want to go back. I don't think I want to do something like that again."

"I know that feeling," Avery said.

"See, that's just it. Like I told you when we were at the farm, I know I wasn't as empathetic as I could have been when you were recovering from the thing at the pond. And now . . . I get it. For sure. So I wanted you to hear that."

"Thank you. You really might not go back to being a cop?"

He rubbed his chin again. "I might not. It's . . . it's tough to imagine."

"Wow."

"Hard to believe, right?"

"No, not so hard."

"In a way, it's kind of put us in the same place. For the first time in a long time."

Avery couldn't help it. A smile spread across her face.

"What is it?" Hank asked.

"I've been thinking a lot. Obviously."

"And?"

"And I think I want to be a cop again."

Hank's eyes widened. "Now, that's a wow."

"Yeah. It is."

"Then I guess we do have a lot to talk about. You know, while I heal."

"Are you planning on staying here for a bit? While you heal?"

"If the invitation stands, yes. As you can see, I'm still recovering."

She leaned back against the couch, pressed her body against his. "That's something I know a little bit about."

Acknowledgments

Thanks once again to everyone at Berkley/Penguin for their hard work on my behalf—with special thanks to Loren Jaggers, Jin Yu, Bridget O'Toole, Hilary Tacuri, Tina Joelle, Ivan Held, Christine Ball, Claire Zion, Jeanne-Marie Hudson, and Craig Burke.

Special thanks to Jen Carl for my newsletter.

Special thanks to Kara Thurmond for her website prowess.

Special thanks to my wonderful editor, Tracy Bernstein, for her tireless efforts to make the book better.

Special thanks to my outstanding agent, David Hale Smith, for always keeping things running smoothly. And thanks to Naomi Eisenbeiss and everyone at Inkwell Management.

Thanks to my family and friends.

Thanks to Molly McCaffrey for everything else.

TRY

NOT

TO

BREATHE

DAVID BELL

READERS GUIDE

Questions for Discussion

1. Anna and Kayla are roommates and good friends, but they're also very different from each other. Did you have friendships like this in college or since then?

2. Anna has had a falling-out with her father, and she's failing out of school and partying too much. Do you empathize with the way Anna's life is spiraling out of control, or does she seem immature?

3. Avery has grown distant from Anna and associates her with the failure of her parents' marriage. Do you understand Avery's resentment? Is it fair?

4. Avery feels like she has disappointed her father by leaving the police force. Can you relate to her sense that she has let him down? Is it always difficult to follow a parent into a career? Is it especially so in this case?

5. Alisha tries to play the role of peacemaker in the family, both between her sisters and between her sisters and their father. Do you have a family member who plays this role?

6. Anna feels close to her mom's cousin Libby, and Avery has a friend and mentor in her dad's friend Charlie. Did an adult other than your parents play an important role in your life growing up? What did the relationship offer you?

7. Avery agrees to try to find Anna and bring her home even though she isn't sure why she does it. Why do *you* think she goes after Anna?

8. Hank regrets that he was not as understanding of Avery's PTSD as he should have been. Have you ever been in a situation where you didn't fully understand the challenges someone else was dealing with?

9. What do you think happens to the Rogers family once Anna and Avery return home? How will they move forward?

10. Why do you think Avery is rethinking her decision to stop being a police officer? Does it surprise you?

Photo © Glen Rose Photography

David Bell is a *New York Times* bestselling, award-winning author whose work has been translated into multiple foreign languages. He's currently a professor of English at Western Kentucky University in Bowling Green, Kentucky. He received an MA in creative writing from Miami University in Oxford, Ohio, and a PhD in American literature and creative writing from the University of Cincinnati. His previous novels include *The Finalists*, *Kill All Your Darlings*, *The Request*, *Layover*, *Somebody's Daughter*, and *Cemetery Girl*.

CONNECT ONLINE

DavidBellNovels.com
🅕 DavidBellNovels
🐦 DavidBellNovels
📷 DavidBellNovels